DIMENSION M

ALSO BY SCOTT WYATT

Beyond the Sand Creek Bridge

DIMENSION M

To Ellie —
Scott Wyatt

SCOTT WYATT

ISBN 1492197009
ISBN-13: 9781492197003
Library of Congress Control Number: 2013916028
CreateSpace Independent Publishing Platform
North Charleston, South Carolina

*

Also available in electronic form for most e-readers

*

HIGHLAND HOUSE PRESS
P.O. Box 350
Issaquah, WA 98027

FOR AVA, ROGAN, SKYE, ELLA AND WILLIAM
—AND GRANDCHILDREN EVERYWHERE

ACKNOWLEDGMENTS

I have known from the outset that a successful conclusion to the task of writing *Dimension M* lay in finding appropriate help. To this end, I am grateful to all who have offered their encouragement and expertise. I wish to particularly thank Dustin Harrison, without whom I could not have completed "The Sanori Flag Debate." At my request, with only my thanks in the bargain, Dustin took the negative side of the debate and graciously lent his voice, considerable wisdom, and practical insight to my fictional interlocutors Professor O'Neil, Rabbi Levenson, Secretary-General Romero, and Monsignor Doyle.

Cheryl Hauser, Barbara Carole, Sandy Nygaard, Kim Pearson, Molly Strange, Frank Winningham, Sandy Rainey Maras, Scott Jarol, Amy Dahl, and Linda Deiner top the list of people who bear some of the credit but none of the blame for the novel.

I am, as always, thankful for the skill and patience of my copyeditor, Sandra Judd.

A special thank you goes out to my mother, Betty Wyatt, to my sister, Christine, and to my children, Aaron Wyatt, Todd Wyatt, Aaron Denke, and Teija Bielas, for their unique contributions and ongoing love and support.

The multiple contributions of my wife, Rochelle, defy adequate description here. I could point to her hours of encouragement, her unfailing willingness to listen and offer "edits," her unlimited patience, and so on, but these would barely scratch the surface. Hopefully, she has taken me at my word the countless times—after enlisting her help and guidance—I have said, "Thank you, Sweetie." I've meant it.

FOREWORD

Historical references in my first novel, *Beyond the Sand Creek Bridge*, resulted from research into the lives of Chinese immigrants who came to the American West to build the great transcontinental railroads. In *Dimension M*, set slightly but indeterminately in the future, the chief "historical" references are, with few exceptions, fictional. There is no Şahin Diary, for instance (pronounced: sha-*heen*). The African nation of Tashir does not exist, and there is no capital city of Sanori. The characters and plot of *Dimension M* are the products of my imagination.

One thing that is real and that plays a small role in the novel is the companion flag project. The companion flag project is a not-for-profit initiative I founded in 1999. *Dimension M* is a dramatic story of love, friendship, loyalty, and crisis and is not a monograph on the companion flag idea. Readers interested in learning more about the companion flag initiative are encouraged to read the optional appendix, "The Sanori Flag Debate."

SCOTT WYATT
SAMMAMISH, WA

Gandhi was asked, "How can you make another man do good?" He answered, "You cannot make another man do good. You can only create the conditions under which he will choose to do good."

I

―――

"We're in," whispered Fatimah. Her flashlight tore a hole through the darkness. The shaking circle darted from one side of the foyer to the other. Fatimah put her free hand on her chest and commanded her heart to stop pounding. Pretty much like any other school in this part of the world, she thought. Soviet style: brightly painted cement walls, distorted attempts at Western cartoon figures, bare wooden tables with no obvious role to play, and a futuristic indoor fountain, circa 1960, as dry as the Aral Sea.

A hand-painted paper banner in Russian hung from the ceiling. When the light from a second flashlight, Alden's, caught it, she asked in English, "What does it say?"

Alden hesitated, then translated, "We are proud sons and daughters of Uzbekistan."

He'd barely gotten the words out when Fatimah brushed past him. "The stairs are over here."

They tiptoed up the wide staircase. When they reached the landing, their traveling lights fused and slid past colorful student artwork, much of it depicting scenes of warfare: falling planes, tanks, streams of bullets. They kept the elongated ovals of white light ascending two or three steps ahead of them.

The second floor was dark save for two small red exit signs glowing at either end of a long hallway. Their smudged reflections were visible on the polished cement floor.

"Up one more," whispered Fatimah. Alden nodded.

Partway up, they found the stairwell lit by moonlight pouring in through a two-panel window high overhead. They quickened their steps.

Alden clung to the banister, breathing heavily, by the time they arrived at the third-floor landing. "All right, it'll be an unnumbered door. You go that way," he said, pointing to his right.

The third floor copied the second, except for a rectangle of moonlight that reached across the floor and climbed a few inches up the opposite wall. It had a tentative grip on their shadows, as though the irregular shapes had been borrowed momentarily from the dark expanses left and right. "I'll look down here," Alden said, indicating the other direction. "Wave your flashlight if you find something."

They had not gotten far when Alden signaled her. Fatimah ran to him. "Here it is," he said. He began to fumble at the bottom of a black duffel bag. She knew he was after the lock pick set.

He lowered himself to the floor with some difficulty. A slight wheeze escaped the sixty-three-year-old as he edged the half-diamond pick into the lock.

"Hold the light still, please," he said.

The door clicked open. Alden clambered to his feet and pushed against it slowly. He and Fatimah looked over their shoulders, then sidled into a small, windowless utility room. Alden switched on the light to reveal metal shelves with paint cans—in shades of maroon, blue, and yellow—cleansers, rags, a clipboard, two boxes of nails, paper towels, a deeply scarred pine toolbox, and a pyramid of rolls of coarse, gray toilet paper. In one corner a copse of mop and broom handles was visible behind an ancient, pewter-colored electric floor polisher with a threadbare cord. In another, next to a black metal staircase, lay an oil-stained cardboard box filled with lost or abandoned children's sweaters, gloves, hats, coats, scarves, and backpacks. Moving on, Alden and Fatimah climbed the four steps of the metal staircase to a second door that opened onto the roof. The flat roof, with its overlapping vents and heating units, was a mystery of moonlight and shadows. Alden used his flashlight to prop open the door.

"Let's get this done and get out," he said to his companion. He nodded toward a spotlight a few yards away. It was pointed up at the flag of Uzbekistan, three horizontal stripes—sky blue, white, lime green—separated by thin red lines. The flag hung limply at the top of a flagpole. It was a cool, windless night on the Central Asian steppes.

Fatimah took the duffel bag and moved toward the spotlight, unbuttoning her black *abaya*. Alden made his way to the base of the pole and started unwinding the flag's halyard. As she set up the tripod and camera, Fatimah heard the rope thudding against the steel pole. She made eye contact with Alden, and at his signal tossed the folded *abaya* over the spotlight, dousing it. Alden began lowering the flag. Fatimah, dressed in black designer pants and a long black damask blouse, was next to him in time to catch the flag's leading edge and prevent it from touching the roof.

Alden tied off the rope and fished two flag clips out of his front pants pocket. Spreading his hand to measure approximately eight inches below the bottom of the Uzbekistan flag, he attached one clip there.

"Hurry," said Fatimah.

"I know," Alden replied. He pulled a second flag out from under his shirt, a mostly white banner with indistinct markings visible in the folds. Fatimah took hold of the attached clip while Alden searched for the grommets. They had done this dozens of times. Fatimah watched closely, silently timing his actions. He attached the new banner to the clip and started to raise the two flags together. The pulley at the top of the flagpole squeaked softly.

Once the new flag stretched open it was only a matter of holding its lower grommet against the halyard to see where the second clip should go. When it was done, he quickly raised both flags to the top of the flagpole.

Fatimah ran to the spotlight, removed her *abaya* from its perch, unfolded it, and quickly put it on. The two flags, now companion banners, were suddenly awash in bright light. She let the camera run a few more seconds. "Got it. Let's go," she said. She separated the camera from the tripod with a flick of the quick-release lever, folded the tripod, and stuffed both back into the bag. She hurried toward the door. Alden met her there. Both turned to look at the two flags one more time before hurrying down the metal steps.

Alden slowly and silently closed the utility room door while Fatimah waited on the third-floor landing. Alden hesitated.

"What is it?" whispered Fatimah, standing knee-deep in moonlight. A stippling of golden threads shimmered in the red-and-black *hijab* that covered her head and neck. Her dark face was lit by three or four points of light.

"Let's put the sign *here*," Alden said.

"All right." Fatimah hurried back. She produced a piece of paper and a roll of masking tape from a side pocket of the duffel bag.

Alden held the sheet against the door as Fatimah secured it with long strips of tape. She could read below his splayed fingers ". . . and all that we share in common with people everywhere."

When they were done securing the sheet, Alden said, "Good. Let's get out of here."

They ran to the top of the stairs and descended through the swath of lunar light into the deep pool of gloom below. Fatimah switched on her flashlight. She turned at the second-floor landing with Alden close on her heels. They made the intermediate landing and turned again, their footfalls now a rapid thrumming. How many times have students run down these stairs just like this? she wondered. But not in the dark. At last they reached the foyer. Fatimah turned off her flashlight. They dashed toward the glass doors and accelerated out into the night.

*   *   *

"You two got in late last night," said Dilbar, as she set a plate of lamb kabobs and another piled high with potato-stuffed *manty* in front of them.

"We stopped after the movie to feed our coffee habits and ended up talking to the people at the next table for an eternity," said Fatimah, reaching for the *manty*. "These look wonderful. Are they—?"

"Steamed dough with rosemary potato filling," said Dilbar.

"Mmmm."

Alden sat quietly, lost in his thoughts, only vaguely aware of the dishes being placed in front of them. Dilbar's husband, Sasha, added a bowl of sliced cucumbers and another filled with savory *plov*. Their daughter, Christina, followed from the kitchen with *chuchvara*, a beef filling wrapped in dough, and a moist salad of shredded cabbage, shredded carrots, tomatoes, and sliced almonds. Sasha disappeared into the kitchen again and brought out a bottle of vodka. He filled Alden's glass without asking, and then stopped to offer some to Fatimah, who declined the liquid in a practiced way that gave no offense.

"And today's events, Fatimah," continued Dilbar, "you must tell us about this. You were interviewed and photographed for *Tashkent Today*. What kind of questions did they ask? Who interviewed you? Was it Irina Sadikov?"

"Yes, it was Irina."

"Tell us what she's like. Sasha believes she is much older than she looks on TV, but I say she is not yet thirty-five. Maybe you can settle this for us?"

Fatimah laughed. "I'm not very good with ages. She is a striking woman, but she wears a lot of makeup. I think Sasha may be right."

Sasha raised his glass. "There. My day is made." He drank his vodka down in one gulp.

Alden, smiling faintly, his mind obviously somewhere else, followed suit, taking a small sip of the fiery spirit.

Dilbar laughed. "Don't worry, Fatimah. If you'd have said she was under thirty-five, he would have toasted my health and drank it anyway. Isn't that right, Sasha?"

Her husband was pouring another glass for himself and topping off Alden's glass as well. "Perhaps, my flower," he said.

Watching the glittering drops slide from the bottle, Alden remembered the images of the night before, the floodlight on the roof, the vertical folds of the companion flag underneath the limp material of the flag of Uzbekistan, the two tones—milky gray and blue-black—of the night sky beyond. He saw the low clouds lit by the moon and the luminance of the city and heard the distant rumble of traffic on some unseen street. Yet another city of millions, he thought forlornly, letting his eyes drift toward the Rishtan blue-and-white glazed bowl at the center of the table. Where are we now? he wondered. Oh, yes—Tashkent. And where have I been these last months? Does it matter?

"Oh, it must," he imagined saying to his thirty-six-year-old son Derek, whom he hadn't seen in over four years. Derek's wide blue eyes stared out doubtfully over a balled fist partially hiding his goatee, mustache, and thin lips. The younger man looked past his father, distracted. Where were they? It was an airport somewhere in the States, perhaps Kansas City International—in a coffee shop. Derek seemed to gather himself. He sat back, took a deep breath. "You're missing the chance to see your grand-kids," he said. "You must realize that. Cassie and El, and Sarah's kids, too. You're unable to watch . . ." The imagined voice faded momentarily as Alden observed Christina, elbows high, dish-ing salad from an oversized bowl. He watched as Dilbar got the bowl of *chuchvara* moving clockwise around the table. Then Derek, who was there again, said, "The kids don't even know you, Dad. And I don't know what to tell them."

Alden felt the doors and windows shuttering closed around his heart. Why had he allowed them to open in the first place? "Was it a mistake to call you?" he imagined saying to Derek. "No. You're my son. How could it be a mistake?"

What have I done, leaving everything and everyone behind? Alden wondered. Sometimes I don't know, but when I think of stopping I realize . . . no, I have to go on. If I don't do this, no one will. Sometimes I wish this idea had never occurred to me. If I'd been happier with things back then, I would have been like Teflon. The idea wouldn't have stuck at all.

While the others dished food onto their plates, Alden brought the vodka to his lips again, and his world was drawn in and made small. Will I ever have a home again? he wondered. Not since Wichita, since Deborah, had he felt at home in a place like this. Shared furnishings, the colors and angles of comfort, rooms branded with family. He had the strange feeling of cross-ing back through time. He remembered Deborah not as a dis-satisfied and censorious wife, but as a friend and lover.

In his mind he began to consider the layout of their liv-ing room in the house on North Elder Street. The orange, threadbare couch, the gold, hand-me-down, hourglass-shaped lamps, the thickly painted brick fireplace, mauve, jaundiced in the midday light. With the memory came the hint of a smell, of the afghan Deborah had crocheted for him on their third anniversary, before the kids came along. Not for its own sake, he knew, did he imagine that smallish living room, or its accoutrements, or the smell of the afghan. He had been part of a family once, and things were not so different from this, he thought, glancing up furtively at the group gathered around the table. Had he rejected it all—family and home? He'd left it, but no, he hadn't rejected it. Deborah had wanted out, and then when this idea took hold . . . He couldn't imagine marrying again, but a home? Surely, someday, he would have a home again.

"How do you keep going?" It was Deborah asking now, not Derek. And they were not in the airport. They were seated across from each other in the sunny breakfast nook at the back of the house on North Elder. "One foot in front of another," he answered with a strained smile, tasting the vodka on his tongue. "That's the key." It was an old formulation, something he'd heard his grandmother say, apropos of nothing, but it worked now, and he'd erected it again and again in recent months as a paper-thin divide between himself and a yawning abyss of loneliness.

Fatimah's familiar voice interrupted his rumination and was a comfort. She represented energy and youthfulness to him. And besides, she had been with him in Lucknow, in Katmandu, in Bishkek, and in a dozen other cities and towns. But who was she? What was this divine creature doing here? Was she a friend? Of course, but where did the roots of friendship take hold, with so little in common and so many years between them, he wondered. Was she a confidant? Yes. A disciple? To him, no, but to the idea of the companion flag, yes.

Alden smiled inwardly. She was known as one of the world's most beautiful women, and for good reason. It was nearly impossible to find a magazine from the year before without Fatimah Ibrahim's picture on the cover or somewhere inside. He listened to the youthful inflection of her voice as she exchanged lighthearted banter with Dilbar in English, but he did not turn to look at her. He did not raise his eyes at all. He had grown used to not looking at her, had made it a practice, even, without going overboard. It was far from easy, although he had found it easier in countries like India and Pakistan where Fatimah had worn the *niqab*, the face veil, out of respect for a practice widely observed there. What good did it do to stare at a sublime object over-much? At his age. And besides, he thought, beauty is a human difference.

He was glad for her company, and when she had approached him in Lucknow ten months earlier and asked to join him, he'd entertained the thought that this would quell his frequent bouts of loneliness, his pangs of road weariness, his self-doubts. Things had gone only so far in that direction. He had grown to like her, to admire her, and to avoid looking at her in the self-saving spirit of age and discretion. But his loneliness had remained with him in spite of her company. In India, in Pakistan, in Kazakhstan, in Russia, and now in Uzbekistan, still it was there.

He remembered the faint odor of her perfume the night before, as she stood next to him by the flag pole . . . They've no doubt discovered the flag and the sign, and removed both, he thought. As though it never happened. But of course it did. Just like at all the other schools. Fatimah's video would prove it, even if the headmaster or the police denied it. Imagining points of light around the globe, he reminded himself that the companion flag had also flown in Sydney, in Singapore, and in Karachi. They could take it down, but it had been there.

"Shall we toast?" Sasha set the bottle down. "Alden, would you care to begin?"

Dilbar, Fatimah, and Christina raised delicate teacups.

Alden, mildly startled to hear his name being spoken, said, "What? Oh, yes, I would be happy to." He stood up, his pale face showing some color above the line of white stubble on his chin. He smiled at his three hosts in turn, including young Christina. "To all who seek friendship—may their journeys end as ours has ended this evening. Thank you, Sasha, Dilbar, and Christina for opening your home to us last night and again tonight, and for this wonderful meal. The memory that is fed with love lives a thousand years."

"Here, here," whispered Fatimah while Dilbar and Sasha uttered a phrase in Uzbek that seemed to seal the sentiment.

Sasha followed with a toast of his own that surpassed Alden's in length by a factor of four or five and seemed to leave nothing to chance—although, again, much of it was in Uzbek. When they had drunk at last, Sasha broke the round *tandir non* bread into pieces and distributed them. He urged them all to begin, leaving nothing untasted.

As they lifted their forks, Dilbar asked, "And you, Alden— what did you do today? You were gone so early in the morning."

Alden spoke slowly as he carefully dished a large spoonful of the cucumber mix onto his plate. "In truth, nothing at all. I went for a long walk. I walked to Alayski Bazaar, and I browsed an open market on Anasova. There wasn't much—"

Just then there came a loud knocking at the door of the apartment, a racket so abrupt that all activity stopped at once.

"What in the world?" cried Dilbar. She wiped the corners of her mouth with her cloth napkin as if preparing to get up, but her husband raised his hand to stop her.

Fatimah saw a shadow of fear cross over Dilbar's face. She felt a sudden heaviness invade her own stomach.

"Open up! Police!" came a male voice in Russian.

Fatimah looked at Alden, and their eyes met and held as though each had been caught in a trap. Alden put down his fork and pushed the plate away from him.

Sasha was en route to the door. "Coming!" he called. In the next instant he was shouldered aside as three uniformed men rushed past him with pistols drawn.

"Alden Frost and Fatimah Ibrahim?" the leader demanded from the foyer. He didn't wait for an answer, but moved forward, flanked by his comrades, into the living room that doubled this evening as the dining room.

"I'm Alden Frost," said Alden, in Russian, rising from the table and dropping his napkin on his chair. Christina stood up and moved away from Alden, closer to her mother.

Fatimah stood up in turn. "And I am Ms. Ibrahim," she said in English.

Three gray steel barrels were pointed across the table. "You're both under arrest. Come with us."

"But—" Dilbar began softly. "There must be some mistake. They—"

"There's no mistake," said the lead man. He did not remove his eyes from Fatimah. "Get your things. Let's go."

II

From: XX5 – Executive Director CO-9 (London)
To: undisclosed recipients
Date: Sun., 3 September 20ZZ 04:14:42
Subject: Fatimah Ibrahim
Encryption/Decryption Enabled: B72ZZ256-9102 (All Threads)

TO ALL COMMITTEE OF NINE (CO-9) MEMBERS:

JUST RECEIVED:

INTERPOL ADVISORY BULLETIN 12LQ5334, 3 SEPT. 20ZZ
03:44:19 +0200: "INTERNATIONAL CELEBRITY FATIMAH
IBRAHIM, 22 (REPUBLIC OF TASHIR) ARRESTED, TASHKENT,
UZBEKISTAN, 2 SEPT. 20ZZ 15:22:00 +0500 UTC/GMT.
ALSO ARRESTED: ALDEN FROST, 63 (USA). BOTH BOOKED INTO
TASHKENT MUNICIPAL JAIL FOLLOWING BREAK-IN AT PUBLIC
SCHOOL 32. CHARGES UNSPECIFIED."

COMMENT/REACTION?

*　　*　　*

From: XX8 – CO-9 (Bangalore)
Date: Sun., 3 September 20ZZ 04:25:01 +5030

PS 32? ISN'T THIS WHERE THE ALI ŞAHIN DIARY IS KEPT? HAS THE DIARY BEEN DISTURBED?

*   *   *

From: X16 – CO-9 (Sao Paulo)
Date: Sun., 3 September 20ZZ 04:25:01 -0300

THE ALI ŞAHIN DIARY? I DON'T FIND IT IN THE LITERATURE. PLEASE ELABORATE.

*   *   *

From: XX5 – Executive Director CO-9 (London)
Date: Sun., 3 September 20ZZ 04:34:06

TO ALL COMMITTEE OF NINE (CO-9) MEMBERS:

WE ARE ENDEAVORING TO CONFIRM THE DIARY'S STATUS AT THIS TIME. X16, CALL ME ON A SECURE LINE, TRANSCRIPTION CODE 9.

*   *   *

"This is Sixteen."

Henry Matheson made a little popping noise over the bit of his pipe, then, with an adder of smoke climbing his face past squinting eyes, he set the pipe down in an ashtray. "Hello,

Sixteen," he said in a deep, gravelly, reluctant tone. The office was dark. The migrainous seventy-two-year-old leaned back in his chair. A narrow band of silver-white hair picked up, momentarily, feebly, the lights of East London beyond the window. "How are things in Sao Paulo?"

"They're fine," answered the caller. In matters touching the activities of the Committee of Nine this man went by "X-sixteen" or "Sixteen." "*Assim-assim*" (so-so), Sixteen added in his native Portuguese.

"The Şahin Diary," said Matheson flatly. Matheson was the Committee of Nine's executive director. He was not known as Matheson in this regard, but as "XX-five" or "Five."

"Yes, Five."

"It's an exposé on the Armenian genocide. Ali Şahin was an aide-de-camp during the First World War—a Turk."

"I see."

"His diary—he'd been a journalist before the war. His diary fell into the hands of British Naval Intelligence, and the Turks wanted it back."

"So I assume it doesn't support Turkey's denials about the Armenian genocide," said Sixteen.

"No. Well, actually, no one knows. That's the assumption, clearly."

"No one's read it?"

"No one who's alive today."

"What about Şahin?"

"He was assassinated, shot through the window of his home in 1922."

"And there are no copies?" asked Sixteen.

Matheson sat up, adjusted the Bluetooth receiver in his right ear. "No." He reached for the mouse, jiggled it, brought his computer screen to life. A harsh white light assaulted his thin, surprised face, his high cheekbones and his sharp, aquiline nose. He leaned forward to read the pop-up window in the lower right corner: TELEPHONE CONFERENCE IN PROGRESS, TRANSCRIPTION CODE 9 (AUTHORIZED). The director sat back. "It was the subject of secret negotiations conducted by the Turkish envoy Abdul Paşa and Lord Worthington on behalf of the British Naval Intelligence in June of twenty-three, following the end of hostilities in the Turkish war of independence."

"Okay."

"In August of that year," Matheson continued, "it was turned over to Caliph Abdülmecid II in exchange for the release of thirty-three British prisoners. With Ataturk's approval, and approval of the national assembly—"

"Wait a minute!" said Sixteen. "Then someone must have read it."

"It's unlikely, I'm afraid. The Armenians have been turning over that stone for almost a century. No copies, and no survivors with knowledge of the diary's contents. Abdülmecid ordered it sealed and held in a secret underground repository for two hundred years. Western intelligence has placed the Şahin Diary in an unmarked vault beneath a building located in Tashkent, at 72-208 Shukhrat Street."

"And that's—?"

"Today, that's the address of Public School 32."

"The location of last night's break-in."

"Right."

Sixteen was silent. Matheson picked up his pipe and knocked its bowl against the side of the ashtray. "So, as I said, we're awaiting confirmation that the diary was not disturbed. Hold on. I'm getting another Interpol bulletin . . ."

"I'll let you go. Send it on when you get it decrypted. Thank you for the briefing, Five."

"Not at all."

*   *   *

From: XX5 – Executive Director CO-9 (London)
Date: Sun., 3 September 20ZZ 04:58:19

TO ALL COMMITTEE OF NINE (CO-9) MEMBERS:

JUST RECEIVED:

INTERPOL ADVISORY BULLETIN 12LQ5348, 3 SEPT. 20ZZ
04:09:26 +0200: "PRESIDENT MOHAMED MOHADJI, ISLAMIC
REPUBLIC OF TASHIR, HAS SCHEDULED A PRESS CONFERENCE
CONCERNING THE ARREST OF HIS GRANDDAUGHTER FATIMAH
IBRAHIM FOR 6 SEPT. 20ZZ, 13:30:00 +0300."

*　　*　　*

From: X22 – CO-9 (New York)
Date: Sun., 3 September 20ZZ 04:47:41 -0500

RECOMMEND ACTIVATION OF CONTINGENCY PLAN 44 (PAGE 266).
XX5 CONTINUE MONITORING.

*　　*　　*

From: X14 – CO-9 (Sydney)
Date: Sun., 3 September 20ZZ 04:59:19 +1000

NEWS HAS NOT HIT THE WIRES HERE IN SYDNEY. AGREE WITH X22.
ACTIVATE CONTINGENCY PLAN 44 (PAGE 266). XX5 CONTINUE
MONITORING.

III

———

Len steered the silver Hyundai Genesis—property of the American taxpayer—around a series of deep, jagged potholes and received a honk from a nervous oncoming driver. Len waved out of habit. His hands-free cell phone dialed audibly through the car's speakers, followed by the sound of a phone ringing.

"Hello. This is Sharon."

"Hi, Sharon. This is Len Williams—in Tashkent. I hope I'm not calling too late? My first meeting this morning took longer than expected."

"Oh, no worries."

"I e-mailed you the other day about the gray split-level in North Seattle." He sped up, for the time being having put the worst of the potholes in his rearview mirror.

"Yes. How are—?"

"As I mentioned, I like the look of that house. I'm fine, thanks. I particularly like the location. According to Google Maps, it's about a twenty-minute drive to my soon-to-be office." He imagined tree-lined streets of solid, never-ending asphalt, without potholes.

"Where's that?"

"Majestic International. They're in—"

"Oh, yes. In Edmonds. Pretty hard to miss the new Majestic building."

"That's what I hear. I haven't been there yet. In fact, I've never been to Seattle. I hear it's nice."

"Oh, it's more than nice. You're going to love it here."

"My wife was there once, as a kid, but she doesn't remember anything." Len made a face behind his sunglasses. "Strike that. I can't start the day with perjury. She hated it. She said it rained nonstop." The eight speakers surrounding the black leather interior of the car erupted with bright female laughter originating more than 6,200 miles away. Len used his left thumb to turn the volume down. "There's a bit of an enthusiasm gap over here."

"Where are you, again?"

"Uzbekistan."

"Where's that?"

"You've seen the face in the moon, haven't you, Sharon?"

"Yes."

"Anyway, Uzbekistan is right below the right eye. On a really clear night—" he continued, but there was no competing with the real estate agent's laughter.

"You're funny," she said.

"Actually, we're just north of Afghanistan, if you know where that is. It used to be part of the Soviet Union."

"Oh, it's one of those 'stans.' Aren't there just a whole bunch of those huddled right there together?"

Len had had the advantage of seeing Sharon Jordan's photo on her broker's web page, so he could imagine her—or some facsimile (who knew how recent the photo was)—standing or sitting in a well-appointed office, or perhaps sitting at home or in her car encased in the waning, orange-red light of a late summer evening. But, he thought, it wasn't until now—the way she'd asked the question, the lilt and intonation in her voice—that he would have known without seeing the photo that she was black. He wondered if she had detected the same thing about him.

"Yup," he continued, "there's Kazakhstan to the north, Kyrgyzstan and Tajikistan to the—"

"You live there?" she interrupted.

"For the last couple of years. Before that, I was in Kabul. My wife's been here for four-plus years. We wanted to be close, but didn't want her in a war zone, you understand."

"Sure. What do you do, if I may ask?"

"Political officer for the State Department. Negotiator. Conflict resolution, that sort of thing." Len checked the clock on the dashboard. "In fact, that's where I'm headed now. I have a negotiation out at the airport this morning."

"Oh, okay." Three seconds of silence beamed down from the satellite. Len had imagined a different response, something like, "Did you say conflict resolution in *Afghanistan*? You're kidding, right?"

"So you're leaving government service?"

"Right. After twenty-three years it's time to make an honest living." Time to make some real money, he thought as he checked the rearview mirror and maneuvered around a line of taxis double-parked in front of the Silk Road Hotel. A jolt of self-consciousness passed through him. Where's that coming from? he wondered. Is there something wrong with getting paid what you're worth? The question appeared suddenly, seemed to calve off something larger: all right, he had debts, and if the cards had gone differently . . . if he could have drawn to an inside straight just once . . . He banished the splashy red, yellow, and blue Poker All-Stars website from his mind by concentrating on the road.

"Do you and your wife have children, Len?"

"What? No." Now there's another sore subject, Len thought. He turned the Hyundai eastbound onto Navoi and lowered the visor. The sun was a furious ball of flame caught in a net of haze up ahead. He shielded his eyes with his hand and metaphorically shielded himself from the arguments that had punctuated the first twelve years of his marriage—before he had dropped the idea of children for good.

Another day above one hundred degrees, he guessed. The familiar roadside market, a blur traversing the passenger-side window, teemed with people—dark-haired men in black or navy suits with white shirts open at the collar. Women in long, loose-fitting tunics and intricately patterned ethnic dresses. He'd seen it hundreds of times: colorfully dressed women with straining plastic bags bulging with fresh fruits and a variety of salad greens—"green grass," they called it here—and golden discs of Uzbek bread, *tandir non,* converging on the market's narrow exits.

"The split-level on Eleventh Avenue Northwest is just over 1,400 square feet. Most of the price is in the location, I'm afraid, but there are some nice upgrades. It's got a great view of the Olympic Mountains and the shipping lanes."

"Yes, I saw that. What I'd—"

"It'd be a bit small for a family with children though. If you and your wife . . . what's her name?"

"Laura. What I'd—"

"If you and Laura decide to have children, there's potential for expansion downstairs. And the elementary school up there is top-notch."

"Got it."

As if she could safely have children at forty-four, Len thought. But even if that were possible, she wouldn't. Hell, I could still have a kid, Len thought. Forty-seven is nothing. But it was all counterweight to the memory of Laura, thirteen years earlier, declaring once and for all that she would never give up her figure for a child—that she found the postpartum female form repulsive. Len exhaled through clenched teeth and set up a little rhythm with his tongue. He sought to rid himself of the disagreeable recollection by concentrating on the road. He cleared his throat. "I'd like to take a look when I get there, if it's still on the market. I arrive in Seattle on the twenty-fourth. I'm due at the office the next day, but if we could meet that Wednesday or Thursday evening, that would be great."

"Of course. I can pick you and your wife up at the airport if you'd like."

"No, no, that's all right. They're handling that at Majestic. Thanks just the same. Oh, and it'll be just me. Laura's staying a few weeks to sell our furniture and take care of some last-minute things around here."

"I see. She trusts you, huh?"

I like this woman, Len thought. His cheeks rose suddenly beneath the rims of his dark glasses, and his smile exposed to the sunlight two rows of exceedingly white, straight teeth. She can dish it out, can't she? She reminded him of his older sister, Connie. No minced words, but kindhearted just the same. Her voice was similar, too.

"Well, to a point," he answered Sharon's question. "Tell me something, Sharon. How far is it from Majestic up to the Tulalip Casino? Am I saying that right?"

"The Tulalip. Let's see, it's not far. Right up the freeway. I'd say twenty miles or so."

"All right. Excellent."

"Would you like me to—?" A high-pitched dual tone reverberated in the speakers. "What's that?" asked Sharon.

"That's another call coming in. I better take it. I'll e-mail you and we can confirm the details."

"That'd be great. Say, how do they say good-bye in Uzbek?"

"*Salomat bo-ling.*"

"Sad-o-mat bowling, then." She giggled. The call-waiting signal sounded again. "Have a good day over there, Len."

"Will do." Len clicked her off, waited a beat. "Len Williams here."

"Len, it's Abbas."

"Hey, man, how's it going?"

"Don't know. Too early to tell."

"I was going to say. It's only—what? Ten fifteen? I thought nobody showed up at the Interior Ministry till noon or one on Mondays."

"Very funny."

Len had a ready image in his mind of his friend, thirty-six-year-old Abbas Ahkmedova: almond-colored skin, dark eyes, a strong chin, a guileless smile, short-cropped, straight black hair. "That flat hair's going to take you exactly nowhere," Len had once teased, rubbing his own short, afro-textured hair gingerly. "Maybe we can do something with it." Now Len turned down the fan on the AC. "What's up?"

"I'm not sure. You're not in the office?"

"No. I have a negotiation at the airport this morning."

"Okay. I just heard we arrested two people Saturday night: one an American, white, sixty-three, the other . . . well, you won't believe it."

"Try me."

"Fatimah Ibrahim. *The* Fatimah Ibrahim."

"Who's that?"

"You're kidding, right?"

"No, I'm afraid not."

"The heiress? The granddaughter of the president of the Islamic Republic of Tashir?"

"Oh."

"Probably one of the most photographed people in the world. Where have you been, man? Last year she was on the cover of about six thousand magazines."

"Is that right?"

"I know you know who I'm talking about. Dark. Beautiful. Great eyes—unusual eyes. Came up with the PR campaign for

Doctors for Peace a couple of years ago. Raised over $400 million in less than twenty-four hours, or something like that."

"Ah. Okay."

"You really don't know who I'm talking about, do you?"

"Not a clue."

"You've got to get out more."

"So you arrested her. What for?"

"Depends who you ask. They'll say they were raising a flag."

"What?"

"Yeah. No joke." Abbas's voice became reticent, as though someone or something at the other end were distracting him.

"Where?"

"At a school. Again, that's what they'll say."

Len stopped and waved a jaywalker across the street in front of him. "Okay, and who's the American again?"

"Alden Frost."

"Frost. Should I have heard of him, too?"

"No, not necessarily."

"What was he? The first astronaut or something?"

"You're in a rare mood. So, I take it you're in the dark on this?"

"I'd say so, yes." Len brought his car back up to speed. He checked the passenger side mirror, hoping to change lanes. No luck, the lane was full.

"All right. You're no help. Something tells me you'll know more by the end of the day."

"Oh?"

"I've asked the interior minister to call Ambassador Tompkins and request that he put you on the case. I figured I owed you a favor. Plus, it'll give us a chance to work together one last time."

Len chuckled. "No, I don't think so, old man." He slowed again, this time for traffic up ahead. "I'm a short-timer. You know that. I'm out of here in a couple of weeks."

"I know. I was scheduled to come over to your office tomorrow morning for cake, but then this came up, so now—"

"*Cake?*"

Abbas groaned. "Oh no! Don't tell me it was a surprise. Your secretary didn't tell me. She just said 'Come by at ten on Tuesday for a piece of cake and a good-bye party for Len.' She's going to kill me."

Len laughed. "Don't worry about it. I'm in the State Department, remember? 'Blown secrets' is my middle name. She'll never know. I'll break down crying or something."

"I'm counting on it. I've got to live with Karen long after you've gone off to the wilds of America." Len rubbed his perpetual five o' clock shadow with his knuckles.

"That's right. And my retirement is exactly why I won't be getting involved in this—whatever it is—flag caper." It took him a second, but he didn't like the way the word "retirement" sounded coming out of his own mouth. I'm forty-seven but I sound like sixty, he said to himself. "I'm sure the ambassador will give it to a consular officer," he continued.

"No, I think this one may require more of an experienced hand."

"What do you mean?"

Abbas hesitated. "You're going to find out soon enough," he said, exuding more confidence than Len wanted to hear. "Let's just say these two broke into a building that isn't . . . well, it's more than a school. We're sure Washington knows what it's used for, and where it's located. On top of that, Fatimah Ibrahim has been officially listed with Interpol as missing for the last nine months."

"Huh. Interesting. But no, it won't be me. I'm cleaning out my desk, closing files—that sort of thing. I'm done after this morning's negotiation." Len put on his turn signal to enter the airport off-ramp. "You say they were raising a flag. What kind of flag?"

"I don't know. A peace flag, I think. I need to find out more about it."

Len chuckled. "Ah, world peace. Good times."

* * *

"You understand, my clients have lost everything. Their children, Ahmed's brothers, Maqbool and Muhammad, and both of their mothers. Mr. Williams, you cannot believe $350,000 is a fair offer."

Len fought the temptation to look up, to make eye contact with the thirty-two-year-old woman wrapped in a gray *chador* and wearing a black veil or the thirty-six-year -old man dressed in an ill-fitting black suit with open collar and vest. They sat to the left of their Pakistani attorney, facing the window, staring past Len's shoulder at what for them, he knew, was nothingness—or worse— and for others was the busy tarmac of Tashkent International Airport. The roar of jet engines came and went, overwhelming the ticking clock that hung at one end of the small, sparsely appointed conference room. They were perfectly still, these two.

Sitting to Len's left was General Stuart L. Martin—hometown Carbondale, Pennsylvania, avid fisherman and hunter, church deacon, grandfather to seven. This and more Len had learned while they had waited for the plane from Peshawar. The questions, however, had gone both ways.

"And you? Where are you from?" the general had asked.

"Tucson by way of Bakersfield and Flagstaff," Len had replied.

"I guess that's a different brand of hunting down there?"

"I suppose. It's never been my thing. City kid."

"You a church-goer?"

"Was for a time. After my father was killed, my mom stopped insisting we go. You know how kids are."

"That's a tough thing, losing a father."

Each man had given only a small fraction of his attention—maybe 10 percent—to this conversation, 90 percent to e-mail and text messages, and to letting their eyes rove over people—women mostly—bustling about the busy airport. But now they sat shoulder to shoulder, hands in their laps, their eyes veiled behind half-closed lids. Across the width of the mahogany table between them and the man and woman field reports, bomb damage assessments, and black-and-white aerial photographs were strewn in conspicuous confusion. The Peshawar attorney waited for an answer.

A little silence won't hurt, Len thought, as he reached for his legal pad and leaned back, letting his scribbled notes blur and his mind wander in a new direction. He wrote a series of Zs with heavy serifs across the top of the page and wondered how long it would take for everyone in the room to see that fairness had nothing to do with any of this.

It wasn't fair when Dad died, he thought. He recalled a piece of that day thirty-nine years earlier when he'd heard his name and his older brother's name called out over the school PA system. "Arthur Williams and Leonard Williams, please come to the office immediately." Marching into the office to find Arthur already there, crying in his mother's arms—how fair was any of it? Little boys shouldn't lose their fathers, even police officer fathers.

Len took a drink of tepid coffee. He had grown past certain concepts popular in the culture—was, "alas, disabused" of them his mother would have said—the idea of objective fairness being one. Life isn't fair. It's a gamble. There are winners and losers. Two older sisters and his mother, Henrietta Williams, had ushered in the new reality. "What is fair to you, *mon ami*, may not be fair to Henrietta Darlene Williams, pleased to meet you." Len sensed a hint of a smile pulling at the muscles of his face as the memory flooded back. He kept his eyes downcast. "Fair? I'll tell you what's fair!" his mother had yelled from the kitchen as she dropped two bulging bags of groceries on the table and marched into the living room to break up a fight between Len and his older brother. "Fair is my not having to come home to a messy house and two spoiled boys who think nothing of kicking over the lamps."

"But Mom!" Arthur had pleaded in a high, bleating, thirteen-year-old voice. "That's not fair. Leonard started it." She had held up her hand. "What's fair to you, *mon ami*, may not be fair to Henrietta Darlene Williams, pleased to meet you."

This phrase had struck a chord with Len and Arthur's older sisters, Elsie and Connie, and not two days had elapsed before "What's fair to you, *mon ami*, may not be fair to Henrietta Darlene Williams, pleased to meet you," became the lingua franca of the tormentor—even, at times, the tormented. It was repeated in every room and hallway. It reverberated across the closed—and only—bathroom door in the small, stucco house on Maple Street. In less than a week, common usage had shorn the expression of needless wool. "Pleased to meet you" was the ultimate put-down in the Williams' Tucson home in the ensuing epoch. Even Henrietta used it on occasion.

A great wave of noise swallowed the room again as a jet thundered down the runway, bringing Len back to the present. Seconds later, quiet. Len became aware of the subtle movement of the grieving father's lips as he whispered something to no one—to himself.

Len had been startled by two lines of discolored, misshapen teeth when they were introduced. The man had an unpleasant odor, and his cheeks, not sufficiently hidden by a full black beard, were sallow and pockmarked. He seemed disproportionately tall and lanky—although Len, at six foot one, had looked straight across into his eyes when they shook hands. Yet it was odd: the slope of his shoulders and the forward lean of his neck and head suggested a body wishing to be shorter. Would he be considered handsome in his homeland—in the tribal areas of Waziristan? Perhaps, Len thought, for in spite of all else there was a hint of strength, even a reserved nobility in the set of his large, brown eyes. Len guessed he was a man of innate intelligence, whatever his schooling.

Len turned his pen over and drummed its nonbusiness end on the pad. Pursing his lips, he thought of asking questions about these people, of taking to his breast some sense of their lives. Flipping the pen back deftly, he drew a squiggled line one way and then the other through all the Zs. No, he thought, I'll stick with the information provided by their attorney. Nothing is gained by familiarity. In twenty-one years of negotiating, he had learned the art of silence.

The attorney cleared his throat. Len felt General Martin's hand on his arm. He leaned toward the officer. The general cupped his hand and whispered behind it. "Godammit, I haven't got time for this, Williams. Tell him that's our best offer. If they can give us actionable intelligence on the whereabouts of Abdul Rahimi, we'll go to 400. Otherwise they can jolly well—"

Len nodded and raised his hand, stopping the general. "Right," Len said.

"May I have a word with you alone, Mr. Williams?" said the Pakistani attorney. He leaned over and said something to his clients in Hindko, then, facing Len again, in English said, "Perhaps we can take a five-minute break?"

Len looked at General Martin, who signaled begrudging consent.

In the hallway, the attorney adopted a conciliatory tone. "Mr. Williams, I understand the position you have to take, but I want to appeal to your sense of justice—to what you know is the right thing to do. My firm has taken this case *pro bono*. I have no personal stake in this matter. But I am interested—as I believe you must be—in seeing justice done. Why the United States government is offering $350,000 for the lives of nine innocent people I don't know. I suspect the Army may think my clients are withholding intelligence, but I can assure you they are not. Mr. Siddiqui is a simple goat farmer. He has tried assiduously to stay out of local politics for fear that the very thing that has happened would happen.

"Last month, the United States government paid the family of Shaheen Shahzad, the six-year-old son of the local magistrate, who was killed by a drone attack, three-quarters of a million dollars. Now, it offers these parents $350,000 for five children and four other loved ones. Can you tell me this is right?" The legal counsel did not release Len from his stare, but neither did he insinuate by his expression that Len was responsible for the current state of affairs. He saw in Len only a last hope.

Len knew of the case of the magistrate's son, and, of course, the attorney was right. What motive would he have had to lie? "I understand your frustration," Len said in an even, professional tone. "The government has a policy of handling each of these cases separately . . . but let me talk to the general and see what I can do. Why don't you ask your clients to step out of the room for a few minutes?"

The attorney smiled and nodded. "I'll do that."

It is impossible to say what impact Len might have had on the general had he pressed him for more money. He's out of cards, Len thought, smiling inwardly. Shit, I could use $350,000, he thought, taking his seat beside the general. He took a moment's satisfaction imagining the phone call he'd place to Adam Smythe, the "banker" at Poker All-Stars. "It's done. I've deposited the full $63,000 . . . yes, it's there. I told you I was good for it."

"What did he want?" the general asked.

Len turned to the man with the deep voice beside him. He could read impatience in the parenthetical lines on either side of the general's face. "Listen. He's brought up the Shahzad case, the fact that we paid Abdul Shahzad $750,000 for the death of one child. I tried to explain—" Len stopped in deference to a long, slow, loud exhale by General Martin. "Yeah, I know. I tried to tell him—"

"Godammit, why the hell are we wasting our time with these people?"

"You're right, General," Len heard himself say. "They're done. They know it. Wait a couple minutes, then we'll call them back and tell them."

"If Mr. Siddiqui can give us the whereabouts of Abdul Rahimi or any members of his immediate family, I'll go to $400,000. But otherwise, we're at $350,000, period."

"Yup. Makes sense."

With that Len sat back and checked for messages on his cell phone. After a couple of minutes, he went to the door and waved the attorney and his clients back into the room. He waited for them to retake their seats. Looking across the table into the eyes of the Peshawar attorney, he said, "We absolutely do think our offer is fair, Mr. Khalili. We, of course, are sorry for your clients' loss, but the drone program is an essential part of the War on Terror. It's not perfect. We flew you and your clients here to negotiate a fair compensation package, and that's exactly what we're trying to accomplish."

"But $350,000 for five children and four adults? It's—"

"It's a small fortune. I assume your clients intend to live in Waziristan, and that Mr. Siddiqui will continue to raise sheep and goats? Am I right?"

The attorney frowned and turned to his clients. He spoke to them in Hindko. Now Len did look up. The father of Rama, age 9; Shazia, 8; Syed, 6; Tahir, 3; and Naveed, 4 months—all dead; the brother of Maqbool and Muhammad—both dead; the son of Saba Bukhari and the son-in-law of Alina Shahzadi—dead—did not turn to look at his representative, or at his wife, or at anyone else in the room.

The right thing to do.

For an uncomfortable half minute, the bereaved man's large brown eyes were fixed on the surface of the table as in a death stare.

*　　*　　*

It was palpable. Never mind the Islamic calls to prayer or the miles of gray, monolithic Soviet-era apartment buildings lining the boulevards. Forget the *duppi* hats worn by swarthy Uzbek men, or the variety of Turkic languages spoken on the sun-drenched streets four floors below. The Silk Road? No, this was a little piece of America. Len knew it. They all did. Steelcase cubicles, Hewlett-Packard computers, a Jimi Hendrix poster, the stars and stripes flying straight out in one child's patriotic drawing pinned to a cubicle wall after another, a dreamcatcher in the window. What struck Len as he entered the back rooms—the working rooms—of U.S. embassy Tashkent was the pleasant sensation of American soil.

Len stopped to get the latest Diamondbacks score from a fellow Arizonan on the way to his office. He tried to ignore his secretary, Karen Blair, who rose up out of her cubicle sentry-like and took a position near his office door, arms folded. She watched through oversized, horn-rimmed glasses as Anthony Cotton, a security analyst, wadded a piece of paper and bounced it off Len's shoulder like a tennis ball. There was general laughter. "Short-timer!" shouted Cotton.

Len chuckled. "Yeah, yeah. I know."

Karen Blair wasn't laughing. She was all business as she handed Len a pile of mail and phone messages and followed him into his office. "The ambassador has been down here twice looking for you. He wants to see you the minute you walk in— his words."

"Let me guess. He didn't say what he wanted."

"No, but he seemed agitated."

Len put his briefcase down on the desk and began looking through the mail. "Probably wants to have a going-away party for me." He was careful not to look up. When he did at last, Karen was blushing.

She marched over and took the mail out of his hands. "He was serious. Now if you don't go up there, I'm the one who looks bad." She tamped the mail on the desk to neaten the pile, then laid it down. "And unlike some people, I need this job." She took a step back and folded her hands. Under the thick lenses of her glasses a mist gathered.

Len smiled. "I'm going to miss you, too, Karen. I was serious about you coming with me . . . getting a job at Majestic."

"I know you were. Just go—please."

Len removed his jacket and swung it over the back of his chair. "I will." He walked toward the door and then spun around. "Call Abbas Ahkmedova at the Interior Ministry. Ask him to meet me here tomorrow morning at 10:50. Tell him it'll take only a few minutes . . . and coffee's on me."

Karen's face brightened. She suppressed a smile. "Right away."

The door to Ambassador Harold Tompkins's office was open. The ambassador, a gray-haired man of sixty-seven, lean and fit, with pale blue eyes and long vertical lines on either side of his mouth, looked up from a phone call and waved Len in. Len closed the door and walked to the window, sensing it would be awhile. The ambassador fed staccato utterances and long silences into the receiver. Len looked out over the skyline of Tashkent and at the park below. A pigeon swooped close then veered off when Len raised his hand to cover a yawn. The blue dome of the Amir Temur Museum winked up through a windswept canopy of trees. Len wondered for the first time if he would miss this place. He would certainly miss his friends—Abbas, Karen. But the place? It had its good points. He liked the heat. Being from Tucson, he was a heat worshiper. All of a sudden, Len felt a pressure rise up in his head, a weariness associated with this morning's negotiation at the airport. He closed his eyes and pinched the bridge of his nose, willing the stress away.

"Yes, well, that's what I told Jacobson," the ambassador was saying into his phone.

Len opened his eyes and stared out at the dust-colored, sun-suffused horizon. Seattle's weather is going to be a challenge, he thought. He'd been warned not to put too much stock in the photographs he'd seen of Puget Sound, the mountains and lakes— when the sun was shining they were unbelievable. Everything is so green there, he mused. Still, give me the desert.

I'll miss not being able to use my Russian, he thought, as he tried not to eavesdrop on the ambassador's conversation. I'm going to miss the staff at Tariq's Café, too. Perhaps if Laura liked it better here, he thought. She doesn't seem happy, especially since I've returned from Kabul. I can't say she's chomping at the bit to get to Seattle, either, though. An unsettled feeling drove Len away from the window. He walked over and sat in one of the chairs facing the ambassador's desk.

Tompkins frowned, saying "uh-huh" into the receiver for the umpteenth time. He picked up a piece of paper from a stack on his desk and tossed it at Len. He pointed at it as if to say, "Read it." It was an "overnight note" from the Central Asian Desk in Washington marked "Top Secret":

SECURE IMMEDIATE RELEASE OF US CITIZEN ALDEN W. FROST FROM TASHKENT MUNICIPAL JAIL. OFFER SAFE PASSAGE TO WASHINGTON *WITH PACKAGE.*

It was signed by the secretary of state herself. Len felt a shudder. He looked at Tompkins, who, far from being distracted, lifted his eyebrows for emphasis. Shit, thought Len, looking down at the cable again, this is the guy Abbas was talking about.

"I've got to get back to work, Bob. I'll check with Betsy and we'll figure something out. Alright . . . you bet . . . good-bye." The ambassador exhaled heavily and shook his head as he hung up the phone. Shifting gears, he asked, "So, what do you think?"

"I don't know. Who is this guy?" Len placed the cable back on the desk. "And what—?"

"No idea. You'd think they'd tell us a bit more, wouldn't you."

"The package, I mean."

"Yeah. I don't know. I've got my staff making some calls to find out."

"Hmm. I got a call from Abbas Ahkmedova this morning telling me they'd arrested this fellow along with some gal from Tashir—the president's granddaughter or something. Something about putting up a flag. Apparently they'd broken into a building to do it."

"All right. We need to get to the bottom of it, whatever it is. You can see what our marching orders are."

Len waited a few seconds, hoping the ambassador would remember that he was leaving the State Department in a matter of days. Evidently, Tompkins didn't remember—or didn't care. "I'm done here at the end of next week, Ambassador. I'm taking the following week off to pack, and then I fly out on the twenty-third."

"The end of next week," repeated Tompkins, as though recalling the detail over a span of years. "That's right. But you'll have plenty of time." The ambassador trained his blue eyes on Len. "I need you on this one. When the orders come down from the secretary like this, I get a little jumpy. Something's up. And why they didn't send more details I can't imagine."

Len wondered if the ambassador would tell him what he already knew: that the Uzbek interior minister, Salim Guryanov, had called that morning to ask that Len be put on the case. Thanks a million, Abbas, Len thought as he watched the ambassador rise, walk around his desk, and make his way to the door, where his suit jacket was hanging on a brass hook. He put on the jacket. "I've got a lunch meeting."

Len stood up. A new assignment was the last thing he'd expected. He began, "Harold, I really think—"

"No, I want you on this. Find out what's going on, will you? And negotiate this man's release. If the secretary says its top priority, that's what it must be. Though I suspect it's pretty minor. Otherwise they wouldn't expect us to waltz in and get him out just like that. Take $15,000 with you. That should do it. I'm guessing you'll have him out this afternoon."

IV

——

A third round of knocks on the steel door was so far out of keeping with her dream that Fatimah awakened. She lifted her head off the pillow. As her eyes adjusted, the unadorned gray walls barely visible through the gloom seemed to hum with a low, ambient sound—a distant furnace perhaps. There was a small, spare table near her head, familiar now, and a wooden chair. Next to the door was a sink with a cold water tap. The scratched and dented stainless steel mirror above the sink reflected a horizontal window—two feet by six inches. Beyond its frosted glass the indistinct impression of prison bars. More knocking. The air was cold.

"What is it?" asked Fatimah. She cleared her throat and rose up on an elbow.

There was a jingle of keys, then the sound of a door being unlocked. A female guard appeared, a black silhouette framed in bright artificial light. "Someone here to see you," she said in a struggling English.

Squinting, with one eye shut, Fatimah tried to clear her throat. "Who is it?" But before the guard could answer Fatimah asked in a gravelly voice, "What time is it?"

"It's 4:20. Get up. Mr. Msaidie from the Tashiri Foreign Ministry is here. He's received permission from our government to see you at once. He's waiting."

"At this hour?" Fatimah frowned. "I don't think so." She rolled all the way over onto her other hip and flopped down on the pillow, pulling the blanket up to her chin.

The guard waited.

"*Up!*"

Fatimah was a silent mountain range under the covers.

"Get up and get dressed. You have ten minutes." The overhead light went on, then the door closed with a click-clicking of the lock.

Is there any reason to believe she isn't serious? Fatimah wondered, her nose pressed to the pillow. She really will be back, won't she? And if I were an ordinary prisoner—if they weren't giving me this special treatment—she would have sworn at me, pulled me out of bed by now, or beat me with a baton . . .

*   *   *

Ali Msaidie rose when Fatimah entered the interrogation room. His height—six foot three—startled her, as did the width of his broad shoulders. His black suit could not have held a larger man. He reacted first by observing her hands closely, to see if she were carrying anything. The guard who opened the door cleared her throat, held up the key insinuatingly, and stepped back into the hallway, locking the door after her.

"Ms. Ibrahim," Msaidie said in greeting. He bowed his head and switched from English to Tashiri. "I'm sorry to have disturbed you at this hour, but my orders are to get you out of Uzbekistan and back to Sanori as quickly as possible. Please, have a seat."

Fatimah complied. She blinked repeatedly, trying to wake up. The cold water she'd splashed on her face, the elevator ride, and the long shuffle down the silent hallway in ill-fitting flip-flops hadn't been enough. "Who are you again?"

The man produced a wallet. He flipped it open to a plastic window and showed her an official-looking ID card. "My name is Ali Msaidie, Ms. Ibrahim. I'm with the Tashiri Foreign Ministry." He replaced the wallet, then leaned over and reached into a side pocket to produce another piece of paper, this one a letter-size sheet folded in thirds. He opened it with large dark hands and handed it to Fatimah. "I have authority from the Uzbek government to take you into my custody and transport you home."

"At four in the morning?"

Msaidie looked at his watch. "It's almost five now. I've been meeting with local authorities most of the night, you understand." Impatience twitched just beneath the surface of his coffee-colored skin. She noticed for the first time a scar on his right cheek. She could smell him, too—smell him in the still air of the small conference room. His odor was not unappealing, although in a split second she stamped his odor with indifference and didn't think of it again.

Fatimah frowned as she glanced down at the paper. It was an official-looking something-or-other—a form printed in Uzbek or some other language she couldn't read. The blanks appeared to have been hurriedly filled in. She recognized her name and Mr. Msaidie's, but nothing else made sense—not a bit. There were two scribbled signatures in the bottom right corner and an embossed seal in the bottom left corner.

"My grandfather sent you?" Fatimah said, yawning.

Msaidie swallowed uncomfortably. "Yes. Although that's not . . . that's not for me to say, Ms. Ibrahim. I take my orders from the foreign minister."

Fatimah pulled at the sleeves of her prison-issue *abaya*. I know the foreign minister, she told herself. I've met several of his deputies, including his chief deputy. Why wouldn't he have sent someone familiar to me? I've never seen this man before—or heard of him. "I see. And did the foreign minister tell you to arrange for Mr. Frost's release, as well?"

"Mr. Frost?"

"The man I was with when I was arrested."

"No. It's my understanding he's . . . isn't he an American?"

"So?"

"So, his release is not a concern of the government of Tashir. However, if there's anything you wish to take—"

"But it's a concern to *me*." Fatimah trained her large brown eyes on Msaidie. "I'm not leaving without him."

"*What?*"

Fatimah sat up stiffly, arms folded. She knew her celebrity meant power and, to a certain extent, protection. She hadn't been blind to the guards' sheepishness and embarrassment. Even the arresting officers grew reticent once they realized who she was. She was determined not to abandon Alden—not to remove this protection from him.

"There's nothing we can do for Mr. Frost. I wish it were different, but you see, he's under the jurisdiction of the U.S. embassy."

Fatimah stared blankly at Msaidie.

"Each of you is a separate case. But as I say, if—"

"We'll have to see about that," she said. "I'm meeting with him and . . . someone from the U.S. embassy at one o'clock tomorrow afternoon."

"I'm afraid that's impossible, Ms. Ibrahim. We have a jet waiting at the airport. There's no time. You're being released now, and I'm under orders to get you out of here as quickly as possible."

Fatimah leaned back heavily in her chair. "Perhaps *you're* under orders, Mr. Msaidie, but I'm not. I'm an adult, and . . . I don't do things at the beck and call of my grandfather, or the foreign minister, or anyone else. I shan't go with you, not unless you've arranged for Mr. Frost's release, as well."

I don't want to go back to Tashir anyway, she thought, remembering Jamaal. It would kill me to see him again, but could I resist seeing him if I were there?

"I hope I'm making myself clear," she said aloud. She squeezed her eyes shut and touched her temple. It was hard to be forceful when you were only half awake, Fatimah realized.

"So you're choosing to stay in jail?"

"Yes—in so many words."

Msaidie's brow arched. "You . . . do you . . . realize, Ms. Ibrahim, the danger you're in here? Your status in the world will not save you. Uzbek prisons are notorious for their—"

"I don't want to debate you at four . . . or five . . . in the morning, Mr. Msaidie. I'm simply telling you that I will not leave without Mr. Frost." She covered a deep yawn with a fist. "We were putting up companion flags as an encouragement to children. That's all. Our crime was trespassing, nothing more . . . to get to a bloody flagpole." The last two words she said in English with a thick British accent, a legacy of seven English teachers and three tutors all hailing from Britain, followed by four years spent studying philosophy at Oxford.

Their eyes met for several seconds. Msaidie relented and looked down at his fingers thrumming the table top. Then he pulled out his wallet again and extracted a card. "Perhaps I should give you more time to think about it. I will return tomorrow afternoon, Ms. Ibrahim, after you've had your meeting with . . . Did they say who they're sending from the embassy?"

"No. They just said they're sending someone."

"If you'd like to contact me, here's my number." Msaidie left the card on the table, got up, walked to the door, and put his hand on the doorknob. "I'll see that you have access to a telephone."

V
___

From: XX5 – Executive Director CO-9 (London)
To: undisclosed recipients
Date: Tues., 5 September 20ZZ 05:10:01
Subject: Fatimah Ibrahim
Encryption/Decryption Enabled: B72ZZ256-9102 (All Threads)

___

TO ALL COMMITTEE OF NINE (CO-9) MEMBERS:

THE ŞAHIN DIARY IS MISSING.

OUR SOURCE AT THE CITY JAIL CONFIRMS THAT FATIMAH IBRAHIM HAS REFUSED EXTRICATION/TRANSPORT. THE TASHIRI AGENT WHO VISITED HER WILL RETURN 6 SEPTEMBER AT 11:15:00 +0500.

*　　*　　*

From: X19 – CO-9 (Buenos Aires)
Date: Tues., 5 September 20ZZ 05:19:30 -0300

IF SHE LEAVES, THE DIARY MAY LEAVE WITH HER. DO WE HAVE ASSETS IN TASHIR? IF SHE HAS IT, CAN IT BE ACQUIRED BY OTHER MEANS? RECOMMEND XX5 CONTINUE MONITORING.

*　　*　　*

From: X14 – CO-9 (Sydney)
Date: Tues., 5 September 20ZZ 05:24:49 +1000

STILL QUIET HERE. STORY KILLED BY ADDINGTON. PLEASE ADVISE NEXT STEPS.

*　　*　　*

From: X22– CO-9 (NY)
Date: Tues., 5 September 20ZZ 05:37:22 -0500

THE STATE DEPARTMENT HAS ASSIGNED LEONARD DANIEL WILLIAMS (CO-9 PROFILE XTY734-99), US EMBASSY TASHKENT, TO SECURE RELEASE OF ALDEN FROST. WILLIAMS WAS RECENTLY HIRED BY MAJESTIC INTERNATIONAL, EDMONDS, WA, AS CONFLICT RESOLUTION SPECIALIST. STARTING DATE: 25 SEPTEMBER. DO WE HAVE ANYONE INSIDE MAJESTIC? XX5 CONTINUE MONITORING.

*　　*　　*

From: XX8 – CO-9 (Bangalore)
Date: Tues., 5 September 20ZZ 05:44:29 +0530

THIS MAY BE OF INTEREST. ON 26 AUGUST THE INTERNATIONAL COURT OF JUSTICE THREW OUT A KEY PIECE OF EVIDENCE IN THE REPARATIONS CASE BROUGHT BY ARMENIAN RELIEF AGAINST THE REPUBLIC OF TURKEY. THE COURT'S MINUTE ENTRY READS, IN PART, "A CLAIM FOR REPARATIONS CANNOT STAND WITHOUT DIRECT EVIDENCE THAT THE CRIMES ALLEGED TO HAVE OCCURRED DID IN FACT OCCUR. THE PETITIONER HAS REQUESTED A STAY OF NINETY DAYS. AT THE END OF THAT PERIOD, ABSENT THE PRESENTATION OF NEW EVIDENCE SHOWING THAT THE ALLEGED ATROCITIES IN EAST ANATOLIA DID OCCUR AT THE BEHEST OF THE TURKISH GOVERNMENT DURING THE PERIOD 1917-18, THE COMPLAINT FILED BY ARMENIAN RELIEF WILL BE DISMISSED WITH PREJUDICE."

VI

Laura Williams was late to the farewell party, but her entrance, with red, white, and blue balloons and a dozen red roses, raised the volume in the break room.

"You're not too late—there's cake left," someone said as she hugged her way across the room.

Laura laughed. "My eyes say yes, my hips say no."

"Oh, come on. Embassy rules."

One of the women relieved her of the bouquet and went in search of a vase. Laura arrived in front of Len and Abbas, handed the balloons to Len, and gave his friend a hug. "Hi, Abbas. How are you?"

Abbas was holding a piece of cake in a paper plate. His free arm encircled her narrow waist without touching it. He leaned over to kiss her smooth, mocha-colored cheek, but then thought better of it. "I'm fine, Laura. Not thrilled about the reason for this party, though."

She embraced Len with the side of her head pressed against his chest. "I know."

Len had expected a kiss but was happy to feel the fullness of her breasts nestled against him. He kissed the top of her head and greedily breathed in the familiar smell of her. "I'm glad you made it, sweetheart. Was the traffic bad?"

"Don't get me started. But, hey, here I am." She looked around the room and exchanged smiles and waves with a couple of women from the consular section. Then she turned back to Abbas. "How's your mother, Abbas?"

The Uzbek stood with a white plastic fork and a small piece of white cake poised inches from his mouth. "Oh, she's fine. Thanks." He held that position until Laura turned to her husband.

"We still have her red and black serving dish," she said. "You keep saying you're going to return it."

"I know. I will."

Laura raised her eyebrows skeptically. "Time is runnin' out."

"I'll bring it in tomorrow," Len said. He looked over his wife's head at Abbas and shook his head no.

Laura delivered a backhand to Len's midsection.

"I will!" Len insisted.

"It was given to my mother as a thank you for saving three children and a dog in a fire," Abbas said, struggling to keep a straight face.

All three broke into laughter, which contributed to the general state of the break room.

"Hey, Williams!" shouted Anthony Cotton. "Now that your wife's here, why don't you tell us how you're going to conquer the world once you get to Seattle?"

Len laughed. "One juicy federal contract at a time," he said. "Isn't that how it's done?"

"That's right!" someone shouted, and a murmur of agreement spread throughout the room.

Another deep male voice rose above the din. "But you're not leaving town until you pay off your gambling debts, right?" Len looked to see a red-faced Sam Davis, a liaison officer, standing at the back of the room. Davis's tone had held some of the brightness of a jest, enough to leave a smile on about half the people in attendance. Laura's body tensed visibly. She turned her head away from her husband.

Len laughed deeply. "Of course not. You'll be two hundred dollars richer by the end of next week, Sam. That is, unless you want to go another round." This last he said with an insouciance and spiritedness designed to take back the advantage, a ploy that seemed to work.

"Fair enough," answered Davis.

Now Laura turned to him, partly to hide her face. Staring at his chest, she struggled to control a paroxysm of anger. In a disguised whisper, she said, "So you're gambling here, too?"

Len held her arms and shook them gently. "No. It's not what you think."

"What is it then? Why did he say—?"

Abbas had started to turn away, but then Len said in his direction, "Abbas and I were just talking about a last-minute assignment." Len looked at his friend entreatingly. "Shouldn't take more than a day or two, but who knew I'd be opening a new file at this stage."

"You're kidding," said Laura, swallowing back her anger and composing herself. Her dark eyebrows dipped slightly and her voice betrayed a new level of concern. She turned to look at Abbas, then back at her husband. "Who gave you this—"

"Tompkins," Len replied. "Yesterday."

"Why didn't you tell me?" She stopped herself on "me" and her eyes flashed to the side.

Because you didn't get home from your book club meeting until after midnight, Len said to himself. He knew from her expression that she was thinking the same thing.

"But Majestic's expecting you on the twenty-fifth."

"I know."

Laura's eyes narrowed critically. "What is this assignment? Can you talk about it?"

"Sure, if I knew what to say. An American was arrested here Saturday night. Abbas knows more than I do, but he's not talking."

Abbas gave a short, embarrassed smile. He held up his plate. "I'm just here for the cake."

Laura rolled large eyes at the Uzbek. "Sure you are," she said.

"Anyway, that's all I know," Len continued. "The orders are to get him released and get him on a plane to Washington, so I guess that's my job. We're going over to the city jail tomorrow. Abbas has agreed to run interference for me."

"What was he arrested for?"

Len looked at Abbas questioningly.

Abbas shrugged. "Let's just say breaking and entering. I'm not really at liberty—"

"Oh, I get it. You're cast in the role of Len's minder again," Laura said. She took a step back and put her hands on her hips, then made an elaborate face. "I swear, I don't know how you two do it."

Abbas choked and began to cough, evidently caught off guard by Laura's tone. "Oh." He began coughing uncontrollably. "Sorry!" he wheezed, between Len's blows to his back.

*   *   *

"We're ten minutes out," Abbas said, adjusting the fit of his Bluetooth ear piece. "Have Mr. Frost and Ms. Ibrahim ready in the large conference room at one-fifteen, will you? . . . Right . . . Len Williams, U.S. State Department . . . There is? Who?" Abbas turned in the passenger seat. "Do you know a Charlotte Yacoubi?"

"Don't think so," Len said. "Who is she?"

"International Committee of the Red Cross." Abbas shot another inquisitive look at Len. Len shook his head. "What? No. Stall her. I'll talk to her when I get there."

Len nosed the silver Genesis into a roundabout and exited on to Mirobad ko'chasi. He heard the rest of Abbas's conversation without listening, with a slight smile on his face. He was grateful for Abbas's company. Never mind that the single, thirty-six-year-old Uzbek was repeatedly tasked with watching him like a hawk and reporting anything and everything, telling and otherwise, to higher-ups. This was business as usual in this part of the world. It didn't mean he and Abbas couldn't have constructive and candid dialogues or keep confidences, within limits.

He thought back to their first meeting, four years earlier. Len had been ordered to fly from Kabul to Karshi-Khanabad airbase in southeastern Uzbekistan to negotiate a dispute over hours of military use of the narrow, Soviet-built Friendship Bridge connecting Uzbekistan and Afghanistan. Fuel and supply convoys were routinely clogging the single southbound lane, making it impossible for farmers and shippers on the Uzbekistan side to get their produce to Hairaton on market days. The Uzbek Interior Ministry sent Abbas to negotiate on behalf of Uzbek interests. Len found in him a fair, pragmatic, and tough negotiator who kept his cool and, like Len, had an unfailing sense of when he was, and was not, on the clock. Off the clock, the quiet Uzbek matched Len's propensity for candor, compromise, and self-deprecation—a refusal to take oneself too seriously. He introduced Len to Uzbek *plov*, the national dish of rice and lamb, and mailed him his mother's recipe in English within the week. So, similar in temperament, imbued with mutual respect, the two found it easy to carve out a workable solution to the bridge problem.

Abbas, whose slightly bent boxer's nose seemed to favor the left side of his face, was fluent in English, French, and Uzbek—and, of course, Russian. The dossier that Len had pored over on the flight to Karshi-Khanabad revealed that Abbas was from Chukurkul, in the Bukhara region. After four years at a local lyceum, he'd trained at a technical institute for a career in geotechnical engineering. He evidently grew bored with numbers and formulas, and failed his proficiency exams. He served four years in the military. As a member of the Qongrat tribe, whose leadership had the ear of many in the national government, Abbas was hired by a deputy minister of the interior to work as an inter-agency liaison officer, first in Bukhara and then in Tashkent. His exceptional interpersonal and communication skills, as well as his unshakable sense of political loyalty and proper decorum, were noticed. He enjoyed a steady climb in responsibility and title and soon had the trust of the interior minister himself.

Abbas stared out the passenger window now at the colorful storefronts racing by. "Someone from the ICRC wants to see Mr. Frost."

"News travels fast," Len said, steering around another constellation of potholes. "By the way, what about these potholes?" He flashed a quick smile at his "host."

"What do you mean?" Abbas looked at Len, nonplused. After a few seconds he understood. "Very funny. I'll get right on it."

Len's cell phone rang on a secure line. He picked it up, disengaging the hands-free. "Williams here."

It was Karen. "Len, I just got a message from the ambassador's office with instructions to contact you ASAP. Have you seen Mr. Frost yet?"

"No, not yet."

"All right. It turns out the building he and Ms. Ibrahim broke into on Saturday night holds an archive of the Uzbek Secret Service. He wanted you to know."

What the hell? Len hesitated, glanced sidelong at Abbas. Time to dissemble. "Yeah, I get that a lot."

"Is Abbas there with you?"

"Yup. Look in my upper left-hand drawer. It should be there."

Karen was no stranger to two-sided conversations. "And they discovered something missing. The Ali Şahin Diary."

"All right. I'm not sure what—?"

"I'm not exactly sure either. It has something to do with Turkey. It's being held there—or *was* being held there—as part of an agreement not to disclose the contents of the diary for two hundred years following the end of hostilities in World War I. Part of a treaty obligation. It's missing. The CIA wants it recovered *pronto*."

Good Lord! No wonder the secretary of state had gotten involved. "What about his partner? What's his name—Frederick something . . . ?" Len watched Abbas out of the corner of his eye, looking for any sign that he suspected anything out of the ordinary.

"They didn't find anything on either of them at the time of their arrest," Karen said. "They searched the house where they were staying. Nothing."

Len felt a churning in his stomach. Suddenly, this had the look and feel of a much different kind of case. What was all this nonsense about a flag? "Huh. I guess I can talk to him tomorrow. You say he's in LA?"

"Okay. Well, he wants you to keep him posted—the ambassador, I mean."

"Yup. Nine-thirty is fine. Good-bye, Karen."

Abbas waited a few beats. He was staring out the passenger window again, then looked down at his fingers. "It's called the Şahin Diary," he said nonchalantly.

What the hell? Len thought. How did Abbas know what we were talking about? Len kept his eyes on the road. The ground was shifting under him now in more ways than one. "All right."

"Ali Şahin. He was an aide-de-camp for the Turkish general in charge of the Special Operations Division from 1914 to 1918. Şahin was killed in March of '22."

"And you know this because . . . ?"

"Studied it in school. Şahin kept a diary of every order and communication from the Ittihadist leaders in Istanbul to the Fifteenth Army, East Anatolia—particularly those concerning the Armenian Question."

"The Armenian—?"

"What to do about the Armenian population in parts of East Anatolia. They stood between Istanbul and the rest of the Muslim world."

"Ah. And the Ittihadists?"

"Young Turks. When the orders were executed, Şahin described the events in graphic detail—at least that's the rumor." Abbas lowered his voice and stared out the passenger window. "No one knows for sure what the diary says." He pulled his phone out to check for text messages, then replaced it. "Within a few months of Şahin's death, the diary fell into the hands of a British war profiteer, a contractor, Alastair something, who made no secret of its availability on the black market. He, too, fell off the face of the earth, and the diary found its way into the hands of British Naval Intelligence. After the Turkish war of independence, Turkey negotiated for its return. It was sealed and placed in hiding for two hundred years by order of the last Ottoman Caliph. He hid it as far away from Turkey as possible—here, in our fair city of Tashkent."

"All right, but why would these two want it? Frost and Ibrahim? What use could they have for it?"

"I don't know. That's a good question." Abbas adjusted the AC vent in front of him. "I don't think they took it, for one thing."

Len looked at him quizzically. "All right. So there's one theory. And you're saying no one really knows what's in it?"

"No. There are plenty of opinions—stories, really, most of them apocryphal. Nothing's been confirmed. The consensus is that it contains damning revelations about the Armenian genocide, but in what detail, and with what proof, who can say?"

"The Armenian genocide . . . hadn't that been going on for decades?"

"Yes. But in the shadows of World War I it exploded. Over a million and a half were killed. It's thought that the Şahin Diary puts the lie—once and for all—to Turkey's official position, which is to deny that the genocide ever occurred, that its leaders ever carried out the systematic slaughter of the Armenians."

Len worked his teeth over his lower lip for a moment. "So . . . this is why Turkey negotiated to get it back . . . Hmm. Weird." Len spun the steering wheel with one hand, bringing the large, gray municipal jail building into view. "And who would benefit now? I guess that's the question. Who would want those facts revealed now—all these years later? *Not* Turkey, that's for sure."

Abbas nodded. "No. This won't go over well in Ankara. It could spell disaster for the Aslan government."

"How so?"

"Ankara's denials have been steadfast—President Aslan's as well. For decades, they have presented a united front to the West, even gaining admission to NATO in part on the strength of their denials. The current coalition is hanging by a thread in any event, and if this comes out—well, it's doubtful it could survive. The IRP will sweep into power."

"The IRP?"

"The ultra-nationalist Islamist Republican Party. They've been advocating closer ties with Iran and Syria and want to cut ties with NATO and most of Europe—certainly England, France, and the United States. They've gained credibility and strength since the first Arab Spring."

"So if the diary went public, the Aslan government could fall?"

"It could. If it says what most people think it does."

Len took a deep breath. "Well, then, there's no mystery why Washington wants us to jump." Checking the side rearview mirror, he mumbled to himself in a singsong, "And now I know what 'the package' is."

"If Turkey goes Islamist," Abbas continued, "the balance of power in the region will be destabilized."

"And so the ante goes up—economically, culturally, militarily. The pipelines—Kirkuk-Ceyhan and others . . . I wonder if the Committee of Nine will get involved?" Len said this while slowing down and craning his neck to look for a parking space.

"The Committee of Nine? Yes, I suppose they could," replied Abbas, "with so much at stake."

Len remembered a grainy black-and-white image from an old *Time* magazine article he'd read years before. Four young men in their twenties, in dark suits, all wearing sunglasses, sitting around a sunlit poolside table in Monte Carlo. The man furthest away, with his legs crossed and his face partially obscured by the shadow of a palm, was reputed to be Henry Matheson. It was the only known photo of the elusive Englishman, whom many believed was now the executive director of the Committee of Nine. Its activities—if it existed—were clandestine. Its mission: targeting and eliminating threats to Western global business interests.

"This situation is at least as serious as Zimbabwe was last year," Len continued. "Can you imagine Turkey turning its back on the West?"

Abbas took a few seconds to ponder the question. "Of course, there are the Armenians themselves," he said. "They still share a border."

Len glanced quickly at his friend. "That's right. If the diary were to surface, tensions along that border could . . . " Len had slowed the car to a near stop opposite an opening between two parked cars but then accelerated again when he realized that the space was too small. "What would *they* do, do you suppose?—the Armenians."

Abbas hesitated. "I don't know, to be honest. If my great-grandmother were alive, I could ask her."

"Your great-grandmother?"

"Yes. She was Armenian."

"You're kidding."

"No. I guess I never told you that. My great-grandma Gayane."

Len smiled. "I thought you were straight-up Uzbek. Dyed-in-the-wool."

"On my grandfather's side I am . . . and my father's Uzbek, as well. So yes, I'm Uzbek. But Great-Grandma Gayane was Armenian. My mother's one-quarter Armenian."

Len found a parking space and began to back into it. "Will wonders never cease," he said facetiously, twisting around to look out the back window.

VII

———

There was a knock at the door. Fatimah was sitting up in bed with her back pressed against the wall of her cell, reading a prison copy of the Qur'an. "Yes?"

Again, the jangling of keys, the turning of the lock. The door opened. It was a different female guard. Above the glint of her badge her eyes widened and she stifled a smile. So they were taking turns now. They wanted to be able to say, "I've seen Fatimah Ibrahim in person." This one carried a cell phone. "It's a Mr. Jamaal Rachadi for you. Also, I've got orders to take you to Conference Room 14 downstairs."

Fatimah realized she was being treated more like a guest at a hotel than a prisoner. In a strange way, she had grown used to it. She took the phone. "Yes, yes. Give me a moment." She waited for the guard to leave. "Is it really you?"

"Hi Fayruz, precious gemstone."

"I can't believe it. How did you find me?"

"Your sister called from Paris. She found out from your mother, who found out from your grandmother. Everybody's worried sick, Fatimah. Me included."

Fatimah felt the first sting of tears since her arrest. She blinked them back. How often had she imagined Jamaal's voice since that day so many months ago? Boarding the plane bound for Lucknow, feeling the surge of takeoff and watching the lights of Sanori spread out over the horizon, giving shape to the relative emptiness of Port Hikma. Knowing he was down there.

"I need you to tell me again, Jamaal. I don't understand," she'd said an hour before leaving for the airport. "Why would you throw what we have away?"

"I can't do it anymore, Fayruz. Not with what's happened to you. You live in a different world now, and it's not my world. There's no place for me. I am a simple man."

"But we—"

He had pulled her close. "No. Listen to me. We managed—*I* managed—while you studied in England. But that was going to be temporary—remember? You and I were going to live a quiet life on South Island. That's what you used to say. Now you've been discovered, Fayruz. People in every part of the world see you as I always have. You're everyone's precious gemstone now. You're jetting all over, and you're gone more than you are here. I can't relate to your life anymore, Fatimah. You have handlers for your agents and agents for your handlers." He had guided her to a bench and they had sat, their knees touching. "It's enough that you are the granddaughter of the president, and heir to an oil fortune. My family has hardly known how to handle that, as you know. But they're in an utter state of confusion now. Two weeks ago they woke up to the sound of a CNN satellite truck backing up their driveway. It's gone too far."

Too far. Those were words she'd heard again and again in her mind, lying awake in yet another lodging or stranger's home, her backpack standing up in the corner, Alden's snoring—or someone else's—audible through the walls on most nights. Now she wanted to hear him say anything *but* those words. Talk to me, Jamaal. I've missed you. "Did you . . . how did they find out? About me, I mean?"

"Your sister said the foreign ministry picked up an Interpol bulletin. It mentioned you by name."

Fatimah wiped a tear from her cheek with the flat of her hand and then nodded. She drew a ragged breath. "There was a man here from the foreign ministry yesterday. An Ali Msaidie." She picked up his card from the table and examined it front and back. "They've got clearance to take me out of here, but . . ."

"But what?"

Fatimah bit her lip. Do I dare tell you, she wondered. Can I tell you that it is too painful for me to return to Tashir knowing you're there with someone else? She closed her eyes: how his face had appeared, then disappeared, how with his pleasant talking he had moved side to side before the blazing noonday sun. They were twelve. He had called to her, beckoned her to the chain-link gate separating the two playgrounds. Her friends had watched in stunned silence as she had strode boldly over to speak to this impetuous boy dressed in drab brown street clothes. But he was not a complete stranger to her. She had seen him three days earlier outside the main entrance to the school, comforting a crying child. Was it his sister? She didn't know, but it didn't matter. He had shown such a focused tenderness with the frightened child, kneeling down to face her at her own level and wiping away her tears with a handkerchief, that it had touched her heart.

Jamaal had reached up to take hold of the metal links. It was a prelude to a smile that she would remember forever. "At last," he'd said, as though this moment counted for him above all others. "I'm Jamaal."

"I am—"

"Yes, I know who you are. Fatimah Ibrahim."

She'd passed a gentle curse over the sun that had swept his lovely smile into blackness and left her squinting up at a silhouette. Certain that her squinting made her look ridiculous, she'd turned away. Suddenly the afternoon bell sounded behind them.

Tell me about you. Isn't that what she'd tried to say, stepping back and forcing her chin up in spite of the sun's glare? But the words came out, "How do you know who I am?"

"My father is an engineer," he'd blurted. He was answering the question she'd intended. "My mother is a teacher here. Perhaps you know her—Madame Rachadi. Anyway, we live nearby. I am in the sixth form. I have wanted to meet you."

"Thank you," she'd said, stepping away in response to the bell.

"Don't go." Jamaal's round, dark eyes grew intense.

"I must go."

"But . . . what form are you in?"

She'd giggled at the fervency in his voice. "The sixth form, like you." She'd turned and begun to run as fast as she could to catch up with her friends.

"I will talk to you again," he'd called after her.

She'd stopped, turned, smiled, and waved.

She wished she could be back at that moment. She would give anything to be back there, but reality thundered around her. Fatimah opened her eyes and saw the open Qur'an on her lap. "There are technical issues here that have to be worked out," she said at last. "Someone from the U.S. embassy is coming at 1:00. I think they're here now. Hopefully, I'll have a better idea after we've talked. Tell me about you, Jamaal. How have you been?"

"Wait a minute! You're imprisoned in Uzbekistan and you want to know how *I'm* doing? Tell me what happened. What were you doing there? Why were you arrested? They said you broke into a building. What—"

"I don't trust this phone, Jamaal." She looked around. "Or this room. I don't think I should talk about it. I can tell you we did nothing wrong."

"We? You and the—"

"Alden Frost."

"The American."

"Yes." Fatimah closed her eyes again and her brow furrowed. "Are you still with Zainab?"

Jamaal didn't answer. The line held a heavy silence.

Fatimah exhaled slowly, shaking her head. "She's very lucky, Jamaal."

"Is there anything I can do to help?"

She felt a weight in the pit of her stomach. "No, but thank you." She thought: Now I am in a different world, Jamaal—just like you said. I am so far away from you.

Fatimah leaned her head back against the bare wall of her cell. She could almost hear her mother say, "You think you love him. Look what you have accomplished. Do you think you would have been able to do this had you married him and moved to South Island?"

"I love him, Mother," she imagined saying.

She listened for Jamaal's breathing—any sound of him—on the phone. The world you talked about, Jamaal, of glamour magazines and penthouse parties—that was just a game. Don't you understand? That's not me. I have dreamt of a different world, Jamaal, it's true, but it's not what you think.

*   *   *

Abbas's badge and ID card put one uniformed officer after another into motion unlocking and opening doors. They took an elevator to the prison basement. Abbas waved Len down a long, poorly lit corridor. Turning a corner, he spoke to a middle-aged guard with prominent brows who was seated at a wooden desk. A small table light illuminated the guard's folded hands but nothing else. The desktop was empty. One had the feeling the drawers were empty, as well. Len's cell phone rang.

"Len, Brett Perkins, chief operating officer for the China and Far East Division, Majestic International."

"Oh?" Len was caught off guard. Although he'd been hired by Majestic, he wasn't scheduled to start for another two and a half weeks. What could this be about? He balanced the phone on his shoulder and pulled a pen from the inside breast pocket of his jacket. "Okay."

"We've got a problem with our Swan River Dam project. Are you familiar with it?"

"No. I haven't . . . could you hold on a minute?" Abbas had turned to him and was waiting to say something. "I'm with somebody. Hold on just a second."

Abbas said, "Mr. Frost and Ms. Ibrahim are in Room 14. You finish your call, and I'll go in and talk to Ms. Yacoubi in Room 9. Ms. Yacoubi is the woman from the International Committee of the Red Cross."

"All right," Len answered, nodding. He pivoted and started walking back down the hall. "Mr. Perkins? Yes, thank you for waiting."

"Listen, Len, I know you're not on board yet, but I've got authority from Richardson to move your start date up—at least on a temporary basis."

Len stopped. Move my start date up? What are you talking about? Are you kidding?

"This thing's gone from a nuisance to a crisis overnight," Perkins continued, his speech pressured.

"I'm afraid I—"

"The local government, they . . . we're in Xining, the capital of Qinghai Province, if you know where that is . . . western China . . . they assured us everything was taken care of. Put it in writing. Now we've got a committee of goddam village elders coming out of the woodwork complaining about the road. They say the right-of-way we've staked out from the main highway to the construction site cuts across a sacred burial ground dating back 2,100 years to the Han Dynasty or something. They've come up with some kind of proof—a hieroglyph of some kind. If we don't pioneer that road in by the first of December, we'll lose an entire season. That's what I keep telling them. And we're not getting any help from Beijing. It's a regular Mexican standoff here."

Len held the phone away from his ear and stared at it. Little wonder you're having problems with that kind of cultural insensitivity, he thought to himself. He squeezed his eyes shut and shook his head. Why is this happening now? He put the phone to his ear again. "Hold on a minute. Let me get a piece of paper." As he fished in the pocket of his jacket, he said, "I'm afraid this is hitting me pretty cold, Brett. You understand, I'm still with the State Department . . . finishing things up here. I'm going to Seattle on the twenty-third." Moving to the wall, he held up the scrap of paper and repositioned the phone between his ear and shoulder. "Okay, what is it exactly I can help you with?" Before Perkins could answer, Len added, "You're in China, right?"

"Yes. And we need you to come out here this weekend. I'm sending the Gulfstream to Tashkent to pick you up first thing Friday morning. We'll have you back Sunday night. I need you to negotiate this thing."

"You mean—?"

"My secretary will contact you with the details. She's arranging your visa and hotel right now."

Len lowered the scrap of paper. "Wait a minute, I—"

"And I'll bring you up to speed on the details when you get here. In fact, I'll have Elaine e-mail some of the background documents this afternoon."

"Hold on, Brett. I can't come out there this weekend. I've got other plans, and something's come up here at the last minute—top priority. From the secretary herself." Even if I get Frost out of jail today, I don't want to go to China on a last-minute boondoggle, Len thought. He caught sight of himself in the glass panel of a door. He'd never liked his look, the ovoid head, the dark, distended eyebrows, the half-full lips that yielded a smile too broad, he thought, for his face. It seemed the women in his life knew better. "You're easy on the eyes," Laura was fond of saying.

But now his lips were twisted up in an unnatural scowl. There was nothing about this call he was enjoying. "I'm not sure what I can do for you on such short notice," he said, turning away from his reflection.

"I need you to apply your negotiating skills here. That's what you do, isn't it? That's why we've hired you—right? Crisis management, that sort of thing?" The questions were clipped, rhetorical. "Give me a name or reference of some kind on this other project. I'll see what we can do."

"What do you mean?"

"This matter with the secretary of state. Let me make a call to Edmonds and see what they can work out with Washington, DC. We're tied in pretty close there."

Len hesitated. "Frost."

"Spell that."

"F-r-o-s-t. Alden Frost. Look, Brett, I can't get away this weekend. I'd like to help but—"

"Let me stop you right there, Len. This thing came up unexpectedly—okay? And now we're faced with a potential $50 to

$70 million hit if construction of the dam is delayed another year over this fucking road. This is why we hired a conflict resolution specialist. If I can work things out with the secretary of state, I expect to see you here Friday around midday. If you're joining this company, a little advance loyalty is not too much to ask. In fact, if you want to think in starker terms, you could say your job depends on it."

Len was speechless.

Perkins gave him an extra few seconds, then concluded in a brighter tone. "I'll have my secretary get back to you. You have a good day out there."

*   *   *

Charlotte Yacoubi leaned over in her chair. Her legs were crossed beneath a long black skirt, and she held a cell phone to her ear. Her chin rested in her free hand. Speaking in Arabic she said, "I may be a few minutes late. Go ahead and order when you get there. Order me *brik* with egg and *lablabi* if they have it, will you? I don't know—3:30 maybe . . . I've been held up here since 11:00 . . . No, not yet." There were four evenly spaced knocks on the door. "Someone's here," Charlotte said, sitting up. "I've got to go. I'll see you when I get there."

The door opened slowly "Hello?" Abbas said in Russian.

"Yes, come in," Charlotte answered, putting down the phone. The thirty-four-year-old turned in her chair and straightened the sleeves of her red-and-gold tunic. A bracelet of miniature gold sovereigns jangled as she checked her *hijab*.

"Oh, hello. I'm Abbas . . . Ahkme—" He was pulled help-lessly into the two deep, green pools staring back at him. "—dova. I'm . . . I'm with the Interior Ministry."

Charlotte nodded. "Charlotte Yacoubi. International Red Cross." A smile began to spread across Abbas's face, then vanished as he stopped and stood at attention. An observer would have guessed that he'd utterly forgotten why he'd entered the room. Charlotte looked down at her phone to push the silence mode button, then met his gaze again. "It's a pleasure to meet you," she said.

*   *   *

The memory flooded back in an instant. I have never seen such eyes, he'd thought, staring across piles of pomegranates, figs, dates, and cherries, at a woman in a maroon-and-orange *abaya* and white head scarf striding slowly down the aisle opposite him. She was at least ten years older than him. He was sixteen at the time. She was twenty-six or twenty-seven, light complected, with a firmness about the set of her lips, as though she were facing some task that required all of her concentration. Never mind that she was simply examining the fruits and vegetables, or that the greatest of her visible challenges lay in navigating the crowded Saturday morning market with a friend a few steps ahead.

Such eyes! Abbas, barely breathing if at all, had been struck dumb by them, had stopped hearing his sister's patter. In that instant, he had sensed the world doubling in size, the possibilities multiplying. But it had been only an instant. And although he had continued to stare after the woman—he had ignored the polite requests, twice repeated, of an old man asking to pass in front of him—it was no longer her exquisite green eyes he saw, but only her eyelids and lashes from the side, and the dark arch of her eyebrows. No, it was only—and all—that moment before, when the most perfectly shaped orbs he had ever seen were lifted. Bore into him, through him. Set his heart racing. Eyes, he'd thought. What is it about them? At last he'd told himself, ignoring his fourteen-year old sister who was slapping his arm ("Hey, are you listening? Did mother say she wanted us to get grapefruit?"), I've seen what I want. I've seen exactly what I want . . .

It's her, he thought now—back to the present. No, the brow and nose are different. It's not the same woman, but at least the eyes are the same. What had she said? She works for the Red Cross? Charlotte? Was that her name? Yes, that's it. Charlotte. Charlotte.

*   *   *

"I . . . It's my pleasure," Abbas managed.

"Can I help you?" she asked.

Abbas didn't answer.

Is this man sick? Charlotte wondered. Why doesn't he answer? She dared not believe the stranger was flummoxed by her appearance, although the idea presented itself like a wet dog at the door wishing to come in. Such a thing is impossible, she thought. I am not beautiful. A long list of imperfections—a well-rehearsed list—passed like a shadow across her mind. But then, as quickly, and without warning, a memory slid before her eyes—of her grandfather, telling Charlotte in her youth that her beauty was fixed and legendary.

"Your grandmother was the fairest woman in all of Tunisia," her grandfather had been fond of saying, "and one day after sampling figs from an old tree called 'Vanity,' it occurred to your grandmother, 'If I marry an ugly man, I shan't have to put up with beautiful daughters and granddaughters. I can keep all the beauty to myself. But, you see, her plan backfired." Charlotte delighted in the memory of this story, not least because of the jousting that would ensue between her grandmother and grandfather. "Don't listen to him, Charlotte," her grandmother would call out from another room. "Your mother's beauty, and yours, is a sublime gift from Allah. It has nothing to do with fig trees, or with me." To which her grandfather would wink and whisper, "But we know the truth, don't we?" And their teasing, so full of love, came in many forms and seemed designed to please her. Charlotte, at thirty-four, had grown into a practical, clear-eyed woman with far greater things to worry about than her physical appearance, but she knew herself as reasonably attractive and cherished the words of her grandparents nonetheless.

Perhaps, Charlotte thought, I should explain myself. "I am here to see a prisoner, Mr. Ahkmedova. Alden Frost."

"Oh . . . yes, of course," said Abbas, blinking once and breaking free again. He moved forward. "Forgive me. Yes, I'm from the Interior Ministry."

"So you said."

Abbas took a seat. This was a small conference room, with a rectangular steel table and four utilitarian chairs. The table's surface was made up of fake pine planks with knots and black caulking. In the corner of the room stood a small, square console table—real wood here, oiled—holding an empty water pitcher and four small glasses turned upside down on a paper towel. A confident President Karimov assumed his place on the wall opposite the door, in a black frame, next to a long-forgotten three-year-old calendar. Abbas rested one arm on the table. "If you don't mind my asking, what's your interest in Mr. Frost?"

Charlotte was surprised by the question. "What's my interest? As I said, I'm with the International Red Cross." She began to dig into her purse looking for her ID. "Under the Geneva Conven—"

"No, no. I understand. I'm just curious about timing. Mr. Frost and Ms. Ibrahim haven't been charged. I'm surprised to see someone from the ICRC here already. How'd you even know we were holding him?"

Charlotte sat back. You know I'm not going to answer that, Mr. Ahkmedova, she said with her eyes.

Whatever her eyes were saying, Abbas seemed to devour every word. Several seconds passed. Abbas chuckled self-consciously. "There's no problem whatsoever, you understand. I'm just curious."

"Mmm-hmm." Charlotte smiled with aplomb then looked down momentarily. The effect on Abbas was all out of proportion. His face blanched and he looked away and drew his next breath through his mouth. Is he that smitten, or is it a trick? she wondered. She felt an unwelcome flutter in her own chest. Oh no, she scolded. He's attractive, all right—yes, quite beautiful—but don't let your guard down. He's with the Interior Ministry. The prisons here are infamous for unspeakable cruelties and human rights violations. For all I know, he's been part of that. Her smile quickly receded. Keep your mind on the task at hand, she told herself, then pursed her lips.

"Do you know Mr. Frost?" Abbas ventured.

Charlotte's green eyes betrayed a hint of uncertainty. She recalled the Internet search she had done that morning. "Perhaps. If it's him. I met a man by that name twenty-one years ago."

"And you want to know if this is the same man?"

"Yes. When I saw his name on the list of detainees this morning, I came here at once. I would like to speak to him." She watched an intrusive question — "And what is it you'd like to talk to him about?"—come and go from the corners of Abbas's eyes.

He did not utter the question, but said instead, "I don't work the prison detail, Ms. Yacoubi, but it's my understanding . . . I believe the Red Cross and Red Crescent are admitted only after someone has been charged, or held seventy-two hours."

"Yes, that's normally the case, but—"

"Well, it doesn't matter," Abbas said, waving the subject away with his right hand. "We're meeting with him presently. I'll see if you can join us for a few minutes . . . if you'd like."

"Yes, I would. Thank you."

"You may be asked to leave at some point."

"I understand."

A silence followed that stretched the distance between them. Charlotte lifted her cell phone to check the time. Abbas seemed to take some measure of himself in which he found himself wanting. He exited the room as though it were on fire.

VIII

Len knocked quietly on the door and leaned in. "Mr. Alden Frost?"

Behind a long, rectangular conference table sat a thin-faced man with pale blue eyes, a white stubble on his chin, and disheveled hair, graying at the temples. The table accommodated a host of chairs, fifteen or more, abandoned at various angles. The plaster walls were bare except for a dusty, decades-old photograph of a statue of Tamerlane.

"Yes."

"May I come in?" Len inclined further until he spotted Fatimah seated at the end of the table. He entered, then closed the door. "Hello. You must be Ms. Ibrahim. I'm Len Williams. I'm with the U.S. State Department."

Fatimah's slender dark brown arm emerged from beneath the black folds of her *khimar*. It was unexpected. Len approached and took her hand. "Good afternoon."

I have seen her before, Len realized. What a face! Yes—on magazine covers, on posters, online. He'd assumed she was a model. What did Abbas say? She came up with some kind of fundraising campaign? Anyway, that's not what made *this face* famous.

He took in her enormous, round, brown eyes, the elevated cheek-bones, the graceful turn of her lips. A modern day Aphrodite.

With difficulty Len diverted his attention to Alden. "Mr. Frost, Len Williams." The man whose hand he grasped had a well-shaped, almost effeminate-looking mouth, but his cheeks were sallow and sunken, a condition accentuated by the shadows cast by the overhead fluorescent lights. His wide shoulders seemed to end in bony points, and there was no evidence of a chest beneath the black prison overalls. Len produced a legal pad and pen from his briefcase. "I'm here to help you."

Alden smiled crookedly. "I see."

"Have you been treated all right so far?" Len looked up. Alden and Fatimah exchanged a perfunctory glance.

"Yes."

"And how about you, Ms. Ibrahim?"

"Yes. Fine, thank you."

"Are you both getting enough food and water?"

"Yes," answered Alden. Fatimah nodded.

"Do either of you need medical attention?"

"No," they said together.

"Mr. Frost, I'm going to want to talk to you alone, but I thought we'd start out this way. You understand, I'm not an attorney."

"Okay."

"We received a cable from the secretary of state this morning instructing us to try to secure your release. Do you know about that?"

"No."

"You have no idea why the secretary of state would be involved personally?"

"No. Not at all."

"She also said something about a package—bringing a package back to Washington. Do you know what that refers to?"

Alden answered, "No, I have no idea."

"Ms. Ibrahim, do you have any—?"

"No."

"All right. Before we go on, there are two other people out-side who would like to see you. One came with me. His name is Abbas Ahkmedova. He's with the Uzbek Interior Ministry. He's well connected. I'd like to use him as a liaison to communicate with the foreign minister, if you don't mind. I've done this in the past with good effect. Your release will not be up to him, mind you, but he can be a very effective spokesperson with the right people. The other is a young woman with the International Committee of the Red Cross. She says she may know you from years ago in Tunisia." Len took a slip of paper from his shirt pocket. "Her name is Charlotte Yacoubi."

Alden cocked his head. "That name doesn't sound famil-iar to me."

"Should I invite them to join us, or . . . ?"

Fatimah and Alden exchanged similar expressions. Alden said, "Yes, I guess so." Fatimah nodded.

Len stepped out and a moment later returned, walking ahead of Abbas and Charlotte. Abbas stepped around Charlotte, pulled out a chair for her and, once she was seated, sat next to her. Len remained standing to make introductions.

Charlotte said to Alden, "Mr. Frost, you wouldn't remember me, but you came to my school in Tunis twenty years ago to introduce the companion flag. I've never forgotten you—or the idea."

Alden smiled. "Ah, that's wonderful. Thank you. It's a plea-sure to meet you, Ms. Yacoubi."

Len retook his seat, stealing a quick glance at Fatimah. Yes, she's beautiful, he thought. But she reminds me of some-one. Then it came to him. Fatimah reminded him of his niece Lynnette—his sister Connie's oldest daughter. Same large eyes, same open expression, he thought. I wonder if she's as stuck on herself as Lynnette is? he mused as he looked down at his notes. "Shall we continue?"

"Of course," said Fatimah.

"Alden," Len said, "let me get some background information. What is your full legal name?"

"Alden Frost. My middle name is Wilson, but I don't use it. Feel free to call me Alden."

Len smiled as he wrote. "All right. Thank you. You can call me Len. Do you have your passport, Alden?"

"No, they took everything."

"Do you . . .You're a U.S. citizen, is that right?"

"Yes."

"And Ms. Ibrahim, I understand you're a citizen of the Republic of Tashir."

"Yes, that's correct."

"But you were together when you were apprehended?

Fatimah's voice was high-pitched, youthful. In an older person, the light rasp might have accredited a kind of nervousness. "Yes."

"Mr. Frost—Alden, what's your address in the States?"

"I don't have a home there anymore. My last address was in Emporia, Kansas. 509 Farm-to-Market Road."

"Are you married?"

"No. Divorced."

"Do you have children?"

"Two boys, both adults."

"Is there anyone you'd like me to contact . . . to let them know you're all right?"

Alden hesitated. "No. I'm . . . not at this time."

"What time were you arrested on Saturday night?"

"It was . . . uh . . ." Alden looked at Fatimah. "Eight, maybe?"

"After eight," said Fatimah.

"And where were you at the time?"

"At the home of friends," answered Fatimah.

"You were arrested for breaking into a building. Do you know what this building was used for?"

"A school," replied Alden.

"Are you sure it was a school?"

"Oh, yes. We go to schools only. Do you remember the number, Fatimah? Thirty-two? Thirty-one?"

"Public School 32," Fatimah answered.

Len laid the yellow legal pad on the table, sat back, and rubbed his thumb and forefinger over a mustache that wasn't there. "We've been informed that it may have been a repository of some kind. A government repository."

"Oh?" Alden's voice rose in pitch. "I wouldn't know about that."

Len continued to watch him in the periphery of his vision as he turned to Fatimah. He was looking for a telltale movement, an uncomfortable fidget of some kind. "How about you, Ms. Ibrahim? Do you know anything about this?"

Fatimah opened her eyes wide and shook her head. "No, I'm afraid not. What kind of repository?"

The question caught Len off guard. "I, uh . . . well, let me get back to that. I want to keep going with background, if that's all right. Mr. Frost—Alden—what's your line of work?"

"I'm retired, I guess you'd say. I was a FedEx driver many years ago, but I occupy my time working on the companion flag project." Alden smiled at Charlotte, evidently in response to a smile from her. "Have for the last twenty-four years now."

"What's the companion flag project?"

"It's an initiative to introduce and get people to adopt and fly the companion flag around the globe. It's a reminder of—"

"I've never heard of the companion flag."

Alden smiled weakly. "No. It's been . . . tough sledding. It's a big world."

"You started to say it's a reminder of something."

"Yes, a symbol of what human beings have in common around the world in spite of their differences. Things like the love of children and the desire for health and knowledge. Concern for the safety of loved ones. The need for friendship, that sort of thing."

"I see. So this is—"

"In spite of our differences."

"Yes. And—"

"This is what I was . . . this is what *we* were doing."

Len looked up from his writing. "What do you mean?"

"At Public School 32 we installed a companion flag below the Uzbek flag. This was the day before our arrest."

Len made eye contact with Abbas and raised his eyebrows as if to say, there's the flag you were talking about. Turning back to Alden, he said, "*We* being you and Ms. Ibrahim?"

"That's right."

"So you installed a companion flag? Where exactly did you do this?"

"We put up flags at two different schools that night. Public School 32 was the second one."

"And the earlier one?"

"PS 17, I think," said Alden. "We just look for schools with accessible flagpoles. I don't pay much attention to the names anymore. Fatimah, do you know?"

Fatimah looked up. Alden continued, "Fatimah is documenting this."

Len turned his legal pad sideways to write in the margin: PEACE FLAG? "What do you mean she's documenting this?" he asked.

Fatimah placed one hand on the table and turned it on its side to explain. "I guess you could call me his videographer. I'm documenting the flag raisings, posting what we do on YouTube, Vine, and Facebook, sending Tweets, that sort of thing. This is preliminary to a media campaign I'm working on to get this project to a different level internationally."

Len's lower lip protruded as he wrote, then he turned back to Alden. "So you put up companion flags at these two schools on Saturday night—*and that's all you did?*" Alden and Fatimah both nodded. Len stared at his notes. "Wait a minute. I may have misunderstood something. The companion flag is flown with another flag?"

"Always, yes," said Alden. "That's where it gets its name. It's a companion to the other flags of the world—to each country's flag."

"Oh. I thought 'companion' referred to people getting along: friendship, companionship, that sort of thing."

"No. This is a common misconception. Feelings of friendship toward other people are not something human beings have—or experience—in common around the world. Neither is the desire for peace. These are not what the companion flag stands for." Alden looked into the faces of all three people sitting across from him.

"Okay," Len said under his breath, crossing out the words "Peace Flag?" Godammit, he thought, avoiding eye contact with Alden. This guy's a nut. And he won't shut up about this damn flag. He pictured Ambassador Tompkins sitting at his desk, imagined telling him exactly what he'd learned. "He denies taking the diary—they both do. This is the kind of thing Stanton or *someone* from the consular section could have handled easily," he would tell him—"and they should be handling it."

Len suddenly realized that Alden was still talking. "I'm sorry?"

"I was just explaining what the companion flag looks like. It's a white flag with a single stripe of color across the top. The stripe of color matches any color that appears in the host flag above it."

Len flipped the page of his legal pad and then quickly glanced at Abbas as if to say, are you getting this? He scratched out a few more notes and underlined them needlessly, saying to himself, as if I give a shit about your crazy flag. God, the things people will do! Could this have been a diversionary tactic? He pursed his lips and drew a moment's comfort from the silence in the room—that is, until he realized the others were waiting on him. He looked up. "Mr. Fr—Alden, are you saying there were already flags flying at these two schools on Saturday night?"

"Yes. The flag of Uzbekistan."

"And you didn't remove them?"

"No. As I said, the companion flag is attached and flown below the world's existing flags. We added a companion flag below each of those Uzbek flags."

"How did you know those flags would be there?"

"We walked past the night before and saw them there. They were illuminated, which told us they were kept up at all times."

"And you left the companion flags as a gift?"

"Yes." Alden returned a smile from Charlotte. "We always leave them as gifts."

"Did you take anything from either school . . . or building?"

Alden furrowed his brow. "Of course not. We're in the business of leaving flags. That's all."

"You didn't take any computer data, papers, books, that sort of thing?"

Fatimah laughed beautifully. "Computer data? Books? Why would we do that?" she asked.

"No," said Alden flatly.

Len looked from one to the other. "You didn't take anything at all? From the second building?"

"No. Of course not." Alden's eyes narrowed. "We went in, raised the flag, and left. We're not thieves, Mr. Williams."

"Did you break into these two schools?

"The second one, yes, to get to the flagpole on the roof. The first one had its flagpole next to the playground."

"Did you go into the basement of the second one?" Len looked at Abbas, who nodded back.

"The *basement*? No, of course not."

"Why didn't you ask permission to put these flags up?"

Alden hesitated. "That's a long story. The short version is that most adults aren't amenable to new ideas—they find it the easiest thing in the world to say no. Young people don't do that. They're open to new ideas."

Len's eyebrows rose wrinkling his forehead as he wrote on his notepad. "All right. You were arrested almost twenty-four hours after the break-in at Public School 32. Can you tell me what you did during that interval—I guess this was Saturday?"

Fatimah and Alden hesitated, each waiting for the other. At last, Fatimah said, "We had breakfast with our hosts, Dilbar and Sasha. That was about 9:30. At 11:15, I met with Irina Sadikov. Photographs were taken and I was interviewed for *Tashkent Today*. I returned home at 3:00, took a bath, read for a while, then helped Dilbar prepare the evening meal. That's it. We were arrested during dinner."

"And you, Alden?"

"I didn't really do anything. Walked around town is all. Visited the Alayski Bazaar."

"So you weren't together for large parts of the day?"

"No," said Fatimah.

Which means Alden could have disposed of the diary any-where, Len thought. Or passed it off to someone. He cleared his throat then reached up under his suit jacket to feel for the thick stack of one-hundred-dollar bills in his breast pocket. It was the $15,000 Tompkins had ordered him to take along for bribe money, to secure Frost's release. He pretended to chase an itch. Perhaps it was time to tender this sum to Abbas—he would see that it got into the right hands.

"I have just a couple more questions," Len said. "Unfortunately, I need to step outside for a minute to call my office. Abbas, can I have a word?" The two men slid their chairs back and made their way to the door. Len had partially opened the door when his movements were arrested by the sound of Charlotte's voice.

"I've never forgotten," she began, her voice trailing off as though she were pursuing a memory. She seemed oblivious to the looks of surprise all around, and when she continued, it was with an enthusiasm that lifted the corners of her mouth and sent her gaze to every person in the room, beginning with Alden. "You see, we had hoped to adopt the flag at our school when you left—to be the first in Tunisia to fly it. My friends and I formed a companion flag committee. We held a student forum so that the idea could be debated and voted on. The vote was overwhelmingly in favor, but that was just the students."

Len moved to open the door wider, but Abbas touched him on the arm and nodded as if to say, "Wait a minute. I want to hear this."

"One of the teachers, who had served in the Tunisian armed forces, complained that it would be unpatriotic to fly another flag with the flag of Tunisia. He said it would sully the sacrifices made by those who had died defending the national symbol." Charlotte turned a beacon-like stare on Abbas. Any semblance of a smile had vanished. "Can you imagine? They thought celebrating what human beings have in common was an insult to dead soldiers? It made no sense, but the headmaster saw no way forward. Those were his words. What embarrasses me most is that we dropped it then, too. We let the voices of confusion and human separation drown us out."

*　　*　　*

A minute or two after Len and Abbas had departed, Fatimah and Charlotte started speaking Arabic in tones that suggested a friendly cross-examination. Alden could not understand it—not a word. Twice he let smiling eyes drift up to Charlotte, but he avoided looking at Fatimah, and for the most part he let their voices recede into the background. Touching the tips of his fingers together, he breathed in, slowly gathering a remnant of a long-forgotten day. He closed his eyes. Why was he remembering this? he wondered. It was so many years ago, but the feelings came flooding back, as though it were all happening this minute, as though, were he to open his eyes, the two of them—his wife and Dr. Soderling—would be staring at him in disbelief. As they had then. Sensing that Dr. Soderling, a clinical psychologist, viewed him with strict academic interest, he'd felt his heart go out to Deborah. "How could you do this to the boys?" she'd said.

"I'm doing it *for* them," he'd replied, half believing it. They were boys, after all. In the blink of an eye, they would be of draft age. He didn't have to look beyond that. Yes, he knew that men who returned from war often looked back on their experiences with fondness—a kind of fondness that either bred a kind of sanctimony or played host to that parasite. But those were the ones who returned full-bodied. He'd spent a good number of years in his childhood playing with army men, dreaming himself into the background of old photographs of World War II. It was something in the odds that struck him eventually, that let his mind wander into and behind the upturned eyes of the private who had just seen—and could not bear to bend his neck and look down again to see—that both his legs were missing, or that a foot or two of his small intestine lay damp and clumped over his belt like something dropped from the sky. Or that . . . it doesn't matter. Multiply it and expand it in every direction, and laugh at your inability to conceive the limits—even one limit, one boundary, one not-this-far—of man's inhumanity to man.

"You are depriving them of a father," she'd said, tears filling her eyes. "And all for this silly flag of yours. You've changed so much. I don't even know you anymore."

She was right to wonder, he'd realized. He could hardly explain it to himself. No, that's not true—he could explain it to himself, that was not the problem, but sharing the words with others, sharing the idea, proved difficult. Some people got it, a small percentage. Did that make it less true, that only a small percentage of people got it right away?

How had it originated, this idea of a companion flag, the psychologist had wanted to know. The answer was one he detested for its staleness and familiarity, and because he couldn't be sure of its truth anymore. Early on he had shaped an answer out of the clay of his experiences, but was he giving a full account of himself? When exactly—at what point in time—was a decision *made*? An idea hatched?

The answer he gave by rote was this: that at age thirty-four he took his first-ever trip outside the United States. He had been talked into joining the Emporia Peace Chorus, and the following year that group traveled to Iran under the special auspices of the two governments. He went there expecting to be struck by all the differences he'd known about or heard about, and he *was* struck by them: differences of culture, language, religion, traditions, and so on. But just as there were differences, he noticed similarities—from grandmothers walking their grandbabies in the parks, to teenagers flirting on the bridges, to boys playing soccer in the fields. There were as many similarities as differences.

On the flight home it occurred to him: We humans are, paradoxically, both different and the same. What's more, neither leg of that dyad is more or less true, or, as a starting point, at least, more or less morally relevant, than the other. But we use our symbols to celebrate and highlight our differences only. Symbolically, we are strangely mute on the matter of our commonalities (which itself is a commonality). This was not mere abstraction or idleness on his part. Oh, it might have been initially, but in no time he was galvanized by a new possibility, one that promised not only to capture the truth but, he thought, help heal the world as well. If there is reason to celebrate and elevate with symbols such as flags an awareness of our differences and separation from one another, he thought, then surely there must be reason to join those symbols with another that reminds us of all that we share across our myriad borders and divisions in spite of our differences. The idea of the companion flag was born.

It was something like that, he'd explained to the psychologist.

Alden pushed away the memory of his ex-wife and listened to the singsong of Charlotte's voice in the background. Perhaps she gets it, he thought. To have remembered the idea after all these years . . .

*   *   *

Len stopped at the end of the hallway near an empty glass display case encrusted with dust. He put his hand at the back of his neck. "All right, look," he began. He forced a tone of importance, but abandoned it the moment he turned to find his friend checking his phone for text messages. "What are we going to do here, Abbas? These people are crazy."

The Uzbek, still focused on the phone, raised his eyebrows and answered with silence.

"You can't possibly believe these two took the Sab-heen Diary, or whatever it's called."

Abbas swiped his finger across the screen of his phone. "Şahin. No, it doesn't seem so."

"But can you believe this companion flag thing? That doesn't seem real either."

Abbas smiled absently and returned the phone to the inside breast pocket of his suit. He seemed to brighten at the change of subject. "It's an interesting idea, you have to admit. You have to wonder why someone didn't think of this five hundred years ago. Then these two wouldn't have had to break into schools from here to Lucknow."

Len shook his head. Abbas believes this shit, he thought. When was the last time I thought some leftist idea was interesting? It wasn't an idle question. Oh, he'd been a liberal once, but years had intervened, and the bodies of dead children. He had shaken too many hands, and mumbled condolences to bereaved strangers who could not—would not—make eye contact. And they were real, not some symbol. A flag? Of all that human beings have in common? A *flag*? That door was frozen shut. He sensed it—the door, that is. Laid his hand against it in a fashion; but then whose voice continued to sound in his head uttering, "It's an interesting idea. Why didn't someone think of this five hundred years ago?" Why was he hearing *himself* repeating Abbas's words as though they were his own? What was the meaning of this? Did some part of him agree?

"They're a couple of hippies," Len said at last. "Well, she's not, but he is."

Abbas turned to Len, as though preparing to say something, but then he stopped. Nothing. Seconds later, breaking free of some unspoken thought, he said, "I'll see what I can do."

"Here." Len withdrew the thick envelope bulging with U.S. currency and extended it to his friend. "There's fifteen thousand there. Should be enough to go around."

Abbas hesitated. His glance rose up from the envelope to Len's eyes. "Hold on to that for a minute. Let me call Guryanov."

"The interior minister? I would have thought you could handle this at the departmental level."

Abbas raised his finger and walked away with his phone once again to his ear. Now it was Abbas who placed a hand at the back of his neck. He continued to face away from Len as his call was transferred from one office to another at the Uzbek Interior Ministry. Finally, he ended the call and turned back. "Guryanov's in a meeting. He'll call me in a few minutes."

"You look worried."

"Do I? No, I'm not. It's just that . . . well, I wish Guryanov could have been here to see these people for himself. Like you say, it's pretty inconceivable that they had anything to do with the missing diary. But then . . ."

Len waited. "What?"

"Well, it's missing, right? And they admit to breaking in."

"Yeah, but not to the basement."

Abbas rocked his head back and forth as though weighing the relevance of this distinction. A slight wince betrayed his skepticism.

Len angled the envelope back into his breast pocket. "I just need to get this guy out. I've got a week's worth of packing to do. And you saw Laura's reaction."

"Mmm-hmm. She seemed pretty upset. I wasn't really sure—"

"I'm in the doghouse, that's why."

"In the doghouse?"

"In trouble. On her shit list. It's my damn gambling debt to Smythe. She found out about it."

Abbas sucked in a sibilant, half-commiserating breath.

"It was the freakin' computer repair guy. She couldn't get Outlook to work. He told her to back up all the e-mails before bringing in the laptop. She doesn't know how to do that, right? And she says she didn't want to bother me at work . . . says she was too embarrassed. Anyway, so she takes the laptop in and the guy prints out all the e-mails and gives them to her. Can you believe that? *Prints them out.*"

"Including your correspondence with this Smythe fellow."

"Right. Which is not a friendly exchange. You know, this is why I took the job at Majestic. To make enough to get this guy off my back. I'm tired of the threats.

Abbas shifted from one foot to the other. "No. I didn't know—but I guessed. I mean, I knew things had been going wrong."

"I had a string of bad luck is all. If I didn't have Laura breathing down my neck, I'd take a month's pay and parlay it into the sixty thousand I owe this guy. I'd be done with it."

"And all of this was from online games."

"Yes. What she doesn't know is that I made over twenty in two-and-a-half days last year. Like I say, I had a string of bad luck. It happens." Len sniffed. "All right, so getting back to our flag man and his celebrity tag-along, let's get them out and be done with this. If I never hear of the companion flag again I'll be a happy man."

The ebullient ringtone on Abbas's phone threatened to drown out "happy man." "There he is," Abbas said, turning his back on Len and marching purposefully down the hallway. Abbas stopped twenty feet away, turned, and faced the wall. He launched into a steady stream of Uzbek utterances and answers, echoes of an ancient culture.

Len heard "yes" twice, but otherwise understood none of it. He let the familiar but unintelligible, rapid-fire intonations fade into the background. They were replaced by pieces of a recent argument he'd had with Laura over his "problem gambling"— no, "intolerable problem gambling." If it was so intolerable, he thought, why hadn't she said anything about it before? Well, no . . . but she knew he played cards . . . that he liked to gamble. It was his hobby, for Christ's sake. It had been going on for twenty-four years. So I play online now and then—what's the big deal? he thought. It's not like a guy in Kabul, an American diplomat, can drop by the corner bar for a Thursday night card game with the fellows. What do you expect? You've been well provided for. I just don't see why you're . . .

Len was suddenly aware that Abbas's phone call was coming to an end. He neatly capped his internal monologue with the optimistic thought that Laura's preoccupation with his gambling would, in a similar fashion, quickly die down. He stepped toward his friend. "What did he say?"

Abbas frowned and shook his head. "No. He says no."

"*What?*"

"I'm afraid so."

"But that's—"

Abbas's shell-shocked expression stopped Len in midsentence. "The diary is too important," Abbas said weakly. He seemed unable to look at Len directly. "It must be recovered at all costs. He insists Frost must have it. Frost or . . . probably Frost. He is not to be released."

IX

———

After ten minutes, Len and Abbas re-entered the room and took their seats. Charlotte looked at both men with a light in her eyes. "Fatimah was just telling us about her visitor yesterday."

"Oh?" Len said. "So someone else has heard about your arrest? I didn't think . . . I haven't seen anything about it in the media."

Fatimah glanced nervously at Alden.

"Go ahead," said Alden. "We're all friends here." He showed his palms to Abbas. "I'm right about that, aren't I, Mr. Ahkmedova?"

"What? Oh . . . yes. Of course." Abbas straightened his tie. Something approaching a smile crossed his face.

"It was a Mr. Ali Msaidie," Fatimah began, "sent by my grandfather to get me out of Uzbekistan. He's gotten permission from the Uzbek government, but I told him I wouldn't go without Alden."

"You did?" Len and Alden said at once, with Charlotte providing an echo.

Fatimah nodded. She looked at the tabletop in front of Alden. "I'm not leaving you here. We came in country together. We'll leave together."

Charlotte smiled. Her green eyes sparkled within the frame of her black hair and bright blue head scarf.

"That's very noble of you, Fatimah," said Alden, "but it's entirely unnecessary. You should leave if you can."

"You would not leave me if I were stuck here and *you* were free to go. I know this to be true."

There was no argument. Alden appeared to look inward. The corners of his lips turned up appreciatively.

"Here is his card," said Fatimah, sliding it across the table. "He said he'd be back this afternoon."

Len leaned over and picked it up, examined it. "May I?" he asked, signaling with his pen that he would like to write down the information.

"Of course."

"You say he was sent by your grandfather, the president of Tashir?" asked Charlotte while Len wrote.

"That's what he said."

Charlotte looked down at her fingernails. "It's a pity you can't use that fact to advance the companion flag cause."

"What fact?" Fatimah said in Arabic, looking past Alden. The lilt in her voice betrayed an almost childlike openness.

"The relationship," said Charlotte. "The fact of your grandfather's involvement. What if you were to agree to return to Tashir in exchange for your grandfather's promise to sponsor an initiative . . . or sign an executive order or something adopting the companion flag?"

Fatimah spoke in Arabic, and this time Charlotte nodded and responded "*N'am, n'am,*"—yes, yes—encouraging her. Fatimah explained that she had dreamt of seeing the companion flag fly beneath the green, white, and black flag of Tashir, but had abandoned the idea of approaching her grandfather. Why would he do this, after all? Why would he upset the status quo? He was a pragmatist, and his chief concern was to stay in power long enough to see his democratic reforms put into place. The United Peoples Party and its leader, Muhammad Ngalie, waited in the wings, ready to pounce. The citizenry was closely divided, and the president could not lift a finger without being criticized. No, it would be too risky. When Charlotte replied that his sponsorship of the companion flag might be seen as proof of his commitment to true democratic reform, Fatimah said, "By some, yes, but certainly not all. You see, the opposition is very organized."

While they spoke among themselves in Arabic, Len whispered something into Abbas's ear behind a cupped hand. Both men appeared to resist a smile until Fatimah's eyes flashed up at them.

Fatimah turned to Charlotte again. "You mean adopt the companion flag as a national symbol, don't you?" she asked, switching to English. Her already large eyes widened. "As a condition of my release?"

"Yes. Why not?" answered Charlotte. "But of course you must both go. Perhaps your grandfather would agree to have some kind of deliberation? A debate, maybe . . . or a conference. The public would have to learn about it. There would have to be buy-in."

"Yes," agreed Fatimah. "A televised debate. And let the people in neighboring countries watch, as well."

Alden, visibly startled, turned to Fatimah. "You don't think your grandfather would agree to such a thing, do you?"

"Normally, no. But you see, he's frightened about my being imprisoned. I'm sure of that. You know Uzbekistan's reputation for—" She stopped, looked at Abbas. "I'm sorry."

Abbas lifted his hand and shook his head.

Fatimah continued. "I know he wants me out of here, and I . . . yes . . ." She turned toward Charlotte. "Yes, I think he just might do this. He certainly knows I'm committed to this idea, and that I've put it ahead of almost everything else."

Charlotte looked from Alden to Len to Abbas. "So, what do you think?"

"I like the idea," said Alden. He pivoted to face Fatimah. "That is, if you're okay with returning to Tashir and you think your grandfather will go along. Would you be comfortable arguing for adoption of the flag?"

"Of course!" answered Fatimah. "Are you joking?"

Charlotte turned to Alden. "You must insist on going yourself, Mr. Frost. This is a great opportunity. Perhaps Mr. Msaidie can convince the Uzbek authorities—"

"No," Alden said. "I was the one who broke in. I need to stay and take care of this." His eyes met Len's. "You'll help me find an attorney—assuming I'm charged?

"Of course," Len replied.

"No, wait! Don't you see?" cried Charlotte. "The two of you must leave together!" Charlotte's ardent tone drew curious stares from the others. Charlotte sat back and got control of herself. "To explain the companion flag, I mean . . . certainly you will both be needed."

Alden smiled. "Thank you, Ms. . . . ?"

"Yacoubi," Charlotte said.

"Ms. Yacoubi. But Fatimah is quite capable of doing this alone." He turned to Fatimah and whispered, "If you do this, there is something I want you to take to your grandfather. We can talk about this later."

Charlotte's eyes darted in his direction and back again. She bit her lip to think. "Then I will go!" she blurted, bolting upright and turning toward Fatimah. "I will help you." She leaned over the table for emphasis. "I . . . this is very, very important to me. I'm determined not to let this project pass me by again."

"But you have your work here," Abbas said. "The Red Cross. Don't you risk losing your job?"

Charlotte looked closely at Abbas and her words covered the start of a smile. "That's secondary to me now. This is what I have to do. This is not a coincidence, I'm sure of it. I'll ask for a leave of absence. Even without one, I'll—"

"What about your family?" Len asked.

Charlotte shook her head. "That's not a concern. My family is not here, but they support me."

Len held up the business card and examined it again. "Do you think this Mr. Msaidie will agree to take *two* of you back to Tashir?"

"I'll insist." Fatimah leaned far over the table and faced Charlotte. "Are you sure you want to do this?"

"I am."

"You must get your things and be prepared to leave this afternoon then. He was in a great hurry." Fatimah's brows arched as she looked up and gazed into Alden's eyes. "Are you sure you want me to do this, Alden? If I'm here, the world's attention will be here, as well. You'll be safe. Once I'm gone . . ."

"I'll be fine, Fatimah. Go. This could be a breakthrough. I've always thought, if only one small country would adopt it, surely other nations would follow."

Fatimah put both hands on the table and leveled her gaze at Abbas. "Can you guarantee his safety, Mr. Akhmedova?"

"Can I—?"

"Can you guarantee his safety?"

Abbas cleared his throat, made eye contact with no one. "I will certainly do everything I can. I cannot speak for—"

"Do you see what I mean?" Fatimah cried, turning to Alden again. "This is too dangerous! We should stay together!"

Alden covered one of her hands with his own bony, white hand. "No, dear. I've got Mr. Williams here to help me. Besides, I've been doing this for years. I'll be fine." Alden looked across the table at Len. "You believe us, don't you? That all we were doing was leaving a companion flag at that school?"

Len looked around, surprised. "Uh . . . yeah, sure."

"There. See? I've got the power of the United States behind me. Mr. Williams is here to get me out, and I'm sure he will."

X

"You must be Ms. Yacoubi," said Ali Msaidie in heavily accented Arabic. Charlotte looked up at the tall, dark-skinned man with wary, tired-looking eyes and a fading, self-conscious, not unbecoming smile. The shine over the raised outline of a scar on his right cheek matched the gleam of perspiration that lit up his chin, the tip of his nose, and the breadth of his forehead. Before averting her eyes, she saw that he was handsome in a rugged, mysterious sort of way. He approached her with hands extended. "Here, let me help you."

Her rolling suitcase banged against the door frame, while a stuffed green-and-white duffel bag slung over her shoulder caught on the door behind her. "That's all right," said Charlotte.

"Please." Msaidie took the suitcase, retracted the handle, and deposited it on the couch in one motion, then returned to relieve Charlotte of the heavy duffel. "I'm Ali Msaidie, Ms. Yacoubi. Fatimah has told me about you." He put the bag on top of the suitcase. "She asked me to process your visa, which I've done. You'll be free to enter Tashir when we arrive."

"Oh. Okay. Thank you." Charlotte took a moment to catch her breath. "It's nice to meet you," she said, letting her eyes meet his again and offering her hand. Then she looked around the empty waiting room. "So Fatimah hasn't been released yet?"

"They're getting her now. We have a car waiting outside to take us to the airport."

Charlotte wondered how much this man knew about the condition under which Fatimah was agreeing to return. "Do you know if she's spoken with her grandfather?"

Msaidie smiled obliquely. "Yes, I believe so. You're referring to this flag business?"

"Yes."

"Mmm. I spoke to the foreign minister. He and several cabinet ministers met in emergency session with the president this afternoon. The president has agreed to the condition. Not with a great deal of enthusiasm, I should add. But, as you may know, he is a man of his word."

Msaidie's phone rang. He checked the caller ID. "Excuse me," he said, stepping quickly into the hallway.

As he moved away, Charlotte was startled momentarily. She'd thought she heard him whisper something in Turkish. She knew only a few words in that language, but it was something similar to—No, it couldn't be, she told herself. She shook her head. Why are you so jumpy? she asked herself. It was probably a Tashiri phrase, a greeting of some sort.

Charlotte moved to the couch and sat down next to her luggage. Alone in the waiting room of the municipal jail, she looked around for a few moments then to keep her hands busy she extracted her cell phone, let out a long, nervous breath, and checked the weather in Sanori, capital of Tashir. Not a cloud, not a drop of rain was expected for the next ten days. Good thing I packed light-colored clothes, she told herself. Suddenly, her phone vibrated and the Caller ID came to life. The unsmiling face of a pale, dark-haired woman with deep-set brown eyes, an angular jaw, and thick brows stared back at her. Charlotte covered the phone and instinctively looked up to ensure that no one was there. I have to remember to disable this feature, Charlotte told herself as she turned to the side and put the phone to her ear. I can't afford to have faces and telephone numbers appearing on my phone for the next few days.

"*Barev*, Raisa."

"Charlotte, where are you?"

Charlotte kept her voice to a whisper. "In the waiting room of the city jail. They're bringing Fatimah down now. What is it?" Charlotte's Armenian was laden with Arabic inflections.

"Are you sure this is the right move?" came the voice over the phone.

"Yes. When Mr. Frost said he had something he wanted Fatimah to take to her grandfather, I knew I had to go. She's smuggling it out—don't you see?"

"But how do you know this? He could just as well—"

"He's stuck in jail. That's how I know. He has no other options. And he trusts her."

"Do you have any idea who he's working for?—Why he took the diary?"

"No. It's . . . I can't figure it out. Have you found anything?"

"He was a FedEx driver at one time, but then he came up with this companion flag idea. That was decades ago. That's all I've . . . The web is full of references to him being in various countries, speaking at schools, conferences, that sort of thing, but it's all about this flag. There's no mention of the genocide or of our claims for reparations in the International Court of Justice."

The thought that Frost's possession of the diary might lack rhyme or reason sent a shiver up Charlotte's spine. Was he a mercenary? Did he intend to sell the diary to the highest bidder? Neither supposition matched the impression she'd gotten of the older American. His single-minded concern for the companion flag had struck her as genuine, and all encompassing. But three things were certain for Charlotte: he had broken into Public School 32, he had taken the diary, and by now he'd given it to Fatimah to carry out of Uzbekistan.

Was it all about money? she wondered. She thought about her own commitment, shuddering at the image of her brother Mehdi's smile, the way his brows knit, the eruption of his infectious, boyish laughter. Always, there rushed in on the heels this memory a very different one: her brother's limp body, his head turned unnaturally, his eyes half closed. At twenty-two, he had died in her arms. Time had congealed around that moment. His eyelids, active only seconds before, had stopped moving. But wasn't he trying to close his eyes for her at the moment of death, so that she wouldn't have to see such a thing? How could she think this? I'm a monster, she'd thought, as she'd brought his lifeless head up against her chest and screamed, "*No! No! Great Allah, no!*" And all around her were the thrashing legs and shuffling feet of protesters, hundreds of them, and shouts of every description and pitch. She remembered the thunder of rifle fire, the sudden retreat, and then, inexplicably, the onrush of the unarmed crowd. The crush. Mehdi's outstretched legs moved, not from life, but from being trampled upon, and this—seen through a veil of tears—was hideous to Charlotte, although she bore no lesser assault herself where she crouched, and her head—and Mehdi's—were knocked forward and back in a paroxysm of righteousness. "*Justice for Armenia! Justice for Armenia!*"

"*Help me!*"

"*Justice for Armenia! Death to Turkey!*"

"*Help me! My brother's been shot!*"

"*Justice for Armenia! Death to Turkey!*"

"Charlotte? Are you there? Charlotte?"

Raisa's voice brought her back to the present.

"I'm here," said Charlotte weakly. "Maybe he doesn't know what he has. No, that's impossible. Why would he go to all the trouble of taking it if he didn't know what it was?"

"Be care—"

"There's something else, Raisa. This idea, the companion flag. I researched it before I met with them. I told them . . . I'm not proud of this. I told Frost that I'd met him as a child. I didn't like doing it, but . . . Do you see how its adoption would help us? Can you imagine a better symbol for highlighting the injustices that your people suffered, the denial of their humanity?"

"Perhaps you're right, but what does this have to do with the Şahin Diary?"

"Nothing—not directly. But the companion flag in Tashir would be a start, wouldn't it? If I can help Fatimah Ibrahim get the companion flag adopted in Tashir, I will. I plan to do it, Raisa. It can only help the cause."

"But the diary!"

"I know. Believe me, if she has it, I'll get it." Charlotte looked up to see Msaidie turn at the far end of the hall. He had finished his call and was walking back. "Raisa. I've got to go. One more thing. There was a handler at the meeting this morning, an Uzbek with the Interior Ministry. His name is Abbas Ahkmedova. Can you check him out?"

"Yes, of course."

"All right. And the U.S. representative was someone named Len Williams—probably Leonard Williams. See what you can find out about him, as well, will you?" Msaidie reached the doorway. "Good-bye," she said, pulling the phone hurriedly down from her ear and hitting the Cancel button.

XI

Len heard the throaty roar of motorcycle pipes over his right shoulder. He checked the right rearview mirror of his Kawasaki. At first, nothing: billowing dust (presumably his own), a line of dark green-capped palm trees receding, flat Uzbek farmlands beyond, a thick line of brown stretching back as far as the eye could see. But then: a flash of Day-Glo green. It was Abbas's helmet. Abbas's body and bike leaned into a quick countersteer and swerve. Shimmering chrome took over the center of Len's mirror and suddenly with a rumbling crescendo that grew deafeningly loud, Abbas pulled even. Len saw Abbas's front wheel out of the corner of his eye and pressed more speed out of his own bike. He felt the lift and surge beneath him. There you go, buddy, he thought. The two powerful motorcycles flew across the steppes at eighty miles per hour, wingtip to wingtip.

"There's nothing better than this," Len said aloud inside his full-face helmet, not daring to turn his head. What a way to spend an afternoon! A steep uphill right turn loomed ahead. They throttled back and leaned into the corner in unison as though the two bikes were fused by a single connecting rod. When they reached the apex and crested the hill, they were swallowed by a flash of orange light. The setting sun stamped itself on their visors. Twisting their right wrists over the accelerators, they rolled power on together. Len laughed out loud. Smooth sailing: there were no potholes out here, thanks to the new highway the president had built to reach his summer house in the Tian-Shan Mountains.

A few moments later, Len became aware that something was different. Abbas had fallen back—way back—this time with his turn signal on. Len slowed. There was no one else on the highway. He saw in his rearview mirror that Abbas had angled off onto the shoulder and stopped. "What the hell. . . ?" Len muttered as he applied the brakes and maneuvered his bike into a sharp U-turn. By the time he had pulled up next to the blue Yamaha, Abbas was off his bike, had lifted his visor, and was pacing, speaking excitedly through his helmet-mounted Bluetooth phone.

Len shut off his engine. "What is it?" he yelled through the thick plastic of his helmet.

Abbas held up a hand, then turned his back on Len and resumed an animated exchange in Uzbek. His voice was edged with concern and incredulity.

Len dismounted and loosened his helmet straps. He wished he understood Uzbek. A knowledge of Uzbek wasn't necessary for the job—only Russian and English—but there were times when not speaking Uzbek felt intolerable.

Abbas was shaking his head. He turned around to face Len. He punctuated each exchange with a heated challenge until doubt faded away and resignation had him lowering his voice—and his eyes. "Okay," he said. "Yes . . . I understand."

The switch to English was for his benefit, Len realized. Abbas was trying to get off the phone. He had stopped moving. After looking around impatiently, he settled his gaze on Len's feet. He issued an order of some kind—again, in Uzbek. There was a pause. Now, in English: "All right . . . we're on our way."

"What is it?" asked Len as Abbas felt for the switch next to his chin strap, ending the call.

"It's Msaidie—"

Len's phone rang, startling him. The ringtone was set at the highest volume so as to be heard over the sound of the engines, and it was the double ring reserved for high-priority calls from the embassy. "Msaidie?" said Len, as he reached for the call accept button. "Just a minute . . . Williams here."

His secretary's voice sounded tinny through the earpiece. "Len, it's Karen. We just got an urgent call from someone in Tashir, a Jamaal Rachadi. He's a former boyfriend of Fatimah Ibrahim. They spoke on the phone this morning. Apparently Ms. Ibrahim told him Ali Msaidie was there to take her out of the country. That name sounded familiar to him, but he couldn't figure out why. An hour ago, he checked with the Tashiri foreign minister's office. They told him Ali Msaidie was a field agent killed in a car accident three weeks ago. In Sanori."

"*What?*" Len looked at Abbas, who nodded. Wait a minute. If this man's not Msaidie, who is he? And if he's not with the Tashiri government . . . ?

"Let's go!" Abbas shouted, snapping down his visor.

"He'd read the name in the paper," Karen continued. "He was—"

"All right, all right. Listen, Karen. Here's what I need you to do. We're heading to the airport now—"

Abbas tapped him on the shoulder. The words came muffled through his visor. "I've alerted the police and airport security," Abbas shouted. "And the tower. They're trying to locate the plane."

Len nodded. "Listen, Karen. Tell the ambassador what's going on. Then contact the Tashkent Municipal Jail. Tell them we have reason to believe there may be an attempt on Mr. Frost's life. We need them to double the—"

"I've already done that, Len!" shouted Abbas, mounting his bike and hitting the starter.

"Strike that!" Len cried, regarding Abbas anew. He was vaguely irritated with Abbas for being one step ahead of him, and for his evident calmness under pressure, but at the same time he knew his admiration for the man would last a lifetime.

"Let's go!" Abbas shouted again over the undulating din of his exhaust pipes. The Yamaha was like a racehorse at the starting gate.

Len shouted into his helmet-mounted microphone. "Call me back, Karen, and patch in Abbas on his cell."

Seconds later, Len and Abbas were climbing through the gears on their motorcycles, inching ahead of one another in turns. They negotiated the downhill curve and hit the straightaway at eighty-five miles per hour. Like two gunshots in quick succession they passed a lone road sign: "Tashkent 22 km." Karen's call came in. Len tapped a button on his helmet. "Karen . . . Abbas, are you there?"

"Right here," said Abbas through the speakers.

Len was aware of the Yamaha's front tire inching up beside him. The roar of the wind began to match the sound of the engines. The pavement was a blur. Abbas's calm voice was unnerving. Len tried to speak but couldn't. He was caught in mid-swallow. "All right," he managed. He took two long breaths through his mouth.

"Let me know what you need," Karen said.

Over a long straightaway, the phone went quiet and his attention slipped from the road ahead to flashes of information that seemed to point nowhere. He imagined Alden and Fatimah, at night, on the roof of PS 32. Breaking into schools? Really?

A static spike sounded in his earphones. It was followed by a quick exchange in Uzbek between Abbas and the Uzbek dispatcher. Len listened for Abbas's voice in English, but it didn't come. The earphones went silent again. The high pitch of the two engines, already higher than anything he'd heard before, rose in unison.

All that just to leave a flag? And the Şahin Diary? Why? Who had ever heard of a secret archive in a public school?

A truck and trailer lit up with headlights and running lights appeared a half-mile ahead. Seconds later, it roared past, throwing the screams of the two bikes back into Len's ears.

"Len, it's Karen."

"Go ahead."

"I've notified the ambassador. He's on his way."

"Copy."

Len swallowed again, slowly. Talking and flying down the highway at breakneck speed was a whole new trick for him. It wasn't easy—or safe. How did Abbas manage the calm voice?

They flew past a small road sign: "Tashkent 13 km."

On top of everything else, an international beauty had given up everything to sneak around with this . . . what? Sixty-three-year old itinerant idealist? Len didn't get it. He didn't get it at all.

Abbas began to pull ahead. Len leaned forward, squeezed his knees hard against the gas tank, and increased his speed. Ninety-one. Ninety-two. Len settled in on Abbas's left side, less than fifteen feet behind the blue Yamaha. Biting down on his lip, he was certain of one thing: the calm, uneventful transition from State Department to private sector he'd planned on was DOA.

*　　*　　*

Fatimah cleared her throat and shifted to better see out the window. The passing skyline glowed a deep reddish-purple, an effect made more dramatic by the limousine's dark-tinted glass. In the city's two tallest buildings, the National Bank of Uzbekistan and the Hotel Uzbekistan, the topmost floors flashed with light from the setting sun. The day and the city are winding down, she thought. Perhaps it is saying good-bye—Tashkent, that is. She searched the skyline in vain for the city jail building. Alden's there somewhere, she told herself. She turned and glanced at the back of Msaidie's head, but her thoughts pulled her back again to the city. How could I leave him here? she wondered. I shouldn't have. I should have insisted that he go to Tashir with us. She recalled the meeting earlier with Len Williams and Abbas Ahkmedova—and this woman. She was suddenly conscious of Charlotte in the seat next to her, clothed in a gray *abaya*, her light brown arm looped through the straps of a tan handbag.

I don't think he's forceful enough to negotiate Alden's release, she told herself, thinking of the American. He seemed disinterested—didn't he?—like he was reading from a script, or had something more important to do. And why were they smiling when I was talking?

But grandfather has agreed to sponsor a companion flag initiative, she thought. A smile formed at the corners of her mouth. This could be amazing. There would be a debate, of course, but she was ready for that. She glanced at Charlotte. Their eyes met. Fatimah's half-formed smile disappeared. She looked away again. She hoped this woman was as committed as she said she was.

Just then Fatimah heard a strange thrumming. It grew louder by the second.

"What's that?" Charlotte asked, looking around.

Fatimah checked the side window. It seemed to be coming from above them. Unable to see anything, she twisted around to look out the back window. Charlotte was doing the same.

"It's a helicopter!" Fatimah called out. "It's right behind us!" She glanced into the front seat. Msaidie and the driver were both ducking, trying to see out of their respective side windows. The car swerved.

"What is it? What are they doing?" Charlotte asked, turning first one way and then another.

There was a mechanical clicking. Fatimah saw the black perforated barrel of a submachine gun rise up above the back rest of the front seat.

"What are you doing?" she shrieked.

Msaidie didn't answer. He continued looking up, trying to spot the helicopter overhead.

Charlotte shouted, *"What are you doing? Stop the car!"*

The two men exchanged words excitedly in a language Fatimah had never heard before. It sounded Eastern European. The soundproof glass divider separating the front seat from the extended passenger compartment began to rise.

Fatimah lunged forward to press the control button on the passenger console, but it was too late. It had been overridden. *"Hey, wait a minute! What are you doing?"*

*   *   *

As the traffic picked up, Len and Abbas had to break their close formation. Abbas led the way, winding through cars, trucks, and busses, bound for the airport freeway. Len had to rely on instinct as much as following Abbas, for there were periods when he lost sight of his friend's motorcycle and green helmet. When the traffic opened up again, Len exhaled deeply and his racing heart slowed a beat or two as he spotted his friend flying down the road ahead of him.

Through his earphones, Len heard Abbas and another person—a woman—speaking Uzbek. "Okay," Abbas said. "Len?"

"I'm here."

Abbas's blue Yamaha streaked toward a red light and a major intersection no more than five hundred yards ahead of him. Len's heart jumped into his throat. Did he see it? He was on the verge of crying out "Watch out!" when he saw the flashing red-and-blue lights of four police cars, two on each side of the road. There were a half dozen policemen in black and white uniforms standing with arms raised in front of long lines of cars and pedestrians. They were blocking the intersection for them. Abbas was past them in a split second, and moments later the roar of the engine of Len's Kawasaki filled the intersection with the Doppler effect. Within seconds, the intersection grew preternaturally quiet, with the only sound being that of the two bikes straining to gain speed in the distance.

"Our helicopter has located them," said Abbas. "They're on Barbur Street, heading toward Tolipov. Ground units are converging, but right now we're the closest." More Uzbek—the same calm dispatcher's voice Len had heard earlier, this time with other dispatchers' voices audible behind her—filled the speakers. Abbas's reply was equally relaxed, if breathier. "Okay. Copy that."

Abbas, then Len, flew past another blocked intersection. Len glanced to the side. The faces of pedestrians lining the sidewalk and crowding the street corners blurred together like featureless mannequins. The road ahead bent to the left and both bikes, in turn, slowed and dipped in anticipation. Accelerating out of the turn was a high-pitched affair, but Len was oblivious to anything now but the rear fender and taillight of the blue Yamaha. Follow in his track, he told himself. Just stay on his track.

"We've got ground units coming in behind us," Abbas said, "and four in position at the airport. The plane is a Dassault Falcon 900 parked at the east end of Runway 25. It's registered to a Sadler Transworld Leasing in the Cayman Islands. Have you heard of them?"

"No." Len could barely get the word out, his heart was racing so fast. He wondered how Abbas did it. He hesitated, forced the words: "Karen, are you getting this?"

"We're getting it," came the baritone voice of Ambassador Tompkins. "We've got you on the speaker phone."

"Be safe, Len," said Karen in the background.

"Listen to me," said Tompkins. "You let the Uzbeks handle this. I want you to break off—*now.* You have no business getting involved with—"

There was another dispatch in Uzbek. It drowned out the ambassador. Abbas answered. Calmly. So calmly! Len tilted his head up to get a better look at the tail end of Abbas's bike. The brake light flashed as he rounded another corner. Len realized that he had let a little space open up between them. Perhaps it was his body complying with Tompkins's order to break off, or a reaction to the concern in Karen's voice. It wasn't intentional. He slowed for the corner and countersteered into a steep left-hand lean. As the Kawasaki stood up again he shifted down and rolled on the accelerator. The bike jumped beneath him. Len heard the garbled voice of the ambassador mixed with the voices of the dispatcher. Len was gaining on Abbas again. What you don't realize, Ambassador, Len smiled to himself above the rising voice of the engine, is that that's my friend up ahead. He may need me, and I'll be damned if I'll back off now.

*   *   *

"What's happening?" Charlotte grasped Fatimah's arm. Her mouth opened as though she were preparing to scream, but then she covered it with a hand. She looked into Fatimah's frightened eyes, her own wide with fear.

Suddenly, the limousine accelerated. The driver swerved to get around traffic, first to the left, then sharply to the right. The rear tires spun in loose gravel on the freeway's shoulder as they passed a white delivery van. The vehicle swayed on its long chassis as it veered again, with horns blaring around them, to the left and then back again onto the shoulder. Charlotte screamed. The car sped past the airport exit.

"We've gone past the exit!" cried Fatimah. "That was the exit to the airport!" She sat back, placed a hand on her heart. She turned to Charlotte. "What's happening? What have I gotten you into?"

Charlotte was still covering her mouth. With her free hand she gripped the armrest and turned first one way and then another in a desperate attempt to figure out what to do next. She reached for the door handle on her side of the limousine. It was locked. She tried the latch. The driver had overridden it. Fatimah tried the door handle on her side as well, with the same result. Their bodies pitched forward and back with the vehicle's sudden deceleration and acceleration. Other vehicles were honking now and swerving out of the way. At last the limousine cleared the traffic and angled off the freeway, accelerating up an off-ramp with a deep roar of the engine. The thump-thump-thump-thump of the helicopter was still above them, but more distant-sounding now. Perhaps it was higher. The driver suddenly leaned to the right and spun the wheel. Fatimah and Charlotte both let out a scream as the limousine fishtailed onto a dirt road that pointed back toward the airport.

Msaidie opened the passenger-side window and pointed the submachine gun up toward the sky. A sudden burst of gunfire erupted. The barrel jumped and vibrated in his hands. There was a pause, then more firing. Msaidie fought against the wild yawing and sliding of the limousine over the rutted road as he tried to aim the weapon.

Charlotte twisted around to look out the back window. Through the limousine's brown, rising dust cloud she spotted a flash of Day-Glo green in the distance. It was there and gone.

The screaming engine jumped registers as the driver shifted down and then accelerated again. He shouted something unintelligible to Msaidie, daring to take his eyes off the narrow road for only a second at a time.

"They're going to kill us!" Fatimah shouted.

Charlotte didn't hear her. She had plunged her hand into her purse and was feeling for her cell phone. I must tell Raisa, she thought. Even if I am killed, Raisa must know. She must know where it is. With the car bouncing around her, her body pitching uncontrollably, she brought out the phone and began to imagine telling Fatimah everything. "I must know where the Şahin Diary is," she would scream above the engine's roar and the firing of Msaidie's weapon. "You must tell me!" She would ignore the terror and confusion that would spring into Fatimah's eyes. "Listen to me! I'm working for Armenian Relief. Do you understand? That diary holds the secrets to the Turkish genocide, to the slaughter of millions of Armenians. Don't you see? I must have it. Justice requires that I . . . that it be made public. You must tell me where it is!"

But before she would talk, she would get Raisa on the phone. Charlotte began dialing, misdialed because of the violent jarring of the limousine, and started again. The phone was ringing at the other end. Just as Charlotte opened her mouth to speak to Fatimah, the car veered and dipped heavily to the left then back to the right again. Fatimah screamed. The cell phone flew up into the air, bounced off the leather seat, and landed on the floor opposite her. Charlotte lunged for it, throwing herself across Fatimah's legs.

XII

Twice Charlotte tried, but she could not reach the phone. She heard Raisa's voice. "Hello? Hello? Charlotte, is that you?"

Msaidie pointed the driver down an abandoned, brush-covered utility road. The limousine bounced heavily, three times, over the rough surface, lifting Fatimah and Charlotte off their seats, sending a spiraling dust cloud into the air. Msaidie shouted something to the driver. The vehicle spun to the left, crashing through tall bushes that scraped along the undercarriage of the limo. They were airborne again. A great cloud of sand and debris, like a bow wave, erupted over the hood when the vehicle crashed down again. The car gave up a deep, metallic groan but rose again. Msaidie was barking orders. Bits of green, needle-like foliage poured in through the open passenger-side window. The rear tires spun in the loose soil. The limousine slowed despite the steady roar of the engine. Fatimah and Charlotte embraced in the backseat, invoking Allah's protection between frightened screams. The car lurched forward again. There was no semblance of a road now as they bounced and fishtailed over bushes, stones, and berms.

They were making their way toward the east end of the runway. Suddenly a blur of chrome, blue, and bright green crossed in front of them. It was Abbas, the front tire of his motorcycle bouncing off the ground. He was standing on the foot pegs, knees flexed. The driver of the limousine took evasive action, spinning the wheel to the left. His head bent against the ceiling of the car and his cry was audible through the glass in the backseat. The two women braced for the impact and managed to protect their heads as the rear of the limo jumped skyward and crashed down.

"Look!" Fatimah shouted. Charlotte lifted her head and leaned forward to see past her. Flashing in and out of view behind a row of bushes was a second motorcycle, its engine roaring in fits and starts as if complaining, its rear tire throwing back great shovelfuls of dirt. This rider was also standing on his foot pegs, letting the bike bounce beneath him.

The black limousine emerged into a clearing—a maintained area, part of the airport's approach. A wire fence separated it from the asphalt runway stretching away to the west. A white-and-blue jet with the strobes on its wingtips flashing stood just off the runway, its engines whining softly. The car stopped. Both men scrambled out and stepped back to the rear passenger doors. The driver pulled a GSh-18 semiautomatic pistol out of his shoulder holster. He held it at the ready, looked around, then opened Charlotte's door.

"Get out!" shouted Msaidie. He saw the cell phone on the floor, grabbed it, and threw it several yards from the car. It broke apart on impact.

"What are you doing?" Fatimah demanded. "Who are you? What do you want?"

"Get out, I said." Msaidie looked around nervously. "Hurry up!"

"No! I demand to know who you are. Where do you think you're taking us?"

With his submachine gun pointed to the side, he reached in, took her by the arm, and pulled her out of the car.

"Leave me alone!"

He pushed her toward the fence. "Get the cutters," he told the driver.

The driver hesitated. "What about *her*?" He jabbed his pistol in the direction of Charlotte.

"Kill her."

"No!" Fatimah screamed, stepping back toward the limousine. Msaidie yanked her around, forced her toward the fence again.

A gunshot rang out.

Fatimah stumbled forward, then turned back. "*Charlotte!*" Fatimah saw the driver lower his gun. Charlotte was bent over in the car. Time seemed to slow. Fatimah couldn't make sense of it. The driver leaned back. Why was he leaning back? In the next instant he was falling. He fell backward like one expecting to be caught. His body hit the ground with a thud.

Fatimah saw something out of the corner of her eye. The barrel of Msaidie's submachine gun was swinging up. Msaidie pulled her toward the gun as though he thought to use her as a shield. A second gunshot split the air. She felt Msaidie's grip loosen. At the same time, the submachine gun emitted an arcing spray of bullets up into the sky. Now Msaidie was spinning around, falling away from her. She turned back. A man in a Day-Glo green motorcycle helmet stood sixty feet away with his arms extended. The outline of a pistol was visible between his two hands.

"Ms. Ibrahim!" someone shouted behind her. Another man was running toward her, removing his helmet. She recognized him, and by the time she turned back to face the man with the pistol, he had lowered it and was running toward the open door of the limousine. He, too, raised the visor on his helmet.

A terrified scream erupted from inside the car.

"Ms. Yacoubi," Abbas yelled. "It's me! Abbas! You're okay now!"

Just as Len reached Fatimah and gently took her shoulders to steady her, the voice of an uninjured Charlotte sounded from inside the vehicle, barely audible over the high-pitched whine of the jet and the thrum of the lowering helicopter. "Abbas? Oh, Abbas! Oh, praise Allah!"

XIII

—

Len entered Abbas's office carrying two large, white paper cups. He set one in front of Abbas. "Welcome to latte world."

Abbas sat back, frowning. "You know I don't drink coffee."

"Look. If you're going to visit us in Seattle, you have to drink coffee. It's mandatory—and not just any ol' coffee. And, yes, you're coming for a visit. So drink up."

Abbas reached for the cup. "Don't they have tea in—?"

"Try it. Tariq made it special for you."

Abbas raised the cup toward his lips. "My secretary would probably like this, but she's out sick today. Food poisoning." He sipped miserably and made a face.

"So," said Len, ignoring him and taking a seat. "Do you have an ID on this fellow who came in as Ali Msaidie?"

Abbas set the cup on the far edge of his desk behind his phone. "Unfortunately, no. Neither he nor the driver show up on Interpol's dental or fingerprint databases. We think he's Tashiri, but not recently from there. We're still looking. The plane was leased, and the pilot is a contractor hired through the leasing company. He's clean."

"How'd Msaidie get through?" asked Len. He widened his eyes innocently to assure Abbas he meant no disrespect.

"We don't know. It's an embarrassment for the foreign minister . . . and the president. The fallout is just beginning."

"How do you mean?" asked Len.

"The foreign minister received a pointed communiqué from his counterpart in Tashir this morning. Put it this way. His Excellency raised questions about the competency of our government and closed with a thinly veiled threat should anything further happen to Fatimah. It was sent through a back channel but somehow the Associated Press picked it up."

Len nodded. "The old kick to the ribs. I was thinking on the way over here: whoever these people were, they were willing to bet Fatimah—and only Fatimah—had the diary. She insisted that Frost be allowed to accompany her to Tashir and Msaidie refused—right? What does that tell you?" Len stomped on Abbas's hesitation. "That they weren't interested in Frost at all." Len took a long drink. "In some ways it makes sense. Frost is all about this flag project. Besides, he's old. Fatimah is . . . well, new. New to all this. Maybe malleable. Someone got to her."

Abbas stood up and walked to the window. He thrust his hands into his pants pockets and stared out. "Possibly. Or it could be that they lacked a pretext for freeing Frost. He's not Tashiri, after all."

"True," Len said, licking the rim of his paper cup. "What's the condition of the survivor, our fake Msaidie?"

"Still in a coma," said Abbas, glancing back at Len. "Critical condition, I'm afraid. Whoever's behind this has friends in high places." Responding to a blank stare from Len, Abbas continued, "How else can we explain such an elaborate plot? And don't forget your own secretary of state directed you to secure Frost's release and offer him safe passage *with the package*. They obviously think he has the Şahin Diary. There was nothing said about Fatimah."

"Maybe they think he can get his hands on it," Len offered.

"She's an international superstar and she obviously cares a great deal about Frost and his flag. Why would she risk it all?"

Len ignored the point. "What about the other woman? Charlotte?"

"She's shaken up," Abbas said. His jaw tightened and his eyes betrayed the contemplation of something unpleasant. "Whoever's out there may target her again now that she's been seen with Fatimah. I've convinced her to stay with my sister and her husband for a few days. We've got men watching her flat. Last night, we issued a report that says both men were killed. We want whoever's behind this to think we're in the dark."

Len sat back and loosened his tie. "Are you okay? After the shooting, I mean?"

Abbas hesitated. A fragile smile—a forced smile—crossed his face. He stepped back from the window and stared down at the papers scattered across his desk, then picked one up. "Line of work, I guess."

"I suppose." Len glanced out the window past him. He saw that his friend was in pain. "Truth be told, Abbas, I wasn't sure what we were going to do. I didn't know you were armed. I mean . . ." Abbas opened his mouth, but Len lifted his hand and added, "Don't get me wrong. I knew you could shoot. I'm glad you can. Our options were thinning out fast."

Abbas nodded. "Part of the job." He raised the sheet and took a sudden, if false, interest in an interoffice e-mail listing parking abuses south of the ministry annex.

Len waited for Abbas to look up. All right, Len thought, it's part of the job. I get that—when you're on security detail, or you're guarding the president. But out for a ride on your bike? "So, I'm off to China in the morning. Care to join me?"

"Funny." Abbas put down the memo and sat at his desk.

Len drank from his latte then looked long and hard at his cup. "You know why I dropped by this morning. I've got to get

Frost out, plain and simple. Those are my orders. Look, his only interest is this crazy flag idea. You've met him now. You've seen for yourself. You don't think there's any connection between the Şahin Diary and the crazy companion flag, do you?"

"No."

"Well then . . . ?"

Abbas rocked back in his chair and looked at Len over a steeple of fingers. His eyebrows rose up noncommittally.

"It might even have been a kidnapping for ransom," Len continued. "She's an heiress—right? And Frost is . . . nobody. I don't even want to talk about the building, or the diary. You heard him. He thought it was a school. That's what everyone thinks. You probably thought so yourself until the other day . . . You have the flag, I assume."

"I don't. The police presumably do."

"Right. So there it is. I don't know why the secretary of state got involved. Someone who knows Frost probably knows her. It happens." Len shifted in his chair. "I need to get this off my plate, Abbas. That's the bottom line. Can you see about getting him released today? Strip-search him if you want to. Wrap him in a towel and put him on a plane to New York or Moscow or something."

"If only it were that easy," said Abbas. He looked up as a young man in shirt sleeves with a green-and-gold regimental stripe tie leaned into his office.

"Oh, I'm sorry. I didn't—"

"Never mind," said Abbas. "What is it, Dilshod?"

The young man glanced at Len and nodded a greeting. "The plot thickens," he said in a nearly accent-free English. "The company that leased the plane is a shell corporation based in Martinique. Our agents have traced the address to a vacant lot owned by the Catholic Church."

Len saw that both Uzbeks were staring at him. He threw a hand up. "Don't look at me. My people are straight Southern Baptist."

Abbas laughed.

"On top of that," the young man continued, "the foreign minister just got another communiqué from the foreign minister of Tashir. He's demanding to know what charges we're holding Fatimah on. He wants an answer yesterday."

"Can't blame him for that," Len said genially. There was no response, but a little chill in the room prompted Len to add, "Something tells me they're pretty panicked down there in Tashir. I mean, she's the president's granddaughter—right? . . . Oh, and by the way, I do recognize her now."

Abbas nodded. He explained to his junior associate, "Forty-eight hours ago, our American friend here didn't know who Fatimah Ibrahim was."

The young man looked at Len with an embarrassed smile. "You're kidding."

"Just her name is all. Once I saw her I recognized her."

"Uh-huh." Abbas smiled playfully. "Okay, thanks Dilshod. I'll be done here in a minute." With that the young man was gone.

Len cleared his throat and picked a piece of lint from the sleeve of his jacket. "I'm not unsympathetic to what the Tashiris are trying to do. Think of this as an informal demarche. I'm on a plane to Seattle in nine days, and—"

"Hopefully, when you return from China we'll know more," Abbas said, closing a file on his desk. "If I can arrange to have him released, I will. You know that."

*   *   *

Abbas's sister Zukhra glanced to the side expressively and scratched her head as she opened the door to admit him. It was greeting enough between siblings. "She's just gone into the bedroom," Zukhra whispered as Abbas stripped off his jacket.

"Is she all right?"

Zukhra took his coat, draped it over a wire hanger, and hung it on a brass wall hook in the small, red-tiled foyer. She proceeded into the flat's narrow kitchen, to the hissing gas stove, where she took up a tea kettle with a ragged potholder. "She will be," she said, pouring steaming water into two cups.

Abbas stood behind her, aware that his heart was pounding. He took two deep, quiet breaths to try to settle down. When Zukhra turned and handed him his cup of tea, he was at pains to hide his nervousness.

Zukhra smiled. "Relax."

"I am relaxed," he lied. He brought the cup up to his mouth and held it there uncharacteristically. "Why wouldn't I be?"

She shook her head and brushed past Abbas, leading him into a small room, one of over seven hundred identical living rooms stacked eight deep in this sprawling, monolithic, Soviet-era apartment complex. A red floral tapestry covered one wall, floor to ceiling, while a blue tapestry depicting the Italian Alps disappeared behind a brown leather sofa along the opposite wall. The sofa and love seat, a big-screen TV, a coffee table, and a bookcase set at an angle in one corner, with inexpensive vulpine statuettes and plastic tulips and chrysanthemums in pink and green vases scattered throughout, awaited the arrival and enjoyment of people. Abbas walked to the window facing the courtyard three floors below.

"Sasha's not home?"

"His car's in the shop. I'm going to pick him up in a few minutes. You must stay for dinner."

He nodded absently, watching two boys kick a soccer ball below. I didn't hear the shots, he thought. I heard the bullets flying out of Msaidie's submachine gun, but my own .45? Why can't I remember? There were two shots—pop! pop!

Zukhra said something that he didn't hear.

Pop! There should have been a sound, dammit. I saw the driver's body shudder. It was instantaneous and unnatural. There would have been another pop! Msaidie went down, spinning, with a bullet traversing his lung. His submachine gun spewed smoke in a perfect arc. What a strange thing! I can still feel the recoil. I can feel the grip of the .45 in my hands, but there was no noise. I can only imagine it. Pop! Pop!

"Should we be worried about you, brother?" Zukhra said from the love seat.

"What? Oh, no. I'm fine."

"It had to be terrible."

Her words reached him impersonally, like a telegram. So Charlotte must have told her, he realized—at least some of it. He recalled the look of horror on Charlotte's face when he reached the door of the limousine, the blood splatters on her forehead, cheeks, and hands. What could he possibly have said to her? His eyes had scanned down to see the driver's last movements—the helpless quivering of blood-soaked lips above an exit wound where his Adam's apple should have been. Then he had looked back into the limousine at wide, green eyes misshapen by tears. What could he have said?

He turned away from the window and was brought up short. Zukhra's eyes followed his to a figure standing behind her in the entryway. "Oh, you're up," Zukhra said in bright tones, rising and offering her guest her place on the love seat. "Let me get you some tea. Here, sit. Come."

Charlotte complied, trying to hide her thick, black, mussed hair behind a hastily donned *hijab*. To the sounds of Zukhra making preparations in the kitchen, Abbas moved to the far corner of the sofa and sat down. Oh, but she is beautiful in Zukhra's white robe, he thought. He took advantage of the fact that Charlotte, in this stage of dress, was at pains to avoid looking at him. He felt his heart begin to throb at the base of his throat. Suddenly, he longed to hear her speak, to see the shape of her mouth as it moved around words.

"Ms. Yacoubi, I've come to see if you're all right. I've been worried about you." He pinched down on the words, hoping the sound would not reach the kitchen where Zukhra was busy with the tea kettle.

Charlotte glanced up, then averted her eyes again, and the hint of a smile turned the corners of her mouth.

"Are *you* all right?" she asked, her voice trembling slightly. Now she looked at him full in the face, unhesitatingly, as though some minimum requirement of feminine restraint had been satisfied.

They exchanged a long, unflinching gaze. He could stay in this moment forever, Abbas realized. He nodded, paused a few moments, smiled briefly, then, looking down at his feet, nodded again.

Zukhra brought Charlotte a light covering—red with green flowers—although her legs were already covered, then returned to the kitchen. When Charlotte had thrown the blanket over herself and brought her feet up comfortably on the cushion, she said, "What's wrong, Abbas? Are you unwell?"

He looked up, startled by the question. He felt a new surge in his chest. Surely, no woman could be more becoming, he thought. He even wondered for a time if Charlotte actually possessed this singular beauty, or if it was simply the product of some ephemeral combination of the light in the room and the play of shadow. And to think that she is here with me in my sister's house, Abbas thought, with some amazement. She continued to stare at him now, unabashed, and one side of his mouth formed a grin to cover his foolishness. "I'm fine," he said. "It's just that . . ." He wanted to be known by her, he realized. To have no secrets. *What is it about these marvelous eyes that draws this out of me?* he wondered. *I want to tell her everything. But does this include—?* Remembering the sight of her upturned face, spattered in blood, less than twenty-four hours earlier, he felt an upsurge of words. "It's my fault, Charlotte . . . what happened to you yesterday." *Yes, it's time to come clean,* he told himself. *Tell her.*

"What do you mean? Don't be ridiculous. You saved my life."

She knitted her brow and her voice bore the oblique impatience of a loved one—a sibling, a beloved wife, a friend of years. She trusted him implicitly, he realized. Suddenly, a calm overtook him. It was safe to say nothing, to keep his secrets. A kind of rethinking led him to utter, "My government is responsible for letting this man in, the one who claimed to be Msaidie."

Charlotte smiled humorlessly and threw her head back. "Oh, so now you're responsible for *that?* Please."

XIV

—

"We're going to lose one entire construction season, Williams. Now you see what we're up against." Brett Perkins, 56, dressed in a tired gray wool suit and blue-and-white tie, attempted to turn in the front seat of the small taxi. At six three and built like a lineman, with his knees pressed against the dashboard, it proved impossible. "State Grid Electric Power Company knows we're up against it here, but they're not lifting a finger. They have us under contract, so they can just sit back. We're getting hung out to dry, I tell you."

Len nodded in the backseat.

"I told Richardson last week these villagers have their heels dug in. It's like apples and oranges to them." Perkins's words were half shouted into the ear of the driver, a local man of small stature with disheveled black hair and sauce stains spotting the front of his white-and-forest green striped shirt. If he understood a word of English he didn't show it. Perkins's swiveling head and gesticulating arms did little to quell the quasi-comic, wash-cycle effect as scores of cars, bicycles, small trucks, motor scooters, and handcarts pressed in on all sides. "These people are crazy, Len. You can't talk sense to them."

Who's crazy? Len thought, turning to look out the side window. Did someone put a gun to Majestic's head and make them agree to take financial responsibility for construction delays? Not likely.

The crowded sidewalk teemed with pedestrians—narrow Mongolian eyes, black hair, yellow-brown skin, ethnic clothes in equal number to western. There was a minute measure of relief visible in the faces of office workers emerging from doorways in two and threes, out for lunch or a noontime stroll. Len rolled the window down an inch or two, let the noise in, breathed in the smells of Xining. The calmness at Len's core spoke to years of traveling in strange cities, dropping in and out. He covered a yawn. Different city, different case, love the people, hate the pace. Wasn't that how it went? If all these years in the State Department had taught him anything, it was how to compartmentalize. The motorcycle chase, the shooting, the aftermath: that was Tashkent, that was yesterday. This was Xining.

He reflected on the face of Sheng Jianyao, who had spoken so eloquently for the villagers in the morning session. It happened now and then: he would find himself sitting across from a man or woman of such prepossessing charm and sangfroid that he could not help but cheer for them in a sense. He marveled at these quixotic champions who plied their talents in unwinnable contests against overwhelming opposition. How do you stop the United States from getting what it wants, for example? How do you prevent a multinational behemoth like Majestic International from building a road—in the one place where the road must go? You don't. Len smiled crookedly. That's the simple answer. The die is cast.

Still, Sheng Jianyao was an impressive fellow, and you had to root for him. Len looked forward to reconvening at 14:00. He wondered if he could convince Perkins to think bigger and allow him room to negotiate. To give them something.

"So tell me, Brett, what's our bottom line?"

"We gotta have that road, damn it, and soon. It was approved by Beijing three years ago, and now the national politicians are sitting on their hands. It's like these villagers have got something on them."

"So it would seem . . . but you know how that works, don't you?"

Perkins managed a three-quarter turn against all the disinclining forces. "No. Enlighten me."

Len smiled. "It's called 'my uncle's neighbor plays golf with the prime minister's second cousin.' Six degrees of separation squeezed down to a single, bridgeable gap."

"Huh?"

"Or to use an Americanism, 'all politics is local.'"

"Yeah, okay—great. But how do we get them to sign off on this road?"

The car jerked to a stop. The driver honked and issued a stream of complaints in a dialect Len had never heard before. The driver was still complaining as the car started to move forward again.

Perkins continued. "They're saying no road. The valley floor is a quarter mile wide, and they're saying the whole damn thing is an ancient burial site. We have no other way up there. I say we just punch the damn thing through."

"Damn the torpedoes, huh?"

"Yeah, that's right."

Len took out a pair of sunglasses and put them on. "So where are we going to eat?"

*   *   *

"The problem we face, Mr. Sheng, is that there is no other way to get our equipment up to the construction site. If we can't get the equipment up there, we can't build the dam, and if we can't build the dam, Xining will have to continue to rely on much more costly electricity from the Luijia Gorge Dam. You see the problem?"

Jianyao rubbed his chin. "Yes, Mr. Williams. The Forbidden Gorge route would be impractical. It could not be kept open during the winter months. But you see, don't you, the problem *we* face? My clients' ancestors are buried where the tributary and the valley floor turn west. Here." He directed his laser pointer to a large map hung from an easel, which had been strategically positioned opposite the corner of the table directly in Len's line of sight. The red dot quivered over the page. "It is unfortunate that the valley is so narrow at this point, but for thousands of years this has been sacred ground to the Qiang people. To disturb this land would greatly offend the ancestors."

Len noticed from the corner of his eye that Perkins was loosening his belt. When that was done, the COO for the China and Far East Division sat back in his chair and began examining his fingernails. Not a bad strategy, Len supposed. There was nothing new in Jianyao's argument.

"Do you have any idea, Mr. Sheng, how we might resolve this impasse?" Len asked. "It is a difficult one, with valid concerns on both sides. But, that said, you cannot reasonably expect to halt the construction of a $1.6 billion dam." The third largest in western China, he might have added but didn't.

Sheng Jianyao gazed evenly across the table as though he were still waiting for a point to be made. This guy's good, Len thought, forcing his eyebrows up as if to say, "you've heard my point, now what's your answer?" The stalemate was broken when Jianyao's assistant leaned over to whisper something into his ear.

"My assistant reminds me that I have been a poor host. This, too, is an insult to the ancestors. Allow me to refill your cups," he said, standing and reaching over the table to pour hot tea into the two Americans' cups. The silence and cordiality of the moment belonged entirely to Mr. Sheng. Through the cloud of steam rising from the teapot, he said, "Mrs. Sheng and I request the honor of your presence at our home this evening, for a traditional Chinese dinner."

Oh yeah, you're good all right, Len thought to himself. He smiled broadly and said "Thank you. We would be delighted."

"Why in hell did we agree to dinner with the guy who's trying to put the screws to us?" Perkins would ask, later that afternoon, as he and Len waited on couches in the hotel lobby for Mr. Sheng's driver to arrive. "What's wrong with you anyway? You seem distracted."

"What? Oh. No, it's nothing. They call it *guanxi* here, but you see it in many other parts of the world. The idea is to negotiate on the basis of personal relationships, befriend your adversary and in the process weaken his resolve."

"Well, fuck that," Perkins said, sitting back and crossing his arms across his broad chest. "It's time you told this son of a bitch the road's going in, period. I don't know why you negotiation types dance around everything so much. What good's it doing? Why don't you just come out with it? Isn't that what we're paying you for?"

Len chuckled dryly. "No, you're paying me to keep bullets out of the cabs of your bulldozers and road graders. There's a bit of gamesmanship here, Brett. Play along, and let's see what comes of it."

*   *   *

Len's east-facing room on the fourth floor of the Huangshui River Hotel smelled of cigarettes and cleanser and had a toilet that was constantly running when he arrived. The toilet he fixed in short order, a link in the chain in the tank having become twisted. Fixing the problem and hearing the toilet sing a scale and go quiet—promising him a night of quiet rest—gave him an unexpected sense of well-being. The day was not a total loss, he told himself wryly. They had agreed to meet again in the morning. If experience had taught him anything, it was that success was always just one more meeting away. He took off his suit and hung it up, then slipped into jeans and a gray Northern Arizona University t-shirt. With an hour and a half to kill before he would meet Perkins in the lobby, he flipped on the television and hit the mute button, then went into the bathroom to splash cold water on his face.

Was there a refrigerator somewhere in the room? he wondered, watching water drops fall from his brown skin in the bathroom mirror. He toweled off, emerged from the bathroom, and began his search. There it was, tucked under the nightstand behind a faux drawer, and within it the very thing he wanted: cold beer. His sense of well-being was confirmed and amplified.

Setting his beer on the nightstand, he pulled down the bedspread, blanket, and top sheet on the king-size bed and stacked the three pillows against the headboard. He dug through his open suitcase for his Kindle, then slid onto the bed. He turned on the light. Page 202 of *The Known World*. All right, he thought, reaching for his beer, where is this story going? He was aware that some part of his mind wanted to relive the events of the last few days—the motorcycle chase, the shooting of "Msaidie" and the driver—but he pushed that away. Another time, he thought. Ten minutes later his cell phone rang. It was Laura.

"Hello, babe," said Len. The silence at the other end of the line gave him an instant uneasy feeling. "What's—?"

"Len?"

"Yes." Another pause. Something was wrong.

"Listen, Len, we need to talk. I need to talk to you."

"Okay. I'm listening. What's up, hon?"

"Len, I've wanted to talk to you for a long time. I . . . I couldn't find the right moment."

Now the silence bore through at both ends of the line. Len swung his feet over the edge of the bed and placed them on the floor. He inhaled a great breath and held it, hoping that would steady him.

"I just need to cut to the chase. I've been unhappy, Len . . . I *am* unhappy."

Len felt his heart rise into his throat. Through the receiver, he heard Laura's breath catch. He leaned over his knees. "What do you—"

"I want a separation."

He couldn't believe what was happening—if this was happening. "A separa—"

"I need time to think."

"Think? What are you talking about? Think about what?"

"I—"

"What do you mean you want a separation? What's going on? I'm in China. What—"

"I know. I'm sorry, Len. I should have told you earlier . . . or waited."

"Told me what?"

"I know it's not right . . . oh, none of this is right. I didn't know how else—"

"Wait. You're unhappy? What do you mean you're unhappy? I . . . did I do something?" He stood up and started pacing. It was his gambling debt—to Smythe. Or his gambling. Even the penny ante stuff. He knew it, but couldn't bring himself to admit it. "God, I can't even believe you're telling me this. What in the world's going on, Laura?" Surprise began to make room for anger. The latter edged in. "I'm 1,700 miles away, for Christ's sake. You couldn't have waited until tomorrow night when I get home?"

"I'm sorry. I . . . "

"You're serious about this. You're actually calling to tell me this." Len turned on his heels, his free hand on his forehead. He was prepared to pace again when he was stopped short by an image flashing on the television. *What?* Is it possible, he wondered, stepping toward the screen and leaning over, his mind now reeling more than ever. It *was* her. In the upper left-hand corner of the screen, superimposed over video showing hundreds of dark-skinned people rioting, of tear gas canisters being thrown, of cars burning in the streets of Sanori, was a picture of Fatimah Ibrahim. What in the world? Len thought. What the hell's going on?

"Len? Are you there?"

Dumbfounded, he sank down on the end of the bed. Bright yellow Chinese ideograms scrolled across the news ticker left to right. The video loop jumped from one location to another in the Tashiri capital, from street level to overhead images taken, presumably, from a helicopter. Police in riot gear, surging crowds, windows being smashed with sticks and poles, youths and young men throwing rocks and Molotov cocktails. A ground-level camera showed a tan, mansion-like building visible behind a sliding veil of smoke and a double phalanx of riot police. Next to its high arched doorway were a round seal and the flag of Uzbekistan. When the camera zoomed in, it was easy to read the words written in English: EMBASSY OF THE REPUBLIC OF UZBEKISTAN.

"Good God," Len whispered.

"What?"

Laura's voice was thinner than he had ever heard it before and yet, he thought—averting his eyes from the TV for a moment and finding himself looking back in the mirror above the desk—the same as it had been for a long, long time. "Nothing. I . . . Nothing." Intruding on Len's thoughts was the memory of his mother's voice growing thinner in the days and weeks after his father's passing.

How withdrawn she became. He had experienced her suffering as a punishment.

"I'm moving in with Barbara for now," said Laura. "Today. This is why . . . Glenn is on assignment in Bukhara and she could use the company."

Len stood up, moved to the window, separated the gauze curtains with his fingertips. He bit down on his lower lip. You've thought this all out, haven't you? This is why you're not coming to Seattle with me. It wasn't just for a few weeks. It wasn't to sell the furniture. It was never that. He felt the sting of angry tears and fought them back. He concentrated on a line of mountains visible in the distance, beyond Xining's city center—the rise and fall of peaks.

"Len, I'm sorry."

I can't deal with this, he said to himself. I can't believe it for one thing—I don't believe it. He pasted these words over what he knew to be true. This is—

"Len? Did you hear me?"

Why the hell are you doing this? he thought, shaking his head and turning back to the TV. The memory of Laura smiling wearily at his facetious parries when they were first married, his unrepentant defensiveness, passed through his mind. "I play cards with my friends," he'd said, counting out twenty-dollar bills at the kitchen table of their small Bakersfield apartment. "Some guys play ball. I play cards. I mean, lighten up." Len felt a weight, a hardness, form at the bottom of his throat. I can't deal with this right now, he reminded himself. Besides, it's not me. Maybe she just needs time. "Listen, I've got to go, Laura. Something's come up."

"*What?*"

The same images were playing on the television. What a strange juxtaposition: Fatimah's smiling face—a picture no doubt taken in a studio for a magazine cover or publicity spread in Cairo or New York or Tokyo—superimposed over images of rioting in her hometown. It had to be a reaction to the attempt on her life and possibly news of her incarceration in Tashkent, he thought. He guessed that Abbas would try to contact him. Perhaps he already had. He held the phone away from his ear. Sure enough, there were two text messages, both marked urgent. "I'll call you when I get back. Good-bye, Laura."

The first message was from Karen Blair, his secretary. "Top priority. Call immediately. Amb. wants to meet you Monday 07:30. Have you seen news from Tashir?" The second message was from Abbas. "Plz call ASAP."

Abbas took the call while in a meeting, whispering, with someone else speaking in the background. He excused himself and a few moments later said in full voice, "Len, thanks for getting back to me. Sorry to bother you."

"Not at all. I'm watching pictures on the TV here, but I don't know what's happening."

"Riots broke out overnight in Tashir. Reuters is reporting Fatimah's arrest and the kidnapping attempt. Every news agency in the world is running with it."

"It looks like they're rioting in front of the Uzbek embassy."

"They're blaming us for giving Msaidie access to Fatimah. We're in a difficult spot. We've filed a protest and have even threatened to recall our ambassador. It's an embarrassment for President Karimov. The whole country's in a very unwelcome spotlight."

"Yes, I see that."

"There's a counterprotest here this afternoon in front of the Tashiri embassy, and possibly the American embassy as well. That's what I wanted to talk to you about."

"The American embassy?"

"Yes. I've gotten clearance to handle this back-channel. We're going to charge Alden Frost with espionage, and—"

"*Espionage?*"

"Yes. Fatimah will be charged as an accessory. She will be allowed to leave, however, in exchange for a signed confession and apology to the people of Uzbekistan."

"You can't be serious. Espionage? He'll face the death penalty."

"I'm passing on what I've been told. I tried to talk them out of it. You know how this works, Len."

"But that's insane. You know damn well he's no spy."

"I do. But look, what I know doesn't . . . I've spent the last four hours trying to convince Guryanov that they're innocent. He keeps asking me how I know. The president, the foreign minister, and now the interior minister have all been humiliated, and it grows worse by the minute. No one can explain how Msaidie got in, or how he managed to fool us."

Len detected something different in his friend's voice, as though this were no longer just business, as though he had some personal stake in the matter. He thought of asking him about it, but Abbas was still talking.

"Msaidie's still unconscious. We've got a medical team doing everything they can to revive him so we can find out who he really is. The fact remains, he did it, he took her right out from under our noses, and it makes us look . . . well, worse than incompetent. Every media outlet in the world is asking why we arrested Fatimah Ibrahim in the first place—why we put her in this position. It can't be for putting up a flag as a gift to children."

"So Frost is caught in the middle of this?"

"I'm afraid so."

XV

———

"Son of a—!" Drops of sweat glistened on Len's face, neck, and arms as he gathered himself for one final push. His elbows shook as he lowered the barbell. He felt the moist bench cushion against his back. One more, he told himself, grimacing. And keep your back straight. He took a deep, sibilant breath. The bar began to rise, but then it stopped unexpectedly. The muscles in his shoulders seemed to give out, sending a spasm of alarm into his brain. He sucked more air between his teeth and redoubled his effort. The silver bar began to rise again, tentatively. He willed his elbows to lock, emptying his lungs in a great rush of air. His eyes lost focus momentarily. At last he held the 205 pounds at arms' length. He took two quick breaths and let the bar ease back over his head and clank into its cradle. The instantaneous relief in his shoulders and pectorals was warm and palpable. He let his arms fall to either side of the bench and rolled his eyes. What the hell, he thought, I must be going backward. That felt like 400 pounds. He felt blood surging rhythmically in his neck as he lay staring up at the tile ceiling of the hotel's small workout room. He closed his eyes for a few seconds, then turned to look at the clock above a trapezoidal swath of early morning sunlight illuminating colorful anatomical charts on the wall. Six forty.

He knew why he felt weak. It was the same reason he'd sought out the hotel's gym in the first place. The same reason he hadn't slept well. Laura. After twenty-four years of marriage, she was prepared to leave him. And then, if that weren't enough, there was Frost. They were going to kill him. They were making him the fall guy.

Len heard the sounds of people approaching and sat up. A Chinese man who looked to be in his forties, accompanied by an adolescent, the two wearing identical red-and-white gym shorts and red t-shirts, entered the room. The boy was laughing after what sounded like a quick repartee in the hallway, although Len couldn't understand their speech. The two had identical reactions to the sight of a foreigner occupying the space: they stopped within inches of each other and quickly replaced blank stares with friendly smiles and rapid, almost childlike waves. Father and son, Len thought. Maybe uncle and nephew. He nodded and waved back, releasing them from further embarrassment by looking down and wiping the sweat from his forearms.

"Good morning," said the man, trusting a muddled English.

Len looked up again. "Good morning."

"Do you mind?" The man pointed toward two treadmills and a television mounted on the wall.

Len waved him off. "No, no. Not at all. Go ahead."

They each gave something like a head bow and then they mounted the two machines. The older man took up the remote control and switched on the television.

Len replaced the plates on the barbell with two ten-kilogram weights. He removed the barbell from the bench press rack and turned toward the mirror, preparing to begin an upright row routine, but then lowered the barbell to the floor when an idea occurred to him. He walked to the windowsill where he'd placed his towel and cell phone, picked up the phone, and stepped into the hall. He used the phone's voice activation program to dictate a text message to Abbas: "Urgent. Can you arrange meeting with the foreign minister before charging Frost? Late tonight—I arrive Tashkent 18:30—or after 09:00 tomorrow? Let me know."

We've got to talk them out of it, he thought, entering the gym again. If Abbas can arrange this, there's a chance, he thought. Abbas is certainly motivated. I've never heard that tone of voice from him before. Once Frost is charged, though, it'll be next to impossible. It'll go public. They'll have to go forward.

Close by, Len heard the chatter and music of one television station after another as the Chinese man and his son cycled through the options. From the sound of it, they selected a news channel. Then they turned the volume down—way down—to just above a whisper. He knew this was for his benefit.

What am I going to say to the foreign minister? he wondered, centering his feet beneath the barbell. He squatted, then lifted the weight to the starting position. He started the upright row, feeling the strain in his upper chest. He watched the barbell rise and fall in a smooth motion. What would Frost say if he could speak for himself? he wondered. Probably what he'd told them already, Len realized: that he didn't know anything about any secret service archives or hundred-year-old diary. But that's what he and Abbas had been telling the Uzbek authorities, and they knew it anyway. Alden would talk about the flag. Naturally. He'd tell them that human beings were different and the same.

"Seven . . . eight," Len counted.

That they tended to see only differences.

"Ten . . . eleven . . . twelve."

Suddenly Len was aware of a change in the room. He lowered the barbell to the floor and turned to find the man and the teenager whispering excitedly to each other while looking up at the television, then back at Len. The man nodded and smiled at

Len, and pointed up at the screen. "Very good, very good," he said.

"I'm sorry—what?" Len asked. The boy spoke in a rapid and excited whisper. The older man signaled agreement, but his tone changed to one of caution. Len stood up. He stepped around the older man's treadmill until he could see the picture. The man pointed the remote control and raised the volume. Len's eyes grew wide and his jaw dropped open. On the screen was a photograph of Len and Abbas, and next to the crawl at the bottom was the same photograph of Fatimah Ibrahim he had seen the night before.

Len gaped in stunned silence. He turned around to see the man and boy both smiling widely. The boy gave an enthusiastic two thumbs up.

The man said, "You save Fatimah. Very good. You are hero. That is you, right?"

Oh, shit! Len said to himself. He turned and smiled obliquely. He let out a little chuckle. "No. It does look like me, though, doesn't it?" He wasn't sure why he'd said it, why he'd denied the truth, but there it was. He looked back at the screen and shook his head. "I'll be damned. That guy looks just like me."

When Len turned again, the man and the boy were both nodding. As they began to grasp Len's meaning, doubt clouded faces, interfering with their smiles.

*   *   *

A half hour later Len emerged from the shower, wrapped himself in a towel without drying off, and dashed for the ringing phone on the nightstand next to his hotel bed. "Williams here."

"Len, it's Perkins. I just got a call from Seattle. Have you turned the TV on this morning?"

"Yeah, I saw it."

"So, what is this? You and this other fellow have been identified by Fatimah Ibrahim as the men who saved her life. Is that true? What's going on here?"

Len frowned. "I was in the area is all. It's nothing."

"Nothing? Your face is being broadcast all around the world. They're saying you saved Fatimah's life, for Christ's sake."

"Look, Brett. I told you I had something going on this week."

Perkins let loose a brittle laugh. "Jesus, Williams, you're a real piece of work. Why the hell didn't you tell me about this?"

"It's State Department business, for one. For the other, it's not true. I was with the guy who . . . well, never mind. I can't go into it. If she said that, she's mistaken."

"You're one of those false modest types, huh?" When Len didn't answer, Perkins went on. "Listen. Two things. I want you to be damn careful. This thing could screw the pooch."

"What?"

"That's right. Don't get us mixed up in it—whatever it is. And second, we need to make a real push this morning. I know we might not get it done . . . I know that. But I've got to have your best. We had our 'get chummy dinner' last night, but now it's time to put this thing to rest. Tell him thanks and here come the bulldozers."

Len hesitated. "Here, let me write that down, Brett."

"Well, you know what I mean, godammit."

"Yes, I know. Listen, Brett. I had an idea this morning that I want to run by you. If you like it, you can run it by the CEO . . ."

*　　*　　*

"Good morning, Jianyao," Len said, as he and Brett Perkins entered the meeting room at 09:00. Len and Sheng Jianyao shook hands as Perkins pulled out his chair and sat where he'd sat the day before.

Jianyao's assistant also rose to his feet and reached for Len's hand. "Good morning, sir," he said in fractured English. Both hosts shook Perkins's hand, as well, although the reticent project director was never more than halfway out of his chair, and seemed anxious to have his hand back.

So they've seen the news, as well, Len said to himself as he extracted the previous day's notes and papers from his briefcase. Let's hope they don't bring it up. "Jianyao, Brett and I want to thank you and Mrs. Sheng again for an absolutely wonderful dinner last night, and for inviting us to your home." He turned to Brett, who signaled his agreement in the briefest possible manner. Len knew the game, and no doubt Jianyao did, too. Perkins was the stakeholder here. He wanted to convey that his patience was running out. It was not a bad tactic, especially with the clock ticking before Len's return flight to Tashkent.

"It was an honor to have you in our home," Jianyao said. "Of course, at the time we did not know that—"

"May I interrupt you?" said Len. He took out his cell phone. "You see, I have until 10:30, but then I must leave to get to the airport. It's already after nine. We left things at an impasse yesterday and . . . well, I would like to begin at once in hopes that we might get this issue unstuck."

"Yes, of course," answered Jianyao. "I agree entirely. If I may steal just a moment of my clients' time, my wife has asked me to make sure that I get a photograph of the two of us before you leave town. It is a silly request, I know, but—"

"No. It's fine. I—" Let's make this quick, he thought. So he wants my picture. I can't refuse him, not under these circumstances. As long as he doesn't ask me any questions.

"Excellent." Jianyao raised his hand and snapped his fingers in the direction of a glass panel with partially closed blinds that faced the hallway. Len turned to see three figures sidling toward the door. They were very young women dressed in black skirts, white shirts, and maroon vests, with gold-plated name tags and other pins on their lapels: the uniform of the hotel staff. The one in front had a large camera slung over her neck. She knocked on the door and entered on Jianyao's command. The other two stood in the open doorway. Jianyao took control of the photo session and had the three whispering girls on their way three minutes later, closing the door behind them. By the time they left, two other young hotel staffers were gazing in through the glass partition. "Pardon me for that," he said, flushing. Jianyao moved to the interior window, wagging his finger. He closed the blinds in a hurry. "My wife's orders were remarkably unambiguous."

Len and Perkins smiled in spite of themselves. "It's all right," Len said, taking his seat.

Perkins leaned over and whispered into Len's ear. "All right, big shot, here's your chance."

Len dissembled with a cough. "We'll see about that, Brett. One step at a time."

When Jianyao was resettled, Len sat back in his chair and tossed his pen onto the pile of unopened files and papers in front of him. He waited for Jianyao's eyes to find his. "Jianyao, I want to resolve this matter, and I think the only way to do that is to think outside the box. Here's my suggestion. Your clients' concern for the sanctity of their ancestral burial ground is understandable. There's no getting around that. This isn't about money. You've made that clear. You've also acknowledged that there's no way to build this dam on time or on budget unless we're able to build the road across the western edge of that sacred ground. So far, all that's agreed, right?"

Jianyao nodded. His assistant whispered something to him behind a cupped hand. "Agreed," said Jianyao.

"This morning I got approval from my client—from Majestic—to make an unusual but sincere offer of compromise," Len continued, glancing sidelong at Perkins. "I'd like your reaction to it." Len thought for a moment of Alden sitting in jail. In his mind, he said to the American, "Here's your companion flag idea, Mr. Frost. Now let's see if it works."

Jianyao sat back and folded his arms. "Very well."

"Honoring the Qiang people's ancestors can be thought of in two ways," began Len. "As a concern of the Qiang people alone—that is, as something unique to them. Or, as an example of the desire by people everywhere to keep alive the memories of loved ones who have passed on. If it's looked at in the former way, it's seen as something possessed and jealously guarded by one group of people to the exclusion of others. Others— take us, for example—are on the outside, forced in this case to stand down for an interest claimed and identified exclusively by the Qiangs and their descendants. But if remembering the Qiang ancestors is seen as one facet of a multifaceted jewel that is shared by people everywhere . . . well, then the circumstances shift."

Len swiveled in his chair toward the map hung on the easel, studied it for several seconds, then turned back to face Jianyao. "The plan is to pave this road after the dam is built. What if this were to be named the Remembrance Highway? And above the bend in the river . . ." Len got up and pointed to a spot on the map. "*Here*, overlooking the Qiang burial grounds, what if Majestic were to build a world-class interpretive center for the study and contemplation not only of Qiang burial traditions, but of all the world's traditions for honoring and keeping alive the memories of those who have gone before us? This could be a destination not just for scholars, but for locals from Qinghai Province and tourists from around the world. Perhaps a meditation garden could be added. And trails along the river, or on the bluffs overlooking the burial grounds—here and here." Len stood back from the map and nodded. "There are any number of possibilities. I have in mind a beautiful spot . . . a restful place honoring the Qiang ancestors as well as all human ancestors." He turned and walked toward the window. Staring out at the mountains outside of Xining, he said, "I don't see why the dam itself couldn't be named Remembrance Dam. There's no reason why it has to be called Swan River Dam, is there, Brett?"

"No, I guess not."

Len spun around, returned the stares of each of the three men at the table, then walked back to the map. "There are logistical issues with something like this, of course. We'd want to use a local architect and make sure the buildings and grounds were approved by your people. Once in place, staffing and operations would provide jobs for your clients, Jianyao, and financing—well, as I see it, that would fall to the dam operator."

Len became aware that Jianyao's assistant was once again whispering something to Jianyao. He turned to find Jianyao nodding and walked back to his seat. He leaned forward and folded his arms on the table. "What we have here is an opportunity to honor something common to all of us. The question, Jianyao, is whether your clients will take it—whether this will provide a basis for agreement allowing Majestic to begin construction of the road. If you think it might, I'll ask Mr. Perkins to get started with permissions, finding someone to work with you on design, and so on." Len turned to Perkins. "I'm talking about something world-class here, with a construction budget up to $12 million. That's the authority we've gotten, right?"

Perkins cleared his throat. "Yes, $12 million."

Jianyao nodded reflectively. "It is an interesting idea, Mr. Williams. A novel idea. I will need to make a few phone calls. Can we take a few minutes?"

Len checked the time on his cell phone. "Yes, of course."

Jianyao, whose assistant was already dialing and stepping away from the table, allowed himself a wide grin. "You are having a good week."

XVI

——

As the taxi sped toward his home in the Unus-Abad district of Tashkent, the pain in Len's chest grew intense. Would he really be returning to an empty apartment? It seemed on the one hand impossible. But on the other, there hadn't been any doubt in Laura's voice. He took out his cell phone and navigated through his contacts to Glenn and Barbara Elston. The idea of calling to see if Laura was there sounded good one minute, unbearable the next. Frowning, he replaced the phone and stared out at the passing apartment buildings. Babushkas in threadbare coats stooped along the cracked and uneven sidewalks, carrying bulging shopping bags. Young men and women, in twos and threes, walked or half-ran in the throes of some excited conversation. How foreign it all seemed to him now. Not that it was. He had lived in this part of the world for years. But he wanted Laura, and the life he had thought he had. Without that, everything seemed foreign.

The driver mumbled something and pointed toward a giant, gray monolithic building with scores of identical windows reflecting a pearly blue, the last remnants of daylight.

"That's it," Len said. "7B. Around the back."

"Hello, Laura," he imagined saying. What would she say? "In here, sweetheart," or "I'll be right there."

The taxi turned onto the rutted, unpaved side road.

Len felt a dryness in his throat. "Just to the left up here, past that hedge." This was the last place he wanted to be right now, he admitted to himself.

The taxi slowed for two boys chasing a third across the narrow, gravel drive. Its headlights scrolled across the midline of a dark laurel hedge as the car swung to the right, then sharply left again, back toward a large parking area. As the car jerked to a stop, Len looked up. His mouth fell open then slowly formed a wide smile. There, sitting on the cement stoop, was Abbas, dressed in blue jeans and a white t-shirt. On one side of him, half hidden under his black leather jacket, were two six-packs of Heineken. On the other side, his green helmet. A few feet away, his motorcycle rested on its kickstand, entertaining two boys and a girl who stood on tiptoes arguing over its dials and instruments.

When Len had paid the driver and taken his coat and suitcase out of the trunk, he approached Abbas with a nonchalance—a feigned indifference—that Abbas mimicked seamlessly.

"Nice bike."

Abbas nodded, leaned back on his elbows, and let his lower lip protrude. "It runs."

Len set his suitcase and jacket on the ground and plopped down next to his friend. Vaguely aware of the sound of a beer bottle cap being removed, he watched the taxi back out and disappear over the noisy gravel. When the taxi was gone, he felt a nudge on his arm and turned to find an open Heineken at his side. Len took it, and when Abbas had opened a second beer Len raised his, said "*Za vas!*" (To you!), and took a long drink. He loosened his tie, then leaned forward, stretching his forearms over his knees. "Were you able to arrange a meeting with the foreign minister?"

Abbas was staring up at an old man wearing a blue bathrobe, removing clothes from a clothesline on a balcony five floors above the courtyard. "What? Oh. Yeah. Tomorrow morning, 10:15. My office."

"Thanks."

They drank in silence, watching the surroundings disappear in darkness, listening to the squeals of children playing in the shadows. One subject after another breached the surface of Len's consciousness and sank back again. It wasn't until Abbas opened a third beer for each of them that Len turned toward him and said, "I didn't think you drank."

"I don't."

Len looked at his friend and smiled. He offered the neck of his green bottle for a toast. Abbas repeated "I don't" to the first stars appearing in the sky a few minutes later, but that was all that either man said until, at last, Len whispered in the perfumed wake of a young woman climbing the stairs next to them, bound for her apartment, "How'd you find out?"

"About?"

"Laura."

Abbas stared at his empty bottle. "She texted me last night. Said she was moving out. That you two were having difficulties."

So she's talking to people, Len thought, unsure what to make of that. I know why she told Abbas though. She knew he'd be here for me. He felt another stabbing pain in his heart and shook his head slowly. "I didn't see it coming. Isn't that the shits?"

Abbas turned to him and nodded. "That *is* the shits. That's the shitty-shits." He leaned heavily on Len, who then began to laugh in spite of himself. "I love English," Abbas added.

"So that's English, huh?" It is tempting, Len thought, pushing his friend upright again and taking a long drink from his beer. Get drunk and forget this whole damn thing.

Abbas answered a question about his motorcycle from one of the boys standing nearby. Is Abbas drunk? Len wondered. Probably—he's feeling it anyway. One motorcycle question led to another. Len began picking at the label on his Heineken. Laura's gone, he thought. That's an empty apartment in there. I don't feel like getting drunk. I just want her—here. He tipped his bottle back, let two mouthfuls go down. What did I do to deserve this anyway? I guess I haven't been the most attentive husband in the world. Rather than think about gambling, or his debt to Smythe, he thought about the way she'd looked at him of late when he came home from work, how she'd presented a cool front even when he'd said "I love you," often responding with a curt "You do, huh?" and giving him a rapid-fire smile and a peck on the cheek for his troubles. Maybe I was in Kabul too long, he thought, as he watched the three children drift away from Abbas's motorcycle. Has she found someone else? Is it Abbas? Oh good God, what am I thinking?

"Hey," said Abbas, "what are you—don't bring Charlotte into this."

"Charlotte? What are you talking about?"

Abbas reached unsteadily for another beer. He shook his head. "I don't know. I think I'm drunk. What do you think of that name—*Charlotte?* I kind of like it. *Char-lotte.* Sometimes I . . ."

"It's all right, I guess," Len said, leaning back on his elbows. The night had grown cooler all of a sudden, and quieter. The sound of a window sliding shut in the distance was sharp against the reigning silence.

"What about Fatimah?" asked Abbas. He stifled a hiccup with a sudden, involuntary inhalation, then said, "You don't seem—"

"What do you mean? The name?"

"No. The person. What do you think of her? Would you ever consider . . . you know. Would you . . . if that were possible?"

Len scowled. "No." He *is* drunk, Len thought, sitting up and taking a sip. "Hell no." I'm not going there, he thought. Just give me Laura back.

"She's very attractive," Abbas continued after several long seconds.

"So is Laura." Len turned to face his friend. "I *am* forty-seven, you know."

Abbas blinked dully. "I was just thinking, what if Charlotte and I, and you and Fatimah—"

"Okay, my good friend," Len said suddenly, rising to his feet, "enough of your thinking. You're not going anywhere tonight. I'm going to make you the best spaghetti dinner you've ever had." Len reached for Abbas's arm and helped him to his feet. They made their way to the elevator. "I can't tell you how much I appreciate your dropping by tonight."

"Not at all," Abbas said. "I can do that."

*   *   *

Len emerged from the kitchen with a steaming bowl of pasta in each hand and a small, round loaf of Uzbek bread under his arm. He set one bowl in front of Abbas, the bread between them, and his own bowl where Laura normally sat. "Are you still working on that soldier?" he asked, picking up the bottle and finding an inch of liquid at the bottom.

"I'll take another," said Abbas, forcing his eyes open and turning the bowl as though searching for the right angle of approach. He looked under each side of the bowl for a fork or spoon.

"Oh, yeah," Len said. "Hold on." When he returned, he set two forks down followed by a pair of freshly opened beers. "Don't say I never did anything for you."

"No, sir."

Len knew what he wanted to say. He wanted to ask Abbas if he knew why Laura had left, if she'd said anything about his gambling or the $63,000 he owed Terrence Smythe. But he couldn't find the words, and besides, what would Abbas know about Laura's motives? All she'd said to him was "we're having difficulties." He felt a wave of grief, but in the next instant it all seemed pitiful. Pitifully weak. Why had he let things go so far? He let four gulps of beer slide down his throat. That's what I am, he decided. *Weak.* Len stabbed the spaghetti and began to twirl his fork. He was busy wondering if Laura had been right about his gambling when the image of the Pakistani man with the misshapen yellow teeth and pock-marked face came to mind. For a moment—a second or two—he *was* that man. He felt himself wrapped in the man's olive skin. Each of my five dead children is worth $38,000, he said to himself. The deal has been made.

"Let me ask you something, Len."

Len looked up to see Abbas attempting to twirl spaghetti noodles on his fork using both hands. He had gathered such a prodigious coil that he gave up and set the fork down against the bowl. Picking up his bread and tearing off a chunk, he dipped it in the marinara sauce.

"Have you ever done something you regret but don't regret? Something that could hurt the people closest to you, but you never intended it—never saw it coming, not in a million years?"

There it is, Len thought. She did tell him. "Not really. Not that I want to talk about anyway." There. He'd pushed it aside. I know one thing, he said to himself, measuring off a bite of spaghetti, I don't want this to come between us, Abbas and me. Besides, I'm drunk. Hell, what could he have to say about it anyway? It's my business. I'm the gambler.

"Oh."

Len looked up again to see surprise and disappointment registered in Abbas's alcohol-dulled eyes. "You don't mind if we talk about something else, do you?"

"No, I guess not. I was just going to . . ." Abbas caught himself and stopped. He took several bites of *tandir non* in a row, peeled them off one by one with his fingers.

Len said, "You're never going to believe this. I used to pretend that if I made seven out of ten free throws, Sally Johnson would tell me she loved me, or kiss me out of the blue, or something."

"Sally Johnson?"

"This girl I fell in love with in high school. She never so much as looked at me, but I was sure I was in love with her. I obsessed over her for years. I was still obsessing over her when I met Laura."

Abbas kissed the lip of his Heineken and tipped it back. He crafted an answer out of silence.

"The strange part is, it didn't matter that none of it ever came true. I could make seven out of ten free throws—or I'd keep trying until I did—but Sally never changed. Had a boyfriend all those years. In fact, they're married now. Weird thing is, it never stopped me. I kept placing the odds on shots, or some other event. If this happens next—if the chemistry teacher uses the word algorithm twice before the bell rings—Sally Johnson will fall in love with me. Do you see what I mean?

"Yes, I think so."

"I wasn't doing it all the time, but enough, you know." Len tore off a small piece of *tandir non* and began to dip it, copying his friend. "I kept it up. And here's the kicker: I still find myself doing it now and then."

"Still hoping for that kiss, you mean?" Abbas smiled out of one side of his mouth.

Len involuntarily spit some beer back into the bottle. "No. That's not what I mean."

"I know. I was kidding."

"Thinking if I do this or that, this or that will happen—or not happen." Len looked closely at his friend. "Have you ever done that?"

"Hmm. When I was a kid, I guess. I don't remember."

"It's funny. I never thought anything about it, and then a counselor told me once it was some serious thing. He got this worried look on his face, even said something about hospitalizing me. Called it cabalistic thinking." Len took a long draft of beer. "Needless to say, I didn't go back. He apparently didn't hear the part about my not taking it seriously anymore. In fact, I don't ever think I took it seriously. It was just a way to make shooting baskets by myself in the driveway more interesting."

Abbas was concentrating on his marinara sauce, on the part dripping from a wedge of bread. "That's how I took it. What's his problem?"

"I know, right?"

"What made you think of this?"

Len hesitated. "I'm not sure. The gambling thing, I guess. I stopped this magical thinking stuff long before they sent me to Kabul, and then I wasn't gambling online either. I always enjoyed cards with the fellas, but it was dollar ante stuff, and then maybe once a month or something. You know that. I asked you to join us a couple of times."

Abbas nodded.

"I don't know," Len said, putting his empty down heavily on the table. He pushed his chair back. "Another one?"

"If you're serious about me sleeping on the couch, sure."

"I'm serious. You're not going anywhere," Len's voice reverberated slightly in the empty kitchen. He reappeared a few seconds later and set two more sweating bottles between them.

"So maybe it's chaos control," said Abbas, sliding one green bottle closer to him.

"How's that?" said Len.

"An attempt to control chaos—which is really just a way to acknowledge it. I mean, you can't control chaos. Suddenly you're down there negotiating settlements with photos of dead children spread out in front of you. You're not negotiating the hours of bridge use, or trade restrictions on the import of apples. That sounds like chaos to me."

Len tipped his bottle back slowly and with concentration.

Abbas continued. "Maybe that's why you got back into the magical thinking, or why you started in the first place. You said she was never available, this Sally Johnson. That's chaos, to love someone who is truly lost to you. You were trying to get a purchase on uncertainty. Even with gambling, there are odds, right? There's a chance for something. But when there are no chances, no odds, what's left? Those kids under those drones, they . . ." Abbas stopped himself, then seemed to form a determination to go on. "Maybe that's what's going on. You're trying to feel alive . . . Why are you smiling?"

"No, I think you're right," Len said. You're not a quiet drunk, Abbas, he thought. You're a philosopher. I love it. But you're right. Can I deny it? In the last four years, gambling has been my drug.

Abbas took an embarrassed sip of beer and rolled wet lips. His eyes widened slowly to a new subject. "So this Frost arrest has reached back to bite us." He wiped his chin with the back of his wrist, then pealed off another large piece of *tandir non* and placed it beside Len's bowl. "If we'd have known what we were getting ourselves into, we—"

"What?"

"With Fatimah, I mean. She's too hot to handle. How do you say it? She's a hot potato."

Len was trying to catch up. "Wait a minute. I thought you had a plan. You said you were going to charge her as an accessory, get her to make a public apology, then release her."

"That's what I thought. But this morning the Tashiri foreign minister arrived. He met with her. She's again refusing to leave without Frost. Says a confession and public apology are out of the question, unless *we're the ones prepared to apologize*."

Len smiled. "Sounds about right." He kept his eyes on Abbas until he was sure his friend saw that he was joking.

"The foreign minister is beside himself," Abbas went on. "They've got a plane at the airport—a Tashir Airlines 737 this time—loaded with fuel and waiting. She says not without Frost, and not unless her grandfather agrees to introduce legislation calling for the adoption of the companion flag. And she's upped the ante. She wants it displayed below the Tashiri flag on the arm of every soldier and policeman."

"Jesus."

"Right."

"And what about this other woman, Charlotte? The one you've been ogling."

"*Ogling?* I'm not ogling her. What are you talking about? What does ogling mean?"

Len laughed. "It means to stare at a woman like a love-sick puppy."

"Well, then, there's no way I have been ogling her!"

"Uh-huh." Len stuffed a thick coil of dripping spaghetti into his mouth. He chewed around a smug grin. "Whatever."

"I haven't. I respect her. She's kind and thoughtful, and she has a unique way about her that . . . " Abbas picked up his lagging beer and finished it off. He took a quick sip of the new beer as though it were necessary to clean his palate. "But I don't know, to answer your question. She'd want to go, I suppose, but who knows if—"

"So what's the hot potato part?"

"She's calling the shots! Fatimah, I mean. Who's ever heard of a prisoner refusing to leave prison? Especially an Uzbek prison. And every word she breathes ends up in news reports above the fold from here to Lima. It's like we've put ourselves under a microscope. Suddenly, everyone's an expert on Uzbekistan's internal affairs."

"It's not going to get any easier if you charge Frost with espionage. You realize that, don't you?"

"I do, but try convincing Guryanov. He won't let go. I've tried. Frost is his man—and that's a quote."

"Crazy."

"Yes, and throw in protests and rioting in two countries and you've got a hot potato."

"Uh-huh."

The two fell to eating in silence, Abbas preferring to dip his bread in the marinara sauce rather than mimic Len's fork twirling. He reached into his bowl to good effect but with deepening lines furrowing his brow as the minutes passed. He looked around the room, into the gloomy recesses and corridors, as if feeling Laura's absence for the first time. When his eyes met Len's again, he found the American staring at him expectantly. "I don't know what it is, Len," he began. "To me, Charlotte's the most beautiful woman I've ever seen. I know she's no Fatimah . . . but, well, to me she's stunning."

Len nodded while he chewed. "I thought so."

"But I didn't ogle her."

"No, of course not. You just took her off to your sister's house for safekeeping." Len smiled against the rim of his Heineken. After taking a long draft, he said, "Not that anyone noticed. I know I didn't. It was very subtle, start to finish."

"Do you think she knows?" Abbas asked.

Len burst out laughing. "Oh, no. Not a clue."

"Well, she might not. I don't think she does."

Len saw that his friend wanted to believe this, so he let it go with a shrug.

XVII

From: XX5 – Executive Director CO-9 (London)
To: undisclosed recipients
Date: Sun., 10 September 20ZZ 22:19:41
Subject: Fatimah Ibrahim
Encryption/Decryption Enabled: B72ZZ256-9102 (All Threads)

TO ALL COMMITTEE OF NINE (CO-9) MEMBERS:

JUST RECEIVED:

INTERPOL ADVISORY BULLETIN 12LQ5451, 10 SEPT. 20ZZ 21:54:10 +0200: "UZBEKISTAN INTERIOR MINISTER SALIM GURYANOV CONFIRMED ATTEMPTED KIDNAPPING OF FATIMAH IBRAHIM NEAR TASHKENT INTERNATIONAL AIRPORT ON 6 SEPT. 20ZZ, 20:34:00 +0500. TWO ASSAILANTS KILLED, IDENTITIES UNKNOWN."

COMMENT/REACTION?

*   *   *

From: X12 – CO-9 (Vatican City)
Date: Sun., 10 September 20ZZ 22:55:13 +0100

HAVE BEEN ADVISED THAT FATIMAH IBRAHIM CONDITIONED RELEASE ON GRANDFATHER'S PROMISE TO SPONSOR LEGISLATIVE INITIATIVE FOR COMPANION FLAG ADOPTION IN TASHIR. GRANTED THIS IS A SECONDARY CONCERN, BUT WHAT DO WE KNOW ABOUT THIS COMPANION FLAG? WHAT INTERDICTIONS ARE POSSIBLE HERE? DO WE HAVE ASSETS IN SANORI? XX5 CONTINUE MONITORING.

*   *   *

From: X22 – CO-9 (NY)
Date: Sun., 10 September 20ZZ 23:14:36 -0500

AMOS ALBISHIR, DEPUTY DIRECTOR OF THE UNITED PEOPLES PARTY, IS FRIENDLY. CONTACT THROUGH BACK CHANNEL. XX5 CONTINUE MONITORING.

*   *   *

From: XX5 – Executive Director CO-9 (London)
Date: Sun., 10 September 20ZZ 23:49:40

TO ALL COMMITTEE OF NINE (CO-9) MEMBERS:

ŞAHIN DIARY STILL UNACCOUNTED FOR. THREE ADDITIONAL AGENTS HAVE BEEN SENT TO TASHKENT TO ASSIST WITH SEARCH.

CONTACTS IN TASHKENT AND SAMARKAND CONFIRM CONDITIONS

OF RELEASE. SUBJECT IS DEMANDING PUBLIC (TELEVISED) DEBATE IN TASHIR ON ISSUE OF CF ADOPTION NATIONWIDE. PROTESTS IN SANORI AND TASHKENT CONTINUE. AT 05:30:00 +0500 THIS MORNING, TASHIRI FOREIGN MINISTER REQUESTED EXPEDITED ENTRY INTO UZBEKISTAN TO INTERVIEW F. IBRAHIM.

COMMENT/REACTION?

*   *   *

From: X14 – CO-9 (Sydney)
Date: Mon., 11 September 20ZZ 02:48:59 +1000

ALL NEWS SERVICES NOW REPORTING ATTEMPTED KIDNAPPING, ARREST OF FATIMAH IBRAHIM. NO MENTION OF DIARY. IMPOSSIBLE TO CONTAIN WIDER STORY PER ADDINGTON. RECOMMEND WE FORGET COMPANION FLAG AND CONCENTRATE ON RECOVERING ŞAHIN DIARY. XX5 CONTINUE MONITORING.

XVIII

———

Ambassador Tompkins set one cup of coffee in front of Len. The other he carried around his desk and lowered onto a torn manila envelope—the overnight pouch. He sat down, scooted his chair in, put on his reading glasses, and began shuffling papers here and there, making room on his blotter. "Here's where we're at with this thing," he said, his attention still divided. "Akbar Turaev called me last night. He'd just gotten out of a meeting with his counterpart, the Tashiri foreign minister. Ms. Ibrahim, it seems, is running the show with these people." Tompkins carefully airlifted his cup onto the newly cleared space then licked the tips of his fingers to cool them. "The Uzbeks have painted themselves into a corner. The Tashiris want her home, if for no other reason than to stop the street protests that have resulted in several serious injuries. But here's the deal: she's refusing to go unless Frost flies out with her and her grandfather agrees to sponsor some sort of public airing of this flag idea. She's informed the foreign minister that she'll stay put if the Uzbeks follow through on their threat to charge Frost with theft of the Şahin Diary. She's guaranteeing them more negative publicity than they'll know what to do with."

Len's eyes followed the path of the Harvard crest emblazoned on the side of the ambassador's crimson cup. Tompkins sipped his steaming coffee and lowered the cup again before continuing. Len noticed that Tompkins's eyes were ringed with red. Perhaps he hadn't slept well either.

"On top of that, Turaev and the Uzbek interior minister, Guryanov, are at dagger points over releasing Frost. Guryanov wants to embarrass Ankara—at a minimum. He won't come out and say he wants the diary made public, but that's the upshot. He wants to interrogate the prisoners until the diary is disgorged. Turaev wants Ms. Ibrahim out of the country and will do just about anything to make that happen. He'd put Frost on the plane himself if he could."

"Without charging him?" asked Len.

"If it were up to him. At least that's the impression I get. I think he believes them when they say they know nothing about the diary. But it's moot now. Guryanov is adamant . . . and he seems to have President Karimov's ear on this one. So they've come up with a compromise. They'll charge Frost under a secret indictment and release him provisionally to travel to Tashir under guard. When this debate is over, he'll be brought back here to stand trial."

Len sat up straight. "And Frost has agreed to this?"

"Apparently. Either that or they don't think they need his agreement. Uzbekistan and Tashir have an extradition treaty."

Len let his eyes drift up to a photograph of Tompkins and his wife at a white-tie event with the president and first lady. He was thinking about Abbas and whether all this would be news to him. Probably not, he concluded. "I'm guessing Frost knows," Len said at length, "and that they've sworn him to secrecy. For Frost, it's all about the flag." Len looked back into the ambassador's pale blue eyes. "He's worked in anonymity for decades. He'd be willing to keep this from Fatimah—the part about coming back to stand trial.

They would have insisted on it, right? For Frost this is a chance of a lifetime."

"Oh, and speaking of insisting," said the ambassador, "Ms. Ibrahim insists that this other woman go along, too, if she wants to—the one who was in the car with her. What's her name? Charlotte something."

"Charlotte Yacoubi."

"Yes, that's right."

It figures, Len thought. Charlotte would insist, wouldn't she? And Frost would give his right arm to be part of a national debate over the merits of his flag idea. "And the president of Tashir?" Len asked. "Fatimah's grandfather—has he agreed to this debate, or whatever it is?"

"Yes, according to Turaev. He's prepared to give it the highest priority, whatever it takes to get his granddaughter back. They'll file the paperwork and schedule a televised debate sometime in the next two weeks."

"Televised?"

"That's another condition. Don't forget, she's a PR maven. Doesn't miss much. Anyway, after the debate the Tashiri legislature will vote up or down on adopting this company flag—or whatever it's called."

"Companion flag."

"Companion flag—okay. They'll vote on whether to add the companion flag as a national symbol."

She might just pull it off, Len thought, half chuckling to himself. Who can say no to Fatimah Ibrahim? On the other hand, no prophet is accepted in her own hometown.

"And when it's over, the debate I mean, and they bring Frost back, what's to prevent Fatimah from returning and raising hell?" Len asked.

The ambassador lowered his head and looked over his glasses. "She won't be allowed back in the country would be my guess.

Right now, the priority is getting her on that plane." The ambassador's chair squealed softly as he turned toward his credenza. Once again he was looking through piles of papers for something. "Which leaves our own secretary of state. I called her chief of staff as soon as I got off the phone with Turaev." The ambassador seemed to forget what he was looking for. Hunched over, he pulled on his lower lip and stared forlornly at the corner of his desk. Suddenly, he bolted upright again and pivoted to the other side of the desk, reaching for a small pile of papers tucked under his computer screen. "I didn't know what the secretary would say."

The ambassador picked a sheet out of the pile. He glanced over it, then looked up into Len's eyes. "She wants nothing more to do with this. The CIA is taking over. That's according to the chief of staff. This came in with the overnight pouch."

Len knew there were times when it didn't pay to ask questions or to peer over fences. "I guess that means she doesn't have an opinion on the plan to fly Frost to Tashir?"

"No. Our orders are to let Frost know that the consular section is there to assist, period. Help him get a lawyer if he wants one. Other than that, we're out of it."

"*Out* of it? Just like that?"

The ambassador nodded. He held the sheet up. "This is dated last night at 21:04 Washington time. 'Suspend all efforts on behalf of Alden Frost. Provide consular services upon request. Make no public statements whatsoever concerning Frost or the Şahin Diary.'"

Len set his cup on the edge of the desk and sat back. What in the world? he thought, rubbing his chin. One minute she wants the political section involved, the next they're telling us to stand down. He looked up to see concern etched in the corners of the ambassador's eyes as he reread the cable. After a few beats Len felt a sudden upwelling of relief—Friday was his last day, after all. At least one problem was solved. Now he'd have time to pack. Len cleared his throat and slapped the arms of his chair, preparing to get up. "All right. Well, I'm done here then."

Tompkins nodded, and his face began to color above the temples. "Yeah. But something doesn't smell right. And I'll be damned if I know what's going on."

Tompkins's tone told Len the conversation wasn't over. Len sat back in his chair once again.

Tompkins picked up his cup and held it in front of his lips. "The CIA thinks Frost and Fatimah were unwitting covers for someone else."

"Someone else?"

"Possibly Armenian Relief." He drank the hot liquid noisily. "They've been interested in the diary for years. Or it could be the Islamist Republican Party seeking to overthrow the Aslan government. They don't know."

"But how could any of these people have known that Frost and Fatimah Ibrahim were going to break into Public School 32?"

"That's what I'm saying," said the ambassador. After setting his cup down, he removed his glasses and began to rub his eyes with the thumb and middle finger of his right hand. "Something doesn't smell right."

*   *   *

Having shaken hands with Salim Guryanov and Abbas and settled into one of the chairs facing Abbas's desk, Len found that his newly minted relief was alloyed to a strange pang of doubt. He watched Abbas leave the room to say something to his secretary, then reenter and walk to his desk. Len wondered at the odd feeling coursing through him. Was he grieving the sudden termination of this last opportunity to work with his friend? he wondered. After all, within the last hour it had been wiped away as quickly and as unexpectedly as it had come up. And the activities of the last several days hadn't been without excitement. No, he realized, that's not it. *I'm going to see him again—and soon. I'll get him to Seattle if I have to drag him there myself. And we'll stay in touch by phone and e-mail. Now that I've taught him to drink, hell, maybe we can drink a Heineken together once a week over Videochat.* A slight smile played at the corners of his mouth.

"Well, gentleman," Len began, carefully modulating his voice to squeeze out any hint of the personal. "I may owe you an apology. I asked Abbas to arrange this meeting in hopes that I could prevail upon you, Mr. Minister, to reconsider your decision to charge Alden Frost with espionage. However, I've just come from a meeting with Ambassador Tompkins. He's taken me off the case."

"*What?*"

"Yes. I've been told to stand down."

"But why?" asked Abbas. Guryanov's body language conveyed the same question.

"I'm told that Mr. Turaev and the Tashiri foreign minister have worked out a deal—if that's the right way to put it. Frost will be allowed to leave the country to attend this debate in Tashir, and after the debate—"

"That's right," said the interior minister.

"Salim and I were just discussing this," said Abbas. "But I don't see how this changes anything as far as the embassy's concerned."

Len sank back in his chair. "The secretary wants it handled by the consular section. They'll no doubt get him counsel when he returns, but in the meantime he's heading out of the jurisdiction. I guess maybe that counts as getting him released or something."

"Thanks to Ms. Ibrahim," muttered the interior minister, sitting back and staring vacantly at no one. A sudden thought seemed to lift him out of that position a moment later. "President Karimov has asked me to thank the two of you for your quick action the other day. Without that, we'd be in a much more difficult position."

Len waited for Abbas to say something. When he didn't, he pointed to his friend and said, "This guy here deserves all the credit."

"No," said Abbas. "Not true."

"It doesn't matter," said Guryanov, waving the argument away. "We're indebted to you both. And I'm not surprised that Ms. Ibrahim has asked the two of you to accompany them to Tashir."

"I'm sorry . . . What are you talking about?" Len asked, sitting up.

"It's true as you say," Abbas began. "Frost is being allowed to leave the country. I've been assigned to guard him, to ensure that he comes back." Abbas averted his eyes to something on his desk. "The other woman who you and I met—what was her name?"

Len glanced sidelong at the interior minister. "Oh yes, the . . . the woman in the car. The Red Cross lady."

"Yes," Abbas mumbled. He shifted papers from one side of his desk to the other.

"Charlotte something."

"Yes. She's going to Tashir, as well. The two of them—Ms. Ibrahim and this Charlotte—spoke and apparently agreed that they'd feel safer if both of us went. They're leaving on Thursday."

"Both of us?"

"The two of you," blurted the minister. He sat back impatiently and showed his palms. "It's not so hard to understand, is it? You saved their lives, and they'd like you to be there."

Preposterous, thought Len. We're not bodyguards—at least I'm not. Why can't people understand that I didn't do anything?

I was there in case Abbas needed me, but he didn't. It all happened so fast that Fatimah and Charlotte think I was part of it, that I helped save their lives. Just then he thought of the warning delivered by Majestic's Brett Perkins. "Don't get us mixed up in it—whatever it is."

Abbas fixed Len with round, brown eyes. "Fatimah will have police and secret service protection and will no doubt stay in her family's compound. Mr. Frost and I will stay at the Al Maseer Hotel, as will this other woman, Charlotte. I'll have my hands full and could use another set of eyes. It's just a couple of weeks. A little tropical sun might do you good."

Len smiled good-naturedly at his friend's pitch. Two weeks on a tropical island. Tough duty. You know, I'd do it if I could, he thought. How many times had he seen colorful posters of Tashir's famous flower-laden boulevards; its shimmering white marble buildings, many left over from colonial times; and the steep green mountains surrounding—in some cases reaching down to touch—the white-sand beaches of Port Hikma. Someday, he thought, ahead of saying, "I'm afraid it's out of the question. I'm still with the State Department through Friday, and I have packing to do the following week. I fly out on the twenty-third." Len hesitated. I really do wish I could go. He couldn't deny that having Frost to worry about would distract him from his marital troubles, but, then, what if Laura were ready to talk while he was gone? How long could he avoid confronting the inevitable? Something veiled in Abbas's expression caused him to ask, "Are you expecting trouble down there?"

"Who can say? We still don't know who's behind the attempt on Fatimah's life. This man who identified himself as Ali Msaidie is still in a coma. No one has claimed responsibility."

Was this part of the reason for his sense of foreboding when he entered Abbas's office? Len wondered. Either way, it's not my problem anymore. The CIA is on the case. "As of the twenty-fifth,

I'm officially on the payroll of Majestic International," Len said, looking from Abbas to Guryanov, but saying it as much to hear it himself as anything. "I've got meetings scheduled in Edmonds."

"Perhaps you could delay your start date for a few weeks," said Abbas hopefully.

Len squeezed the bridge of his nose and closed his eyes, grimacing. "No. A job is a job. This is my career we're talking about, and I could lose this job before it starts. They want me to steer clear, if you know what I. . . Listen, I've got to decline. I'm sure you'll find someone else. Besides, I'm a negotiator, not a bodyguard. I don't know what good I could do you."

Abbas didn't attempt to disguise the resignation in his voice. "Fatimah will be disappointed. She trusts you."

XIX

———

Len frowned when he saw how short he had tied his tie. Staring into the mirror above Laura's vanity, he pulled violently at the knot. Why am I wearing this damn thing? I should wear the blue-and-gold one she got me for Christmas. He reached into the half-empty closet, shoving away his dress shirts to get at the tie caddy. "Let's try this again," he said aloud, checking the clock on the nightstand.

More significant questions vied for his attention, but he had spent the last hour pushing them away. They would be answered soon enough, he thought, as he imagined Laura sitting across a candlelit table at their favorite Tashkent restaurant, Dmitri's. In his mind's eye, she would be dressed in her maroon dress, the tight one that put up a pretty resistance to her breasts and showed off her narrow waist. Her smile would sparkle above the Victorian fringe diamond necklace she'd inherited from her grandmother. Perhaps the diamond solitaire earrings he'd given her on their twentieth anniversary would appear from behind carefully coifed curls.

It was this picture he'd painted over the confusion and trepidation caused by her leaving, by the lack of meaningful communication with her since he'd returned from China. But now she'd agreed to meet him for dinner—thank goodness for text messages. There it was in writing, a step in the right direction.

Without hearing the words, he imagined her mouth—her exceptionally white, straight teeth—rising and falling to form utterances of despair and rapprochement. He saw her downcast eyes and felt a surge of pity. "I've neglected you—us," he would confess. "I've been too busy at work, too distracted. This new case I got, and then the unexpected thing in Xining." Her hand would snake across the table in search of his—how many times had that happened when they were dating, and after they were first married?

This tie was the right one. It hung at the right length. He pulled his suit jacket from the closet. As he turned he was arrested by the sight of the empty nightstand on Laura's side of the bed. Everything was missing, even her reading light. The images he had nurtured only seconds earlier vanished. He was left with a searing pain in his gut. She's gone, and she may never come back, he thought.

"I'll just meet you there, OK?" she'd texted back when he'd offered to pick her up. He couldn't imagine her saying it that way—"I'll just meet you there, OK?"—it wasn't like her. But then, she'd removed herself from him, hadn't she?

I've got to get her back, he told himself. He picked up his shoes and walked into the living room. If I leave now, I'll be early, he thought. The parody of a frown lingered on his lips. He didn't want to be early. He looked around the sparsely furnished room and exhaled loudly. His eyes settled on the computer in the corner. I'll check the news, he thought.

He sat down and clicked the icon for CNN.com. The familiar red-and-white page flashed onto the screen. In the corner of his eye, he saw the word "Tashir" in a video link listed in a column of opinion pieces further down the page. He leaned closer. The full title was "Eagleton: A Sad Day for Tashir." What the devil? he thought, clicking on the link. He didn't need the two second load time to know that Eagleton referred to the bombastic syndicated U.S. radio talk show host Ed Eagleton who'd grown to unprecedented levels of popularity in recent years. It always surprised Len when the mainstream press gave his comments the imprimatur of news. Len waited for the commercial to end, then watched as the image of the pear-shaped, balding Eagleton sitting in his Denver radio station filled his screen.

"What in the world is going on in the small, sub-Saharan country of Tashir?" Eagleton bellowed. "After three days of rioting by street thugs over the arrest of Fatimah Ibrahim in Uzbekistan, Reuters reports that President Mohamed Mohadji, Fatimah's grandfather, has buckled to her demands that Tashir consider adopting something called a 'companion flag.' This is a condition *she* has imposed, ladies and gentlemen—a condition placed on her own release. You heard me right. You have to wonder about President Mohadji. Who exactly is he working for down there in that little island country? Folks, this is the kind of thing that would be funny if it weren't so threatening to freedom-loving people everywhere. Do you know what this . . ." here Eagleton took on a snooty, aristocratic tone familiar to his regular listeners, "this com-*pan*-ion flag is? It's a flag that's meant to be flown on the same pole—*that's right*, on the same pole—as each nation's national flag . . . and it represents what people everywhere have in common. That's what I'm told. Now, if that doesn't put the fear of God in you, nothing will. Can you imagine the same flag flying below the flags of Iran, China, and the United States? That's exactly what this wacky dame is up to . . .Well, I know I shouldn't use language like that, Johnny, but sometimes when my head spins with the crazy ideas I hear out there, it's hard to think of alternatives. This Fatimah Ibrahim is obviously touched in some way, and now we're about to witness some kind of a circus debate over adoption of this flag in Tashir. Stay tuned, ladies and gentlemen. That's all I can say. It's a sad day in Tashir, my friends . . . let's hope cooler heads prevail."

"Tell me you're not serious," Len said aloud. He felt a half smile spread over his lips as he clicked back to the main news page. He wondered how many people would be affected by Eagleton's fearmongering. No doubt a couple of million at least, he thought. Maybe it's a silly idea, this companion flag—but a dangerous one? Hardly. You've overstated your case as usual, Eagleton.

Len continued to surf his preferred news sites, checking the time every couple of minutes. He didn't want to be late any more than he wanted to be early. Better to get there a few minutes early, even if he'd have to wait in the car. Another headline drew his attention, this one on abcnews.com: Tashir to Debate New Flag. He clicked on the link. His eyes quickly scanned the article and settled on a quote near the bottom of the piece: "Amos Albishir, a spokesperson for the opposition Tashiri United Peoples Party, promises a rigorous campaign to defeat the initiative. 'This misguided nostrum will weaken the cultural and national bonds of the Tashiri people. Such a watered-down symbol denigrates the sacrifices of our forefathers and threatens to sap the will of the people.'"

*   *   *

No maroon dress. She wore a khaki shift with white buttons and a wide, white patent leather belt—no diamond necklace, no diamond earrings. She touched the table with both hands as she sat down. Not a good sign, Len thought. It felt as though those hands were symbolically pushing him away. Subtle changes came over her countenance as her eyes darted around their familiar meeting spot. These made her seem like a stranger to him, like she were seeing the place for the first time.

"Thank you for meeting me." He heard in his voice the high-pitched rasp of a scared child. He took a drink of water.

Laura made a show of examining the menu. "Of course." She smiled without looking up. "We need to talk."

Len felt a tectonic movement, a rising bubble in the molten sea of anger that he'd hidden so well below the surface.

"Would you like a drink?" Len asked as he watched the waiter approach.

"Yes, several."

"Two gin and tonics—tall," Len said to the waiter.

"No," said Laura. "Make mine a Manhattan."

"Really?" Len said. She avoided his eyes. So you really are changing things up, he thought. He saw the beginning of a determination taking shape in the set of her eyes.

When the waiter walked away Laura said, "I shouldn't have told you on the phone, or left the way I did, or when I did, but . . . well, it was the best I could do. I am not feeling particularly strong these days, to put it mildly."

Len's reaction was silent but strong. If you're expecting me to feel sorry for you, that's not going to work. I'm the one who's getting left. He waited her out.

"I haven't been happy since you returned from Kabul, Len," she said. "I should have told you much sooner."

"Why? What's wrong? What's different since I got back?"

Laura hesitated, looked past him. "Everything. I don't know—maybe nothing. Maybe I've been unhappy a lot longer. I . . . I don't think I love you anymore, Len. I mean, I love you, but not in that way. That way is gone."

"What? What do you—?"

"I know. It's . . . I don't know what I want. You were gone too long. I waited a long time, a very long time, to feel connected, but then when you were in Kabul and the work you were doing . . . it all seemed so empty to me, so cowardly. I couldn't—"

"*Cowardly?* What are you taking about?"

"Negotiating payments to the families of babies killed at checkpoints, in middle-of-the-night, house-to-house raids, in so-called targeting mistakes. You've become Uncle Sam's 'fix-it man'—a few thousand dollars here, a few thousand dollars there. And I never heard you complain about it. Not once. You'd fly home every few weeks and you were the same as always—like nothing out of the ordinary was happening."

Len stared at her with his mouth open. He wanted to shout: *Are you serious? I was doing my job! What do you think a negotiator does? I work for the government, for Christ's sake. I follow orders. You know this. Why haven't you said anything about this before?*

He wanted to, but didn't.

"And then when I read the e-mails about your gambling, the $63,000, I—"

"That's it, isn't it? Why don't you just come out with it?"

Laura returned a tense, prolonged stare. What did it mean? Judgment? Disgust? Recrimination? All of the above? How different it felt. Laura's brow contracted and she closed her eyes momentarily as though she were bearing an intense pain.

Len remembered apropos of nothing the moment when he knew he would ask Laura to marry him. He was twenty-three, she, twenty. They had argued the night before, although he couldn't remember why. Whatever it was, it had been built on a pretense. The real issue had been his fear of commitment, some permutation there, and it was enough that she didn't project into the night sky the same warning flares that he felt were called for, and were her responsibility. She withstood his silent anger with gently smiling eyes, and then at some point, so far from fleeing, she did the unthinkable. She slid forward off the edge of her chair across the room, assuming the posture of a baseball catcher. Over her outstretched right hand and splayed fingers, she said, "Go ahead. Give it to me. I can take it." *Give me your* best pitch. I'll catch whatever's bothering you. Together we'll deal with it. I'm not going anywhere. It had melted his heart, this simple, playful gesture.

"What were you thinking?" she asked now. "Were you ever going to tell me about *Mister* Smythe, or was this just another game between friends . . . friends who threaten to kill each other? And, of course, now I hear that you're gambling at the office, as well."

Len felt a lopsided orange rage begin to burn in his chest. Begin, but then stop almost as suddenly as it had started. A moment later it was gone. Controlling chaos—wasn't that what Abbas had said? Controlling what cannot be controlled. He felt numb then, and out of numbness said in a low voice, "I was going to tell you, but I didn't want you to worry."

Laura worked her tongue against the inside of her cheek as though that were the price of patience. "That's bullshit," she said at last. She turned in her chair and crossed her arms beneath her breasts. "You've owed Smythe this money for months . . . since before you took the job in Seattle." She swung one leg over the other and fixed him with a look that said, I'm barely containing myself here. "That's why you're taking that job, isn't it? That's why you want to move to the rainiest place on the planet?"

Len thought of lying, and that led him to a dark closet of lie fragments that needed sorting and culling. Laura experienced this as silence. She touched her forehead. "Len, I've met someone else."

He had already stopped breathing, and now he had to breathe but couldn't. He swallowed against an up-rushing pressure. At last, a ragged breath. "Someone else? What? You've—"

"He works at Christoffel Blindenmission. He's an American field agent for CBM here in Tashkent. I met him a couple of years ago at a fundraiser . . . but, no, it's not what you think. We're friends. But things have grown into a new place in the last couple of months . . . and it's because I feel I don't really know you any-more. When you announced you were going to work for Majestic, that's when I knew. I knew I couldn't go with you. I knew I had to end it."

The waiter returned and set the drinks in front of them. "Can I take your orders?"

Len looked at Laura, who simply shook her head no. He picked up the menu without seeing it. Should they leave? Should he stand up and walk out? And what then? Never talk to her again except through lawyers? Dmitri's had been their favorite restaurant. They'd eaten here twenty-five times if once. He knew what she liked, what she usually ordered. "We'll take one order of *moussaka* with two plates. And bring us some *tandir non*, will you? Oh, and a side of *tzatziki*." He wore his certitude like a loud pink shirt. He watched the waiter walk away then he turned and stared evenly at Laura. "So, you want a divorce? Just like that?"

Laura dabbed at the corners of her eyes with a white hand-kerchief she had produced from her purse. "I . . . I don't know, Len. Yes, I think so. I'm sorry."

"Do you love this—? Who is this? What's his name?"

Laura seemed to hide behind the handkerchief for a minute, even with her large, moist brown eyes directed at her husband. "You don't know him," she allowed at last. "This isn't about him anyway. Like I say, we're friends."

The rage that Len sought to contain threatened to burst forth. "No, no. Some guy I don't know is sleeping with my wife, and it's not about him at all."

"Len! Stop!"

He leaned forward, seething. "How long have you been sleep-ing with him, Laura? When did it start? When I was in Kabul? Or was it before? And by the way, is that where you're living now? Did you move in with him, or are you really at Barbara and Glenn's?"

Laura slid her chair back suddenly, startling the only other couple in the restaurant. Then she stopped and imposed a semblance of calm upon herself. She fixed Len with a stare that said, "Are you done?"

"I almost called Barbara when I got in from China. I'm glad I didn't." He said this without making eye contact.

She slid her chair back in and leaned forward. "I'm at Barbara's. I told you that. Len, I don't want to argue with you. I can't go with you to Seattle."

Len picked up his gin and tonic. "Are you in love with this guy?" His changed tone left room for whatever the answer would be and even for the silence that followed. He sat back, resigned. "What are you going to do, then? Are you planning to stay here in Tashkent?" He heard the questions as though someone else were speaking.

Laura looked away momentarily. "I don't know. For a while, I guess."

He stared into his drink. In the glistening pieces of ice he found a portal back to a moment never forgotten, the moment he'd first laid eyes on Laura. He was sitting on the sunny steps of the University Union building at NAU. Laura, eighteen at the time, approached from the south, from Raymond Hall, hugging a large blue chemistry book and a red spiral notebook to her chest. She was alone. She wore her hair straight then, above her shoulders, and the wind tossed its edges as she walked. She smiled at him as she passed. Several paces later she turned to look back. He nodded at her. She smiled, more self-consciously this time, but still, he thought, he had never seen anything more lovely.

Len tilted back his gin and tonic but did not drink. It hardly seemed possible that this was the same woman that he'd fallen in love with so many years before. He shook his head slowly as he realized that Laura had lied about wanting to stay in Tashkent two or three weeks past the twenty-third to sell the furniture and tie up loose ends before joining him in Seattle. He recalled the balloons and roses she'd brought to his going-away party. His anger, surprisingly, did not grow. The blade could go no deeper.

XX

—

They strode five-across down the empty concourse—Fatimah, the Tashiri foreign minister, Abdul Sissoko, Charlotte, Alden, and Abbas—their moist, travel-weary faces luminous in the heat and bright sunlight pouring through the skylights. The evacuation of the concourse for their arrival was just the first abnormality in a series that would punctuate Fatimah's return to her native country. When they reached an open airway, a crosswind wafting through palm fronds lifted their spirits and quickened their steps. A hundred yards ahead lay wide, navy blue double doors, each with a small panel window. A few faces and indistinct movements were visible through the glass.

"Are you sure you won't come with me?" Fatimah asked Alden. "We have more than enough room."

Charlotte jumped. "What are you talking about?" Her eyes pivoted from Fatimah to Alden and back again. "Of course we're going with you."

Alden gave her a smile that was three parts reassurance. "No, no, we'll be fine at the hotel." He turned to Fatimah and stopped. The others stopped with him. "Your family wants you to themselves for a few days. You've been gone a long time. We'll see you on Sunday."

"*What?*" cried Charlotte. "No." Her face clouded with the effort to remain calm, and her large green eyes continued to beseech both Fatimah and Alden. "I mean, we should stay together, right? We have to prepare." At last she turned to Abbas for support. "You agree, don't you?"

Abbas said, "Yes, I guess so," but his statement stopped just short of a question.

"We have a week and a half," said Alden. "That's plenty of time. Enjoy your reunion."

"I'd feel better if you were all staying at our family's compound," Fatimah said, touching Charlotte's arm.

Charlotte nodded swiftly and mechanically as if to say "that settles it."

Just then a tall man in a gray military-style tunic, lighter gray officer's cap, and white trousers appeared through a side door. "Ahmed!" Fatimah ran to him and reached out to take both his hands, then kissed him on both cheeks. It was a greeting usually reserved for family members. "Oh, it's so wonderful to see you again!" she said in Arabic.

"And you, Miss Fayruz," the man said, smiling broadly.

Fatimah turned and waited for the others to draw near. She introduced them to the family's driver of many years. The driver and the foreign minister, Sissoko, greeted each other as acquaintances.

"Ms. Yacoubi?"

The deep baritone startled Charlotte. She turned to find a stranger in a blue uniform with gold stars on the epaulettes. He had spoken through a thick mat of soot-colored facial hair that hid all but the thinnest margin of lips, lips now set in a frozen half-smile. Her green eyes met his dark brown ones. "Yes? Can I help you?"

"Please come with me."

"I'm sorry? What—?"

"Tashiri Customs, ma'am. We have some questions about your visa. If you'll step this way." He pivoted toward an office adjacent to the concourse visible through a large wire glass window. Inside, behind a narrow counter, stood two men and a woman, also in uniform, engaged in animated conversation.

Charlotte looked with desperation at Abbas. He turned toward the agent. "Excuse me, officer. Is there a problem?"

"I don't think so, sir. But we need to check a few things." He seemed to recognize Fatimah in the group for the first time. He performed something of a bow. "Miss." He glanced back at Charlotte. "This won't take long. If you'll kindly come with me."

Abbas touched Charlotte's elbow. "I'll go with you. It's probably just a mix-up of some kind."

"No. I can handle it," said Charlotte, a shadow of concern darkening her eyes.

Abbas smiled. "Let me help you."

They followed the man into the office and remained there with their backs to the glass panel for the next several minutes, although no fewer than a dozen times Charlotte turned to make sure Fatimah was there.

"I've got the car waiting, Miss Fayruz," said Ahmed, nodding toward the side door. "We have your luggage."

"Miss Fayruz?" said Alden genially.

"It means precious stone," Fatimah explained. She shook her head and smiled self-deprecatingly. "It's been my nickname since I was a child. Everyone calls me this. It's nothing." She checked the time on her cell phone, then glanced past Alden into the customs office. "Perhaps I should stay to make sure there's no problem."

Alden smiled and touched Fatimah on the shoulder. "No, no, your family's waiting. We can take care of things here."

"You're sure you won't come stay with us? I would really prefer—"

"Positive."

Fatimah smiled weakly. "All right then." She turned to the foreign minister. "Mr. Sissoko, would you be so kind as to make sure that a vehicle is waiting to take my friends to the Hotel Al Maseer?"

Over the course of the next several minutes, Alden and Fatimah talked excitedly about the upcoming debate and confirmed a plan to meet again in three days. Ahmed's phone buzzed. After reading a text message, the driver said to Fatimah, "The foreign minister confirms that their car is waiting, Miss Fayruz. We can go."

Fatimah at last said good-bye. Before departing, she glanced into the customs office again, and even waved at the backs of Charlotte and Abbas.

When Charlotte turned and saw Alden standing alone, she sprang away from the counter and ran toward the door. Abbas, who was holding a piece of paper in one hand, and pointing at it with the other, spun on his heels. His voice was audible through the black metal door. "Charlotte?"

She ran out of the office and called to Alden. "Where did she go? Where's Fatimah?" She continued to run until she reached the American, and barely stopped in time. Abbas and the customs officer were a few steps behind.

"Oh. There you are," said Alden. "She left. She wanted to wait, but her driver insisted—"

"*No!*" Charlotte reached out for Alden's arms, then stepped toward the double doors. Stopping abruptly, she turned and swung her arms out to the side. "Where is she? We have to stop her!"

"*What is it?*" asked Alden. "What do you mean?" Alden looked to Abbas and the customs officer for answers.

"I need to go with her!"

"I told you . . . she needs time with her family. We'll see her again in—"

"But that's crazy!" What began as a shout ended in a barely controlled sibilant plea. "Don't you see? We should be together—all of us. There's so much work to do. We have to stop her—now."

Abbas stepped toward her. "Charlotte, what is it? What's wrong?"

She stared up at the Uzbek and her head shook uncontrollably. She mouthed some words in Arabic then looked away, exasperated. She let her arms fall. Her hands thudded against her thighs.

"We're getting together again on Sunday morning," Alden said calmly. "We have time. Plenty of time."

Charlotte turned back. Her mouth was frozen open. Her eyes seemed to chase something across the concourse that only she could see.

"Charlotte?" said Abbas.

She blinked and looked up at him.

His voice was rich with solicitude, a contrast to Alden's. "Are you okay? Is there anything I can do?"

"I'm okay," she allowed miserably.

The customs officer stepped up to them, made eye contact with Abbas, and handed Charlotte her passport. "You're free to go. Thank you."

"What was the problem?" Alden asked confidentially, tilting his head toward the retreating customs officer.

"They didn't have a record of her visa," said Abbas. "It wasn't on their registry. When I explained that we were traveling with you and Fatimah, and they saw that the foreign minister was with us, they let it go. Took a photocopy of her passport is all."

"All right," said Alden. "I think we all need to get to the hotel and relax. Ms. Yacoubi, are you sure you're okay?"

Charlotte closed her eyes and took a deep breath. "No . . . I mean, yes. Listen, I'm going to call her." She turned away, plunging her hand into her purse. "I want to go with her." With her phone in her hand she turned back to face Alden. "Do you have her number?"

Alden didn't answer.

"Her number. Surely you must have it?"

"I do." Under the press of her unrelenting gaze, Alden spoke slowly. "Ms. Yacoubi. I'm pleased that you wanted to come, but . . . look, I think it's important that we not make trouble for each other. We will see Fatimah on Sunday." Alden released her from his equally penetrating gaze and forced a smile. "Now, if you don't mind," he said, standing straight and shifting the shoulder strap on his carry-on, "let's go find our car."

Abbas's eyes held questions that were slow to materialize. As he and Charlotte turned to follow Alden, he leaned over to whisper in her ear. "Are you all right? I'm sorry . . . can you please tell me what's wrong?"

Charlotte pressed her lips together and shook her head. Her eyes flashed up at Abbas. "I can't believe it is all."

Alden led them toward the blue double doors. They passed under a large sign in Arabic, English, and French: "MAIN TERMINAL, BAGGAGE CLAIM, TAXIS." When they pushed through the doors, they were startled by an explosion of camera flashes. They stopped. Reporters surged toward them, shouting, most with a microphone or a small silver or black recording device extended out in front of them.

"Mr. Frost!"

"Mr. Frost! Over here!"

Alden inched forward into the crowd, as did Charlotte and Abbas, although Charlotte took pains to hide herself behind the two men as they advanced.

"Mr. Frost!"

Accents from every corner of the globe seemed to fill the room at once.

"What's going on?" Alden asked no one in particular.

The microphones, forming a wide arc like rifles at an execution, bore flags of every color. Above the heads of the reporters long black sound booms stretched and drooped. In the back cameramen and women adjusted long, black lenses.

"Mr. Frost! Can we have a word?"

The microphones began to bob up and down as reporters spoke into them ("He's here" . . . "They've just arrived" . . . "Starting in three, two, one . . .") and then stretched them out again.

"Mr. Frost—over here. Excuse me, Mr.—"

"Mr. Frost! If you don't mind—"

Charlotte lifted her hands and held them inches from Alden's back as they inched forward. Abbas shouldered ahead of them both. Looking left and right, he instinctively put his arms out to maintain a safe margin. "What do you want to do here, Mr. Frost?" he shouted.

"What's that? Oh, if they have questions about the companion flag I guess I can take a few," Alden said, turning to face a reporter from the BBC.

"Mr. Frost, where is the diary?"

A shadow crossed Alden's face. "I . . . I have no idea. I don't—"

"Where is Fatimah Ibrahim?"

"She's . . . she'll be here for the debate."

"Mr. Frost. Over here. Sydney Bozier, *Associated Press*." Alden turned to the sound of the reporter's voice. He nodded to indicate his readiness. "Does she have the diary? When did you—?"

"No. I mean, I don't—"

"So she might have it?"

Another reporter shouted, "What is it you hope to gain from this debate and the vote in the Tashiri parliament?

Alden looked at each man in turn. "No, to your question. And to yours, I've learned to keep my expectations low. For me, a good day is one in which at least one more person has learned about the companion flag—what it is and what it represents. You'll have to ask Ms. Ibrahim about her goals."

"Mr. Frost—over here! Sergei Kirilenko of the *Moscow Times*. "Are you claiming you don't have the Şahin Diary?"

"Yes."

"But you'll admit that you broke into the archive—"

"No. I did no such thing."

Another reporter called out, "Mr. Frost, what is your interest in the Armenian genocide?"

"I'm sorry. Who are you?"

"Gohar Gevorgyan, *Armenia Now*."

"I'm here to participate in the debate over adoption of the companion flag. I'm no expert on the Armenian genocide."

"Mr. Frost. Cardia Miando, *Tashir Times*. The debate is scheduled to begin in eleven days. The United Peoples Party has identified four international experts they will use to try to defeat the initiative, including UN Secretary-General Romero. Can you understand why this proposal has generated such strong opposition?"

Alden opened his mouth, but then another reporter shouted from the back, "Is this a one-world government flag?"

"No, it most certainly is not," Alden said, trying to locate the speaker. "The desire for a one-world government is not something shared by people everywhere. That's the test, you see. If it's not an experience shared by people everywhere, it's not represented by the companion flag."

"*Khaleej Times*. Is there a connection between the companion flag and the Şahin Diary?"

"None. As I was—"

"Mr. Frost, Abdel Quran, *Palestine News Network*. Among the speakers scheduled to argue against the companion flag are the Jewish scholar Rabbi Daniel Levenson and the Catholic theologian Monsignor Marc Doyle."

"They are?" said Alden.

"Yes. Can I infer that you weren't aware of this until now?"

Alden hesitated. "Yes, I'm not aware of the debate protocol just yet, or who's planning to speak against the motion."

"Do you—"

"I'd ask you to remember," Alden added, "that the companion flag stands for one thing: all that human beings have in common in spite of their differences. We'll have to hear from Rabbi Levenson and Monsignor Doyle as to why they oppose it."

"Mr. Frost, Antoine Moreau, *France Télévisions*. Would you be willing to identify the other members of your party?"

Alden glanced sidelong at Abbas. "I'll let them speak for themselves." He turned to make room for Charlotte, who was stepping forward.

"My name is Charlotte Yacoubi," she said, with eyes downcast. "I will be assisting Fatimah Ibrahim and Alden Frost." Charlotte ignored a flurry of questions by looking to the side and taking a step back, but one questioner would not relent. It was Mr. Gevorgyan of *Armenia Now*. He had been pushed back by the press of reporters, but now stood on his toes, leaning left and right, and repeated his question over their heads. "Ms. Yacoubi. Excuse me. Over here. You look familiar. Have you been—"

Charlotte began to shake her head even before he had finished the question. She shrunk back further.

"Mr. Frost! Allen Keene, *San Francisco Chronicle*. What were you doing at Public School 32 on September first? Did you make a statement to the police?"

"Yes. I am cooperating fully. We both are."

"So is that a no?" the Armenian reporter shouted to Charlotte. "You've never been to Yerevan?"

Charlotte had stepped fully behind Alden and did not answer. She avoided looking into the eyes of those around her.

When a question was put to him directly ("Who are you, sir?"), Abbas leaned over awkwardly in front of the nearest microphone. "I am with the Republic of Uzbekistan."

* * *

"Your mother has spared no detail in getting the house ready for you, Miss Fayruz," said Ahmed, turning down the radio and glancing into the rearview mirror. "We have all missed you very much, indeed." He maneuvered the black Mercedes SUV into a high-occupancy lane and pressed on the gas.

Fatimah smiled but did not remove her eyes from the spectacle coming into view: hundreds of sign- and flag-carrying protesters lining the Southern Cross Expressway. Ahmed put on the SUV's turn signal.

"It's all right, Ahmed. Keep going."

"Are you sure, Miss? It's just as easy taking Loaloat."

"Yes, I'm sure."

Within moments they were passing scores of wind-driven Tashiri flags and people holding large, professionally printed signs saying "One Flag is Enough," "Leave Our Flag Alone," and "We Love You, Fatimah, Not the Companion Flag!" Fatimah turned and stared back at them through the darkly tinted window.

"It gets better," said the driver.

"What?" Fatimah asked. She turned to find Ahmed pointing up ahead. She scooted forward until she could see in the distance another line of people standing below a row of tall palm trees in front of the Enterprise Center. These people, too, carried signs and flags, but the flags were paired: the Tashiri flag above companion flags with green or black stripes. As they passed, Fatimah could read only a few of the signs, all of which appeared to be hand-painted. "WELCOME HOME, FATIMAH." "YES TO THE COMPANION FLAG!" "THANK YOU, PRESIDENT MOHADJI."

"This is incredible!" she said.

"It is, Miss Fayruz. And you'll see more. I counted twelve or thirteen groups on the way in. It is all anyone is talking about."

"I had no idea."

"And, as you can see, the opposition is better organized. Mr. Ngalie was on the news last night calling on all supporters of the United People's Party to take to the streets today and every day until this initiative is defeated."

Fatimah sat back and tried to absorb it all. *Alden has toiled in obscurity for over twenty-six years, and he and I have worked virtually unnoticed the last nine months! Nothing like this has ever happened before. Is it all because I have brought the issue home with me? Or do they think we have the Şahin Diary?* She looked out the window at the buildings and towers of Central Sanori passing by. *There is something else. The men who tried to kidnap me—could they have been put up by the UPP? No, that's impossible. Why would they go to such lengths? It must have had something to do with the diary.*

A quarter of a mile ahead she saw another large group of people gathered at the side of the road. Others, carrying signs and flags, were running to join them from behind. Swarms of Tashiri flags fluttered in the wind without companion flags, telling her which side these people were on.

The sun came out from behind a cloud and she saw from the corner of her eye her own reflection—bright, clean lines—in the rear passenger side window. It was as though her hologram were projected there. *It was so much simpler before,* she thought, turning away from the image. Before the Doctors for Peace campaign

I could go anywhere without being recognized. I should never have agreed to those photo shoots and interviews after the video went viral, after all that money was raised. I knew when I said yes to *Time* that I'd made a mistake—that my ego would warm to such uncommon attention and adoration. Is it attention, or fixation? She remembered the look of confused despair that had crossed Jamaal's face—three times, or was it four?—as one plan after another was trumped, as he contended with her apologies and assurances. "We'll still go to South Island to visit your grandmother," she'd promised the last time, "but it will have to be next month, when I'm back from Milan and Paris."

"Will we?" he'd replied sullenly. Had he known that New York and Toronto would intervene? That she would crown one excuse with another?

Closing her eyes behind dark sunglasses, she reexperienced the pain of his announcement that he could not take it anymore, that although he loved her, he could not continue in the relationship. Exhaling and glancing up at Ahmed, she surrendered to the temptation to call him. All of a sudden, she *had* to hear Jamaal's voice. She reached for her purse. Feeling for her phone, her hand struck an object that seemed unfamiliar. She pulled it out. It was an envelope, a handwritten letter from Alden to President Mohadji. Now that he's here, he can present it himself, she thought, placing it back. I must remember to give it to Alden on Wednesday. She looked into her purse and pulled out her cell phone. She began to dial, ignoring the warning voice in her head.

"Hello."

"Jamaal, it's me. I've just arrived in town." She looked up into the rearview mirror and saw that Ahmed was glancing back at her.

The delay at the other end was not long. "Thank Allah you're safe, Fatimah."

Fatimah? What happened to Fayruz? It could mean only one thing: Zainab was there with him. Her heart sank, pulling her breath back into her lungs.

Jamaal spoke again. "Fatimah, are you there?"

"Yes," she said, collecting herself as much for the driver's sake as for her own. "Yes, I . . . I just wanted to call and tell you I'd arrived, and . . . to thank you for saving my life. If you hadn't called and told them about Msaidie—"

"The men on the motorcycles saved your life, Fatimah, not me. I only remembered that I'd just read that name somewhere—Msaidie—and it only took me a minute to find the article online."

"No, Jamaal! They would never have known, had you not called. *Never.* And I would be dead. Or tied up in a basement somewhere. Why can't you see that? Are you trying to be cute? Or is this your way of pushing me—" Fatimah felt a helpless anger rise up in her. She put her fingers to her forehead, screening off the driver. Why did I say that? she thought. What a fool I am! But that sentiment brought with it another, a bitterness at the thought that he was choosing Zainab over her. She could not bring herself to apologize. The seconds passed, while beyond the window hundreds of protesters shouted and waved signs, unnoticed. A tear slid onto her cheek below the rim of her sunglasses.

"Fatimah," Jamaal said at last. His businesslike tone expanded the distance between them. "This matter of the companion flag. Is it worth it?"

"What do you mean?" she asked, unable to disguise her annoyance.

"What happened in Uzbekistan, and—"

"What happened in Tashkent had nothing to do with the companion flag. It was a kidnapping attempt. They thought I had the Şahin Diary."

"How do you know that?"

"They were after *me*, Jamaal. There was no attempt on Mr. Frost's life, and they had every opportunity to kill me if they'd wanted to. It was the diary they were after. They were going to blackmail my parents, or the board of Tashir Oil, or something. I'm positive."

"And how do you explain what's happening here?"

"What do you mean? What's—"

"This debate. The experts they're bringing in. How did they arrange that—almost overnight? How'd they even find these people, and who's paying to bring them here? They're running commercials, Fatimah. *Commercials*. Who paid to produce them? Something's going on."

She wiped away the tear and took a deep breath. "I don't know, Jamaal."

It's no use, she thought. Will I even see you again, Jamaal? Do you care? She summoned her courage. "I would like to see you. It doesn't mean anything, I would just like to—"

"I can't, Fatimah. You know that."

Fatimah closed her eyes as he paused. Oh please, let this not be happening, she thought. Wipe away these words.

"I'm sorry, Fatimah. I support what you're doing. So does Zainab. If there's anything we can do to help you . . ."

A few moments later she was startled by silence. Zainab. *We.* The hum of the engine was the first sound to come back to her. She looked down to see her phone cradled in her hand in her lap. Had she even said good-bye?

XXI

From: X13 – CO-9 (Tokyo)
To: undisclosed recipients
Date: Mon., 18 September 20ZZ 08:05:22 +0900
Subject: Fatimah Ibrahim
Encryption/Decryption Enabled: B72ZZ256-9102 (All Threads)

CO-9:

AGENTS CONFIRM F. IBRAHIM AND A. FROST ARRIVED SANORI 14 SEPT., 10:30 LOCAL. NO SIGN OF ṢAHIN DIARY. IBRAHIM TRANSPORTED TO FAMILY COMPOUND 13.6 KM EAST OF CITY. FROST AND TWO OTHERS—YACOUBI (TUNISIA), AHKMEDOVA (UZBEKISTAN)—DRIVEN TO HOTEL AL MASEER. ALL MOVEMENTS MONITORED.

YESTERDAY, 17 SEPT., THE FOUR SUBJECTS MET AT THE CALIPH AL-MA'MUN LIBRARY, DEPARTMENT OF PHILOSOPHY, PORT HIKMA UNIVERSITY. ALSO ATTENDING: PROFESSOR OF PHILOSOPHY, DR. ABDUL MUSTAFA, AND PROFESSOR OF SOCIOLOGY, DR. RAMIZI BEGISU. MEETINGS LASTING THREE TO SIX HOURS.

PLEASE ADVISE NEXT STEPS.

*   *   *

From: XX5 – Executive Director CO-9 (London)
Date: Mon., 18 September 20ZZ 11:45:10

URGENT. DIARY'S WHEREABOUTS UNKNOWN. EXECUTIVE COMMITTEE HAS ORDERED IMPLEMENTATION OF CONTINGENCY PLAN RT2983 WITHIN 24 HOURS. X13 CONFIRM ASSETS IN PLACE.

* * *

From: X13 – CO-9 (Tokyo)
Date: Mon., 18 September 20ZZ 12:04:19 +0900

ASSETS IN PLACE. CONTINGENCY PLAN RT2983 IS GO/GREEN. DEADLINE TO CANCEL: 19 SEPT. 03:00:00 +0400.

* * *

From: X19 – CO-9 (Buenos Aires)
Date: Mon., 18 September 20ZZ 16:36:50 -0300

XX4 IS IN TASHIR TO COORDINATE DEBATE PRESENTERS. RABBI LEVENSON, MONSIGNOR DOYLE, PROF. DONALD O'NEIL, DEPT. OF PHILOSOPHY, HARVARD UNIVERSITY, ALL CONFIRMED. ARRANGE TRAVEL, EXPENSES, AND REMUNERATION THROUGH XX7.

X15 IS IN COUNTRY TO WORK WITH MUHAMMAD NGALIE AND UPP OPPOSITION. WILL CONTINUE TO EXPLORE PROCUREMENT OF NO VOTES IN PARLIAMENT. XX5 CONFIRM FUND AVAILABILITY THROUGH CAYMAN ACCOUNT.

* * *

From: X20 – CO-9 (Moscow)
Date: Mon., 18 September 20ZZ 16:49:01 +0400

I OBJECT TO CO-9 INVOLVEMENT IN CF DEBATE. A NEEDLESS DISTRACTION. SOLE PRIORITY SHOULD BE RECOVERY OF ŞAHIN DIARY.

*　　*　　*

From: X19 – CO-9 (Buenos Aires)
Date: Mon., 18 September 20ZZ 16:55:22 -0300

CIPHER FROM EXECUTIVE COMMITTEE CONCLUDES "REDUCTION OF GLOBAL MILITARY EXPENDITURES MAY RESULT IF COMPANION FLAG ADOPTED BEYOND TASHIR. EFFORTS TO DEFEAT TASHIR INITIATIVE ARE WARRANTED."

*　　*　　*

From: XX5 – Executive Director CO-9 (London)
Date: Mon., 18 September 20ZZ 18:21:01

TO ALL COMMITTEE OF NINE (CO-9) MEMBERS:

X11 CONFIRMS SET-ASIDE OF $10.25M CAYMAN EQUITY VENTURES ACCOUNT. AWAITING WIRING INSTRUCTIONS.

ELEVATING PRIORITY AS OF 18 SEPTEMBER 20:00:00 – ALL MEMBERS – RED/DELTA. ALL STATIONS MONITOR ON ¼ HOUR FOR INSTRUCTIONS. SEARCH FOR DIARY CONTINUES IN UZBEKISTAN AND TASHIR.

*　　*　　*

From: X19 – CO-9 (Buenos Aires)
Date: Mon., 18 September 20ZZ 18:35:02 -0300

DEBATE PROTOCOL. 25 SEPTEMBER, 13:00 LOCAL. THE QUESTION: SHOULD THE ISLAMIC REPUBLIC OF TASHIR ADOPT THE COMPANION FLAG AND DISPLAY IT BELOW THE NATIONAL FLAG? LOCATION: CIVIC AUDITORIUM, SANORI. TIMING: TWO HOURS PER SIDE AS NEEDED. MODERATOR AND PARTICIPANT QUESTIONS—OPEN FORMAT. PARLIAMENT TO VOTE NO LATER THAN 18:00 LOCAL, 25 SEPTEMBER (IMMEDIATELY FOLLOWING DEBATE). ALL PROCEEDINGS TELEVISED AND STREAMED ON TASHIRTIMES.COM.

XXII

"How did you sleep?" Charlotte asked with a smile as she exited her room, pulling her wheeled suitcase and trying to pin her *hijab* with her free hand. She went back to get her duffel, then reemerged and closed the door behind her.

Abbas stammered, "Where are you——? What are you doing?"

"I spoke to Fatimah last night. I'm going to her family's compound after breakfast." Charlotte felt for the long end of the scarf as it fell open. Abbas took the liberty of swinging it over her shoulder where she could reach it. "Thank you." Her smile deepened. "Shall we get Alden?"

"Sure. I thought we were going to stay at the hotel is all." His tone betrayed his disappointment. He reached for the handle of the suitcase, but she touched his arm, stopping him.

"Don't take it personally—please. I just wanted to get to know Fatimah better." She sought to embrace him with her green eyes. "I'm serious . . . I also want to get to know you better. It's just that this is my only chance. If I thought——"

"I understand."

"If I thought I could not spend time with you at home, there is no way I would leave now."

Abbas felt his heart awaken in his chest.

Charlotte continued, "We'll take time to do that, won't we?"

Abbas thrilled at the possibilities that seemed to linger in her upturned eyes.

"You can say no," she said. Her voice had turned playful.

His own smile widened, and by the slow licking of her lips she welcomed it.

"We should," he said, moving a step closer to her. And then another.

To see his face now she would have had to turn up her head very far, but she didn't. Instead, she lowered her gaze and held her ground, letting the strap of the duffel bag slip off her shoulder, and the bag fall to the ground. She stood trembling, staring at his chest and its width as if to say, "Yes, this is what I want! I want you this close. You will not see me move away from you, Abbas Ahkmedova. Never! Look down on me. Be free with your eyes. See the rise of my cheeks as I smile. Look at my body. It hungers for you." Finally she turned her face up to meet his gaze. She lifted herself on her toes and closed her eyes.

Their kiss was a paragraph, not a sentence—a medley of pressures and messages over soft lips. Oh Allah, this is all I ever wanted, Abbas whispered silently. Is this really happening? And then he felt the narrowness of her waist in his hands, the bevel of her hips starting where his fingers lay. He felt her lean into his chest, pressing herself against him. In what universe are there words to describe this? he wondered. Where but here— with her—is such joy possible? Thank Allah for you, Charlotte Yacoubi.

He felt her pull away. He opened his eyes. Her expression held a thousand promises, a thousand questions, each of which he tried to answer with a reassuring smile. He stole a second kiss, a needful one, which she returned, but then she pulled back a second time, covering his mouth with her fingers.

She whispered. "Someone will see."

Abbas felt an urgency rise up and take over. "Let them," he said. "I don't—"

"No. Shhhh." Charlotte lifted herself up on her toes again and kissed Abbas's cheek. "There will be other times. But not now." She covered one of his hands, pressing it against her waist. "Please." Then she pried the hand gently from her waist and stepped away from him. She lifted the duffel bag again. He took it from her before she could place the strap over her shoulder.

"We must get Alden," she continued. "He'll be waiting for us, and I'm sure the car is waiting to take us to the library."

"Charlotte, I—"

She covered his mouth again, then took his hand and started to pull him down the empty hallway.

He swept up the handle of her suitcase with an athlete's agility.

"Please. Let's go. Okay?" she said.

*   *   *

"Coming!" yelled Alden from beyond the door. Charlotte and Abbas gazed at each other's faces until the last possible moment, turning away only when they heard a hand on the doorknob.

Alden smiled at them both. "Hello! You two look happy this morning. Did I miss something?"

"N-no," stammered Charlotte, averting her eyes and reaching to adjust a fold in her *hijab*. A moment later, she was smiling up at Alden with a new story. "We were just saying how much we're both enjoying this tropical climate."

Alden looked from one to the other. He seemed not to notice that Abbas carried Charlotte's luggage. "Yes, it's quite nice, isn't it?" He stepped into the hallway, carrying a file of papers, and shut the door. Moving toward the elevator, he added, "I was lying in bed last night wondering if they have hurricanes in this part of the world. It seems like they would, but I don't think I've ever heard of one in the Indian Ocean."

Abbas brushed Charlotte's fingers with his own as they walked behind Alden. She slapped his hand away.

"I'm not aware of any," she said, in a voice noticeably elevated. She cleared her throat. "That's an interesting question though." She looked up at Abbas and made a warning face.

He smiled mischievously.

Alden leaned over to press the down button, then turned back to face Charlotte. "So, how do you think it's going? Do you think we'll be ready for Monday? It's less than a week away."

"Yes, I think so," said Charlotte as the elevator doors opened.

Alden led them into the empty car and pushed the button for the lobby. "I'm glad you're confident. The two professors have been a great help. I'm very interested in the latest research showing what I've thought for years: that our moral choices start with subconscious impulses."

"The passionate and compassionate impulses you've talked about," said Charlotte. She found a moment to fire a telling glance at Abbas, one that seemed to say "Yes, this is how he talks. I've gotten used to a whole new vocabulary."

"Exactly—with compassionate impulses arising from awareness of those parts of *other* that are shared by people everywhere."

Charlotte nodded. Seeing the shadow of a doubt cross Abbas's face, she said, "The love of family, the desire for health and knowledge, our desire to be understood when we speak . . . and on and on."

"Yes," said Alden.

Abbas looked at Charlotte and suppressed a smile. She's a woman of immense intelligence and concern for the world, he thought. That's sexy. I'll gladly take that, especially if she has feelings for me.

The elevator stopped on the second floor, and a man and woman, preceded by a girl of six or seven, stepped in. Good mornings were exchanged, but that marked the limit of the conversation until the doors opened at the lobby and the child jumped out, landed on both feet, and stopped, causing the adults behind her to bump into each other. She earned a stern reprimand from her father.

The lobby shone, with long streaks of sunlight reaching in through open windows on the east-facing wall. Fingers of potted palms situated throughout the lobby performed delicate dances in the thrall of a gentle cross-wind. At the reception desk, uniformed clerks greeted guests checking in or checking out, while nearby bellhops, some already bright with sweat, loaded luggage onto brass carts. A middle-aged European man and woman, dressed in khaki trousers and short-sleeved shirts and apparently outfitted for a morning walk, were getting instructions from the concierge. Beyond the open doors of the main entrance stretched a long, U-shaped drive filled with taxis and private vehicles, and a sidewalk teeming with people—guests and drivers, mostly, but also porters and doormen whose practiced enthusiasms and ready hands were a calming influence.

Abbas waited a few feet from the elevator, letting Alden and then Charlotte pass in front of him. He noted the shift to warm, tropical air as they padded across the ornate red carpet, past reading chairs and couches, toward a collection of enormous Ming-inspired vases and a tableau of tropical flowers near the room's midpoint. He told himself to stop looking at Charlotte's gracefully swinging backside. At least don't be conspicuous about it, he thought. Say something to her—that will do the trick. He tapped her on the shoulder. She stopped, glanced quickly at Alden marching away a few steps behind the young girl, and then turned back to Abbas. A hint of impatience darkened her green eyes, then quickly melted. She smiled. "Yes?"

"When we get there, I want to go out and get you breakfast. What would you like this morning?"

*   *   *

The explosion was heard fourteen miles away. Its echo took a serpentine path down Mount Sapitwa's steep ravines, accounting for more than three dozen reports to the Sanori police of multiple explosions, and two reports of an imagined invasion "near the port." The structural integrity of the Hotel Al Maseer was severely compromised, with the partial collapse of three floors. Shards of glass and debris were blown three thousand feet—over half a mile—from the gaping holes that had been the hotel's entrance. Investigators would later determine that the bomb had been planted in one of four oversized vases located near the center of the lobby and detonated by remote control.

XXIII

Len taped boxes on the dining room table and threw them in a jumbled pile on the living room floor. Hip hop beats blared in his ear buds. His only care—besides his obvious mountain of cares—was working around empty bottles of Carlsberg, and one newly opened one. He heard the screech of the packing tape, but not the phone ringing in the kitchen or Laura's voice on the answering machine.

"Len, I can't believe what I just heard. Barbara told me you and Abbas saved the life of Fatimah Ibrahim two weeks ago? Is this true? I can't . . . I've been so distracted. Why didn't you tell me at dinner? I didn't even know she was in Uzbekistan . . . And since when do you chase after bad guys on your motorcycle and shoot them? Call me, will you?"

Another call five and a half hours later roused him from a deep sleep. The ringing was incessant. With one eye opened he checked the caller ID. It was his secretary. "Karen?"

"Len, we just got word. There's been a bombing in Sanori. Alden Frost is dead."

"*What?*" Len bolted upright. He winced at a sudden throbbing pain in his head, and remembered the beers he'd drunk before going to bed.

"A bomb exploded at the hotel where they were staying. Frost was killed. Len, I'm sorry to have to tell you this, but Abbas was injured, too. I knew you'd want to know immediately."

"Injured?" Len couldn't believe what he was hearing. He looked around the room desperately and through the gloom saw a stack of boxes in the corner. He remembered that he'd packed them and put them there hours before. This made it real. "How bad is he? What's his condi—?"

"I don't know. Bad, I think. The other woman, Charlotte Yacoubi—she was injured, too."

"Oh my God." Len was standing now, turning in place, unsure what to do. "And Fatimah? What about—?"

"From what we know she wasn't there."

"I can't believe this," Len said helplessly.

"Interpol issued a bulletin a half hour ago confirming Frost's death. There were thirty-six casualties in all, over a hundred wounded. The Tashiri Interior Ministry is investigating . . . I'm sorry, Len."

Len sat on the edge of his bed. Karen waited for Len to collect himself. He rubbed his forehead while his thoughts raced in all directions. Wait a minute! Bombings don't just happen. "Who did this? Was anyone arrested?"

"No. The CIA is picking up chatter from MİT—the Turkish secret service. They've apparently got agents down there, and so does Armenian Relief. They've also intercepted some traffic from the Committee of Nine."

A bombing? In a hotel lobby? Len remembered the surgical extraction and mysterious disappearance of the Zimbabwean oil minister within days of a speech in Harare the previous year threatening to nationalize that country's oil reserves. That the

Committee of Nine was responsible for the minister's disappearance was widely accepted in diplomatic circles—for one, because of the suddenness and cleanliness of the operation. Would the same organization resort to a terrorist-type bombing now? Len stroked his chin with his knuckles. "Jesus."

"Yeah. Sanori police have located a room in an adjacent office building from which the assailants apparently used a telescope to see into the lobby. It looks like Frost was the target. They've dusted for fingerprints and are talking to witnesses . . . but so far, no leads."

"And Abbas, he's . . . ?"

"Alive. That's all we know."

Len commanded his mind to slow down, to focus, but it was no use. He stood up again and started pacing. He had to think, but it was all too much. Walking seemed to help. "Listen, Karen. I'm going to call you back."

He raced to the living room. The minute and a half it took his laptop to boot up was the longest minute and a half of his life. He clicked on CNN.com. The bombing was the lead story. Len stared in disbelief at photos of the bombed-out lobby of the Hotel Al Maseer. "Thirty-six killed . . . scores wounded . . . one American dead." He pored through one article after another, desperate for new information. "No one has claimed responsibility. . . 'A cowardly and desperate act' says Muhammad Ngalie, leader of the opposition UPP. . . dozens admitted to local hospitals in critical condition." He scanned still pictures of the opposition leader, of Fatimah, of President Mohadji, and of Alden speaking to reporters at the airport.

Len shook his head. "My God." He clicked on BBC.com, then Reuters World News. Seconds after the Reuters page came up, it refreshed, and a news alert appeared above the headline "Sanori Hotel Bombing." It read "Raw Video Feed: Fatimah Ibrahim Statement on Tashir Bombing." Len clicked the link.

Fatimah was surrounded by four tall, frowning men. Brothers? Len thought—more likely bodyguards. An older woman with gray hair stood at Fatimah's side, touching her arm as Fatimah spoke. Fatimah's face was drawn, and her eyes were puffy from crying. She was dressed in a bright blue-and-orange kaftan and matching head scarf, evidence of a day hijacked by tragedy. She read from a statement in Tashiri, then switched to English. Her voice broke. She paused twice but struggled on. With her first words in English, Len sat back in his chair, dumbstruck.

"I am devastated by the loss of my friend and mentor, Alden Frost, and by the deaths of so many innocent people this morning. My prayers go out to their families and loved ones, and to the families and loved ones of the injured, as well. This needless act of violence has caused great harm to the human family, not just here in Tashir but around the world.

"My friend Alden Frost did not run from the world. He was running toward it."

Len felt his mouth and throat go dry. He stared at the screen unblinking. Something began to stir deep within him.

Fatimah continued, "His purpose in living was to help us discover for ourselves a new moral dimension—to proclaim it and bear witness to it. His particular genius was the creation of a universal symbol, a flag that, when displayed with the world's other flags, portrays this moral dimension—"Dimension M," he once called it . . ."

Len thought back to the first moment that he'd seen Frost and Fatimah in the conference room at the Tashkent city jail. Frost had been tired and drawn, a wisp of a man. But behind that weariness, behind those pale blue eyes, was passion, Len realized. He had spent twenty-six years traveling around the world, only to find himself there in that room. How strangely open he had been to whatever came next.

"But the journey was difficult," Fatimah continued, her famously youthful voice sounding much deeper. "He told me once that when he began, he was beset by self-doubts. How could one simple man hope to introduce an idea—any idea—to the entire world? But then he reached a point where it was the clarity of his vision that kept him going, the odds be damned. I have been honored to share that vision with him since November of last year."

And where is my passion? Len thought. Abbas had had enough to race to Msaidie's car and shoot him and the driver to save Fatimah and Charlotte. He had had enough to travel to Tashir as Alden's bodyguard. Fatimah? Enough to turn her back on fame and fortune and go into relative hiding for something more important. Charlotte? She practically crawled into their bags to get to Tashir. *Me?*

Fatimah continued, her mouth twisting with the effort to avoid crying. "Yes, Alden Frost walked toward the world, not away from it. He sought to help us all in the one area that proved his undoing: man's inhumanity to man.

"Someone asked me if this morning's tragedy would result in the cancellation of the debate scheduled for next week. It will not. I am prepared to go forward. I *will* go forward. For Alden. For . . . He dreamed of a day when a small country such as ours would deliberate on the wisdom of adopting the companion flag. I am hardly worthy to share his dream, but I have . . . and I do."

The video clip ended abruptly, leaving Len staring at a blank screen. The replay option tempted him, but then he knew he had seen enough. He was transfixed by Fatimah's courage, her clarity of purpose. It withstood the heaviest blows. This is who she is, he thought, remembering a particular moment when she turned to the old woman next to her and touched her hand consolingly. This woman is amazing. "Beyond that," he whispered.

An idea suddenly occurred to him. "I'm documenting the flag raisings, posting what we do on YouTube, Vine, Facebook . . .," she'd said. He leaned forward, typed "youtube.com" into the search engine, then "companion flag." There were more than two dozen videos: "Flag raising, Mayur Public School, New Delhi, India," "Flag raising, Bidhannager Municipal School, Kolkata, India," "Flag raising, Lahore Grammar School, Faisalabad, Pakistan," and on and on. Len chose a video halfway down the list: "Bishkek School for the Deaf, Bishkek, Kyrgyzstan." The music of Amr Diab, the drums of "El Alem Allah," ushered in an expanding image of a rectangular red-and-gold Kyrgyz flag with a red-striped companion flag below it, and then the title emerged as if from a mist:

THE COMPANION FLAG IN KYRGYZSTAN
BISHKEK SCHOOL FOR THE DEAF

Len watched footage depicting the nighttime lowering of the Kyrgyz flag, the slow, deliberate addition of a companion flag, and then the re-raising of the two flags together. It was all just as he'd imagined it at Public School 32, the only differences being the host flag and the fact that the Bishkek flagpole was near the school's entrance, not on the roof.

He clicked a second video. Shymkent, Kazakhstan. The same motif, this time accompanied by the music of John Barry, "The Beyondness of Things." This is what you are, Fatimah, he thought, as he watched Alden's back and saw the flag of Kazakhstan carefully lowered, Fatimah coming into the picture late. Alden was the idea man. Since when do you debate, Fatimah? That can't be in your comfort zone.

Len rocked back in his chair, closed his eyes, and rubbed both hands through his hair. Recalling the look of disappointment on Abbas's face when he'd declined to go with them to Tashir, he winced. "Lord Almighty. The comfort zone. Dammit, Abbas, I'm sorry." Then he jumped up from the chair and stomped into the kitchen. He put his hands on the edge of the draining board and leaned forward. He lowered his head between his arms, fighting back tears. "Don't die, Abbas. Please." He looked up and stretched one hand over the nape of his neck. I should have been there. I should have.

Suddenly, he was rocked by a realization, a possibility so far-fetched that his first instinct was to dismiss it out of hand. "It couldn't be," he said aloud, but in less than a second he was running back to his laptop and conjuring up the memory of Ali Msaidie lying in the gravel next to his submachine gun, his left arm outstretched. The tattoo he'd seen. What was it? Just above the wrist. A starfish. "It couldn't be." Len shoved the mouse violently, and the screen came to life. Reaching over the back of his chair, then slowly seating himself, he navigated through the articles and pictures he had just viewed until he came to the photo taken in the airport, the one of the press crowded around Alden, Charlotte, and Abbas. He leaned forward. There it was. A man with dark skin in a white shirt standing behind one of the reporters. He wasn't carrying a microphone, a camera—anything. He was standing there, staring coldly forward. By some miracle, his left hand was visible, through a thick copse of legs, arms, and jackets, and on his wrist was the same starfish tattoo Len had seen on Msaidie's wrist. To be certain, Len opened the picture in Photoshop and magnified the man's hand by 400 percent. "Oh my God," he whispered.

Len straightened. Think! he said to himself, touching his lower lip. And then it occurred to him. Abbas and Charlotte are still in danger. I've got to get down there! He stood up and looked helplessly around the room. What about Majestic? "Forget it," he heard himself whisper. Then he spun around, unsure which way to turn. "Christ!" I need to call the Uzbek interior minister. No, they can't do anything in

Tashir, he realized. The Uzbeks and the Tashiris are at dagger points. Len took a step away from the desk, then turned and looked back at the computer screen. I could call Fatimah and ask her to post guards at the hospital, he thought. But the man with the starfish tattoo looked like a Tashiri. He could be on the inside. Msaidie had said he was with the foreign ministry. What if—? No. There was something amiss. Tompkins was right. Who can I trust, then? Len wondered. Perhaps only myself. I've got to get down there! He ran into the bedroom to get his phone. He wondered what Richardson would say. They had practically fired him in advance when he'd hesitated about going to Xining. Len began dialing Majestic International, certain that he was about to lose his job. "So be it, godammit," he muttered, walking back into the living room as the phone began to ring half a world away. It's about time I took a stand.

"Majestic International. This is Rebecca. How can I help you?"

"Rebecca, this is Len Williams in Tashkent. Can you put me through to Mr. Richardson."

"Oh, hello, Mr. Williams. The CEO is in a meeting. Can I have him call you back?"

"I'm afraid it's an emergency. Is there any way to get through to him?"

"Hold just a minute."

The next voice on the line was a deep baritone. "Len, we were just talking about you. You didn't get mixed up in this business in Tashir, I hope."

Len bristled at the implication. Mixed up? I didn't have the guts, if that's what you mean. "No," he answered. "You heard about the bombing?"

"Of course," said Richardson. "They're out to stop this companion flag nonsense. That's pretty plain."

"Who is?" Len asked, suddenly confused.

Richardson hesitated. "Damned if I know. Some Tashiris, I suppose. What's up?"

"I need to get down there, Bill. A close friend of mine was hurt in the attack—actually, two friends. I need to check on them—see if there's anything I can do." A silence stretched out and turned menacing. "I need to delay my start date a week."

"Uh . . . that's not going to work for us, Len. You know you're scheduled for meetings here next week. And we need to get you up to speed on a problem we're dealing with in Argentina. We were just talking about it. I'm sure these friends of yours—"

"I understand, Bill, but this is an emergency. I need to ask you for some leeway here."

"I'm afraid that's not—"

"Normally, I wouldn't ask."

"No, I'm sure you wouldn't. The answer is no." Richardson's clipped tone seemed to surprise even him. The CEO took a breath. "Look, Len, I'm sorry to hear about your friends. I really am. But I'm sure they're getting the medical attention they need. There's nothing we can do for you. We need you here on Monday."

Len stared at the wall, nonplussed. "I'm . . . There's no way I can . . ."

"I'm somewhat sympathetic to this companion flag idea—more than you think," said Richardson. "Especially after what you did in Xining. That was remarkable. But the board wants nothing to do with it, and they want to make sure there's plenty of daylight between you and this Fatimah Ibrahim, this Frost character, and the whole debate thing."

"Frost is dead," Len said.

"I know that. The bombing down there makes it twice as important that our name not be brought into it."

Len waited, sensing that Richardson had more to say.

"If you want to work here, you stay away from Tashir—you hear? We'll plan on seeing you on the twenty-fifth."

Len said good-bye and hung up. He stared at his half-bare closet and at the boxes stacked in the corner. An idea struck him. As he dialed Karen's number, he imagined Laura standing beside him in disbelief. "So that's it? You're giving up your job at Majestic? Just like that? So much for making your fortune in the private sector. So much for paying your gambling debts, and any real ambition."

Len thought back to the moment when Ambassador Tompkins had tried to call him off the motorcycle chase through Tashkent. *What you don't understand, Ambassador, is that's my friend up there.*

Laura is leaving me anyway, he thought. And who needs Seattle's rain?

"Karen, I need you to get me down to Tashir. Are there any aid or military flights scheduled? I need to get down there now."

"What about your status, Len? Technically, you're not with the State Department anymore. Friday was your last—"

"You gotta help me. Talk to Harold if you have to. Extend me a week or two. He'll do what you say—right? We can ship medical supplies down there, or maybe search-and-rescue dogs. Whatever it is, I've got to get down there. I'll take a commercial flight if I have to, but I need you to extend my diplomatic visa."

"OK, let me get to work on that."

Karen was a fixer. He knew she could do it. "Thanks, Karen. I'll start packing."

"I'm proud of you, Len."

Len closed his eyes. The words came unexpectedly, caught him off guard. A soft groan escaped his lips. All he wanted at that moment was to be someone else, someone who had said yes to his friend nine days earlier.

XXIV

———

Len walked with a bouquet of irises down the eggshell-white corridor of Sanori General Hospital. He stopped in front of an armed guard. "I'm Len Williams. Are you—"

"Yes, Mr. Williams," the guard said, straightening. "May I see your passport, please?"

While the guard examined the document, Len read the brightly colored embroidered patch over the man's breast pocket. He recognized the name and logo of the security company he'd hired before leaving Tashkent. "Are you Mr. Mesona, then?"

"No, sir," the guard answered, returning the passport. "He's upstairs, with Ms. Yacoubi. Room 804. I'm Amidu."

"All right. This is Mr. Ahkmedova then?" Len said, peering over the guard's shoulder at the partially opened door to Room 612.

"Yes, sir," said Amidu in a low voice. He stepped aside.

Len knocked quietly. "Abbas? Are you in there?"

"Len?" The voice was unmistakable, if weaker than he'd remembered. Len stepped tentatively past the curtain, then froze. Abbas was partially sitting up in bed. His left leg, held in place with pins and suspended in a sling, his torso, his right arm, and his right shoulder were heavily bandaged, as was his head. His face and hands were spotted with cuts and abrasions. He leaned partially to the side to take the pressure off a surgical incision through which his spleen and part of his liver had been removed.

"Jesus," exhaled Len, letting the curtain fall behind him.

Abbas managed to raise his eyebrows. "The guard told me to expect you, but I still can't believe . . ." Seeing the alarmed look on Len's face, Abbas stopped and looked down at his suspended leg, adding, "Not what I had in mind."

"No, I guess not," Len said in a thick tone. "What do the doctors say?"

"The impression I get is that they're glad they're not me," Abbas moaned. He followed this with a laugh that Len knew he paid for in pain.

Len smiled despite an upwelling of emotion that caught him by surprise.

Abbas seemed to detect his difficulty. "Actually, they say I'll recover completely."

"And Charlotte?"

"She was burned pretty bad. The right side of her face, her right arm. She broke her collar bone and a bone in her wrist . . . or so they tell me."

"You haven't been able to talk to her?" Len struggled to control his voice.

Abbas shook his head. "Will you go see her? Tell her I'm okay?

"Of course. I'm a negotiator. I can lie about anything."

Abbas smiled crookedly. "I've asked the nurses to talk to her, but I doubt they've taken the time. She's in the burn unit. Things are hectic around here." Abbas's eyes misted. "I *am* okay, Len. But I just want her to recover. That's . . . I want that more than anything."

"Sure. Do you want me to go up there now?"

Abbas nodded.

"All right." Len commanded his voice not to break. "But I want you to know I'm here for you. I should never have let you come down here alone."

Abbas's chuckle seemed designed to lift Len's spirits. "Suddenly, we're brothers. And you're my older brother." He shifted again to find a more comfortable position. "The guards? That was your idea?"

Len cleared his throat. He didn't think he could talk anymore. Besides, how could he explain his suspicions? So two men wore the same tattoo. Was that a conspiracy? He stood staring into space until Abbas began to wave the fingers of his free hand.

"Go, please. Take the flowers. Tell her I picked them myself."

Len managed to make a face. "Charlotte this, Charlotte that. We need to talk." He slapped the curtain aside. "Don't go anywhere." Had he succeeded in saying this without his voice cracking, he probably would have found the strength to go directly to Charlotte's room. It was not to be. He knew it as he stepped past the guard and felt the muscles in his face pull and burn with the need to cry. Damn it, he thought. I can't stop this! He rushed toward a door marked with an exit sign and entered a stairwell. He lowered himself onto the top step. "Godammit," he moaned as the first full sob rose in his lungs. He dropped the irises by his side.

A question began to reveal itself between convulsions. Was he incapable of caring enough about anyone or anything else? He pushed the question away. He tried to imagine the explosion that injured Abbas. The orange-red flash, the thunderous boom. Whatever he conjured up was insufficient, he knew. He tried to double it—double its intensity—but it was no good. What had happened to Alden's body? Was it torn to pieces? Did the concussion kill him? Or was it shrapnel that—? Len's lungs erupted again and a deep growl preceded the wailing that came out half formed, weighted, and was eventually swallowed back. "Shit." He drove a fist down against his knee. He listened for anyone else in the stairwell. He had to recover, and quickly. The question came back, and he tried to block it with images of Charlotte's face surrounded by flame. It didn't work.

How could I not care enough—and still care this much? I've played it safe my whole life. He remembered the blank expression on Abbas's face when he told him he wouldn't come to Tashir. I yawned at Fatimah's and Charlotte's concern for their safety. Abbas didn't judge me. He said they would be disappointed. But he was disappointed, too—he just didn't show it. "To each his own," he would have said. But that leaves you with yourself, doesn't it? To each his own. What is "my own?" Gambling, staring at poker hands on a computer screen late at night while my wife sleeps? Negotiating on behalf of the United States government, making damn sure we pay as little as possible to the families of our victims? Is that all I'm about?

He threw his head back and closed his eyes. Money. That's been my whole motivation. The winning hand. Give me the winning hand. Isn't that what I'm saying to Majestic? Isn't that at the heart of my decision to leave the State Department? Let me pay off Smythe, and get back to the winning side.

He heard the roar of a jet passing over the hospital. The sound reverberated in the hollow cement stairwell. That's how they came to Tashir, he thought. He imagined Alden, Abbas, Fatimah, and Charlotte sitting back in their seats, getting ready to land. Flying into the jaws of danger—without knowing it. Len was suddenly proud of them all, almost overwhelmed with pride. They came in armed with—what? Only an idea. A quixotic one, yes, but so what? They were on a mission. At some level they had to know they might be targeted. Nothing was certain after what had happened in Tashkent.

Hanging up a flag. Len shook his head and through a ragged breath thought, how many have perished for the sake of a flag? Marched, or sailed, or flown into harm's way? He looked at the blank wall of the stairwell. A little wave of relief swept over him as the need to cry was abating. Stay focused, he thought. He pulled himself up. Yes, it was leaving him. He wiped his eyes with the back of his hand. I need a washroom, he said to himself. I'll freshen up and then find Charlotte.

*   *   *

Len was stopped at the nurses' station on the way to Charlotte's room by a gaunt-looking nurse whose dark cheeks, and the lenses of her glasses, shone blue in the light of her computer screen. "I'm sorry, sir. She's asleep. I can take the flowers if you'd like."

Len looked down the hall to see an armed guard standing in front of Room 804, then checked the time. 18:40. "Do you know when—?"

"No. But the morning is her best time. Can you come back tomorrow?"

Len nodded, then pointed. "Let me talk to the guard for a minute." Still carrying the irises, he walked quietly down the hall, introduced himself to the guard, and presented his passport. The door to Charlotte's room was open. He tiptoed in. Stepping around the curtain, he was arrested by the smell of burned flesh and the sight of an angry swath of red, twisted skin that shimmered with moistness over the right side of Charlotte's sleeping face and down her right arm, bright against the sheet. He felt a sudden shock of phantom pain over his own skin— over his hands and face. He took an involuntary step back, and forced a short breath in and out through his mouth. The IV dispenser clicked over Charlotte's left shoulder. He looked around the room for a place to deposit the flowers, but none was in reach and he knew he risked waking her if he moved too much. He would leave them with the nurse after all, he decided. He inched back against the curtain, stopped, commanded himself to look at Charlotte's face once more before leaving. But then his gaze rose up and before his mind's eye appeared a montage of images floating above Charlotte's head: Alden and Fatimah on the rooftop of Public School 32. Abbas streaking ahead of him on his motorcycle through the streets of Tashkent. The sparkle in Charlotte's eyes as she explained her passion for the companion flag project. Len felt a sudden heaviness in his heart and he turned away, extinguishing the images. Another wave of remorse threatened to overtake him. What did I do when Abbas asked me to join them? "Who, me?" I said. "Oh, no, I have to make money—thanks anyway." You stepped back when they stepped forward, he told himself.

But a moment or two later he felt a change of heart. It was as though a hand were lifting him partially off the floor, as though a strange force were bearing part of his weight. He heard the high-pitched whine and receding roar of another jet descending over the hospital. He moved quickly and quietly past the foot of Charlotte's bed to the window, for the force seemed somehow bound to this noise—to the jet itself. It was a 737 on its final approach to Sanori International. He remembered sitting on just such a plane only hours earlier. This campaign isn't over, he realized. It hasn't even begun—not really. Len felt a surge in his chest, felt himself transported into that descending aircraft, smoothly arriving on the tiny island nation. And suddenly he realized that he, too, had set a course for the jaws of danger. In a plane just like that one, he, too, had sped his way here. It was not just to make sure Abbas was safe. That might have been the first priority, but that was only *part* of his motivation. He thought back to the video of Fatimah speaking in the hours after Alden's death, to the strange way his heart turned when she looked up into the camera and said, in effect, "The debate will go on. This idea will never die." That's when he knew, he realized now. Knew without knowing. When he saw a chance for clarity and purpose—*for him*. A childlike clarity?—Okay, yes, he would admit that. It was something—at least *something*—to believe in. Something larger than himself, something larger than money, more permanent than political expediency. Wasn't that it? But I don't care if it's meteoric, he argued with himself. I want it. Flash and gone, it doesn't matter. I knew when I heard Fatimah's voice that I wanted to join this fight. That's why I've come, isn't it? They're out to kill her, or if not to kill her, to kill this idea. Well, to hell with them.

*   *   *

Later that night, the window of Abbas's hospital room was a black mirror reflecting in vivid detail, hologram-like, Abbas sitting up higher than before, the heart monitor with its active green-and-yellow lights, the IV drip and lines, and Len, sitting forward in an orange-and-blue flower-print chair in the corner of the room. He was asking a question. He'd just returned from getting up to refill Abbas's water glass.

"Thanks," said Abbas, leaning back. "He told me they were finally able to rouse the man who came in as Msaidie . . . gave him something. He was weak and refused to talk, demanded that he be given a lawyer."

"And?" said Len.

"The lawyer never came, if that's what you mean. They took him downstairs in the . . . for enhanced interrogation. They asked about the bombing. He denied knowing anything about it. Then they asked who hired him, who put him up to the kidnapping attempt. He refused to answer. The doctors were eventually called back to administer a chemical reactant. He resisted for about an hour. He was re-injected several times. Finally, he mumbled something about a meeting in Montreal and Arturo Demir. That's when his heart gave out. That's all they got."

"Arturo Demir? The arms dealer?"

Abbas nodded.

"Starfish Industries." Len remembered the tattoos and turned to look at Abbas. "What kind of meeting, I wonder?"

"There was an annual meeting of the American-Turkish Defense Alliance in June, thirty miles outside of Montreal . . . but Demir had been ousted from the ATDA in 2011 for his extremist anti-Armenian views. He'd been a long-time financier for the organization and it's believed he wanted back in. It's likely Demir wanted to get his hands on the diary before its contents went public."

"And this man, this Msaidie, worked for Demir."

"They're looking into that. They didn't find anything on his person, and there was nothing on the driver, either."

"So first Demir comes after Fatimah, and now Frost," said Len, looking out the window again, past his own reflection. The folded foothills of Mount Sapitwa were swept by glittering city lights. High above—impossibly high—the island's signature peak was a blackness visible against a riot of stars. "Somehow the word gets out that these two broke into the school where the Şahin Diary was kept. The book's missing, and Demir assumes—like everyone else—that Frost and Fatimah took it."

"It would seem so," said Abbas, shifting from one hip to the other in search of relief, or something like it.

Len saw his friend's movement in the window's reflection but didn't say anything. When you're that banged-up, you're bound to be miserable, he thought. "So he thinks 'I've got to get my hands on that diary. If I can keep its contents from going public, if I can destroy it, or deliver it to Ankara on a silver platter, the ATDA'll take me back.' What better way to accomplish this than to kidnap Fatimah? Either she has it, or if Frost has it, they'll torture her, or threaten to kill her, until Frost turns it over." Len plunged his hands into his pockets. "He has men working for him who'll do anything, whatever it takes."

"It's possible," said Abbas skeptically, painfully. "But what did he have to gain by killing Alden?"

Len considered the question, gazing up at the flashing strobe and alternating green-and-red navigation lights of a 787 Dreamliner descending over the hospital. It looked lonely up there, he thought, a magnificent, roaring hulk with only the stars for company. "Maybe the idea was to destroy the diary," he said at last, "or at least intimidate Fatimah." Len turned slowly toward his friend, who was probing the skin under the bandage on his shoulder. "We may never know. But I'm sure they're working on it in Tashkent." Len sought to change the subject. "Can I get anything for you?"

"No."

Len turned back to the window. "I'm going to join this debate . . . if Fatimah will agree."

"What?"

"I'm going to help her if I can." Len smiled uncertainly, turning back again, taking a seat in the flowered chair. "Don't ask me what I can do, but . . . she must need help, right? I mean, she's not a politician, she's not a debater. I've got to be able to contribute something."

Abbas studied him for a few seconds. Len's eyes were wide with excitement. "You're serious, aren't you?" was Abbas's question.

"Absolutely."

"Where's this coming from? I thought you thought the idea was silly."

Staring at the foot of Abbas's bed, Len said, "Maybe I did. Maybe it is. But it's just crazy enough to make sense, too."

They were silent then, each man lost in his own thoughts.

"There's still the question of whether Fatimah will want my help," Len said.

"She was here this morning. She'll be here tomorrow. Comes every day at around nine-thirty. You can ask her yourself, and then go talk to Charlotte. By the way, what about Seattle? I thought you started there next week."

"Screw 'em if they can't take a joke."

"You've talked to them about this?"

"Briefly."

Abbas regarded Len skeptically. "Ok, maybe it's my turn to play the older brother."

"No, don't worry about it. I'm finally seeing beyond my nose."

A nurse came in with a tray of pills and a hypodermic needle. Abbas greeted her with a relieved look in his eyes. As she gingerly put a blood pressure cuff on his good arm, he lifted his face to Len. "You're a good man, Len."

Len pasted on a smile that appeared painful. I'm looking right back at one is what he thought, but what he managed was, "You're just happy to see that needle."

Abbas glanced down at the blood pressure cuff as it started to inflate. He suppressed a grimace. "I don't know what Fatimah's going to say, but if you're going to do this, have Charlotte tell you about the two sides of the brain."

"The what?"

"Yeah. The left brain being all about seeing the parts, the right brain about seeing the whole—the unity of things. How both are needed to see the human condition." His grimace reappeared, and then he sucked in his next breath through pursed lips. "The companion flag does this . . . Mr. Frost was telling her about it on the flight down here, and they were talking about it at the morning meetings at the library. He said it's the best way to explain the companion flag, the reason behind it, I mean . . . and why it's necessary. Charlotte was going to handle that part in the debate."

"You're serious?"

"Mmm." Abbas pressed his lips together and closed his eyes momentarily as the nurse removed the blood pressure cuff rather more roughly than she'd put it on. "Yes. It's what they're finding." Between taking pills and sipping his water he said, "Two halves connected by the corpus cal . . . callosum, or something. One side is . . . keen to human differences, the other, to human samenesses—our connections. That's how Alden explained it." The nurse gave him a shot in the same arm. "This is probably going to put me to sleep."

"That's all right. You rest."

"No, it's . . . the other side, the one holding all of our samenesses . . . Alden called . . . the gold sphere. Do you see?"

"Sure." Len watched the tension go out of Abbas's face, the lines of his forehead growing shallow.

"So, the question . . . is . . . whether we see . . . only . . . one sphere . . . or both . . . when we encounter . . . other people. Charlotte knows . . ." Abbas's head sank back against the pillow and he closed his eyes. He opened them again with an effort. "Len?" he whispered.

Len got up from the chair and moved closer. "What is it?"

Abbas's eyes began to roll up in his head. He struggled to bring them back into focus, to awaken. "I have the . . ."

"You have the what?" Len asked. He moved closer and raised his voice: "What do you have, Abbas? I didn't hear you." But Abbas had lost his battle with the drug. He was unconscious. Len and the nurse exchanged something like a smile.

"Did you hear?" Len asked.

The nurse shook her head.

Len thought of touching his friend to try to awaken him, but quickly gave up the idea. What does he have? he wondered. It's probably nothing. As he straightened and prepared to leave, a twinge of electricity ran up Len's spine, but then it was gone. The two sides of the brain, he thought. Maybe Frost had notes. "You can tell me later, old friend." He gently touched Abbas's foot through the covers and left the room.

XXV

——

Henry Matheson walked slowly, his shoulders bent beneath a black umbrella. He tilted his head back and forth while thin lips worked over the kernels of an imagined conversation. A taxi passed on his right, its tires hissing on the wet pavement. His earpiece buzzed. He stopped, pressed it closer to his ear. "This is Five," he said.

"Five, Seventeen. You wanted me to call."

"I did." The connection between Tashkent and London was clear. Matheson walked a few steps up a private drive to get away from road noise. "The bombing in Sanori. What do you make of it?"

"We're trying to figure that out."

"So it wasn't ours?"

"No."

"I didn't hear you."

"That's a no."

"Let's stand down until we get this sorted out. Have you heard from Arturo Demir?"

"No."

*　　*　　*

Len knew he would be recognized throughout Sanori. The stares he'd received on the plane, the whispers that had begun even before his flight took off from Tashkent left little room for doubt ("That's him—one of the men who saved Fatimah's life"). He was glad to exit the hospital into darkness. He turned up the collar of his jacket and strode along a deserted sidewalk, away from the bright lights of a busy intersection. After meandering six or seven blocks through a quiet residential neighborhood, he spotted a footbridge over a canal. Perhaps there he could stop and think, he thought to himself. He found a path through a large, open area covered with grass. The ocean smells, smells of low tide, of rotting kelp, grew more intense with each step.

*   *   *

Nine thousand miles away, Ed Eagleton emerged from the private bathroom that adjoined his radio studio. The sound of a toilet flushing was cut off by the closing of the door. He sang an old Journey song—"Don't Stop Believing"—under his breath as he put on his earphones. He couldn't sustain the tune when the final bars of a jingle for a mattress company erupted in his ears, followed by the voice of his producer. "We have Muhammad Ngalie in three . . . two . . . one."

"Ladies and gentlemen," Eagleton began, his familiar voice beaming out to 527 affiliate stations and an estimated audience of seventeen million throughout the United States and Canada. Another six hundred thousand listened over Armed Services Radio or online. "I have on the phone Mr. Muhammad Ngalie from Sanori. Mr. Ngalie is a member of the Tashiri parliament and leader of the United People's Party, the party in opposition to President Mohamed Mohadji. Mr. Ngalie, welcome."

"Thank you. It's good to be with you." Ngalie spoke with a heavy British accent.

"Tell us what the mood is like there in Sanori with the world's attention focused on you. I mean, let's be honest, this is now stacking up to be the most important week in Tashiri history."

"Well—"

"From the standpoint of clear-thinking, freedom-loving people throughout the rest of the world. We have the companion flag debate starting in four days, and now the bombing that killed Alden Frost."

"Right. We are, of course, saddened by the senseless act that took Mr. Frost's life and the lives of so many others. I would describe the mood here as tense, Ed, but I'm still optimistic that we'll have the votes necessary to defeat the companion flag initiative."

"Let's hope so . . . Are you concerned, as I am, that the murder of Mr. Frost will create a backlash that will skew the results—?"

"Excuse me, Ed. I've just been handed a note. The debate . . . let me make sure I've got this right . . . yes, the debate has been postponed for two weeks . . . citing security concerns. This is by order of the president. Okay, it will now take place on Monday, October 9, with the vote to follow immediately afterwards."

"I see," said Eagleton. "So not this coming Monday?"

"No. October 9, according to this."

"What we'll never know, of course, is the extent to which Mr. Frost was being propped up by enemies of the United States: China, Russia, or Iran, for instance."

"There is some concern here, yes. But, as I say, I'm optimistic. The debate will, I'm convinced, reveal to the world the fundamental weakness and recklessness of this idea, of this new symbol."

"Are you any closer to identifying who was behind the bombing?" asked Eagleton. "You have to wonder, I think, whether Mr. Frost's demise might have been the handiwork of the very people who are seeking to create sympathy for the companion flag. I don't trade in conspiratorial theories, but what better way to manipulate the results here—to drum up support?"

"We don't—"

"There's no proof that Mr. Frost was killed by anti-companion flag forces, that I'm aware of."

"No, certainly not," replied Ngalie. "We feel it's connected to allegations that he stole the Şahin Diary."

"I get back, folks, to the question of who's really behind this crazy companion flag idea. Let me speak plainly: it's a *dangerous* idea . . . as most of you know by now." Eagleton pounded his fist on his desk before continuing. "Yes, I understand people are concerned about the contents of the Şahin Diary going public. But that news is one hundred years old. This companion flag is being waved in our faces right now."

"I understand, but—"

"It's designed to blot out capitalism and our way of life." Eagleton's voice changed pitch characteristically. "That's what they're up to. What would happen to American exceptionalism, I ask you, if we were to suddenly start raising our children under a flag that says "Oh, by the way, we're all the same?" No, we're *not* all the same. What were the sacrifices of our sons and daughters in Afghanistan and Iraq all about? This is the first step in a project designed to eliminate our freedoms, ladies and gentlemen . . . to end our God-given way of life. And can you imagine the impact this would have on some of our staunchest allies? Think of the companion flag flying below the flags of Israel and Palestine within a few hundred yards of each other. What if the same flag were visible on each side of the separation barrier? Israeli children being told that they are both different and the same as kids in Palestine. Palestinian kids being told the same thing. Israel's leadership should be very worried, my friends . . ."

*   *   *

At 22:10 local time, Jamaal Rachadi sent a text message to Fatimah: "Are you all right? Can I see you?"

Fatimah responded at 22:17: "I'm all right. I want to, but no, you were right. It's best if we don't."

*   *   *

"Len, it's Karen. Where are you?"

Len took a quick drink of bottled water. He moved a few steps away from the room's noisy air conditioner. "In my room at the hotel. Why?"

"We just got word from the CIA. They're picking up chatter. It's Charlotte Yacoubi."

"What do you mean?" He went back, switched off the air conditioner.

"Charlotte Yacoubi. She was the target . . . of the bombing."

"*What*?"

"She's with Armenian Relief. She was tracking Frost and Fatimah. She's after the Şahin Diary."

Len spun on his heels. "Wait a minute. How could—? What about the ICRC?" He crossed the hotel room and swept up the keys to his rental car and shoved them in his pocket. He squeezed the phone between his ear and shoulder and in one motion lifted his jacket from the back of the chair and began to put it on.

"She's with the Red Cross all right. Has been for three years. I confirmed it myself."

"What in the hell . . . ?" Len muttered, picking up his wallet and sliding it into the inside breast pocket of his coat. He glanced around the room quickly, his mind racing. Charlotte Yacoubi— the target? She's with Armenian Relief? Wait a minute—that means they know if she gets her hands on the diary, she'll publish it. What about Frost? Would he have—? Can this be?

Len hit the lights and threw open the door, stepping into the brightly lit, orange-and-gold-carpeted hallway. "She's still in danger then. I'm headed back to the hospital." He swallowed back the last word and turned ninety degrees away from another guest, a man in his mid-thirties with short-cropped brown hair and a goatee, walking toward him. He waited a beat or two. "Listen," he whispered, "I need you to call Fatimah. Tell her to send a car and a doctor to the hospital right away." He looked back over his shoulder to make sure he hadn't been overheard, then set off at a near run toward the elevator. "We need to get Abbas and Charlotte out of there. Ask if she can take them to her family compound. If not, we need to find someplace else. She'll know what to do."

"Right, Len."

"I've got to go."

Len dialed Mesona. He pictured the guard standing outside Charlotte's hospital room reaching for his phone, but Mesona didn't pick up. After the fifth ring, Len cursed himself for not getting the other guard's number, as well. Still holding the phone to his ear, he looked in either direction down the hallway as he waited for the silver elevator doors to open. The car was stopped three floors up. Come on, he mouthed silently. Come on, come on! He turned and spied the exit door. He clicked off the call, jammed the phone into his front pants pocket, then ran. A few seconds later he was flying down four flights of stairs, his mind daring him to leap over two or three steps at a time.

It was a five-minute drive to the hospital. He squealed to a stop in the parking lot and half ran, half walked through the building's main entrance. Once inside, he ran for an empty elevator. He thought about stopping at Abbas's floor—even put his finger over the number 6 on the panel—but no. He had tried Mesona twice more on the way, and still no answer.

He crossed from one side of the oversized elevator car to the other, leaned back against the rail, and ran his hand nervously over the top of his head. Hopefully, the guard's phone was dead. Or he'd just left it at the office. Maybe that wasn't his cell number. Maybe, he'd reached Mesona from Tashkent on a land line. He looked up at the floor indicator display. He was glad to have the car to himself, but this was, without a doubt, the slowest elevator he'd ever ridden. Four . . . okay, four . . . keep going . . . five . . . yes . . . come on . . . six. Don't stop. At last—eight. He exploded through the sliding doors into the sterile whiteness of the corridor. The nursing station, with its chairs pushed back, its monitors blinking, a congeries of files and charts spread over the desktop, seemed to be holding its breath, waiting for someone's return. There was no one in the hallway. The skin at the back of Len's neck contracted. He hadn't been sure what to expect, but this wasn't it.

A distant but soothing female voice called out over the hospital's PA system, "Dr. Hamid Najjar, line four please." Up and down the corridor only inanimate objects were visible beneath buzzing fluorescent lights—empty wheelchairs, gurneys, IV poles, portable computer stations, linen carts. Their silvered parts reflected points of light breaking the hard, cold shine of scrubbed linoleum. Mesona was nowhere to be seen.

Len ran toward Charlotte's room. He had gone only four steps when he nearly collided with a woman emerging from a patient's room rubbing sanitizer over her hands. It was the same nurse he had spoken to hours before. He skidded to a stop. She stepped back, alarmed. "What's going on?" she said in a high, trumpeting voice. She recognized him almost at once, and placing her hand against her chest she gave a relieved smile. "Oh, it's you." But her eyes remained wide behind her horn-rimmed glasses. "My, oh my, you scared me half to death."

"I'm sorry. I'm here to see Charlotte Yacoubi. This time I have to talk to her. Where's the—"

"Oh, okay," she said. A calm self-assurance seeped out of every pore of her face. He could feel his own anxiety moderate under her influence. "No running in the hall," she mothered. "Now, as to Ms. Yacoubi, you'll have to wait your turn. Someone else is with her now."

"Who?"

"Now that I couldn't tell you. He gave me his name, but I've forgotten it."

"Where's the guard?"

She looked down the hallway. "I don't kn—Hey! Where are you going? What did I say about running?"

Len tore past the curtain. "Char—!" Charlotte was gone. "Shit!" He looked around the room. The door to the bathroom was open. Inside, slumped in a corner, was Mesona. His hands and feet were bound, and his mouth was covered with black duct tape. He'd been knocked unconscious. There was no sign of a struggle. A cut drip line lay across the bed, leaving a small wet spot on the sheet where Charlotte had lain. Len looked up at a half-full IV bag. She was just here, he thought. He ran out into the hall. No one—only the nurse twenty yards away, near the spot where he'd left her. She was once again busy at a portable computer terminal, but this time when she saw Len running toward her, she began to run toward him.

"What is it?" she cried out.

They swerved around one another, for he was as intent on the stairwell as she was on reaching Charlotte's room.

"The guard's in there. He needs help. This other man—what time did he arrive?" Len demanded.

"What is it? What's the—?"

"*What time?*"

"Only a few minutes ago!" she said as she turned and ran.

They can't be far, he thought. With her injuries, and the need to keep her hidden, they'll be moving slow. Still, they've probably made it outside the building by now.

Len knew the stairs were the only sure bet. No telling how long the elevator would take. He tried to focus his mind as his legs churned and his body plunged down the gray, unpainted cement stairwell. When he passed the door for the fifth floor, something like a rhythm took hold and he began jumping down four steps at a time and swinging wildly at the landings. At last, he reached the ground floor and crashed through the door, exiting out onto the main concourse, frightening several people on the other side. A teenage girl screamed and was pulled in close by her father.

Len looked each way until he spied the exit to the parking lot. He ran as fast as he could, shouting for a doctor dressed in blue scrubs to get out of the way, and yelling "*Look out!*" when a man and woman walking slowly, arm in arm, veered into his path.

He hit the door with a ferocious impact that sent it banging against the stop. In the next instant, he was swallowed by the windless night, a world of darkness, the light droning of tropical insects, a thin, almost imperceptible fog, dim lights. He stopped only long enough to get his bearings, then ran across a gray margin of lawn toward the parking lot, toward rows of tightly packed automobiles—pale and denatured, or black and featureless beneath inverted cones of misty light. The lot stretched in two directions. His own car was to the right, but because the exit was on the left, he guessed they would have parked to the left. He set off in that direction, his feet pounding on the pavement.

He looked over the tops of cars for any sign—brake lights, a movement, a noise.

Exactly what am I doing? he wondered, as a spasm of fear ran through him. What will happen next? But he didn't slow. He reached the end of the parking lot and turned and ran back. He stopped and jumped up on the bumper of a pickup. Peering out over the cab, he spotted a sudden and violent movement between two vehicles—a white van and a dark sedan. He heard a low, muffled cry edged in anger and desperation. His heart stopped. It had to be her. From this distance, it looked like there was only one assailant, but how could he be sure? Had he seen a third arm swing out? And was he—or were they—armed? Probably. Yes, almost certainly. He realized he had forgotten to check to see if the guard's weapon was missing. He heard another cry, this one ending in a growl of struggle.

"Charlotte," he said, swallowing back a shout. He jumped down. What now? he wondered. Keeping a row of cars between them, he ran, bent over at the waist. He stopped twice to judge the distance remaining. His knees began to ache. His heart raced and set up an uneven drumming in his chest. And I'm going to do what exactly? he thought, stopping with an awkward lurch behind a black Mercedes SUV. He rose up slowly to peer through the vehicle's windows at the spectacle now playing out only thirty yards away. There were two men all right, and Charlotte, the right side of her face and her right arm dark with injury, struggling mightily as they tried to lift her and deposit her in the back of the white van. One man held a towel against her mouth, which made his efforts more difficult. Her muffled cries continued, high-pitched and pained one moment, low and fierce the next. At last the two men—both in their late twenties, dark-skinned, wearing light-colored tunics—managed to hoist Charlotte into the vehicle and slam the door shut.

Suddenly realizing there was no sensible answer to the question what to do next, Len stood up and shouted in his deepest voice, "Hey! What are you doing? Stop!"

The two men, now on either side of the van, opened their respective doors and jumped in. The brake lights went on and its engine roared to life.

Len ran between the Mercedes and sedan parked next to it. He slapped the side of the white Ford van as it backed then screeched to a stop. He heard the gears grinding as the driver slammed into drive. Len continued to pound, but then, realizing it was no use, he tore off in the direction of his rental car as fast as he could run.

XXVI

He jumped in and started the car, shifting into reverse. The tires smoked as the rented Lexus veered to the left then stopped with a violent jerk. He found drive, turned on the headlights, and peeled off, fishtailing between two rows of parked cars. He craned his neck, searching for the white van. At last he spotted it, on the road outside the hospital grounds, driving the opposite direction. He had to think—and quick. In a few seconds they would be lost. Just then a landscaped feature came into view, a traffic divider jutting out between the parked cars. He spun the wheel and hit the curb at fifteen miles per hour. The front end of the red Lexus bounced high in the air and came crashing down on a row of bushes. Len punched the accelerator as the back end shot skyward. When it hit the ground again, the spinning tires chewed up leaves, dirt, flowers, and bark chips by the bushel, sending a cloud of debris more than fifty feet over the tops of a half dozen parked cars. The front end bounced down again in the street. A horn sounded, and in the corner of his eyes Len saw headlights—one second filling the driver's side rearview mirror, the next veering to the left and moving safely past him. An uncanny effect, smooth, deceptive. And all the while Len was spinning the wheel and leaning heavily to the right trying to coax the Lexus into the right-hand lane while the back wheels had yet to find the road's surface. He let out an anticipatory groan, half expecting a crash. One car had gotten past, but what about the next? Surely there was another. But the impact he expected never came. He straightened. The car fishtailed beneath him until it found its footing. Another horn blast, but this one seemed innocuous. "Don't blame you," Len said aloud, checking the rearview mirror then pushing the accelerator to the floor.

The first car had pulled ahead and stopped, and its driver had just begun to step angrily from the car when Len sped past, forcing the man back into the driver's seat.

"All right, where are you?" Len mumbled under his breath as he scanned the road and the brake lights ahead. He soon had the Lexus cruising at sixty-five, slowing but not stopping at intersections, flashing his lights at cars ahead to warn them that he was passing. He had gone two miles from the hospital when he spied the white van a couple blocks ahead. It leaned heavily one way and another as it sped through traffic. Len pressed more speed out of the Lexus until only one block separated them.

Stay with them, he said to himself, honking to discourage the cars in front of him from switching lanes. The van turned right at a busy intersection and Len followed suit. He pivoted around to try to find the name of the street. There it was—Jacaranda Boulevard. And which way are we going? he wondered. He saw the blinking lights of another plane landing at Sanori International. The airport was east of town, he thought. All right, we're heading northbound. He looked down at the gas gauge. Half a tank. That's good. His heart and his thoughts started to settle somewhat.

Len reached for his cell phone. Balancing it above the steering wheel, he was able to locate Fatimah's number and touched it quickly.

"Fatimah, it's Len." He could hear a loud thrumming sound coming from the phone's speaker. "Where are you?" he shouted. Len had to swerve to avoid hitting an on-coming car. The tires squealed loudly.

"We've just picked up Abbas. We're at the hospital. Where are—"

"Listen, Fatimah. I need your help. They've taken Charlotte."

"*What?*"

"Two men in a white van. I'm following them. A late-model Ford. We just turned on Jacaranda Boulevard, northbound. We're traveling at about sixty, sixty-five. Can you notify the police?"

"Of course. Hold on." Fatimah clicked off. Len noticed he'd fallen a bit further behind. He started to speed up, but just then a rusty old Nissan pickup angled into the lane ahead of him. The driver was an old man with white hair as bright as his skin was dark. He was going no more than sixty, fifteen kilometers per hour under the speed limit. Len was on his bumper in no time. He honked and steered the Lexus left and right to try to see past the truck. The white van was quickly doubling then tripling the distance between them, growing noticeably smaller.

Len banged on the steering wheel with his open palm. "Shit!" He was blocked on the right and there was too much oncoming traffic to risk passing on the left. He honked again and flashed his lights, leaving the brights on this time. The old man, his neck and shoulders illuminated beneath a heavily sweat-stained flat hat, waved innocently. He leaned forward and made a playful bouncing gesture as if to say, "I'm getting everything I can out of her."

"Good Lord," moaned Len, ducking down in an attempt to see through the pickup's windows. Were the taillights visible in the distance those of the Ford van, or had another car, or cars, taken its place? A bit of a space opened up, enough to allow him to swerve into the oncoming lane for a split second view.

The Lexus heeled over violently into the southbound lane and righted itself again. Two blocks ahead, in the time it took him to swerve back, he saw a sliver of the white van dipping, preparing to turn sharply to the right. Back in his own lane, Len slowed to create space ahead of him, then ran up and drifted intentionally to the right, squeezing the car next to him. He would have called this "nerfing" back in high school, but it didn't have the same .. . well, it was different. The car to his right, a silver Subaru, sped up, honked. Len glanced over his shoulder and made eye contact with its driver, who was gesturing angrily. At least two other young men—perhaps there was a third—were in the car with him. "Welcome to Tucson, bitch!" he mouthed as his eyes darted to the rearview mirror. He hit the gas and nosed into a moving, ever-narrowing gap of no more than fifteen feet, putting the passenger-side front quarter-panel of his rental car less than four feet from the Subaru's headlight. He was only seconds away from impact with the old truck. If the youthful driver didn't hit the brake—and fast—the game would be up. But Len didn't back off—wouldn't. Sanori rules. Hey, kid, he thought, this'll be all the rage if you play it smart. The young driver slammed on his brakes and his car squealed and yawed to a stop, his horn and several behind him blaring, while Len's Lexus sped happily on in his lane. "I guess I still have it," Len said, glancing back to make sure the boys weren't rear-ended, then he intoned "Mm-hmm, that's right," keeping his mind occupied until he could make the corner ahead.

The cell phone screen lit up. "Len?"

"I'm here."

"They're on the way. Where are you now?"

"Just turning," Len exclaimed excitedly. He looked up at the blue-and-white street sign. "Sbinthi Road. Eastbound." He heard Fatimah repeat, "Jacaranda to Sbinthi Road, eastbound," with her mouth away from the phone. Once on Sbinthi Road,

Len had a clear lane ahead. He unleashed the Lexus's 4.6-liter V8, forcing something like the sound of a high surf from the front end. Within seconds, he saw the white van passing rhythmically under the misty inverted cones of light cast by the streetlights. Len was gaining on it. Suddenly, the van's brake lights lit up. It swerved violently to the left and was swallowed up in the darkness of a side street. Len made the intersection five seconds later, but he had to apply his turn signal and wait for oncoming traffic to clear. "Jesus!" he said, "Come on, come on. Hurry up!"

"What is it?" came Fatimah's voice.

He hit the accelerator and at the same time began shouting down at the cell phone. "Turning again . . . on . . ." But he hadn't yet found a street sign and he began twisting one way and another.

"We're on it," came Fatimah's calm voice.

"*What?*" Just then Len heard the deep thrum and *fit-fit-fit-fit* of helicopter blades slicing the air behind him. It was so loud, so sudden, that he ducked involuntarily, slammed on the brakes, and gazed up through the sunroof. The roar was breathtaking, and no less galvanizing was the sight of a six-thousand-pound jet black Agusta Westland 139 banking across the sky, negotiating a sharp left turn, 150 feet above the ground. It took him a second or two to register the white markings illuminated on the fuselage—the presidential seal—and by that time the sleek vessel was invisible, no more than the sum of its blinking green, red, and white running lights and the banshee cry of its Pratt & Whitney engines in pursuit of a target. Len pictured Fatimah in that screaming vehicle. Of course, he thought. That was the noise he'd heard from the hospital—in the background. They'd come for Abbas in a helicopter—a faster, safer alternative. And now, as the helicopter slowed and hovered over the white van, he smiled to himself and hit the gas with a new thrill of excitement. The van sped up, turned yet again, and the helicopter spun above it, its noise filling the air with an ear-splitting drumming. Len kept pace behind the white van, wondering now what the next move would be—could be—should be. "They're probably armed, Fatimah," he shouted.

"Yes. Copy that."

The black helicopter continued to hover above the van for three or four more miles. Len struggled to keep up, now having no idea what street they were on. He kept one eye on the aircraft and another on the road and unmarked intersections flying by. This is crazy, he thought. Suddenly, the pilot switched on a searchlight, bathing the white van in a sharp, vibrating, blue-white luminance. Was the pilot looking for a place to drop down—away from buildings, trees, and wires? Would he or she try to intimidate the driver into stopping by putting the landing skids only feet from the windshield, like he'd seen in a movie once?

Len watched in anticipation. The van's driver seemed to spot another street—an elevated expressway. He sped up dramatically, turned onto the on-ramp. The helicopter turned with the van, dipped forward, and followed the Ford easily. But then, inexplicably, the copter shot up and angled away. What are you doing? Len thought. Why are they breaking off? In no time, Fatimah's helicopter was more than a mile away.

"Fatimah, what's happening?" Len shouted. He hit the gas hard and fishtailed onto the on-ramp himself. He punched it, hoping to catch sight of the white van the minute he crested the hill, before it could be lost in traffic. When he hit the top of the ramp, Len was traveling over 150 kilometers per hour. But the expressway was empty, and within seconds, on either side of him, two blue-and-white police helicopters screamed past at less than one hundred feet, in tandem. He looked up ahead. There were the taillights of the white van, and another mile or two farther up the abandoned expressway, a row of police vehicles stretched across the road with blue-and-reds flashing, illuminating the guardrails on either side.

"Stay back, Len," came Fatimah's voice. "Let the police handle this." Just as he heard this, a group of seven or eight police cars sped past him with their lights flashing. Len slowed, although his heart continued to race. And slowing, he would later realize, was a relative thing, for he did not drop below eighty kilometers per hour, and he arrived at the scene only moments after the driver and his accomplice had come out of the van with their hands up.

Pulling over at last, he got out and stood by his open door while the police secured the scene. He turned to see Fatimah's grandfather's black helicopter settle on the pavement a short distance away. Fatimah emerged from the aircraft and began running, bent over, toward the white van, followed by a man dressed in a white shirt and dark brown trousers. Len ran to meet them.

Fatimah shouted over the slowly subsiding engines, her head scarf swept back by the helicopter's prop wash. "Len, this is Dr. Sayeed." Len shook the doctor's hand as they continued half-walking, half-running. Fatimah turned. "Is she all right?"

"I don't know," answered Len.

When they reached the white van the driver and his accomplice were lying facedown on the ground with their hands handcuffed behind them. Len noticed something and leaned over to see the starfish tattoo on one man's wrist. When he looked around at the side of the man's face he recognized him as the man he'd seen in the photo taken at the airport. A policeman was just opening the van's side door.

"Please," said Dr. Sayeed, stepping past the policeman. He ducked in but began backing out almost at once.

"Let me out," came Charlotte's voice.

"Are you sure?" said Dr. Sayeed. "Yes, yes, of course. Here, let me help you."

Fatimah and Len both stepped forward and offered their hands, as well, but neither dared touch the enflamed right arm or the bandaged left arm. Charlotte took hold of Fatimah's hand and with difficulty picked herself up and stepped out onto the pavement. Relief and exhaustion settled in her green eyes. She sagged against Len's body and he now held her up almost completely.

"Is it over?" she whimpered. "It is, isn't it?"

"We must get her into bed," said the physician. "I need to restart her IV at once."

Fatimah turned to the officer. "We're taking her out to my father's compound."

The policeman touched the rim of his cap. "Yes, Ms. Ibrahim."

"Do not discuss this with the press, do you understand?" Fatimah held the officer in her stare.

"Yes, of course," the officer replied. "I'll let the men know."

"You may make arrangements to interview her in due time."

The officer stood aside, touched his cap again. "Of course, Ms. Ibrahim."

When they reached the presidential helicopter and opened the passenger door, Len looked for Abbas and found him lying on a stretcher behind the rearmost passenger seats.

"Is she all right?" Abbas asked, forcing himself up on an elbow. His eyes arched with concern as he saw the heavily bandaged woman for the first time since the bombing. "Charlotte! Are you—?"

"She may be in shock," shouted the doctor over the rising din from the engines and the whir of blades accelerating above their heads.

Charlotte looked up at the doctor, then at Abbas. "I'm not in shock," she said slowly, "but I will never ride in a van or limousine again." She locked her eyes on Abbas. "Tell me you don't drive a van."

Abbas grinned. He looked at Len. Their two relieved smiles grew wide together.

Dr. Sayeed got in the helicopter and straightened the second stretcher lying across the cabin in front of the passenger seats, making it ready for Charlotte. Len had begun to back away from the helicopter when he felt Fatimah's hand on his back. "Come with us, Len," she shouted over the noise.

"I've got my car," he shouted back.

Fatimah shook her head. "We'll take care of that. And we'll get your things at the hotel. Get in. We've had enough to worry about for one night."

XXVII

———

Len heard voices beyond the bamboo door to Abbas's room, glottal intonations over music, softly playing—Uzbek music—and in the distance the sound of waves crashing against the shore. Before he could raise his hand to knock, the door swung open. Out stepped a large, dark woman carrying a bundle of tan sheets, towels, and pillowcases. Her wide smile revealed a company of uneven white teeth and a lateral incisor that billowed with gold. Her gums were heavily pigmented. "Well, good morning, sir," she said, turning sideways to let Len by.

"Good morning."

"You're up early."

Len sniffed a pleasant amalgam of the woman's scent and the morning sea air that wafted across Abbas's private deck, past the screens of his windows and open sliding door. "Am I?" Len had already spent a leisurely hour on his own deck with black coffee, a croissant, and a printout of the *New York Times Online*. Now it was past eight. Was that early? "I've been sunning myself for the last hour." He moved into the room backwards. "How's our patient?"

He turned to see Abbas's feet then his hands and torso come into view around a corner. Abbas was holding a remote control, raising his bed, perhaps preparing to answer for himself. "Oh, he's going to be just fine."

Len turned back to the woman. "Are you—?"

"I'm President Mohadji's nurse, Dab. I work with Dr. Sayeed here at the compound. He was just here, by the way. Says Mr. Ahkmedova is doing very well—running out of excuses. That's what he always says. 'Mr. President, you're running out of excuses.' Now Mr. Ahkmedova is running out of excuses." Dab threw her head back and to the side and chuckled roundly.

"Excellent," said Len.

Abbas shifted up higher in the adjustable bed to prepare for Len's visit. Len backed further into the room. "All right then. Well, thank you, Dab."

Dab looked past Len. "You ring if you need anything, Mr. A."

She was already several steps away when Abbas mumbled, "Thank you."

Len closed the door, hesitated. He felt a pang of disappointment to find Abbas so awake—*this* awake, and sitting up. One less reason to delay the inevitable, he thought. He turned and, rubbing his chin, walked slowly toward the windows, toward a long row of tan, translucent curtains settling back into place now that the door was closed and the breezeway was shut off. He gazed out at the sea as though impelled to compare the panoramic view from this room to that from his own. Vaguely aware that Abbas was staring at him, he turned and looked around the room, smiling now at an enormous Gauguin—a giant at forty inches by seventy-two—above the sofa. Len had seen this work a half dozen times over the years in art books and magazines, but this was the real McCoy. "Not bad, huh?" he said, stepping closer to examine the artist's open, thick, accessible signature.

"Not bad," said Abbas. "Can you believe this room?"

"You should see the rest of the place. I had to pack a lunch to get here."

Abbas laughed out loud and immediately put his hand on his chest and closed his eyes. He recovered, still smiling. "Did you hear about the debate—the delay, I mean?" Abbas asked at length.

"Yes, I heard," Len answered, still staring at the artwork. He'd been thinking about the impact of the delay on his job at Majestic, but then he probably didn't have a job waiting for him anymore anyway. At last he turned toward his friend. "Are you all right?"

"Yes. Is your room like this?"

Len moved along the wall to a mounted sculpture, the mottled, blockish likeness of a lion with its right front paw raised. A small plaque in Arabic revealed the date: 1200 B.C. He lightly brushed the animal's ears to touch time. "Oh, yes. *Quite*, as they say."

"Tell me about it."

Len glanced over his shoulder. "My room?"

"No. Last night. How and why we got here. I guess I know the how . . . but why? What happened?"

Still studying the sculpture, Len thought back to the night before, to the slow passage of time that began when the helicopter, with a mighty synchronic roar of engines, lifted off the expressway and, once airborne and tracking toward the compound, passed neatly eastward over the lights of Sanori. He was seated wearing a headset in the dimly lit cabin opposite the head of Charlotte Yacoubi, who lay covered in a tan blanket on a stretcher. Len's right shoulder pressed hard against the left of Dr. Omar Sayeed. Twice he'd looked away to avoid eye contact with Charlotte, and by the expression that crossed her face it seemed that perhaps she understood what had been revealed to him. How else could he have found her? Why else would he have come back to the hospital? In the humming, gently vibrating cabin no one spoke. Fatimah reached over at one point and reassuringly touched Charlotte's ankle through the blanket, but no one spoke—save the pilot to a businesslike female voice on the ground. Len found himself thinking of Abbas lying on a stretcher on the floor behind them. He pictured Abbas for some reason with his uninjured arm raised, his hand on his forehead. He doesn't know, Len thought. For him, Charlotte is still who she said she was. Was Len angry? Hell, yes—and worried about Abbas.

Len turned away from the sculpture and made his way to the foot of Abbas's bed. "Listen, I'm not sure how to tell you this, so I'll just come out with it." He cleared his throat and took a breath. "I got a call from Karen last night at the hotel. They've picked up chatter. Charlotte Yacoubi is an agent for Armenian Relief. She's—"

"*What?*"

"She's not who she says she is." Len hesitated, looked away from the incipient disappointment and disbelief that darkened his friend's face and deepened the lines that stretched over his forehead. "They think she was the intended target of the bombing."

Abbas's mouth fell open. He seemed for a time incapable of speech.

"I know," said Len. "It's—"

Abbas leaned forward. His face turned pale. "But . . . how could that be?"

Len shook his head. "They were after her, and she was after the Şahin Diary. That's what this whole thing has been about."

Abbas stared off into space, then his eyes focused on something closer in. Finally, he looked back at Len. "The diary," he whispered helplessly. "She wanted the diary."

Len nodded. He waited for Abbas to say something else, but nothing came. "I'm sorry, man," said Len at last. He stepped away from the bed, rubbing his fingers over his mouth. Should

I tell him about the Red Cross job? he wondered. Yes, it's a miti-gating fact, isn't it? He turned and sat on the arm of a loveseat, facing Abbas. "Karen says she was recruited. That she really does work for the Red Cross in Tashkent . . . so to that extent she was telling the truth. But someone convinced her to get involved. I don't know how or why, or any . . . details."

Abbas's eyes were following a new thought, but they came back to Len. "And you're sure of this?"

"After last night, can there be any doubt?" Len asked. "I mean—" He saw his friend's attention begin to drift off again, pulled away. "What is it?"

"At the airport . . . they took her aside, said they had no record of her visa. They would have sent her back to Tashkent if I hadn't vouched for her." Abbas sat back, deflated. He stared off toward the picturesque horizon, toward the ocean's dark, undulating, illusory edge, beyond its talkative breakers. "And why do they say she was the target?" he asked distantly.

"Because if she got her hands on the diary, it was going to be published. And I'm guessing they either know, or have a pretty good idea, what's in it."

"About the genocide," Abbas whispered.

Len saw Abbas's distress and slid over, falling into the love-seat. No hurry, he thought. He's hurting. I'll stay for as long as it takes.

Twenty seconds later, Abbas snickered. "She told me she wanted to come out here to get to know Fatimah better. And that business at the airport . . . She was so upset when Fatimah took off. I think that upset her more than the shooting in Tashkent."

What business at the airport? Len wondered. Well, he'd find out later. And then he heard himself say, "It's crazy—she's crazy." He regretted this almost at once. This is the woman he wants more than anything, you idiot. He remembered something he'd seen on television, a psychologist explaining the power of intentional and "*a*ttentional" silence in the presence of suffering. It was time to put it to use.

Abbas continued, "She was after the diary . . . thought Fatimah had it . . . that Msaidie was a friend there to help Fatimah get it out of Uzbekistan." His voice grew stronger and deeper with conviction. "When Msaidie showed his colors, she knew others were after it . . . that they were willing to kill to get it. She saw what she'd gotten herself into." A satisfied smile played briefly at the corners of his mouth. "But she didn't give up."

Len, who was sitting with his right hand over his mouth, let the hand fall into his lap. Was he complimenting her now?

Abbas continued, "When Fatimah got a second chance to fly to Tashir, Charlotte didn't hesitate." He looked closely at Len. "That's amazing, isn't it?"

"Amazing? I guess so . . . I'm not sure. Is it?" *What about the fact that she lied to us? That she's not who she said she was?*

"*I* think so." Abbas settled back against a bright white, creased pillow. His half-smiling mouth went slack, then closed on his next breath. His eyes grew wide as though he were hearing something that swelled in intensity.

Len was glad for the break, glad the Uzbek was looking away from him. He noticed the two-day growth of whiskers against the man's jaw, the unruffled—kempt—look of his black, short-cropped hair. *You're a handsome one*, he thought. *No doubt Charlotte thinks so. But, hey, she lied to you, dude. Have you thought what might have happened had you gotten between her and that diary?* Len imagined Charlotte's oval face before the burns and bandages. He tried to find in her arching brow, in the olive skin and emerald green eyes, a telltale sign of her quest for the Şahin Diary—some warning, some slipup to catch her at her game. But, alas, he couldn't. She'd been too good. He'd believed her: the bit about the companion flag and Frost's alleged visit to her childhood school. *Too good, too quick on her feet*, he decided. She'd have been a hell of a poker player. Len was jarred from his musings by the sound of Abbas's voice.

" . . . when they made the decision to charge them with espionage. You were right, of course. Frost would have been executed—not publicly, but still . . . "

Len leaned closer. "I'm sorry? I missed—"

"He would have been dead within the year," Abbas continued, still staring out blindly. "In prison. I wasn't going to let that happen. Couldn't—couldn't have lived with myself." Abbas bent his good leg up and cupped his hand over his knee. He raised his head off the pillow. "My timing was off, is all . . . thrown off, really. When Guryanov agreed to let Frost and Fatimah come down here, I thought, 'Well, now, wait a minute. Maybe it's not necessary.' I mean, maybe they weren't serious . . . he is an American, after all. Does Guryanov really want to go to the mat with the Americans? At least, I thought, there's more time." Abbas fell silent then, and before he picked up his thread again two sets of waves—three giants in each—crashed ashore, each shattering the morning's tropical ambient calm with a heavy, oddly surprising, earth-crushing thud followed by a long, sibilant *ba-wissshhhh*.

Len could smell the sea and shore, and gave himself—part of himself—over to the ocean's surging rhythms. The art of silence, he thought. He resisted the temptation to break the spell by going out in search of another cup of coffee, although he formed the idea of wanting one desperately. He could see in Abbas's eyes that the man was searching for something, sorting his thoughts.

"I was wrong, of course," Abbas said at last. "Wrong as far as Frost is concerned." Abbas looked down at his broken leg, no longer elevated but fitted with a long, thick, round cast half-hidden beneath a crisp top sheet. "Or Charlotte . . . and hundreds of others."

"I'm afraid I don't follow you, old man," said Len, sliding forward to the edge of the loveseat. He'd reluctantly concluded that his friend was suffering from some mild disorientation, perhaps caused by something Dr. Sayeed had given him along with the shock of the news about Charlotte. And it wouldn't be surprising if Abbas hadn't slept well, or at all.

"I should have taken it back," Abbas mumbled.

"Say, why don't I go get you—"

"I couldn't think of a way."

"—some tea. What's that? I'm sorry?"

Abbas turned to him, clear-eyed. "The diary. The Şahin Diary. I have it."

A shudder ran up Len's back, straightening his spine with a jerk. This was more than disorientation. This was insanity. Len felt his skin contract.

"I have it. I've always had it. For the last nine months. I . . . I took it."

Len sprang to his feet. "Bullshit."

"No. It's true. I was going to take it back. I *was*. It's just that . . . they didn't know it was gone until Frost and Fatimah were arrested. Even then, I thought . . ."

"Wait a minute!" Len's brown eyes were wide open, his head thrust forward. A curved vein bulged at the side of his neck. "Are you saying this is real? That you have the Şahin Diary? Or are you just saying this now because . . . because you know Charlotte wants it?"

Abbas looked away, nodded. "I have it. Not with me of course. In Tashkent. I was going to return it. I just hadn't figured out how and when, and then when Frost and Fatimah were arrested, I knew I had to. I had to find a way . . . and I was going to." Abbas's eyes found Len's again. "But, like I said, when Guryanov gave the go-ahead for them to leave Uzbekistan, to come here, I thought I had more time. I miscalculated—badly.

And it cost Frost his life—Frost and the others. I'm responsible for their deaths."

Len's hands turned up involuntarily, then dropped to his sides. He stood with his mouth open, breathless. "*You* have the diary?" he managed at last.

Abbas wet his lips. "Yes."

When Len next moved, it was to cross the room and return again with his hand on the back of his neck. "Oh my God, I can't believe this. Now wait a minute. You have . . . And no one knew it was missing until Frost and Fatimah were arrested."

"Right," said Abbas. "People had forgotten about it . . . didn't even think to look, I suppose, until . . ."

"Until there was a reason to suspect." Len turned again, staring blindly up at the ceiling. He exhaled through pursed lips.

"Right. And then it was going to be harder to put it back. I knew they'd be watching the school. I was wracking my brain."

And then it dawned on Len: This is what Abbas had tried to tell him in the hospital, before he fell asleep under the influence of the medication.

There were voices, a short peal of laughter, coming from the hallway. Two people passing by. Len waited. "So you just . . . ? *Fuck me*," he groaned, squeezing his eyes shut and touching his forehead with his thumb and forefinger as though magically, fervently, wishing it all away. He turned and began hitting his forehead with the base of his palm. Three times he did this, and then he stopped. "Why'd you take it, for Christ's sake? What did you want with it? I can't believe this!"

"I wanted . . ." Abbas shifted his position to take pressure off one hip and place it on the other. He winced with pain. "To clear my great-grandmother's name, to clear our family's name—on my mother's side." Abbas looked up. The quizzical expression painted on Len's face seemed to catalyze the Uzbek. "My great-grandmother, Gayane Apovian. I told you she was

Armenian. She was accused of fraternizing with the enemy, with the Ittihadists, during World War I . . . of having an affair with an Ottoman colonel named Yilmaz."

Len couldn't believe what he was hearing, but he couldn't gather his thoughts enough to speak, either.

Abbas continued. "He was an adjutant on the staff of General Karabekir of the Fifteenth Army Corps, East Anatolia."

"So this had nothing do with Charlotte," said Len weakly, still trying to get his bearings.

Abbas ignored him, or didn't hear. "The Fifteenth was packed with released criminals, zealots, and thugs. They were the main perpetrators of the genocide, of the mass deportations and killings of Armenians . . . of the *alleged* mass deportations and killings." Abbas set his jaw and squinted as though tasting his own bile. He reached for a cup of water on the bedside table and drank from a straw. He set the cup down again and stared at it for a long moment, collecting his thoughts. "Colonel Yilmaz was a munitions expert, demolitions, that sort of thing."

"What?" said Len.

"It was rumored after the war that he'd ordered the firebombing of a depot at Muş, where over two hundred Armenian families perished. Locked inside. Anyone who tried to escape was shot. Children were shot clambering out the windows. Men died trying to dig their way out with their hands." Abbas looked out to sea again.

Children in windows? Men digging? Why are you talking about this? Who the hell are you? Len wanted to shout. He rubbed the side of his jaw. All of a sudden, Abbas's face took on an unfamiliar aspect. Something in its color, or shape—yes, the angle of the cheekbones, at least in this light—seemed strange. Why hadn't he noticed this before? So you've had the diary this whole time? You've had us trying to protect one of our citizens for something *you* did. Why didn't you tell me, you son of a bitch? And why are you going on now about something that happened a hundred years ago, that no one can prove anyway? Frost is dead. The others are dead. You killed them! None of this would have happened if—. Remembering Charlotte then, he thought, you're both liars—is that it? Maybe you deserve each other. It took several seconds for Len to catch up with the words that had begun to slowly issue out of Abbas's mouth.

"My great-grandmother was a singer. Just seventeen at the time. She performed with a band—Turks and Armenians. It was rumored that she was seduced by Colonel Emir Yilmaz after a performance in Erzurum. That they began a lengthy affair. She denied this, denied knowing him—even meeting him—but she and her family were expelled from Yerevan when the war ended. They were under constant death threats. They came to Uzbekistan. Andijan first, then Bukhara. The rumors followed her and have persisted in the Armenian ex-patriot community ever since. Even my mother, the granddaughter of Gayane Apovian, has received death threats as recently as two months ago. They've started a campaign to ruin my father's business even though he had nothing to do with any of this."

He closed his eyes a moment before going on. "I clearly remember her—my Great-Grandmama Gayane. She was a very old woman defending herself to the end, and I remember the shame that my mother felt—or I should say, she denied feeling, but I knew. Some of my most vivid memories from childhood are of her arguing with neighbors about the unreliability of the rumors that were attached to the name Gayane Apovian. 'She has been defamed,' my mother would say. 'Don't believe everything you hear. My grandmother was beautiful, and the rumors were started by someone jealous of her beauty.'" Abbas carried the weight of his story above his eyes, on arching brows. "When I was older—fifteen, sixteen—I began to get word that people were speaking about me behind my back, that even though I was Uzbek, I was the great-grandson of a famous Armenian traitor. I wanted to ask my mother for more details, but something prevented me. Probably the hurt that I knew it caused her. She would be upset for days after these contentious conversations . . . and it was no better after my great-grandmother died. People continued to spread rumors, to point fingers, to draw my mother's ire—and my own.

"Finally, I began to research this Colonel Yilmaz. I discovered that he was a friend and constant companion of Ali Şahin, the author of the notorious Şahin Diary. I didn't know the diary was in Uzbekistan until I went to work for the Interior Ministry. Even then it was just happenstance . . . someone mentioned to me that the Şahin Diary was being held under the jurisdiction of the minister at Public School 32." Abbas lay his head back. "It was too much of a temptation. Here was a chance to disprove the allegations against my great-grandmother—at least potentially. I could protect my father and mother from these slanders. If they were such close friends, Şahin and Yilmaz, there was a good chance Şahin would have mentioned the colonel, and would have put the lie to rumors about his involvement with an Armenian singer named Gayane Apovian."

Len walked back to the loveseat and sat down. He was not prepared to be persuaded, and showed as much by sitting back, crossing his arms, and lifting his right foot up over his left knee.

Abbas watched him, but only so long as Len's eyes did not meet his, then he looked out to sea again, seeming to wait on the rhythmic crashing waves, to catch the right moment to begin to speak again. "I thought, 'I have to get my hands on the diary.' I wasn't sure what I was going to do with it, but I was sure of one thing: it would prove my great-grandmother's innocence. I didn't know how, but I sensed it—felt this was the only way to absolve my mother's name, to dispel the cloud over our heads."

Abbas looked to Len for understanding. "My father is not even Armenian, and yet they are persecuting him."

Len scoffed. "So you took it. You stole it."

Abbas was not fully called back by the sound of his friend's voice, but he nodded. "I took it. I knew—I could tell—it hadn't been disturbed for over ninety years. It seemed clear that no one would miss it. Not for another hundred years, at least. Like I say, it was all but forgotten."

Abbas stopped, interrupted by some other thought. He began to squeeze and pull on his lower lip.

Len tried to quell a core of anger glowing red-hot in the pit of his stomach. He imagined the gaping hole at what was once the ornate entrance to the Al Maseer Hotel. Then he remembered the trusting expression on the face of Alden Frost when he reassured Fatimah, "I've got the power of the United States behind me. Mr. Williams is here to get me out, and I'm sure he will."

"God damn it, why didn't you tell me? I mean, we could have found a way to—"

"I tried."

"Like hell you did!"

"I did."

"When?"

"At your apartment. You said you didn't want to talk about it. I tried to bring it up. I asked you if you'd ever done something you regretted, something that you knew could hurt people, but you said . . . you cut me off, said you didn't want to talk about it."

Len closed his eyes, grimaced. "Shit. Okay, okay." He exhaled a long breath. "I thought that was about gambling. About Laura. I didn't know you . . ."

"No."

Len was at war with his anger, felt it warming under the skin of his face. He stared at the statue of the lion for a few seconds, then looked across the room at Abbas. "This is fucking incredible. You took the damn thing, and now Frost and more than one hundred others are dead. You're sitting there in pieces, and half of Charlotte's face is . . ." He stopped himself. What good does it do? he thought. You couldn't have known that a book collecting dust for a century would cause all this. "All right, so what does it say," he continued. "Does it mention your great-grandmother?"

Abbas turned toward Len's voice. He tilted his head as though he'd not understood at first, then his face softened with comprehension. "Oh, yes. It mentions her all right."

"So?"

"Gayane Apovian was the lover of Colonel Yilmaz for fourteen months, met with him secretly in three different provinces, and spent a week with him in January 1918 at the home of the Ittihadist leader Emir Aşik in Adana. Secret letters of transit were provided to her, allowing her to pass checkpoints unmolested."

Len heard the disappointment in Abbas's voice, and sat in silence. When Abbas held his gaze, Len pressed his lips together, swallowed back a dry lump of anger, and nodded once. The news had devastated him, Len thought.

"I can't tell my mother," Abbas added, once again speaking in a detached voice. "It would kill her. And there's nothing I can do to protect my father's business."

So your gamble didn't pay off, Len thought, taking a deep breath. Like any gambler, you figured you had things under control, but you didn't. Len thought then of his own gambling debts, of the secrets he'd tried to keep from Laura. And Charlotte, he said to himself several seconds later. I guess she was gambling, too.

Abbas seemed to read his mind. "It's all a gamble. I lost."

I should walk out of here, Len thought. I should have left ten minutes ago—left and written Abbas off for good. Len slowly inhaled, and as he did so he thought: Stop it! This is Abbas, for Christ's sake. My friend. He's been there for me . . . always been there. What am I going to do? Walk out on him? Len looked down at his hands, swallowing back his anger. "And now?" he asked Abbas at length. "What are you going to do now?"

"Like I said, I was going to take it back. I had to. Oh, I thought of destroying it. But what kind of a man would that have made me? To put the fortunes of my family, the reputation of my dead great-grandmother, ahead of the truth about the deaths of 1.8 million people . . . all to be revealed in time." Abbas sniffed and wiped the back of his wrist across the bottom of his nose. "I was planning to . . . waiting for an opportunity to return it undetected. The arrest of Alden Frost and Fatimah Ibrahim changed everything."

Len set both feet on the floor and leaned forward. "And now every thug from Ankara to J-town is after it, and after each other."

Abbas's face clouded over. "Charlotte is not a thug. I doubt Armenian Relief is employing thugs and murderers. They have a legitimate interest in having the diary's contents revealed."

Len regretted the word choice. "You're right, of course. But you know—don't you?—that releasing the diary's contents will topple the Aslan government and plunge the Middle East into turmoil. Who knows how many more people will have to die. We have to return this thing to the Uzbek Interior Ministry— and quick. Publicly and quick."

"Publicly?"

"Yes, the world needs to be convinced. They . . . they need to see with their own eyes that the Şahin Diary has been found and returned. That's the only way the dogs are going to be called off. That's the only way to keep you and Charlotte and Fatimah safe."

Abbas nodded slowly. "Yes, I see your point. But how?"

Len stood up and walked to the open sliding glass door. He stared out past the screen for several seconds. At last he turned. A relieved smile crossed his face. "I know how we can do it."

Abbas sat silently, listening to the plan. When Len was done explaining, Abbas said, "You're right, of course. It would destabilize the Turkish government . . . heaven only knows how many innocent people would die . . . Still, I can't help thinking about the legitimate claims of Armenian Relief—their search for evidence, for justice."

"It's a hard choice," Len agreed. "But in the end you know what we have to do. It has to go back."

*　　*　　*

"So the debate finally starts the day after tomorrow," said Len, interrupting a long silence between himself, Fatimah, and Abbas. "Where's Mr. Rodriguez when I need him?"

"Mr. Rodriguez?" Fatimah asked.

"My high school debate coach." Len raised his hands in mock surprise, letting his fingers frame a plastic smile. "Hi. I'm Leonard Williams. Unaccustomed as I am to 'spublic peaking' . . . "

Fatimah laughed.

Len smiled at her across the table. "Am I inspiring confidence?"

"You're ready," declared Abbas from behind dark sunglasses. "Both of you. Seriously." He lifted his tumbler of orange juice and held it midway between Fatimah and Len. "Here's to success."

Fatimah's white satin pool robe flowed and fluttered in the warm morning breeze that put minute turns in the blue-and-white patio umbrellas. "To success," said Fatimah, her youthful voice melodious beneath the whispering palms overhead and the murmuring leaves of the yellow-flowered hibiscus that hedged the pool and patio. The three touched glasses.

"I hope you're right," said Len.

The wind gusted, and after securing their white linen napkins and loose pages of notes under plates and sweating, half-filled water glasses, the three fell silent again.

"Ahmed will have the car ready Monday at eight o'clock sharp," said Fatimah at length, looking up and making eye contact with Len. "Will you be ready?"

"Eight o' clock," repeated Len. "I'm as ready as I'm going to be. I can't replace Frost—you know that. But I'm determined to do what I can."

Fatimah smiled wistfully. "You'll do just fine. Remember, we will win or lose on the margins. There is no cosmic right or wrong—at least none that we can claim to know. No bolts of lightning. We'll speak for those who stand to gain from the companion flag: the downtrodden, the exploited, the disfavored, and also for the better angels of the rich and powerful. We are speaking for those parts of us all that are the same for everyone."

Len nodded as he chewed a piece of papaya. "I got that." He pulled a piece of paper out from under his plate and began reading it silently. Soon Fatimah followed suit.

"You'll be great, both of you," said Abbas. "I admire you for what you're doing. If there was anything I could do to help, I would."

Fatimah looked up, smiled.

Len picked up his cell phone off the table and muttered absently, "The ceremony in Tashkent should be starting in about twenty minutes."

"What ceremony?" asked Fatimah.

Abbas picked up his own phone and nodded. "Yes. They'll be gathering now."

"I guess I didn't tell you," said Len, behind lidded eyes. He found it easier to keep his attention focused on the cell phone's miniature screen. "The CIA found the Şahin Diary. At least that's the scuttlebutt. Supposedly Ambassador Tompkins has it, and is making a formal presentation to the Uzbek interior minister at a press conference this morning." Len looked up, smiling. "That means you're off the hook. Your days as an international spy are . . . well, let's just say they're over even before they began. Uzbekistan is announcing that they're formally dropping the charges against you, and posthumously, against Alden, as well."

"That's wonderful!" Fatimah exclaimed, but a few moments later her face clouded over. "I only wish . . . " She closed her eyes momentarily, as though listening to a consoling voice inside, and when she opened them again, despite the welling of tears, her smile shone beautifully. "That's wonderful."

Len slid his napkin from under his water glass and wiped his hands. "I was going to tell you, but I wanted to wait. You know how these things are. I wanted to make sure it really happened as planned. At any rate, it's worth another toast," he said, lifting his tumbler of orange juice.

Fatimah clinked Len's glass with a gentle, relieved laugh, and then they both turned to see Abbas craning his neck, staring toward a figure moving slowly past clumps of dark green shore plants and tall grasses down the stone path toward the beach. It was Charlotte, dressed in a flowing red kaftan and white *hijab*. Sensing that Abbas would soon be excusing himself, they smiled at each other and drank from their glasses.

XXVIII

"Charlotte!"

She turned to see him trying to catch up, his aluminum crutches knocking like a metronome over the stone path, his straight left leg cantilevered out to avoid contact with the ground. When he reached the soft sand beyond the grass-knit dunes he had to make adjustments—some quickly abandoned—until, employing a kind of hopping motion, something like success obtained. Charlotte turned away from his little grunts, his labored approach. She leaned forward and stared disconsolately at the ground. Even his "Good morning!" within the last five yards or so went unanswered. The sea thudded and hissed behind her. Only when Abbas stopped did she glance up and give him a pained smile.

She began to walk again, slowly. Abbas kept pace, albeit struggling, with the tips of his crutches sinking an inch or two with each step. She seemed determined to go on. He wondered at her silence, but held his tongue. Several minutes passed. Three times, he saw the hem of her loose kaftan sweep back and caress the leg of his crutch. I hope the wind never stops blowing, he thought. He saw out of the corner of his eye that a wedge of her black, curly hair had escaped her scarf. It danced over the red moist tissue that covered the right side of her face. She made a half-hearted effort to tuck it back into her *hijab*, but without success.

Good! he thought. I want to see your hair. I want nothing more than to touch it with my fingertips, bring it to my lips. You are so beautiful, and your wounds will never change that.

A line of five broad-shouldered, taciturn pelicans drifted by above the foam-etched sand, their heads up as though each were waiting for one of the others to say something. Charlotte kept walking, now embracing herself, arms folded below her breasts. Her head was bent forward. At first Abbas thought she might be looking for something—shells?—in the white sand. But then, stealing a glace at her inward-looking eyes, he realized no, it was something else.

Twice his crutches sank too low and he faltered and hopped on one leg, and rather than press on, Charlotte waited for him without turning. They angled toward a plate-smooth band of drenched sand, crossed a small, uneven berm of washed-up kelp and debris, then kept to the hard brown sand for the sake of the footing.

"Can we sit over there?" Charlotte said after a few minutes of silence, pointing toward a tangle of sun-bleached logs resting well up on the shoulder of the beach within a few yards of a thick, top-heavy jungle growth.

Abbas stopped to examine the place. "Yes, of course." They crossed the berm again and made their way slowly up the incline, back through soft, well-trodden white sands laced with bits of shining black charcoal. Abbas couldn't help but worry about the coolness and preoccupation evident in Charlotte's tone. And he saw it now in the manner of her walking, as well, her arms still stiffly folded even where the walking was difficult.

He sat clumsily on a log of convenient height, collected his crutches, and set them down beside him. Charlotte moved to sit where the crutches had gone, and Abbas shifted them to the other side without complaint. She sent the unruly wisp of hair back under her scarf, took three deep breaths, then said, "I need to talk to you."

"Yes, I think we both need—"

"*Please!* Let me speak," she interrupted. "I have been torturing myself with how to say this." Charlotte wiped the corners of her mouth with her thumb and middle finger. "I must tell you something before it bursts out of me. But you must promise not to tell anyone . . . I have not been honest with you." The gravity of what she was about to say brought tears to her eyes. She sought the solace of the sea for a few moments, then cleared her throat. "I want to explain myself . . . if I can." A rueful little involuntary smile came and went on the scarless side of her face, the side she had chosen to show Abbas. "Four years ago I came to Tashkent. But I did not come directly from Tunisia. For the previous year I had lived in the home of my brother and his wife in Karaköse, Turkey. Mehdi was a teacher of Arabic in the local high school." Intermittently, she allowed herself to glance in Abbas's direction as she spoke. "He had become active in an underground movement seeking reparations for the families of Armenians deported and killed by the Turkish army in World War I. It incensed him . . . he could not believe that even to this day Turkey denies the genocides that took so many lives. He became involved in an organization called Armenian Relief." Charlotte turned to him fully. "Do you know of it?"

Abbas felt his breath leaving him. "I've heard of it."

She turned back, nodding. "Years ago, Armenian Relief filed a claim in the International Court of Justice, but Turkey has resisted it through delays and maneuvers of every kind imaginable. They send their best lawyers to the Netherlands to do this. They challenge the evidence, they argue that too much time has passed, they disqualify witnesses—many of whom have died while waiting to testify. The court has given Armenian Relief only until the end of this year to produce sufficient evidence of the atrocities, and yet the respondent's legal team refuses to hand over millions of pages of documents." Charlotte looked down at her hands. "It's unfair. They say these documents do not exist, but . . . " She swallowed. "More delays, more technicalities." She seemed to ruminate over this for some time before looking up, squinting into the wind. "It didn't matter to Mehdi that the Armenians were Christian. Why should this matter?" She shook her head and looked down again. A tear fell over her lash onto her cheek.

"I was not a member, but I supported Mehdi and the others. I attended their meetings, many of which were secret. I believed what they were doing was right and good. And then they organized a student rally at the university, to build awareness. It started out peacefully enough, but it spilled over into the streets. Mehdi grew nervous. He was worried about my safety. We watched as busload after busload of policemen arrived. He said, 'Come, Charlotte. This is not what we planned. I'm taking you home.' But I knew that, sometimes, it is necessary to confront the police."

It was only then, Abbas realized, that Charlotte allowed herself to look up again. She seemed to gather courage from something distant, a memory that, in coming, caused her to open her eyes wide in spite of the wind in her face.

"I told him it would be okay . . . That we should stay. By our numbers in the street, I said, we could awaken those around us to the cause. He agreed . . . reluctantly. But a half hour later, you see, the crowd had turned onto a main thoroughfare, and shooting began . . . and tear gas was everywhere. People were surging all around us, back and forth, and there was panic. Screaming. I turned to discover Mehdi hunched over, dropping to his knees."

Charlotte wiped away tears with the flat of her hand and sniffed loudly. "He'd been shot, killed." Now she closed her eyes and was slow to open them again. "I'm telling you all this because . . . five weeks ago I got a call from a friend of Mehdi's, an Armenian named Yousuf. This man told me that there had been a break-in at Tashkent's Public School 32, that the Şahin Diary was missing. I had heard Mehdi speak of this diary. It had come up at meetings. It was a dream—I can tell you that— an impossible dream of theirs to acquire this document, for it would provide the definitive proof needed."

"Do you know this?" asked Abbas, unable to eliminate all traces of skepticism.

The interruption evidently surprised her. "Do I know it? Yes. I mean—well, I don't know it personally, but it stands to reason, doesn't it? The diary of an aide who witnessed the killings, a volume that Turkey arranged to place in hiding for two hundred years! One can only imagine . . ."

"I suppose, yes," said Abbas. He felt a heaviness in his chest. Why didn't I just take it back when I had the chance? None of this would have happened, he thought.

Charlotte seemed to be on the verge of asking Abbas something when she sniffed loudly again and swallowed. She collected her thoughts while staring at her hands. "Anyway, he knew I had been with Mehdi that day, and that I would do anything to honor my brother's memory. He asked if I would I try to locate the Şahin Diary. It was the next day that I received word at work that two people—Alden Frost and Fatimah—had been arrested. I arranged to have myself assigned to their cases, and when I met you . . . when I met Mr. Frost and Ms. Ibrahim . . . I made up the story of the companion flag at my school. I knew they had the diary, you see, and I had to get it."

I could have taken it back, Abbas said to himself. The minute I heard about their arrest. How did I miss the fact that they'd be charged with taking the diary? They'd been on the roof, planting this flag. I didn't think—

"When Mr. Frost agreed to let Fatimah leave the country without him . . . with Msaidie . . . I knew *she* would have the diary. He practically said as much, for, you see, I overheard him whisper to her that there was something he wanted her to take out of the country. So I devised the plan of presenting the companion flag to her grandfather here in Tashir . . . as a pretense."

"A pretense?"

"Yes, a reason to go with her. I would distract her, find the diary, and deliver it to Yousuf." Charlotte turned and looked directly into Abbas's eyes. "I'm so sorry I lied to you, but, you see, I know Fatimah has it, and I must . . . get it. I *have to* have it. Hundreds of thousands of people are depending on me. Perhaps millions." In response to the strained expression on Abbas's face, she added, "the relatives of the survivors and victims. It will make all the difference at the International Court of Justice."

"Charlotte, I—"

"It is what Mehdi would have wanted me to do, and I am fortunate to have this opportunity. Truly . . ." She blinked, and her eyes sought the sandy beach stretching away to the south. She raised her fingers up close to the angry, mottled red skin that ravaged the side of her face. "Even though it has cost me a great deal," she whispered. "I will never look the same, never look normal again."

Abbas lifted himself up and shifted his position so that he could face her more easily. "Charlotte, listen to me. I—"

"You don't have to say anything," said Charlotte, raising her hand.

"No, please, let me talk now." He waited, and his patience was rewarded when at last she turned partway back. "You will always be beautiful to me. The most beautiful woman I have ever known. That will never change . . . And you are very brave. I, too, am blessed . . . for having met you."

Charlotte's eyes searched his, wanting—finding, surely—the truth reflected there. She reached up as though to grab his arm, but withdrew her hand at the last minute. He took hold of her hand and kissed her palm. She smiled. "Do you forgive me, then?"

Still pressing his lips to her palm, he nodded.

"Oh, Abbas! You can't imagine how relieved I am." She stood up excitedly, turned to him. "You've made me very happy." She glanced quickly up and down the beach, then leaned toward him in her fluttering red kaftan, barely able to contain her emotions. "I thought . . . I didn't know what to think." She laughed in spite of her tears.

He wanted to reach for her, to pull her toward him, but he dared not. He looked away momentarily, and when he turned to her again he said, "I adore you, Charlotte Yacoubi."

She grinned, then tilted her head. "Why so serious? Don't you know I feel the same about you, Mr. Ahkmedova?"

Abbas smiled, but then he adjusted his sitting position on the log and looked down the beach in the direction they'd come.

"What is it?" said Charlotte, searching the same landscape.

"Nothing."

She held him in her gaze. "It's something. Tell me."

"Oh, it's . . . I don't want to disappoint you."

Charlotte's smile faded. "What is it? You *will* help me, won't you? I only want the truth to come out—what really happened to these people. The world has to know."

"Charlotte, Fatimah doesn't have the Şahin Diary. *I* took it. I took it from the school more than nine months ago."

Charlotte's expression tried to catch up, but it proved too difficult. She closed her eyes. "What are you . . . ? Wait a minute, you—what are you saying?"

"I took it. I can explain . . . but—"

"*You* took it?" Her eyes were open now, stretched open, disbelieving. "Why are you saying this? That is preposterous! Are you trying to be funny? I heard him say—"

Abbas shook his head. "No. Listen, I've had it all along . . . until—"

"You're lying!"

"No. I've told Len . . . I told him the other day . . . now I want you to know. This is my fault, Charlotte. All of it! You would not have been hurt—none of these people would have died—if . . . I should have returned it as soon as I learned of Alden and Fatimah's arrest. It was stupid of me. It didn't occur to me they'd be charged with stealing the diary, or that anyone would even bother checking to see if it was missing. They had planted a flag on the roof of the building, is all! Don't you see? The diary was in the basement. Had been."

Charlotte's mouth gaped open. She held her hands in front of her as though the truth were a bubble that she sought to contain but dared not touch. "You . . . I can't . . . This . . . this can't be true!"

"It is." Abbas swallowed with difficulty. "I needed the diary to prove that my great-grandmother was not—"

"*Your great-grandmother? What are you talking about?*"

"My great-grandmother was Armenian. She's dead now . . . but she was accused . . . her whole life she was accused of consorting with a Turkish officer during the time of the genocides, of being a traitor to her people. We lived under a cloud . . ."

What did Charlotte hear? The more he talked, the more disengaged she appeared—the more she shook her head incredulously, looking left and right as one *in extremis* seeks a clue to her whereabouts, her predicament. That his lips moved, yes, she knew, but nothing beyond—a background noise, perhaps, no match for her own thoughts forming, rising up, tumbling inward. At last, a strange light came into her eyes, and her smile, so ill timed, stopped Abbas in midsentence.

"Then you have it!" she proclaimed.

"What?"

"You have the diary. You must give it to me!" She did not wait for a response. "I must have it!"

Suddenly, Abbas felt a confusion of pains emanating from the sites of his injuries. His leg cast, the long belt of elastic that bound his ribs, the bandages that covered the sutures over his left forearm, chafed like spectral restraints. "No. Listen to me, Charlotte," he said, without knowing what he would say next.

She jumped away from him as if jolted by electricity. She moved into the partial shadow cast by an overhanging palm tree, and the lambent folds of her kaftan appeared to darken and deepen in the wind. "Don't you for one minute deny me this," she warned.

Abbas felt a shudder run up his spine. How dare she speak to me in this way, he thought, but then he silenced his criticism before it could take hold. No, it's not her fault. This is my fault, as well, he told himself. God, if only I had returned it weeks ago—months ago. He regarded her anew, kindly. "Len and I have talked about this. We're giving it back . . . *putting* it back. If the contents of the diary are made public, it will—"

"*No! You can't!*"

"I have to, Charlotte. If the diary is made public, the government of Turkey could fall. Do you realize what this could mean? It could mean civil war—or worse. I know this is not what you—"

"Listen to me, Abbas! You can't do that! Don't you see? This is what the Armenian people have been waiting for." In her strenuousness, little protuberances appeared above her eyebrows. Her elbows were bent, her fingers splayed out and rigid at her sides. "You can't just give it back."

"I've already—"

"Think of what you're saying, Abbas: you took the diary for the sake of one person—your great-grandmother. Okay. I understand that. I need it now for the sake of almost two million victims, for hundreds of thousands of living survivors. Where is the justice if you give it back? What do you mean 'you've already?'" Her face darkened. "What have you done?"

Abbas struggled to his feet, uncoupled the crutches, set the saddles against his armpits, and leaned against them. She won't listen, he told himself. His eyes, two points of light beneath the ridge of his brows, concealed doubts that she had begun to awaken within him. "Do you want a war in the Middle East?" he heard himself say.

"What have you done?"

He felt anger and desperation rise up in his throat. "I've given it to the U.S. ambassador. He's returning it to the Uzbek interior minister today. Now. This morning."

"WHAT?" Charlotte doubled at the waist. Her scream could be heard a thousand yards away. *"You're lying. You didn't."*

Abbas stared helplessly past her, at a trio of small waves converging on shore. He could not maintain that pose, and let his eyes drift back to hers: two green-gold orbs barely focusing, overflowing with furious energy. "You have to understand, Charlotte," he began. "We—"

"No! No, I don't have to understand. Tell me you didn't." She began to walk away. "This can't be happening," she said, her arms swinging wildly. Suddenly, she spun back to him with her hands pressed against the sides of her head. "You can't be serious. *You're not serious, are you? You didn't really give the diary to the U.S. ambassador?"*

The muscles of his jaw pulsed with anger. I can't believe I am letting her talk to me like this—what would she have had me do? For the sake of a claim for reparations, let a revolution break out in Ankara? Let the Middle East go up in flames? Is she mad? I can only reason with her. "With Len's help, I arranged for its delivery," he said at last, his tone even. "Yes, the American ambassador has it now."

Her face contorted, melted into tears. "How . . . how *could* you?" Sinuous red and white lines of scar tissue stretched as she struggled to breathe through gathering sobs. Any semblance of the face of Charlotte Yacoubi as he'd known it was vanishing before his eyes. "*You're a monster!*" she cried.

Abbas sensed only too well what he stood to lose. On the other hand, he couldn't believe this was happening. He stepped toward her. "Charlotte . . ."

"*Don't you come near me,*" she screamed. Spittle flew from between clenched teeth as she took a step back in the sand. She pointed her finger at his face. "*Don't you ever come near me again.*" She continued to step away. Her eyes registered desperation and disbelief, but these emotions were as inconsequential now as passengers on a runaway train. Something else was taking over. "*I hate you!*"

"Charlotte, please, you must—"

"*No! Stay away from me. You've done enough for one day . . . for one lifetime! You're a coward, Abbas Ahkmedova.*" She rocked toward him, her finger jabbing the air. "*Don't you ever talk to me again. Don't you ever so much as—*" She shook her head, then turned and began to stomp heavily through the soft sand back toward the compound. After a few steps, she spun back. Abbas had not moved. "*I am leaving this God-forsaken place—now—do you hear?*" She bent over, picked up a handful of sand, and threw it at him. Not a single grain came close, but something—a whitish dust—rose up and was carried on the wind into a curtain of arrow-leafed bamboo and disappeared. "*You can go to hell!*"

Abbas struggled to breathe, out of time with his pounding heart. He slammed the crutches together and nearly lost his balance.

*   *   *

Minute, battery-driven adjustments, the whirring of over thirty cameras ranging in over the surface of the desk, brought into focus the three raised bands of the book's spine, four brown leather reinforced corners, gilt-edged paper, the bifid tongue of a worn, purple satin bookmark, and on the cover, in a badly deteriorated gold leaf, the remnants of the Turkish word *"Günlük"* (Diary). A cameraman from *Bishkek TV* spoke for the others when he asked the attendant wearing white gloves to please turn the book over and then get his hands out of the shot. The man complied. A fresh eruption of clicks and murmurs, and some shifting of camera positions followed.

"It is not to be opened under any circumstances," the attendant declared, as though anticipating the next question.

"When you're done there, let's get started," said Ambassador Tompkins, making his way toward the dark wooden podium that had been brought into the spacious anteroom of the interior minister's private offices for the occasion. Technicians were still mounting and taping microphones, adjusting key and fill lights. Minister Guryanov gave an order to a deputy, who then barked out in English, "We will begin in three minutes. Please take your places. Bring the diary over here."

The event was timed for live news coverage at the top of the hour. After exchanging a few whispered words with a nodding assistant, the ambassador stood erect and stared out at the pool camera, his pale, pink face bathed in bright light. Interior Minister Guryanov stood behind him at attention. His dark eyes pivoted sentry-like behind sparkling gold-rimmed glasses above the ambassador's right shoulder. A floor manager wearing a headset was counting down with his fingers. "Three . . . two . . ." The room fell quiet.

"Ladies and gentleman," began the ambassador. "Good morning. My name is Harold R. Tompkins. I am the United States ambassador to the Republic of Uzbekistan. We are coming to you today from Tashkent. On behalf of the president, I want to thank Interior Minister Salim Guryanov for arranging this televised event on such short notice.

"As most of you know, Alden Frost was an American citizen. He was arrested here in Tashkent on September 2nd, along with Fatimah Ibrahim, following a break-in at Tashkent's Public School 32. Mr. Frost and Ms. Ibrahim had raised a flag on the roof of the building beneath the Uzbek national flag. They also posted a handwritten note inside the building, before leaving. I have that note here, thanks to Minister Guryanov." Tompkins held up a wrinkled piece of paper, and the cameras clicked like crickets. "Let me read it. It is brief. 'The companion flag is a symbol of all that human beings have in common. It is displayed below the other flags of the world on the same pole. Together, these flags signify the following: Here we are proud of our differences, our diversity, and our special affiliations, but we are mindful, too, of our essential humanity and all that we share in common with people everywhere.'"

The ambassador turned and handed the note back to Guryanov. The minister nodded and handed it off to an assistant. Tompkins cleared his throat behind a closed fist. "Public School 32 was also the repository for the Ali Şahin Diary, a document that has been sealed and kept out of circulation since 1924. This was in keeping with a treaty obligation, as has been thoroughly discussed and dissected in the media over the past several weeks, at the United Nations, and in diplomatic circles throughout the world. International treaties have the force of law. After the break-in, Uzbek authorities discovered that the Şahin Diary was missing. Quite understandably, they suspected Alden Frost and Fatimah Ibrahim . . . as others did. The unfortunate result of the involvement of unknown others around the world has played out all too clearly in the headlines, both here in Tashkent and in Sanori, Tashir. But it has now come to light that neither Mr. Frost nor Ms. Ibrahim had anything to do with the diary's disappearance.

"Thursday at 06:30 local time I was informed that the Şahin Diary had been located by CIA operatives working undercover in Ciudad Juarez, Mexico. It was discovered among the belongings of a known drug lord, Ernesto Concepcion, killed in a firefight with Mexican authorities on Wednesday, October 4. I immediately arranged for the transport of the diary here to Tashkent, and it arrived last night. Evidence recovered at the scene suggests that Concepcion has had the diary for more than six months. There were numerous letters and e-mails uncovered suggesting that he had been trying to sell the diary on the black market.

"We are, of course, pleased to be able to return the Ali Şahin Diary for safekeeping into the hands of the Uzbek government. Minister Guryanov, if you would . . ." The ambassador turned to let Guryanov step up next to him. Both men put on white gloves. The ambassador picked up the book and handed it to the interior minister. The cameras came to life, and through the microphones, throughout the world, went a noise like coins poured from a jar.

XXIX

———

From: XX5 – Executive Director CO-9 (London)
To: undisclosed recipients
Date: Sun., 8 October 20ZZ 05:34:12
Subject: Şahin Diary
Encryption/Decryption Enabled: B72ZZ256-9127 (All Threads)

TO ALL COMMITTEE OF NINE (CO-9) MEMBERS:

ŞAHIN DIARY HAS BEEN RECOVERED AND RETURNED TO UZBEK AUTHORITIES.

RE: CF DEBATE, X15 REPORTS ALLOCATION OF FUNDS COMPLETE. TWO VOTES ARE IN QUESTION: MP SKETHO (SANORI) AND MP NGA-TOT (SOUTH ISLAND). BOTH ARE UNITED PEOPLES PARTY MEMBERS. IT IS BELIEVED THEY WILL COOPERATE. INITIATE PROTOCOL 9. ALL SILENT. CONFIRM.

*   *   *

From: X20 – CO-9 (Moscow)
Date: Sun., 8 October 20ZZ 05:35:41 +0400

CONFIRMED.

*   *   *

From: XX8 – CO-9 (Bangalore)
Date: Sun., 8 October 20ZZ 05:37:03 +0530

PROTOCOL 9. CONFIRMED.

*   *   *

From: X16 – CO-9 (Sao Paulo)
Date: Sun., 8 October 20ZZ 05:41:55 -0300

CONFIRMED.

*   *   *

From: X22 – CO-9 (New York)
Date Sun., 8 October 20ZZ 06.02.15 -0500

CONFIRMED.

*   *   *

From: X14 – CO-9 (Sydney)
Date: Sun., 8 October 20ZZ 06.07.22 +1000

Confirmed. Protocol 9.

* * *

From: X19 – CO-9 (Buenos Aires)
Date: Sun., 8 October 20ZZ 06:15:15 -0300

All silent. Confirmed.

* * *

From: X12 – CO-9 (Vatican City)
Date: Sun., 8 October 20ZZ 06:35:21 +0100

Yes.

* * *

From: X13 – CO-9 (Tokyo)
Date: Sun., 8 October 20ZZ 06:35:49 +0900

Confirmed.

XXX

___

Seven Months Later

"Speak of the devil," said Len, his upturned eyes jumping left to right on Abbas's computer screen. Suddenly, Len's head and shoulders rose up out of view, and Abbas was left staring at Len's midsection. "Hello, sweetheart," came Len's voice from 6,200 miles away. Len turned and leaned partially out of the camera's view. Abbas could see behind his friend's posterior the clutter of an office windowsill, and beyond, below gray, billowy clouds, a row of Douglas fir trees. A wind-tossed U.S. flag flew from a pole in the foreground. Len sat back down. A distracted smile played lightly on his lips. "Laura's here," he said. "Surprised me with a latte." Len held up the white-and-green cup for Abbas to see.

"Lucky you," said Abbas, reaching for his bottle of Heineken and taking a little swig.

"Hi, Abbas," Laura called out. "Here, let me see him."

Abbas waited for Laura's face to appear on the screen. "Hello, Laura. Nice to see you."

"And you, too," said Laura. She squeezed her head in next to Len's, pushing his slightly aside. "You look great."

"Thank you." But for Videochat, Abbas would have leaned all the way back in his chair, set his head back, and closed his eyes, thinking I hope you know what you're doing, my friend. Instead, he smiled dryly and thought the same thing. He looked away from Len's enlarged face as Len reached across Laura at an uncomfortable angle to set his cup down on his desk. The effort seemed to Abbas, for some reason, to heighten the moment's poignancy, and it brought back to mind a video call he had had with Len three months earlier, in which Len had allowed in a low, confidential tone: "I didn't think I'd take her back . . . then when I laid eyes on her at the airport, I knew. . . well, it seemed resistance was futile." I hope you know what you're doing, Abbas had thought then, as well.

In that call, three months earlier, Len had sat encased in the quiet and darkness of his new home, the same gray split-level in North Seattle he'd spoken about with real estate agent Sharon Jordan. Abbas had been at his office. They'd talked about many things, about the surprising way Jianyao had intervened on Len's behalf after Tashir, how he'd threatened to pull his clients' support for the Swan River dam project—now called Remembrance Dam—if Len was dismissed by Majestic. How this intercession had seemed, almost at once, to relieve all sides of an unwanted tension. Len had spoken of how genuinely he'd been welcomed to Seattle, to Majestic, as though nothing had happened.

Much like today, they'd talked for the better part of an hour, and then Len had stopped and, leaning close to the camera, said, "Wait a minute." He'd risen, and Abbas had heard him close the door of his study. It had been a Friday night in Seattle (mid-morning on a Saturday in Tashkent), and for the American three Heinekens were already in the tank. Behind Len's chair, through a large plate glass window, a row of lights, their reflections coming to points over the surface of Puget Sound, marked the eastern shore of Bainbridge Island.

"Do you think—?" Abbas had begun after Len returned to his chair and began to talk about Laura's change of heart. "Do you trust that she really wants to be married?" Abbas had kept an eye on his own office door at the time, to make sure nobody was listening. In hushed tones, Len had replied, "Yes, I think so. She wants to do intensive counseling . . . is committed to it, she says. Similar to what I'm doing with my gambling." Abbas hadn't been able to keep from thinking then about Charlotte. What if *they* had been married? What if *she* had taken another man, and then come back, wanting to try again? He sighed. In a second, he thought. In a split second.

"I wanted to tell her no at first," Len had continued. "But if I learned anything in Tashir, it's that people need to find forgiveness in this world. Find it fast or risk losing everything—people, opportunities, happiness. Forgive yourself, forgive others. Not everything is by the numbers. That's what I learned. I appreciate your concern, Abbas. I do. But this is the right thing. We'll make it right."

Laura's voice brought Abbas back to the present. "I thought you two would be done by now. I didn't want to interrupt."

"You're not interrupting," said Abbas, really looking at Laura for the first time in over eight months. She's beautiful, all right, he said to himself, and something's different now. She has the look of someone who knows what she wants. Perhaps it will work.

Laura glanced quickly at her husband. "When Len told me you'd moved your call up to ten this week, I figured I'd be safe coming by at eleven. I can leave and come back."

"No, no. Don't leave. I had to hear all about Xining," said Abbas, relieved to be in the present moment again—the sultry darkness of his own apartment being cut by the blue-white glare from his computer screen. He lifted his green beer bottle and twirled its contents idly.

"Oh! Are you going to join us in Xining for the opening of the Remembrance Center?" Laura's voice sparkled with enthusiasm.

Her vivacity reminded Abbas of the twelve-hour time difference, of how tired he was after a long day at work. Give me some of that energy, he thought as he adjusted his left ear bud. "No, I'm afraid not. I can't get time off. We're hosting a delegation from Sweden that week, and I've been tasked with the ambassador's security. If I could, you know I would." He watched Laura pout magnificently. "I'm coming out there in July though."

"You'd better."

Len and Abbas stared at each other over the miles in silence. It was somehow plain that Laura still had the floor. "Len tells me you've started giving companion flag presentations at schools throughout Uzbekistan?"

"Yes, that's right."

"And that quite a few schools are adopting it."

"It's gone very well." Abbas took a drink, and his eyes clouded a little, as though he were anticipating some discomfort from what would come next.

"That's great," said Laura. "But tell me, what caused you to get involved with the companion flag? Why did you—?"

"Oh, I don't know, really," said Abbas. He scooted his chair forward. "I owe it to Mr. Frost, I suppose. I owe it to a lot of people. I took the diary, didn't I? I don't regret that—I still don't." Abbas's voice dropped to a near whisper. "But I should have put it back. I'm trying to atone for that."

Len cut in, "I was just telling Abbas about the ten-kilometer flag display they've installed on the road up to the Remembrance Center."

Laura smiled. "With companion flags?"

"Two poles on either side of the road every five hundred meters," Abbas said, grateful for his friend's adroit pivot. Forgive yourself, Len had said. Abbas smiled after drawing a relieved breath. "A different national flag with a companion flag on each pole. It'll be a fantastic approach to an even more fantastic conference center. I would love to attend the opening." Abbas took another drink. He didn't like beer, but this was the deal they'd made, he and Len.

"You'll be there in spirit," said Len.

Abbas nodded and tipped the bottle toward his computer screen, making Laura giggle. She rose up for a moment and then settled back down on Len's leg, her arm snaking around Len's shoulder. The last eleven minutes of this week's conversation would include her.

*   *   *

The joyful laughter that rolled into the hallway—sixty-five young voices—brought a smile to Fatimah's face. She continued to look down at the polished cement floor as they walked.

"They're having a wonderful time," said Bakhtiyar Musaev, the headmaster of the Academic Lyceum of Samarkand. He rubbed bony hands together, and the trousers of his black suit billowed and sank back again over pole-thin legs with each step. She carefully avoided the headmaster's overly eager glances. He turned his torso every four or five steps, hoping to speak to her. His effort to make an impression, to engage Fatimah in conversation, ran to the extreme, but it was not so unusual anymore. Tiresome? Yes.

She nodded. "Indeed." With or without this strange man next to her, it was a joy to hear the children's laughter. She felt— but could not quite remember—a similar light-heartedness. Could it have been so different for me when I was fourteen or fifteen? I wonder what made me laugh then, she asked herself, as their steps echoed in the empty hallway and the laughter died.

"How was your flight? Did you come in directly from Sanori?"

She did not hear Mr. Musaev's questions, for she was suddenly focused on the distant rise and thrum of Abbas's voice, followed by a smattering of vestigial laughter. "Oh, that's him!" Fatimah said. Now she looked up into the headmaster's eyes, wishing to share the moment. "I would know that voice anywhere."

Musaev forced a frown up into a smile. "You know Mr. Ahkmedova, then?"

Fatimah looked up into the man's brown eyes in wonder. Do I know him? Ten at the most, she thought, guessing at the number of Uzbeks who would not know that Abbas Ahkmedova, one of their own, had saved her life in a dramatic shootout near the Tashkent airport and that he had then traveled with her to Tashir. Leave it to a high school headmaster in Uzbekistan's third-largest city to be one of these ten, she thought. Mr. Musaev nevertheless deserves an answer. "Oh, yes. Quite well." The headmaster's needy smile revealed a wish to know more. He raised a finger, but Fatimah spoke first. "I am so looking forward to seeing him." She quickened her steps, but a moment later stopped and reached out in the direction of Musaev's right sleeve. "Oh, he wants to introduce me. He told me to wait in the hallway and listen for my introduction."

"Yes," said the headmaster. He began to rub his hands together again. "I'm sorry. The secret has gotten out. I have no idea how, but the students know of your visit. No one is speaking of anything else."

Fatimah smiled.

"Mr. Ahkmedova wanted to surprise them," he continued. "I tried to tamp down the rumors, but yesterday after the security people came . . . well, I am only a headmaster."

"Of course." Fatimah pointed to an open door on the right. "Is this it, then?"

"Yes, yes." Musaev said. "Everything should be ready for the flag-raising ceremony at eleven."

Fatimah looked back down the long hallway in the direction they had come. "I'm expecting someone else," she said.

"Someone else?" Mr. Musaev's tone betrayed a habituated dislike for surprises. "Does Mr. Ahkmedova . . . ?"

"No. Excuse me, won't you?" Fatimah lifted her handbag and went in search of her cell phone, which had begun to alternately vibrate and buzz. She pulled the phone out and read a text message: I AM HERE. STOPPED BY SECURITY. "Oh! I should have told them," Fatimah stammered as she began to work her thumbs over the phone's keys. She brought the phone up to her ear and waited. "Yes. Please let Ms. Yacoubi pass . . . Yes . . . Correct. All right." She put the phone back and smiled at Mr. Musaev. "Could I impose on you to retrieve my friend? I don't want her to get lost."

She could read disappointment in the headmaster's drooping eyelids even after he'd successfully masked it elsewhere on his face. "Oh, of course, of course."

Fatimah thought of offering him her hand, something she would not ordinarily have done, then dismissed the idea. A Western gesture, not necessary here. "Thank you, Mr. Musaev."

With the headmaster in full retreat, Fatimah had time to step back and lean her head against the wall, listening to Abbas's voice. He was giving a speech, and was fully engaged. She could not understand his Uzbek, but twice heard "companion flag" heavily accented in English. His iterations were a pleasing music to her. She closed her eyes.

"He would not want to see me," Charlotte had told her emphatically during their phone conversation three days earlier. Fatimah had fallen silent. It was her call—that is, she had called

Charlotte, not the other way around. She knew that things said backwards, or inside-out, could untwist themselves in silence. Silence, too, was musical.

"I suspect there may be an error in what you say," she'd told Charlotte at last, staring blindly at a stack of children's letters on her desk. The long, onrushing chorus of waves spending their last upon the shore poured through her open office windows, and if heard by Charlotte at all, 1,830 miles away, would have been mistaken for static.

Ten minutes earlier, not long after Charlotte had expressed surprise at receiving the call, Fatimah had sketched the events of her life since "that time." She had explained to Charlotte how she'd taken a position at Port Hikma University after Jamaal's marriage to Zainab; how she'd kept herself occupied with writing and speaking engagements throughout the world, but mostly in Africa and North America; how now she found loneliness as prevalent as the shadows that pooled and stretched over the manicured lawns of her parents' compound. "No one will ask me out," she'd lamented, half laughing, when what she meant was, "I have not met anyone like Jamaal, and I am beginning to wonder if I ever will."

Charlotte had assured her that such a man would come along in time. "Not every man has the courage to approach you," she'd said. "Who's going to walk up to Fatimah Ibrahim, after all, and say, 'Well, now, I believe you're the one. Care for a Fanta?'"

Fatimah had laughed at this while moving papers back and forth on her desk, but then stopped and changed the phone to her other ear. A long silence had preceded Charlotte's next words. "My friends tell me I'm a fool not to have returned Abbas's calls."

"They're right," Fatimah had replied gently.

"I've tried to make sense of it," Charlotte had said. "I know I . . . I overreacted. He couldn't have known that I was . . . that I wanted the diary. I blamed him. But still, *he gave it back*. And the case in the International Court of Justice has been dismissed."

"Yes."

Every silence was Charlotte's now. She had begun to open her heart to Fatimah. "I'm still at the ICRC, but I've requested a transfer home to Tunis. A position is opening up there next month."

"So you're leaving Uzbekistan?"

"Yes. There's nothing left for me here in Tashkent . . . Oh, and I'm so tired of people averting their eyes when they see me. You have no idea—"

"All the more reason to come with me to Samarkand. Give the poor man a chance, Charlotte. He did only what he thought was right."

"I know, but . . . you weren't there, Fatimah. I asked him . . . I begged him not to give the diary back."

"It was too late," Fatimah had answered. "He'd already given it back."

"I suppose you're right." Charlotte's voice had dropped to a whisper. But then it rose again. "Tell me something. When we were discussing the idea of going to Tashir, in the basement of the jail, Mr. Frost said he wanted you to take something with you . . . something he would give you later. Do you remember?"

"Yes."

"What was it?"

"It was a letter to my grandfather, a thank you for whatever he could do to introduce the companion flag to the people of Tashir . . ."

Fatimah opened her eyes to the present. Glancing up at the lyceum's gray-brown ceiling, at bracketed electrical conduits and enormous ventilation pipes stretching away to the right and left, at a double row of aluminum fluorescent lights hanging from white poles, she felt a smile cross her face. She looked up and down the long hallway with its displays of student artwork, at the shimmering, polished cement floors, at the exit signs glowing red at either end. I'm not sneaking into schools anymore, she realized. And with that awareness came a memory of Alden, as though he were there. "We're in," she whispered.

"Oh, there you are!" It was Charlotte, emerging from a door held open for her by Mr. Musaev.

Fatimah turned and alternately smiled and held her finger to her lips, nodding meaningfully at the open door to the auditorium. "Good morning," she whispered. She embraced Charlotte and kissed both cheeks. "I don't want him to hear. He's right in there."

Charlotte looked uncomfortably toward the rectangle of golden light. Perhaps she heard Abbas then, for a shadow of doubt was suddenly before her eyes. She stepped back. "I don't think this was a good idea after all."

Fatimah reached for her. "Be brave, Charlotte." She rubbed Charlotte's left arm until she could feel some of the tension work its way out. "You've forgiven him? You've thought through what we talked about?"

Charlotte seemed surprised by the question. "Yes, of course. I've thought of nothing else." She tugged at the edge of her *hijab* to cover as much of her scars as possible. "He told me the truth. It was difficult for him. He gave the diary back because . . . because he thought that was the only way to prevent more suffering."

"Yes."

"Including my own . . ."

"Yes, including your life. And your brother, Mehdi. He would have done the same—he would have done exactly what Abbas did for you and the others."

Charlotte looked down and nodded. When she raised her head again, Fatimah saw that a fresh question had taken shape.

It lifted Charlotte's brow, tugging at the sinuous lines of pink tissue on the right side of her face.

"Trust me," Fatimah whispered. Then she held her finger up as if to say, "Wait here." She turned to Mr. Musaev. "Sir, would you kindly tell Mr. Ahkmedova that Fatimah Ibrahim is here? Only Fatimah Ibrahim."

The headmaster looked at both women in turn and smiled, comprehension slowly dawning . "Yes, of course."

They followed him to the edge of the doorway. With their backs to the wall, they listened to the growing murmur from the students as Musaev made his way to the front of the room. Some applauded openly, while others uttered Fatimah's name in sibilant whispers. "She's here. Fatimah's here."

Fatimah turned and winked at Charlotte, giving her a comforting smile. She felt Charlotte's hand slide into her own. Abbas, still speaking in Uzbek, had clearly gotten the message. His tone had changed. Then he switched out of Uzbek altogether. "Boys and girls," he called out. "This is the moment we've been waiting for. We have a special guest to help us with today's flag-raising ceremony."

Fatimah gently pulled Charlotte closer. She whispered, "Wait ten seconds, then come in after me."

"What are you going to do?" Charlotte asked, her voice rising against the crescendo building from within the auditorium.

Fatimah looked deep into Charlotte's eyes. If only this were happening to me, she thought. If only that were Jamaal in there. But I've chosen this life. I made my decision, and it was the right one.

"The one and only Fatimah Ibrahim!" Abbas had finished his introduction.

The auditorium erupted in applause and cheers. Seconds later, the ear-splitting scraping of chairs being pushed back and the screams of teenage girls doubled the commotion. Fatimah slid her hand free of Charlotte's. "Just count to ten, then come in," she shouted, then she turned and disappeared around the corner.

The noise, which had seemed incapable of doubling, doubled again. A wide smile crossed Fatimah's face as she strode forward, both hands high above her head, waving. Then she stopped, and the gesture she made was unmistakable. It was an invitation to all the students to come forward to greet her.

Come forward all of you and shake the hand—at least touch the outstretched hands—of Fatimah Ibrahim. Come! Come!

Through laughing eyes Fatimah watched a flood of adolescents converge around her, pour down the aisles and encircle her, their arms outstretched as though they were reaching out to touch their own mother. She caught Abbas's eye and smiled as if to say, "Hello, friend—but you see it is about the children, not us," and then she pivoted to face the screaming teenagers who surged forward, some in tears. "Hello! Hi! . . . Hello there!" Fatimah said the words again and again. "Yes, it's wonderful to meet you, too! . . . Hi!"

From the corner of her eye, she saw it. She managed to see them both—the instant Charlotte appeared in the doorway, her right hand held up to hide her scars, and the moment of Abbas's realization, of the first change of expression, the dropping jaw. She saw in one direction Charlotte sidling uncertainly along the back wall of the auditorium, like a wild animal thrust into an unfamiliar cage. On the other side there was Abbas, now doing the same thing, moving slowly, holding back with disbelieving eyes.

Jostled by the pressing crowd, Fatimah continued to utter greetings, thrusting her arms and splayed fingers out to be touched. It's not Jamaal, she told herself, as she watched Abbas step slowly along the front of the auditorium, tracking Charlotte step for step. If only it were Jamaal. If only that were me, she thought, facing Charlotte now, peering past the heads of the youngsters. But in the next instant, Fatimah felt a great release. It was joy, such an upwelling as she had never felt before. And it was not for her, but for them—for Charlotte and Abbas, who, having turned and settled their eyes upon one another, first stepped tentatively and then ran headlong into each other's arms.

APPENDIX

THE SANORI FLAG DEBATE

MODERATOR: Ladies and Gentlemen, here in Tashir and around the world, welcome to the Sanori Civic Center Auditorium. I'm Dr. Virander Baweja, Professor of Law and Political Science at the Central University in New Delhi, India.

I have been called on to moderate a debate called under the Emergency Powers Act by the president and Parliament of the Republic of Tashir. The issue is one of first impression: Should the Islamic Republic of Tashir adopt the companion flag and display it in perpetuity below its national flag wherever and whenever the national flag is flown or displayed, at home or abroad?

The following preliminary statement has been approved by the two sides: The companion flag is a symbol of all that human beings have in common, their differences notwithstanding. It is called the companion flag because it is displayed beneath another flag or flags on the same flagpole—never alone. The intended result is a combination symbol honoring both human differences and human commonalities.

The companion flag is a white flag with a single stripe of color across the top 20 percent of the flag by height. The color of the stripe is any color appearing in the "host flag"—that is, the flag appearing directly above the companion flag on the flagpole. The dimensions of the companion flag match those of the host flag.

Posted with the companion flag is an interpretive sign that reads:

> THE COMPANION FLAG IS A SYMBOL
> OF ALL THAT HUMAN BEINGS HAVE IN COMMON.
> IT IS DISPLAYED BELOW THE OTHER FLAGS
> OF THE WORLD, ON THE SAME POLE—NEVER ALONE.
> TOGETHER, THESE FLAGS SIGNIFY:
>
> HERE WE ARE PROUD OF OUR DIFFERENCES,
> DIVERSITY, HERITAGE, AND SPECIAL AFFILIATIONS,
> BUT WE ARE MINDFUL, TOO, OF OUR ESSENTIAL
> HUMANITY AND ALL THAT WE SHARE IN COMMON
> WITH PEOPLE EVERYWHERE.

That concludes the preliminary statement.

We are honored and humbled to have much of the world's attention as we begin this debate, and we will strive—as befits the occasion—to be thorough, fair, responsive, and far-reaching in our inquiry. Nothing is gained—indeed, a great deal is potentially lost—if we fail to acknowledge at the outset the factors that have propelled this event onto the front pages of most of the world's newspapers and news websites. Those factors are, of course, the involvement of Fatimah Ibrahim, an internationally known figure and the granddaughter of President Mohamed Mohadji (she and the other participants are here with us now, and I will introduce them presently) and the tragic events of Tuesday last. That senseless crime, as most of you know, took the lives of a great many people, including Alden Frost, the creator of the companion flag. Mr. Frost was in Sanori to take part in this debate. To honor all who lost their lives, let us now observe a moment of silence.

(Moment of silence observed.)

I will now introduce the participants. Arguing in the affirmative and seated to my left are Ms. Fatimah Ibrahim of Tashir and Mr. Leonard Williams, of the United States. Ms. Ibrahim, as I mentioned earlier, is the granddaughter of His Excellency the President of Tashir, Mohamed Mohadji. She is a graduate of Port Hikma University and holds a doctorate in moral philosophy from the University of Oxford. Ms. Ibrahim has spent the last nine months working and traveling with Alden Frost throughout Asia and the subcontinent, promoting the companion flag.

Mr. Williams was until recently a political officer and conflict resolution specialist with the U.S. Department of State at the U.S. Embassy Tashkent. He has a degree in international relations from Northern Arizona University. He joins Ms. Ibrahim as a private citizen to fill in for Ms. Charlotte Yacoubi, who was injured in the Al Maseer Hotel bombing.

Arguing in the negative and seated to my right are Rabbi Daniel Levenson, Monsignor Marc Doyle, His Excellency the Secretary-General of the United Nations, Federico Romero, and Professor Donald O'Neil.

Rabbi Levenson is a graduate of the Jewish Theological Seminary of Breslau and holds doctorates in Talmudic literature and nineteenth-century European philosophy from the Sorbonne. He is currently a scholar-in-residence at the Hebrew University of Jerusalem and has taught a variety of courses there—and at other universities—since 1989.

Monsignor Doyle is dean of the Department of Comparative Religious Studies at the Pontifical University of the Holy Cross in Rome. He is a graduate of Stonyhurst College and the School of Catholic Theology at Tilburg University. He is the author of four books on the philosophy of religion.

His Excellency Secretary-General Federico Romero is the former president of Uruguay. Prior to holding that office, he worked for the Council of International and Intercultural Relations in Montevideo. He holds masters degrees in economics and international trade from Stanford University.

Professor O'Neil is the Holland Archer Distinguished Professor of Philosophy at Harvard University. He is the author of more than twenty books on moral philosophy. His most recent, *The Value Pluralism of Isaiah Berlin*, received the Pulitzer Prize for nonfiction last year. Professor O'Neil received his doctorate in philosophy from the University of Chicago.

Let me welcome all the presenters.

(Applause.)

With that, let us begin. Ms. Ibrahim or Mr. Williams, if you would.

MS. IBRAHIM: Thank you, Dr. Baweja. On Wednesday, parliament will vote on a resolution to adopt the companion flag. Slide 1, please, Len. Here is the language of the resolution.

(Reading aloud.)

> BE IT RESOLVED, THAT THE ISLAMIC REPUBLIC OF TASHIR SHALL ADOPT AND DISPLAY THE COMPANION FLAG IN PERPETUITY BELOW THE NATIONAL FLAG OF TASHIR WHEREVER AND WHENEVER THE NATIONAL FLAG IS FLOWN OR DISPLAYED, AT HOME OR ABROAD, INCLUDING WITHOUT LIMITATION:
>
> 1. AT ALL TASHIRI GOVERNMENT OFFICES AND MILITARY INSTALLATIONS,
>
> 2. AT ALL PUBLIC SCHOOLS, COLLEGES, AND UNIVERSITIES RECEIVING FEDERAL SUPPORT,
>
> 3. AT ALL LIBRARIES, AIRPORTS, AND DEPOTS,

4. On all ships sailing under the Tashiri flag,

5. At all foreign posts, diplomatic stations, and embassies, and

6. At the United Nations in New York.

The companion flag shall also be displayed below the national flag on all uniforms of the Tashiri military, police, and fire protection services, and on all official vehicles, vessels, and aircraft thereof.

Slide 1

The question for today's debate is whether it is in the best interest of the people of Tashir to adopt the companion flag.

What is the companion flag? It is a flag representing all that human beings have in common, such things as the love of children, the desire for health and knowledge, concern for the safety and happiness of loved ones, our shared susceptibility to pain and pleasure, illness and injury—everything that is done, held, known, or experienced in common by human beings, notwithstanding their differences. As Dr. Baweja noted, it gets its name from the fact that it is flown below the other flags of the world on the same pole, never alone. Where it is displayed on a decal, patch, or insignia, it appears directly below the host flag.

The companion flag creates a dual symbolism. What we as a species have in common across our myriad political, cultural, ethnic, and religious borders is, for the first time in history, confirmed as a category of moral contemplation. Our commonalities do not outstrip our differences or contend against them, but rather both they and our differences are simply brought into focus. The idea is to bring an awareness of all that we have in common—sameness awareness—into the field of moral deliberations, both public and private.

Slide 2, please, Len. This shows the companion flag below the Tashiri flag, and also below the flag of Canada. Alden Frost, the flag's creator, established its design. The stripe across the top of the flag varies in color; it can be any color appearing in the host flag above it. Here in Tashir, the stripe at the top of the white companion flag can be either green or black. In Canada, it will be red. Below the flag of, say, Brazil, it can be green, blue, or gold.

Mr. Frost once explained that the purpose of the variation in color was to depict the constant interplay of human differences and human samenesses. Was this a good idea? Should companion flags look different depending upon the colors appearing in the host flag? Is the flag's overall design—a white field with a stripe of color across the top—satisfactory? We are not here to discuss these topics. We accept the companion flag as it is and ask, "Is it in the best interest of the people of Tashir to adopt it?"

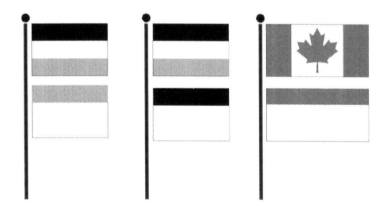

Slide 2
The companion flag below the flags of
Tashir and Canada

We can ask this question on several levels. We can ask, for example, whether what the companion flag stands for—all that human beings have in common—is justification enough for its adoption. Certainly, from a strictly religious point of view, this must be the case. For if God created us all, that which we perceive as common to us all across our differences is something approaching the very essence of His handiwork. We have only to ask, is God's handiwork deserving of our remembrance and celebration through the adoption of a flag? Should God's plan—this interweaving of our lives, our experiences, our natures—be heralded and set before the eyes of our children day in and day out as we, and they, seek ever greater levels of self-identification and moral perspective? Or, do we say to God, "No, these commonalities you've created are of little or no practical interest to us, especially compared to the differences you've created, which, as you've seen, we celebrate day in and day out with flags, and have for centuries. One thing we can say about the wide variety of beautiful flags used throughout the world today: they draw lines of division and separation over the earth's human population. Under each, there is a group of people embraced and included, whereas the rest of the world is, by definition, excluded. This is the way we prefer it."

Even from a nonreligious point of view, is not the companion flag—the world's first symbol of all that human beings have in common—its own justification? To what depths must one plunge to see the merit in this idea? Is it harmful? In what way? Are there advantages to be gained from creating a greater sense of interconnectedness in the world? From walking the talk, as they say? Will the traveler to a far-off country—perhaps someone arriving here on business from Russia or Australia—gain comfort in seeing the companion flag flying beneath the Tashiri flag outside the airport? Or seeing it on the sleeves of our customs agents and policemen?

It's helpful, I think, to imagine the companion flag already in place, already adopted around the country, and to imagine that as one citizen of Tashir you have the power to remove it, to end the practice, once and for all. Would you do it? And more to the point, why? Why would you want our children *not to be reminded* of their interconnectedness to strangers living down the street, or in far-off places? Why would you *not* want Tashir's symbolic landscape to include a symbol representing a new basis for global understanding, a recognition of our partially intertwined identities, common fortunes, and shared existential challenges?

It's interesting to ask yourself if you would remove the companion flag, once established, if you could do so anonymously, without questions asked. This thought experiment eliminates the question of cost and the problem of getting over the stultifying effects of inertia where the evolution of a customary practice is concerned. You're simply undoing something that is relatively new. Would you stop the practice of flying the companion flag if you could?

A similar question might be what you would think of *another* country's adoption of the companion flag. Say South Africa adopted the companion flag. Would you think them shallow or foolhardy? Would their new symbolism paint a more accurate, or a less accurate, picture of the human condition than our flag, for instance, standing alone?

Mr. Frost used to say that there are two questions at the heart of the companion flag project. First, are the things we humans have in common real? And, secondly, if so, are they important enough to justify a symbol of their own? We will answer both questions with a definite yes.

We imagine a world where Tashiri children see these paired symbols constantly. They will understand that both flags have been chosen by the adults around them: their parents, teachers, grandparents, community leaders—all the people who exercise control in the world surrounding them. This is important, for children acquire their moral sensibilities through a kind of unspoken dialogue with these adults. Each day they ask us silently, in effect, "Do you see me?" "Am I important?" "What is it about *me* that has value?" "Where do *I* fit in?" and "How should I treat this person over here, or that one over there who is different?"

What the host flag and the companion flag—together—answer is that people throughout the world are both different and the same; that our differences are important, but so are our commonalities. What the companion flag in particular symbolizes is that each of us has intrinsic value regardless of our differences—regardless of whether we are tall or short, plain or beautiful, intellectual or simple-minded, Tashiri, Japanese, or Costa Rican. We have value by virtue of all that connects us as human beings.

I mentioned that the question before us—Is adopting the companion flag in the best interest of the people of Tashir?—can be answered on several levels, and I daresay some people will need no further convincing. It is a symbol that unites us. It also reflects the true breadth of our cognitive inheritance, for in the last few decades science has shown that the human mind is two-sided; that we are equipped—created, if you like—to see both differences, the world of the left side of the brain, and unities, the work of the right side. It has become evident that integrating both views is our ultimate challenge and destiny, and yet to do this we must overcome with gentleness and understanding the left-side dominance that colors and shapes most of our cultural thinking. We must see each other anew, as brothers and sisters, if we are to avoid tearing each other apart. We have just closed the book on the bloodiest, most lethal century known to man. We are challenged—all of us—to find a new way forward. Awareness of our true natures is the first step in the way forward.

As I mentioned, the idea of the companion flag is to bring awareness of all that we have in common—sameness awareness—into the field of moral contemplation, a field currently dominated by difference awareness.

Will flying the companion flag do this? In what ways can sameness awareness affect our moral choices? These are the questions Mr. Williams and I will attempt to answer in this debate.

MSGR. DOYLE: The question before us is whether the Tashiri Parliament should pass legislation calling for the display of the companion flag below the flag of Tashir wherever it is flown. It is an honor to have been asked to speak in opposition to the resolution, and to be joined by such distinguished panelists.

Seven days ago I had never heard of the companion flag. I daresay if I haven't heard of it, hundreds of millions—perhaps billions—of other people around the globe have not heard of it either, at least not until the very recent events in Uzbekistan and here in Sanori. If we're to believe what we read online, Mr. Frost and, at times, a handful of sympathizers have struggled to bring this idea to the world's attention for more than two decades, traveling throughout Europe, Central Asia, North and South America, and parts of Africa. Granted, it's a big pond, but until last week the ripples had not reached me, or at least I was unaware of them.

Perhaps this is the first piece of evidence against the idea. I don't know. I don't count it the strongest, for the idea of diluting our national symbols with this banner of Mr. Frost's is, in the plainest terms, absurd. This, we must remember, is one man's idea . . . a man whose true motivations, unfortunately, we may never know. Who financed him all these many years? I find nothing about that on the Internet.

The companion flag project smacks of utopianism, and not one word from Ms. Ibrahim argues against that conclusion.

Granted, we are only beginning the debate, but I have heard nothing that grounds this unprecedented idea in popular support, social necessity, or exigency. I'm somewhat surprised, in fact, that Mr. Frost didn't just call it "the Frost flag" and be done with it.

(Laughter.)

We're told the companion flag represents all that human beings have in common. What is that, exactly? That we live and die, that we breathe air and eat plants and animals. Do we really need a flag to remind us of this? Is there anyone here or within the sound of my voice who doesn't know that the folks living in China are people, or that the folks in Brazil are people? And those two-legged creatures dressed in business suits in New York City—the ones who whistle for cabs—we all know that those are people, too.

(Laughter.)

I find it amazing that anyone would suggest we need an extra flag to remind us of what is self-evident. Should we have a third flag to remind us that we have two eyes and two ears? I'm being facetious. The goals for the companion flag, as introduced by Ms. Ibrahim, are far loftier, and we look forward to debating her and Mr. Williams on the particulars of their theory—which at this point I don't pretend to understand. The general idea seems to be that ethical behavior, as concerns humanity, will evolve under the fluttering shadow of this second flag to accompany our current flags; that to begin with, the people of Tashir will adopt a new way of being in the presence of one another that will have us all thinking, one supposes, eventually, of a pre– and post–companion flag world.

I am skeptical, as, indeed, we all should be. As we hear more, let us be alert for appeals to cosmopolitanism. Mark carefully any evidence of the secular humanist canard that we humans can engineer moral progress by tinkering with dials and levers. Keep an ear open for the jargon of world citizenship, multicultural-ism, world governance, social leveling, and the alleged evils of particularism and national identity.

We're familiar, of course, with Moliere's *Misanthrope* who loved humankind in general but could not abide individual men and women. Does this describe the late Mr. Frost? (Present cir-cumstances do not permit me to turn away from the question out of delicacy.) Who was this man who, until the last few months, travelled alone throughout the world, operating oftentimes at night, planting this idea—this flag, which he himself, we're told, named "the companion flag"? What do we know about him? He was divorced, and apparently had lost touch with his wife and children in the United States. He was a former driver for FedEx, we're told.

What did Mr. Frost have in mind when he spoke, as he evi-dently did, of all that human beings have in common? Was it, as we're told, the love of children and our love of music? What would he say about sex-selective abortions in China, or abortion anywhere for that matter? Is this part of what he calls a univer-sal love of children? And what is it that ties Chinese opera to hip-hop? The danger in speaking of universals, of human same-nesses, is that they simply don't exist. Not as such anyway.

How did one writer, Sissela Bok, put it? "Projects for worldwide ethics litter history like tanks abandoned in the desert." Let us be wary, ladies and gentlemen, of this claim that sameness awareness will transform the moral landscape. Do I have that right? Well, in any event, be on guard for sweeping promises of a world—or a coun-try—transformed by sameness awareness. It is simply too broad, too abstract, an idea—too *expensive* an idea—to be tried out on the people of Tashir.

What do I mean by expensive? I'm not talking about the flags themselves. Their cost is a pittance. I'm talking about the inevitable cooling of national pride that will accompany putting a second flag, representing what all of us allegedly have in common, below the Tashiri flag. I'm talking about the calving-off of part of the loyalties and engagement of the people of Tashir—and for what reason? None that is evident to me. Our ethics, as with our loyalties, are not world-encompassing, ladies and gentlemen, they are culturally rooted. Their patterns are visible in the fabric of our local—and by that I mean, at the furthest extreme, our national—histories and identities. There is a natural limit to how far the bonds of our moral commitments can be stretched. Certainly, we agree, do we not, that as parents we owe more to our own children than to the children of people down the street, and more to the children of our friends and neighbors than to the children of families living fifteen thousand miles away, with whom we do not share a language, a culture, or a religion?

Be leery of anything that will dilute the authority of the national symbol—as I believe the companion flag would—for our commitments to each other, and the rights we prize as citizens, are protected by blood and money. Certainly no one who has studied history or lived for two decades or more can doubt that. The only entity authorized and equipped to support our commitments—to our parents, our children, our cultural heritage, and our religious brethren—is the nation in which we live. It is not the world, and not humanity as a whole. It is only with the full engagement of citizens as "national citizens" that this arrangement can continue. Our ability to reason and converse—even with remote others—must, in the first instance, be rooted in a particular history—our history, a particular set of traditions—our traditions, and a particular felicitous (or at least let us say life-sustaining) web of interpersonal and intergroup commitments—ours.

Edmund Burke famously wrote, "To be attached to the subdivision, to love the little platoon we belong to in society, is the first principle (the germ as it were) of public affections. It is the first link in the series by which we proceed towards a love to our country, and to mankind."

The flag of Tashir, like so many national symbols, is beautiful on its own. It has work to do. Let it alone.

(Applause.)

MODERATOR: Ms. Ibrahim or Mr. Williams?

MS. IBRAHIM: Over time, the companion flag will, we submit, reduce man's inhumanity to man. How will it do this? By increasing the production and widening the influence of compassionate impulses in people everywhere.

What we see when we encounter other people—the bits of information about others that enter our conscious or subconscious minds—determines the types of impulses that arise within each of us to inform our moral judgments, opinions, and intentions. The companion flag will initiate and signal a change in a long-standing habit of the mind: a tendency to see only human differences ahead of moral action. It will remind us all, particularly our children and future generations, that we are not just different, we are, paradoxically, both different and the same.

We are pointing, of course, toward a labeling of two distinct types of information about the people around us, a new bifurcation. I'll elaborate on that in a minute. When sameness awareness is part of the content of our awareness of self and "other" (for ease of reference, we'll use "other" in place of "other people or groups of people"), it generates compassionate impulses that promote greater understanding, interpersonal and intergroup regard, and a preference for nonviolent problem solving in people everywhere. It also promotes greater self-love.

Sameness awareness is not a replacement for difference awareness. Sameness awareness sharing the stage with difference awareness is the goal of the companion flag project.

The companion flag is also a corrective. Whatever their social or political origins, the flags of the world today double as markers of human identity. As such, they are inadequate. They impart to the world's children the impoverishing view that their lives are ennobled only by their differences and separation from other human beings, while all that they have in common with people everywhere by virtue of their shared humanity is a trifle unworthy of mention. The companion flag works without denying, speaking to, or diminishing the importance of our differences.

Does it stand for a new moral philosophy or code of ethics? No. The two flags are *de*scriptive, not *pre*scriptive. That is, they portray the human condition but they do not impinge on the free will of any moral actor.

Seeing the companion flag with the flag of Tashir will not tell any Tashiri citizen how to act, or how they should think or feel when human differences collide. There is no hidden agenda here, no philosophy, or code of ethics. The two banners simply remind us that we humans are informed by, and rely upon, not one but two distinct, coexisting, and organically connected spheres of experience: a sphere of human differences (represented by the host flag) and a sphere of human samenesses (represented by the companion flag). The latter is our common bond.

Mahatma Gandhi was once asked, "How can you make a man do good?" He answered, "You cannot make a man do good; you can only create the conditions under which he will choose to do good."

This understanding is reflected in the companion flag project. By adding the companion flag to the world's symbolic landscape, we create for those who come after us a condition under which they will choose to do good. Under the sway of their own compassionate impulses, they will, in ever-increasing numbers, act to reduce man's inhumanity to man, and to reduce as far as possible cruelty, interpersonal and intergroup violence, alienation, and other forms of abuse. (Today and throughout history people have too often shrugged these off as acceptable or inevitable human responses to life's difficulties and challenges.) It is an ambitious project, to be sure, but one buoyed by unequaled simplicity, clarity of purpose, and cost-effectiveness.

To illustrate how the companion flag works—how sameness awareness works—we will introduce two diagrams: the moral continuum, showing the sequence of events leading up to moral action, and the dumbbell analogy, highlighting the coexistence of two distinct spheres of experience, the sphere of human differences and the sphere of human samenesses.

What are human differences and human samenesses, and what are compassionate impulses? A *human difference*, as we use the term, is any human characteristic, experience, concern, desire, or susceptibility that is not shared by all people everywhere. Thus, being Tashiri is a difference; so is being a woman. Being able to speak Chinese is a difference, as is a preference for certain foods, or being over five feet, four inches tall. A *human sameness* is any characteristic, experience, concern, desire, or susceptibility that *is* shared by all people everywhere—no matter who they are, where they live, or how pronounced their differences may be. The desire to be accepted for who you are, concern for the safety and happiness of loved ones, our shared susceptibilities to pain and pleasure, illness and injury—these are examples of samenesses. Other examples include the need for food, water, and air; the desire to be safe in our homes and beds (or wherever we may sleep); the love of stories and music; laughter; our range of emotions; our shared dependence on the plants and animals of the earth; our susceptibility to, and reliance upon, the weather and other forces of nature; our sense of wonder at the mysteries and uncertainties of the universe; our use of sounds and symbols to communicate with others; the knowledge of our own imperfection; our enjoyment of ritual, self-adornment, and art; and our desire to be treated fairly by others.

All human characteristics, experiences, and concerns are either differences or samenesses, and, as you know, the companion flag is a symbol of human samenesses.

Compassionate impulses are the natural fruit of sameness awareness. To continue with our definitions, an impulse is "an impelling force; a sudden spontaneous inclination or urge." Moral impulses are impulses that may, depending on their strength and the strength of opposing factors, influence moral conduct. *Compassionate moral impulses* inspire the actor to privilege over unchecked self-interest or pragmatic gain actions and forbearances that inure to the benefit of other, signal a recognition of other's dignity and equality, and promote compassionate understanding and nonviolence. "Compassion" and "compassionate" are derived from the Latin *comparti*, meaning to suffer together.

There is, as I have already mentioned, a widespread tendency to see in others ahead of moral conduct only the sphere of human differences. If other is an individual, what enters our awareness may be his or her age, ethnicity, gender, skin color, body shape, evidence of nationality, cultural or religious affiliation, evidence of wealth, manner of dress, attractiveness (or unattractiveness), facial expressions, personal bearing, and the like. If the encounter includes verbal clues, we may become aware of his or her language and inflections, his or her emotional state, and possibly his or her beliefs, profession, sociability, and sense of humor.

If other is a group of people, what enters our awareness may be their common interests, physical condition, ethnicity, nationality, skin color, facial features, manner of dress, historical or cultural affiliation, language, and the like. In either case, the picture painted on our awareness is a composite of other's differences.

An active awareness of others' differences is essential and natural. We could not navigate through life without it. It is possible, however, to see and honor these differences in a wider context—that is, as part of an ever-present duality that includes experiences, characteristics, concerns, desires, and susceptibilities that are shared by people everywhere—the context provided by the right side of our brains. A child who grows up surrounded by symbols that consistently honor not only differences and separation but samenesses as well will find it difficult, if not impossible, to do otherwise. He or she will embrace the paradox of humanity effortlessly throughout his or her life.

What accounts for the tendency to see only differences ahead of moral action is a kind of preset of our social and interpersonal consciousness, a left-sided dominance, a pinched and truncated view, something Mr. Frost called "the dumbbell effect." To see only one sphere of experience is to see other incompletely. The companion flag will create a condition under which each of us, in the role of moral actor, will choose to overcome the dumbbell effect and see both spheres of other's experience before making moral judgments.

This project is fact-based. Just as difference awareness is an awareness of facts that may influence moral decision making, so it goes for sameness awareness. Up to the present time, the bifurcation of our life experiences into differences and samenesses has been largely ignored. The companion flag project seeks to rectify this, not because samenesses coexisting with differences is a theory, but because it is a fact; and more to the point, because it can be shown that an active awareness of samenesses in the example of other people is the key to the natural production of compassionate moral impulses.

With free will the moral actor is entitled to form his or her own opinions, judgments, and intentions respecting other, but he or she is not entitled to his or her own facts. Free will does not give us license to deny the warmth or brilliance of the sun, the curvature of the earth, or the charge of a lion. Similarly, we are not free to deny the fundamental structure of our lives—that we humans are, at once, both different and the same. The illusion that there is but a single sphere of human experience relevant to our sense of identity and correct conduct, the sphere of human differences—my family, my tribe, my ethnicity, my religion—is dispelled once and for all by the companion flag.

The function of the companion flag is not to identify or develop a global consensus about all the various ways human beings are the same. It is simply to confirm the fact of our interconnectedness.

So, this is the affirmative claim: the companion flag will promote and sustain an active awareness of what human beings have in common throughout Tashir, cementing in our minds, and in the minds of our children, the fact that people everywhere are not just different from one another; they are, paradoxically, both different and the same. This perspective will extend into the daily lives and moral practices of individuals and groups, defeating once and for all the illusion that we are justified in formulating our moral commitments to others based on awareness of their differences alone. With sameness awareness will come the widespread release and interplay of compassionate impulses. Adoption of the companion flag is therefore in the best interest of the people of Tashir.

In order to further unpack this argument, let me return to some definitions.

Moral conduct is any intentional act or choice that has a foreseeable impact on the well-being of other. *Moral* means "of or concerned with the judgment principles of right and wrong in relation to human action and character." Moral conduct, for our purposes, is not limited to good, beneficent, or positive actions or choices. Feeding a hungry person is moral conduct, but so is assaulting someone or turning your back on someone in need. All are intentional and have a foreseeable impact on the well-being of other.

A person engaging in moral conduct is a *moral actor*. It is the moral actor who must choose to do good under Gandhi's formulation. We are all moral actors in our interactions with the people around us. We are moral actors vis-à-vis our children, parents, siblings, friends, neighbors, and co-workers . . . and, for most of us, a multitude of others as well.

The intention that precedes and informs moral conduct is the third stage of the moral continuum, and we call it the *moral intention*.

I've mentioned two types of impulses that may affect the moral actor's treatment of other and the formation of his moral intention. Mr. Frost called these passionate and compassionate moral impulses. I've also suggested that these have distinct sources in the human psyche. *Passionate moral impulses* arise spontaneously and involuntarily from something we're calling difference awareness, and *compassionate moral impulses* arise spontaneously and involuntarily from something we're calling sameness awareness.

Difference awareness and sameness awareness are the two constitutive parts of the content of a moral actor's awareness of other ahead of his or her moral conduct. *Difference awareness* is the moral actor's awareness of one or more human differences manifested by other. *Sameness awareness* is the moral actor's awareness of one or more human samenesses manifested by other.

Encounter means to be in other's presence or otherwise situated such that the impact (on other) of one's intentional actions and forbearances is reasonably foreseeable.

I encounter a man. I become aware that he is tall, white, Russian, a computer programmer, married, and an expert pianist; has diabetes; and coaches a youth hockey team. Each of these characteristics and experiences is a human difference. The content of my awareness of this man is difference awareness alone.

Now let us say I bring to mind ahead of any moral conduct an awareness that this man wants to be accepted for who he is and is concerned for the safety and happiness of his loved ones. These are human samenesses. Now the content of my awareness is both difference awareness and sameness awareness.

The *content of a moral actor's awareness of other* must be comprised either of difference awareness alone or of both difference awareness and sameness awareness. To see other completely we must see in him or her both differences and samenesses. Generating sameness awareness is, in purely mechanistic terms, the goal of the companion flag.

Passionate moral impulses can be either positive or negative. The operative difference between passionate and compassionate impulses is that while the former may lead a moral actor to endorse either positive or negative moral behaviors or forbearances, the latter evokes a motivation to affirm and preserve humanity in the example of other. Affirmation of other's humanity is commonly expressed through restraint, a check on purposeful, self-centered conduct injurious (or potentially injurious) to other. The urge to preserve humanity in the example of other is frequently seen in selfless acts of protection and saving.

It is hard to imagine a clearer and more compelling acknowledgement of the role of free will in ethical behavior than Gandhi's reply to the question, "How can you make a man do good?" (Each moral actor must choose for himself or herself to do good.) Yet Gandhi's words are also a clarion call to those of us who would leave the world a better place for having lived: we must strive to create conditions under which others will choose to do good.

By adopting the companion flag, the world's first symbol embracing both human inter-connectedness and the paradox of humanity, we answer that call.

(Applause.)

PROF. O'NEIL: What I identify and understand to be the two fundamental claims of the affirmative side are that human beings are paradoxically different and yet the same, and that what we see when we encounter other people determines the types of impulses that arise within each of us to inform our moral judgments, opinions, and intentions. To expand further, my understanding of the affirmative argument is that it is saying the content of human beings' awareness of each other is made up of two parts, awareness of human differences and awareness of human samenesses; that these different aspects of awareness of other lead to different types of moral impulses, passionate and compassionate; and that these impulses play a seminal role in determining moral conduct and behavior.

From here, the affirmative side also suggests that throughout history there has been a predisposition in humankind to view only human differences and therefore act on only passionate impulses. In addition to suggesting that this is not preferable because of its epistemic incompleteness, the supporters of the companion flag also suggest that this "differences only" view of others is not desirable because compassionate impulses arising from sameness awareness are responsible for such seemingly good moral conduct as selflessness, nonviolence, equality, and so on. Therefore, the affirmative side proposes the adoption of the companion flag here in Tashir as a symbol of both human differences and human sameness, to keep the full content of human awareness of other ever present in people's minds. This, we are told, will spark an increase in compassionate moral behavior.

Ms. Ibrahim makes reference to something called the dumbbell effect, an analytical construct devised by Mr. Frost. While I think I have some idea what this refers to, I will await further clarification from the affirmative side before commenting.

Have I adequately summarized the argument in favor of the resolution?

Ms. IBRAHIM: You have.

PROF. O'NEIL. The two main problems with this argument, as I see it now, are that it takes an overly essentialistic view of human nature, and that it deals poorly with Occam's razor, or the principle of parsimony.

The moderator has asked us to limit our use of academic and philosophical jargon, and to define those words and phrases that we are unable or unwilling to avoid. I will certainly have a great deal to say about essentialism and nonessentialism—those can't be avoided here—but let me start with Occam 's razor. This is the principle of philosophy that states that between any given hypotheses to explain a phenomena, the hypothesis that makes the fewest assumptions in offering an adequate explanation is to be preferred.

Is the argument in the affirmative as lean and parsimonious as it can be, or is it weighed down by superfluous and damaging assumptions and claims? The answer to this question seems almost certain to be the latter, for the affirmative argument asserts the existence of new metaphysical phenomena such as "moral impulses," "sameness awareness," "a predisposition toward difference awareness," and so on.

To prove the existence of some new metaphysical phenomenon is a nigh impossible task, so explaining one phenomenon by way of another acts only to compound one's difficulties.

SEC.-GEN. ROMERO: The companion flag, it must be said, is an affront to personal and national identity, acting only to weaken identity, not add to it. Not only does it weaken identities that may otherwise have positive benefits but in working to remove differences and emphasize sameness the companion flag promotes a dangerous homogenizing of persons, cultures, and nations, and causes a chilling effect on people standing too strongly for their distinctions and differences. If adopted, it will inevitably push the people of Tashir toward the lowest common denominator.

Also, while Ms. Ibrahim claims that the companion flag project does not come with a particular political or moral agenda, it undoubtedly does. The flag and project are undeniably ideological, as they embody and promote a particular view of human nature, personhood, and morality, and of how society and politics should be structured. While the companion flag's proponents claim it to be the first true universal flag, almost every overtly ideological flag throughout history has made the same claim: to represent some undeniable and universal aspect of human nature. The companion flag is no more neutral in its agenda and ideological message than are the Stars and Stripes or the Hammer and Sickle. Don't we already have the earth flag, the rainbow flag, the Olympic flag, and the flag of the United Nations?

The companion flag amounts to little more than an attempt by a person, or group of persons, to establish a cultural hegemony and disseminate their own personal worldview on a global scale. One must question whether it is even possible to promote the recognition of human samenesses via a symbol like a flag, considering that flags, as symbols, inherently work to differentiate people, namely those who support and wave the flag proudly and those who do not. The companion flag cannot escape this.

(Applause.)

Ms. IBRAHIM: There are many excellent points here. Let me move ahead with the expectation that these will be met.

To your argument that the earth flag or the rainbow flag, as well as the others you mentioned, are on par with the companion flag, I answer this way. Each of the flags you mentioned represents one or more human differences. The earth flag is a symbol of the environmental or ecology movement, whose agenda and priorities are not held in common by people everywhere. The rainbow flag is a gay pride symbol, or more generally a call to celebrate human diversity. The Olympic flag represents an international organization promoting peace and understanding through international athletic competition. The United Nations flag represents a group of nations acting in concert to affect certain outcomes and priorities of interest to its members. The Stars and Stripes, of course, is one nation's symbol, as was the Hammer and Sickle. We might add the famous peace flag to your list. This is an advocacy symbol promoting peaceful conflict resolution. All of these should be compared to the companion flag, which, far from advocacy, is simply a symbol of all that disparate peoples have in common. The companion flag is *de*scriptive, whereas most of these—certainly the rainbow flag, the earth flag, and the peace flag—are *pre*scriptive. There is an *ought* attached to them. One *ought* to honor diversity, one *ought* to privilege the environment, one *ought* to choose peaceful conflict resolution over other alternatives.

The starting point for one seeking to justify the companion flag is the bifurcation of the human life experience into human differences and human samenesses. That these coexist but are morally distinct must be established. Our differences are plain enough, and I've mentioned several examples of human samenesses.

Seeing both spheres of experience in the people we encounter is problematic, but it is both possible and desirable; and, as Professor O'Neil observed, it is epistemically required in order to see other people completely. For centuries, we have, as a species, not only focused our attention on the sphere of human differences but formulated our moral obligations to others on the basis of difference awareness alone.

Take, for example, the paradigm handed down by the Stoics and prevalent today in one form or another throughout much of the West: concentric circles of concern. Slide 3. This is the idea that humankind's moral commitments are naturally hierarchical and contingent. A person's moral first duty, according to this ancient Greek tradition, is to his or her own self-preservation, a circumstance the Stoics saw as emanating from our basic instinct to survive. Thus, self occupies the innermost circle of concern. Succeeding circles vary from person to person. For a good many of us, the next circle might encompass concern for our children and immediate family members. Once we are certain of our own safety and that of our immediate family, we can extend our moral commitments (our effective concern) to the next circle. Perhaps this will be our friends or neighbors. You get the idea. Beyond neighbors may be our co-religionists; our co-workers; residents of our village or region; members of our tribe; or people who share our ethnicity, our politics, our cultural inheritance, or our nationality.

Slide 3
Concentric circles of concern

The Stoics reasoned that the last or outermost circle of concern must encompass all of humanity, and they held up as an ideal that humankind would someday find a way to bring this circle in closer to the heart of our moral concerns. But that was a distant ideal. The essence of the Stoic model is the frank realization that our moral interests are self-referential, first and foremost seeking our own self-preservation and then, conditionally, and to an ever more attenuated extent, the preservation of people occupying these other circles. What's important for our purposes is to see that each succeeding level of moral concern, up to the last and most contingent, is based on difference awareness, on the content of the moral actor's awareness of other, his comprehension of characteristics, concerns, and desires *not shared* by people everywhere. Are you a member of my family? Of my tribe or nation? Do you share my beliefs? Are you a member of my "little platoon"? These are paradigmatic questions. I will fashion my treatment of you, and be justified, according to the answers to these questions.

We see the same theme in Confucianism. Confucius said, "In their original natures men closely resemble each other. In their required practices they grow wide apart." Confucius was an itinerant teacher who lived in a time of political, economic, and social unraveling in China, and his project, far from being egalitarian or revolutionary, was pragmatic (and ultimately unsuccessful). He was trying to restore the rites and disciplines of an earlier period, around the time of the founding of the Chou dynasty. He believed order and harmony must be sought first in the behavior and psychology of the ruling class. From this others would follow. He taught a doctrine called "the rectification of names," saying, "Let the ruler be ruler, the minister, minister; let the father be father, and the son, son."

Confucius sought to prevent the collapse of traditional social and familial hierarchies by encouraging a heightened awareness of fundamental human differences. The root of good government and social order, he reasoned, was harmony within the family, honoring one's parents, one's elder brother, what we know today as filial piety. That, and self-cultivation. The great Confucian Mencius wrote, "People have a common saying: Empire, state, family. The root of the state is in the family. The root of the family is in the individual." Can you visualize the Stoic model here?

There's no doubt that Confucius, like the Stoics, elevated the love of humanity as a virtue—he spoke of the daily practice of *shu*, of likening others to oneself—but again this was a distant ideal subordinated to the hierarchical duties (prescriptions) that arise from what he considered natural relationships, the fulfillment of which he deemed necessary for the preservation of good order. Those relationships were formed and identified strictly on the basis of human differences: my ruler, my minister, my father, my son, my older brother. Confucianism, like Stoicism, is associated with concentric circles of concern.

We are making the point that these moral systems share what I sometimes call the old paradigm, even though that's a misnomer. It is still the operative paradigm throughout much of the world: the view that we are justified in making our moral commitments to each other on the basis of difference awareness alone.

I mentioned the two schemas Mr. Williams and I will introduce to illustrate our support for the companion flag idea: the moral continuum and the dumbbell analogy. I will turn to the moral continuum next; but first, let me address the claim that there are people who do not love their children, who do not suffer, for whatever reason, from the death of a child, or who do not seek friendship and affiliation with others. These are extreme examples. Our definition of human samenesses encompasses the globe, the great mass of humanity, and is not disproved by the existence of deficits and sociopathologies of one kind or another. Perhaps, Professor O'Neil, if you'd be willing to elaborate on your point . . . ?

PROF. O'NEIL: Yes, of course. There are two general spheres of understanding human nature: essentialism and nonessentialism. Essentialist views posit the existence of some manner of unchanging "essence" or set of requisite components or characteristics that are shared by all members of the species, and as such are taken to be the necessary and sufficient conditions for being a human.

Any time someone posits the existence of some unique thing or set of things that makes us what we are, that person is appealing to an essentialist view of human nature. Put another way, essentialist views of human nature suggest that any and all things possessing the qualities X, Y, and Z are considered human beings, and that all human beings must have the qualities X, Y, and Z. Essentialist views of human nature are predominant throughout Western philosophy, going all the way back to the ancient Greeks. Socrates, Plato, Aristotle, and many of their contemporaries took a teleological view of nature, teleology being the view that each and every thing in the universe has a particular purpose or end for which it is designed and towards which it works, its *telos*. So, for example, the *telos* of an acorn is to grow into an oak tree, the *telos* of a rock is to always fall downward to the lowest resting position, and so on. It is this inherent *telos*, taken to be an objectively existing fact of nature, that counts as the unique essence of a thing, distinguishes it from all other things, and determines its characteristics.

Much of ancient Greek thought on human nature revolves around the idea that the highest good or purpose of human life is to achieve *eudaimonia*, some manner of "the good life." Socrates's and Plato's views of human nature tend toward *eudaimonia* being a state of virtuous living, with Socrates emphasizing rational thinking and Plato a harmonious balancing and operating of moral and intellectual virtues as the key to a life properly lived. Aristotle, for his part, saw human beings as *zoon politkon*, that is, the political animal, and felt that a big part of being human was to live together and organize ourselves into political communities. Aristotle's views on human nature, politics, and ethics had a big influence on later Christian thinkers—Aquinas, for example—who incorporated ideas of free will, sin, and morality as the unique essence of human nature. Much of our thinking today is still based on these notions that there are things that are objectively right and wrong and that it is inherent within human nature to want to be or do good.

Nonessentialism is simply the counter to essentialism; the view that there is no hard and fast unique characteristic or set of characteristics held universally by all human beings that determines our status as human and distinguishes us from all other things. Nonessentialist views can range from the outright denial of the existence of any such essences, instead positing the view that categories such as "human," "rock," "oak tree," and whatever else are just that, subjective categories we come up with, and are not naturally existing demarcations, to a soft acceptance of "human nature," but only with the strong caveat that human nature as such is not solidly determinable as a fixed and identifiable thing but is instead open-ended and subject to change.

Existentialism is a branch of philosophy and literature that has been gaining momentum since the end of World War II and has been largely responsible for triggering the transition in Western thinking from modernism to postmodernism. There are many different views attributed to be "existentialist," both atheistic and non-, but they all roughly hold as their main tenet the idea that existence precedes essence; that is to say, that we are either born without an inherently fixed essence or nature, or that such a thing may exist but we do not have knowledgeable access to it. It is through our actions and decisions that we determine our essence and nature; in short, this is the view that we are what we do, nothing more, nothing less.

Most people are aware of these two broad ways of understanding human nature via their juxtaposition in the nature/nurture debate of psychology: are we the way we are because of some inherent nature, or is it our actions and choices that lead us to become who we are? That the affirmative side is ultimately arguing for the adoption and presence of the companion flag as a means of positively affecting human development and outlook shows a recognition of the variability and constructed nature of who we are, but in my view the foundations of the argument are strongly essentialist. It explicitly points to the existence of a set of characteristics that all humans share, our human samenesses. Beyond this, it also points to the existence of a specifically bipartite sphere of "other awareness" and the existence of passionate and compassionate impulses as human facts and intractable aspects of what determines our morality and makes us who we are.

The difficulties with which all heavily essentialist views of human nature, this one included, must grapple revolve largely around dealing with the exceptions and grey areas and handling the burden of proof. For every conceivable characteristic X, Y, or Z that a person can come up with as a defining human characteristic, for every X, Y, or Z human sameness, we must be ready and able to pass judgment on those things that are seemingly human but lack X, Y, or Z or are in a grey area where they only sort of seem to possess X, Y, or Z.

Taking some of Ms. Ibrahim's examples of human samenesses, I personally know of people whom I consider to be human but who do not love children, do not have loved ones they are concerned about, do not use sounds or symbols to communicate, aren't filled with a sense of wonder, don't have a strong sense of inferiority and imperfection, do not laugh, and so on. You've acknowledged, Ms. Ibrahim, that you yourself do not qualify for most everything on your own list every time you are asleep or unconscious, nor did you when you were an infant incapable of most of these things. Even if I were to not have any ready examples of exceptions or grey areas, or if you were to deny or not accept them, you would have to at least account for the possibility that there could very well exist a thing we would otherwise call "human," except that it does not love children, etc. What, then, of these exceptions and grey areas? Either we are to exclude them from being considered human beings, to say that unconscious persons and babies are not human beings simply because they cannot laugh or self-adorn, which seems inaccurate or unreasonable, or we must whittle down the list of human samenesses, which it seems like we can keep doing until we have nothing left.

Ms. IBRAHIM: Yes, thank you. And the burden of proof concern?

PROF. O'NEIL: The burden of proof concern is that the argument for the adoption of the companion flag is positing the existence of a variety of real-world phenomena: that along with all human beings having the characteristics X, Y, Z, etc., there are these things called "moral impulses," "other awareness," and "moral imagination" that really do exist; that this "other awareness" really does have this particular effect on these "moral impulses," and in turn "moral imagination" and action; that there really is a predisposition in human beings toward seeing "human differences" that really can be corrected by the companion flag; and so on. The direct response to these claims is simple: prove it. What evidence do you have of the existence of these character-istics, impulses, and so on? Where do they exist? How do they actually work—that is, physically or physiologically? Why posit these things and not others as the essential human traits? How do we know this list is comprehensive and complete? What makes it definitive or authoritative? In the end, it is very, very hard, probably impossible, to definitively prove the existence of a sense of wonder or a love of children. And even if you can somehow undeniably prove the existence of such things in yourself or someone else, it is an entirely different task to prove that they invariably exist in every person who has ever lived or will ever live. When faced with such difficulties, people tend to retreat to one of two positions: they either start couching their claims in terms of dealing with human nature only "in general" or "on the whole," or they just outright push their claims as indubitable, often because of their own undeniable experience of such things. The former tack is problematic, and dangerous for that matter, because it leads one to ask what determines the threshold to qualify as "most people" or human nature "as a whole," that is, it leads to the questions of who gets to make this decision, who or what will end up not making the cut, and how to consider and deal with the minority who don't seem to fully qualify as human? The latter tack suffers from the fact that it is completely unverifiable, amounting to saying "this is true because I say it's true." Furthermore, it requires the leap of assuming that what applies to one person applies to everyone, which is again problematic and potentially dangerous. The affir-mative argument we are hearing today falls into the first of these camps, first defining a human sameness as "any human charac-teristic, experience, concern, desire, or susceptibility that is shared by people everywhere—no matter who they are, where they live, or how pronounced their differences may be," then brushing off exceptions as merely "extreme examples" and instead saying that "our definition of human samenesses encompasses the globe, the great mass of humanity, and is not disproved by the existence of deficits and sociopathologies of one kind or another." And just as a final note here, many of the samenesses and differences to which the affirmative side points are not things we actually "see" in each other—that is, literally or physiologically—but rather intersubjective intellectual concepts that we use to interpret and understand what it is that we do actually see. Such concepts did not always exist nor will they always exist, and this is something worth keeping in mind.

Ms. Ibrahim: In law and common practice, we limit moral responsibility for persons with certain disabilities. Examples of this are babies and children, people in a vegetative state or living with severe mental illness, and people who are asleep. True, these people may not, and often do not, exhibit or experience the attributes we are calling human samenesses. I'm quite sure, therefore, that Mr. Frost would have agreed to a point of clarification. Let us redefine human samenesses for our purposes to be experiences, characteristics, concerns, desires, or susceptibilities shared by *morally responsible* (or capable) persons throughout the world, their differences notwithstanding.

Mr. Williams: Coincidentally or otherwise, these are the same people who are alive to the meaning of a symbol.

Ms. Ibrahim: That's quite true. To the extent a mentally disturbed or psychologically handicapped person might not be able to identify with, or embody, human samenesses, it does not follow that others of sound mind will fail to do so. That people of sound mind recognize the common thread of disparate human beings is confirmed in the world's languages, by its legal codes, by religions, and by science. And yes, by its widespread use of symbols. We have words for humankind, do we not? We can say "the world's people" and know what we're talking about. We can count ourselves and declare a global population. We can fashion a comprehensible Universal Declaration of Human Rights. The medical experts among us can assess our wounds and illnesses and address them. If my mother is sick, give me an Austrian physician over a Tashiri test pilot or an Uzbek banker any day.

Are human samenesses real? Take two philosophers, one a Tashiri essentialist, one a French nonessentialist. Let them be picnicking with their families in their respective countries, and let them each discover that their infant child has gone wandering off and is heading straight for a raging river. Which one rushes to retrieve his child? The essentialist or the nonessentialist? Which one uses sounds and symbols to try to communicate with the child? Which one desires to have his communications understood and heeded by the child?

To claim as our opponents do that there are no experiences, characteristics, concerns, desires, and susceptibilities that are shared by people everywhere defies logic. You can fall off a cliff as easily in Singapore as you can in Tupelo. The range of human emotions from sadness to great joy is the same in Johannesburg as it is in Vladivostok. People are born, they grow old, and they die in Santiago and Katmandu alike. People use tools and communicate with each other in Rome just as they do in Buenos Aires. We are a global community of human beings—different in many ways, yes, but the same in others.

There is little to be gained in making this more difficult than it is. Professor O'Neil has posited that the companion flag project violates the rule of Occam's razor. I do not agree. I think it is profoundly simple. But it is also holistic. It requires that we look at those around us and see them completely. It says there are human differences and human samenesses, and however tempted we may be to make our moral commitments on the basis of difference awareness alone, to do so is to act on incomplete information.

I think it is akin to visiting the Louvre and finding the bottom half of the Mona Lisa covered with butcher paper. You are there, and sure enough there are the familiar eyes; there is the veiled hair, the pale sky, and the bucolic Italian landscape stretching out behind. But the enigmatic mouth and androgynous chin, the dress, the folded arms—these are missing. Tell me, have you seen the Mona Lisa completely? Are you justified in taking the part for the whole? Would I violate Occam's razor by insisting that in order to see the Mona Lisa completely you must remove the butcher paper?

People of good will can disagree about whether this or that trait or experience is universal. But the marginal case, or the exception, does not mean human samenesses do not exist. Often, what is common to all of us is the desire or concern underlying a particular experience, behavior, or reaction. Consider the case of the invalid parent who sees her infant moving toward the river but, owing to her disability, can neither move nor shout out. The human sameness there is not the act of rushing toward the child (something the invalid cannot do), but concern for the safety of a loved one.

The essentialist/nonessentialist dichotomy is not relevant here. However they come to be—whether they are innate essences, or the by-products of life experiences—human samenesses exist. The desire to move freely, the use of tools, rational and symbolic thought, the love of stories and music, our susceptibilities to pain and pleasure, our family relationships (we are all sons and daughters, for example), the processes of aging and death are all examples of this.

This is not to deny the dangers of mislabeling. There are, of course, widely shared human differences that to the casual or socially isolated observer may mimic samenesses. A small child growing up in Tashir might be forgiven believing that everyone in the world speaks Tashiri, loves soccer the way she does, or chooses chocolate ice cream over vanilla. A kindergartner might label these samenesses, but only an extremely narrow-minded, socially isolated, or chauvinistic adult would do so. Mr. Frost was fond of telling the story of former Texas governor Miriam "Ma" Ferguson, who, in a speech explaining her opposition to a statewide initiative to introduce bilingual education in Texas, is said to have raised the Bible above her head and cried out, "If English was good enough for Jesus, it's good enough for the children of Texas!"

(Laughter.)

A more nuanced answer is required to meet the challenge voiced by Monsignor Doyle, who would have us believe that morally responsible people living in different parts of the world do not share significant characteristics, experiences, concerns, desires, and susceptibilities. He points to sex-selective abortions in China, or abortions in general, to counter the claim that human beings love children. He asks, if some people love Chinese opera and others listen to hip-hop, can we really say that human beings share a love of music?

His challenge forces us to look carefully at the separate but interconnected spheres of human experience, for both, like twin engines, are constantly at work in our lives, defining us, impelling us, shaping us. Our universally shared human impulses must compete with a multiplicity of local and idiosyncratic factors, and nearly always are colored and shaped by them. There are instances when the impulses we share with humanity writ large are overruled entirely, and at other times they are visible only through the prisms of culture and local practice—but still they are visible. The knowing eye sees them.

In *Cultivating Humanity*, philosopher Martha Nussbaum tells of an American woman living in China who, after adopting a baby, hired a Chinese nurse to help her care for the child. Nussbaum writes,

> Even in the most apparently universal activities of daily life, cultural difference colors her day. Her Chinese nurse follows the common Chinese practice of wrapping the baby's limbs in swaddling bands to immobilize it. As is customary, the nurse interacts little with the child, either facially or vocally, and brings the child immediately anything it appears to want, without encouraging its own effort. Anna's instincts are entirely different; she smiles at the baby, encourages her to wave her hands about, talks to her constantly, wants her to act for herself. The nurse thinks Anna is encouraging nervous tension by this hyperactive American behavior; Anna thinks the nurse is stunting the baby's cognitive development.

What is clear is that both women share a concern for the health and well-being of the child. Different methods of swaddling and interacting with infants are examples of differing manifestations of human samenesses shaped and colored by local influences. Like the multicolored blossoms in the flower garden, their outward differences belie a more complex structure of alloyed impulses including many features and elements in common. The differences we see are real, of course—they answer impulses-to-action spawned by each woman's sphere of differences; but mixed in with these, and just as real and present, are universal impulses (in this case, the love of children, and the desire to protect, care for, and nurture the young) rooted in the sphere of our shared humanity.

Similarly, I would say to Monsignor Doyle, the love of hip-hop and the love of Chinese opera are rooted in two distinct but interconnected spheres of experience, not one. Impulses flowing from each create this overlay, this effect. We may at first see the love of hip-hop, for example, as emanating from the sphere of differences, but that is plainly a mislabeling. It is the product of alloyed impulses.

But I've gotten ahead of myself. Let me turn now to the moral continuum.

MODERATOR: Let us take a fifteen-minute break. (Break taken.)

MS. IBRAHIM: Slide 4, please. The moral continuum is an analytical construct composed of four stages. Although certainly reductionist—what did Alfred North Whitehead say? Seek simplicity, then distrust it—it illustrates the relationship between the content of the moral actor's awareness of other, which is what the companion flag is concerned with, and his moral conduct, which is the companion flag's ultimate concern. Moral conduct, which we've defined as "any intentional act or choice that has a foreseeable impact on the

well-being of other," is the end-point of the moral continuum—stage 4.

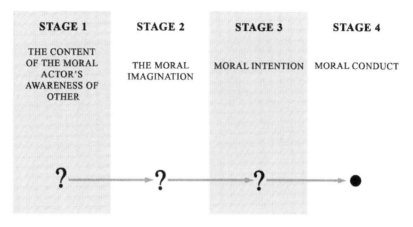

Slide 4
The moral continuum

Slide 5, please. Moral conduct is preceded and informed by
moral intention—stage 3.

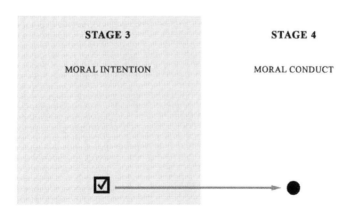

Slide 5
Moral conduct is preceded and informed by intention

Slide 6. Moral intention does not come into being magically or adventitiously. It is formed. It results from a complex mental process we are calling the moral imagination. This is stage 2 of the moral continuum. The *moral imagination* is an undifferentiated mental process by which the moral actor assimilates impulses, sensory perceptions, symbolic thoughts, desires, overlays and prescriptions, and other available data and influences (including free will) to arrive at his or her moral intention.

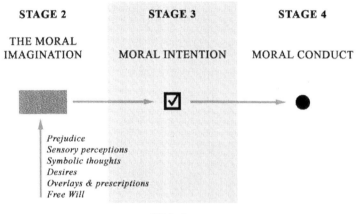

STAGE 2   STAGE 3   STAGE 4

THE MORAL
IMAGINATION   MORAL INTENTION   MORAL CONDUCT

Prejudice
Sensory perceptions
Symbolic thoughts
Desires
Overlays & prescriptions
Free Will

Slide 6
Moral intention, and by extension, moral conduct is
the fruit of the moral imagination

Slide 7. The moral actor's awareness of other precedes and informs the moral imagination. Without the Nazis' prior awareness of the Jews, they would not have—could not have—formed the moral intention resulting in the Holocaust. The schoolyard bully is aware of his victim, just as the Good Samaritan becomes aware of someone in need.

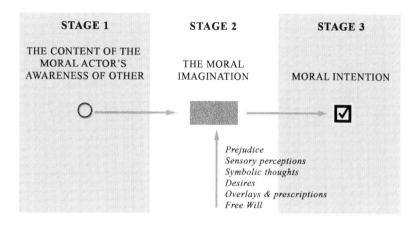

Slide 7
The content of the moral actor's awareness of other informs the moral imagination, and, by extension, moral conduct affecting other

This slide highlights the beginning—stage 1—of the moral continuum. The content of the moral actor's awareness of other necessarily precedes and informs the moral imagination, which in turn necessarily precedes and informs the moral intention. The moral intention necessarily precedes and informs moral conduct.

The companion flag will inaugurate a change in the content of our children's awareness of each other ahead of moral conduct—a change at stage 1. As described by Mr. Frost, the content of one's awareness of other can be—and, in order to see each other completely, *must* be—composed of two distinct cognitive categories, human differences and human samenesses. In contrast, an awareness of other that is limited to just one of these categories, human differences, is our species' default position.

Mr. Frost spoke in terms of spheres: the sphere of human differences and the sphere of human samenesses. This is easily

transposable into a three-dimensional image for illustrative purposes, and it gives us the dumbbell of the dumbbell analogy.
This, in fact, is where the two schemas—the moral continuum
and the dumbbell analogy—intersect.

Slide 8, please. By shifting the content of the moral actor's
awareness of other from difference awareness alone—represented

Slide 8
Silver and gold dumbbell

here by the silver sphere—to both difference awareness and sameness awareness—shown here by the gold sphere and the silver
sphere—we dramatically increase the likelihood of moral actions
being shaped by compassionate impulses. A different world results.

I see we have only black and white slides, so let me clarify:
the silver sphere is the one that appears lighter in color. The gold
sphere is the darker of the two.

The negative side has raised several objections that warrant
discussion, most notably the claim that the two kinds of moral
impulses we've identified, passionate and compassionate, don't

exist, or can't be proven to exist. What we have posited, of course, is that passionate impulses flow from difference awareness in the moral actor, represented by the silver sphere—slide 9, please—while compassionate impulses flow from sameness awareness, represented by the gold sphere—slide 10. Both kinds of impulses may enter the moral imagination, and both are capable of shaping our moral responses and behaviors. The promulgation of sameness awareness and the generation of compassionate impulses in our society—that is, in our moral decisions vis-à-vis one another—is the reason for the companion flag. We don't shrink from the opportunity to illustrate how compassionate impulses come into being, but believe that to do so we must say more about the second interpretive diagram, the dumbbell analogy. Bear in mind that we're turning now to the second question posed by Mr. Frost. We have shown that what we humans have in common is real; now the question is, are our commonalities important enough to justify a flag of their own? Mr. Williams?

Slide 9
Difference awareness

MR. WILLIAMS: Thank you. I'll refer to my notes. I'm passing along what I've learned from Ms. Yacoubi, who was injured in the Al Maseer bombing. She spent many hours with Mr. Frost, preparing for this part of the debate.

Slide 10
Sameness awareness

The two spheres of human experience . . . Each of us embodies the two types of experiences that we've been talking about: those that are shared by people everywhere—samenesses—and those that aren't—differences. On the surface of the silver sphere, imagine that we can see all of a person's human differences. Slide 11. If you were to meet me on the street, or at a party, you might see on my silver sphere that I am a male, forty-seven years old, African-American, and married; that I am trained as a conflict resolution specialist; that I speak English and Russian; that until recently I worked for the United States government; that my skin and eyes are dark; that I'm fairly tall, and so on. On my golden sphere, were you to see it, you might see some of the things Ms. Ibrahim has listed. The gold sphere of all individuals is identical, of course—these are human samenesses—so it's only a matter of imagining what parts of my golden sphere—which of my human samenesses—enter your awareness.

Slide 11
Differences visible on Mr. Williams's silver sphere

The dumbbell shown in slide 8 is a simple but fair representation of every human being on the planet. Each of us is informed, in part, by our differences, our diversity, and special affiliations (the silver sphere), and in part by experiences, characteristics, concerns, desires, and susceptibilities that we share with people everywhere (the golden sphere).

In this figure, we have a three-dimensional representation of the paradox of humanity. It's a paradox, of course, because if two or more people are different, how can they be the same? And if they are the same, how can they be different? Yet, that's exactly what we are.

Mr. Frost's point, as I understand it, is that for most of us, when we encounter another person or group of people, we don't see both spheres of the other's dumbbell; we see only the silver sphere. We see only a composite of human differences, and we formulate our moral commitments to other on that basis alone. This can be illustrated—slide 12, please—by turning the dumbbell on its handle so that only the silver sphere is visible. An important characteristic of a dumbbell is that when it's viewed end-on like this, it no longer looks like a dumbbell at all, but instead, like a sphere. We take in the image of a sphere as a separate object, complete in itself. If this is all we see when we encounter the object, slide 9, we are justified in believing that this is a sphere, not a dumbbell.

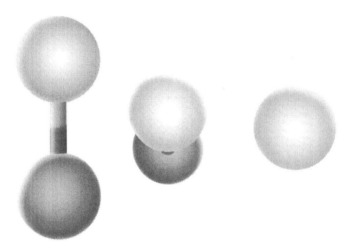

Slide 12
Turning the dumbbell until only the silver sphere is visible

PROF. O'NEIL: *Pars pro toto.*

MODERATOR: I'm sorry, Professor O'Neil?

PROF. O'NEIL: *Pars pro toto.* A part taken for the whole. That's what he's talking about. Go on. I didn't mean to interrupt you.

MR. WILLIAMS: *Pars pro . . . ?*

PROF. O'NEIL: *Pars pro toto.*

MR. WILLIAMS: Yes, thank you. It's an illusion, isn't it? Mistaking the part for the whole. Mr. Frost called it "the dumb-bell effect." If we move around the silver sphere—slide 13—we will begin to see the edge of a golden sphere and soon realize that the silver sphere is part of a larger, more complex structure. At that point we are not justified in calling it a sphere, and must see it for what it is—a dumbbell.

Slide 13
If we move around the silver sphere we will begin to see
the edge of a golden sphere.

Slide 14, please. To better understand and conceptualize how we see each other ahead of our moral conduct, imagine that each dumbbell is encased in a hypothetical, three-dimensional space—a glass box, if you like—which we'll call moral space.

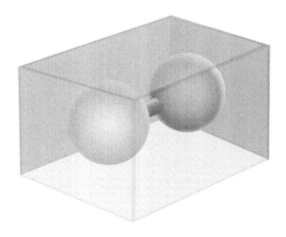

Slide 14
The dumbbell in moral space

Moral space is . . . let me get the definition. Here it is. A hypothetical, three-dimensional universe containing all data and perceptions about other accessible to a moral actor prior to developing his or her moral intention. Remember, in the final analysis, each dumbbell represents a person or a group of people that we may encounter ahead of our moral choices. And more particularly, each dumbbell represents the content of the moral actor's awareness of other, stage 1 of the moral continuum. If I'm the moral actor and I see only your silver sphere ahead of my moral actions—that is, only a composite of your human differences—the content of my awareness of you is limited to difference awareness. If I see both spheres of your dumbbell ahead of my moral actions, the content of my awareness of you is both difference awareness and sameness awareness. Moral space represents my opportunity, typically bounded by time and circumstances, to develop the content of my awareness of other.

Frost's point was that we are drawn inexorably to the silver spheres of other people. As a result . . . slide 15, please . . . this is the way the world of other human beings looks to us most days. We are surrounded by silver spheres.

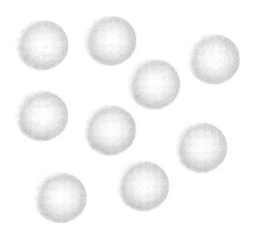

Slide 15
We are drawn to the silver spheres of the people we encounter

When we enter moral space—slide 16—this is the view that informs our moral understanding of other. I ask myself, is he a member of my group—my tribe, my clan, my eth-nic group? Does he have my skin color? Is he speaking my language?

Slide 16
Man encountering other in moral space (View 1)

The content of my awareness of other is limited to difference awareness. What's more, because I see a sphere complete in itself, I have no reason to question the adequacy of this view of things. I take part for the whole. *Pars pro toto.* The silver sphere, I assume, represents other completely. This is a fateful illusion. A kind of blindness results, narrowing the human moral horizon.

Mr. Frost called this phenomenon "the draw of the silver sphere," and he identified several reasons why we are drawn inexorably to the silver sphere of others: the fight or flight response, our cultural definitions of success, and the nurturing of our parents and grandparents, to name a few. He was also studying left-brain dominance with Professor Begisu of Port Hikma University before he died. Mr. Frost referred to imaginary springs holding the dumbbell in place in relation to the moral actor. In other words, unless you purposefully enter moral space with the intention of going behind the silver sphere of other to see their gold sphere, you will see only their silver sphere of differences. He called slides 16 and 17 our default position in moral space.

Think of the eyes of a character in a painting that seem to follow you around the room. No matter where you go, the character in the painting seems to be looking at you. It is the same with the silver sphere of other people's dumbbells. Unless we are reminded of the gold sphere behind them, the dumbbells seem to turn, no matter where we go, so that only the silver spheres are visible. Hopefully, we'll have time to delve into this more deeply. But the point is that, for the great majority of us—virtually all of us, I'll wager—difference awareness is the only thing we rely on to inform our moral imaginations. We formulate our moral commitments to other people on the basis of our awareness of their differences alone. Slide 17, please.

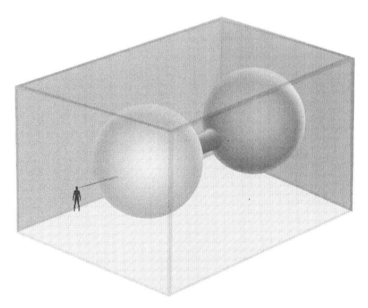

Slide 17
Man encountering other in moral space (View 2)

As you can see, the dumbbell now represents the content of the moral actor's awareness of other. That's how we're going to refer to it from now on. It's stage 1 of the moral continuum.

The alternative—let me be clear—is available to all human beings. Slide 18. That is, it's possible to break the spell of the dumbbell effect—to successfully push against the springs—and turn the dumbbell so that the content of our awareness of other ahead of our moral conduct is difference awareness *and sameness awareness*—not just difference awareness. We may think of turning the dumbbell against the pressure of the springs, or we may think of changing our own position relative to the dumbbell itself so that both spheres are visible to us. Either way, the result is the same as that shown in slide 18.

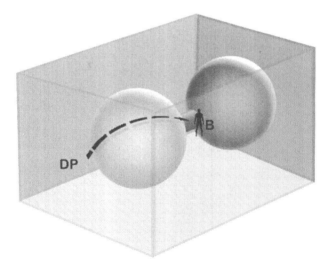

Slide 18
Through an act of will, we can move in moral space from
the default position (DP) to a place where the content of our
awareness of other includes both difference awareness and
sameness awareness (B)

This is the nub of the matter. Difference awareness produces passionate impulses, shown here on slide 19 as a dotted arrow running from the content of the moral actor's awareness of other to the moral imagination, whereas sameness awareness produces compassionate impulses, shown as a double arrow running from the content of the moral actor's awareness of other to the moral imagination. When the moral actor has both difference awareness and sameness awareness, he is producing—and his moral imagination receives—two different kinds of moral impulses, with the chance that his moral intention will be colored and shaped by compassionate impulses.

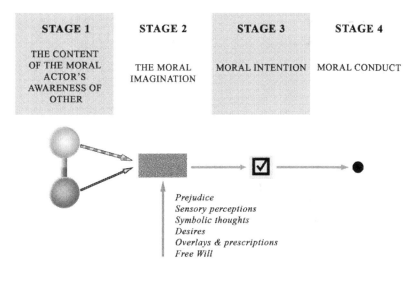

STAGE 1	STAGE 2	STAGE 3	STAGE 4
THE CONTENT OF THE MORAL ACTOR'S AWARENESS OF OTHER	THE MORAL IMAGINATION	MORAL INTENTION	MORAL CONDUCT

Prejudice
Sensory perceptions
Symbolic thoughts
Desires
Overlays & prescriptions
Free Will

Slide 19
Compassionate impulses are released into the moral imagination when the content of the moral actor's awareness of other includes sameness awareness (i.e., when the dumbbell is turned, negating the dumbbell effect).

There is no guarantee that compassionate impulses will carry the day with the moral imagination. Our passionate impulses, or the call of our desires, prejudices, prescriptions and overlays, symbolic thoughts, and so on, may overwhelm them; but certainly the addition of compassionate impulses increases the chances that the moral actor will endorse a compassionate response to other, will eschew cruelty, will privilege restraint over bullying or advantage-taking, and the like.

To sum up, we are all drawn to other's silver sphere, and as a result, absent an effort of the will to see the gold sphere of other, we make our moral calculations and commitments based on difference awareness alone. As Ms. Ibrahim has shown, this is consistent with several historical paradigms—in fact, I think it's safe to assume that those paradigms were developed under the influence of the dumbbell effect. The companion flag's purpose is to remind us that behind the silver sphere of other lies another sphere worthy of our attention, and when it is brought into focus, the human moral horizon expands and a new paradigm is born.

RABBI LEVENSON: Listening to this untried theory—I think we can agree that's exactly what it is—I did not hear an answer to our earlier question about how these alleged passionate and compassionate impulses come to be. Moreover, I'm convinced that no satisfactory answer exists. There is no proof of a cause-and-effect relationship between this so-called companion flag and any change in the behavior of real people living real lives. The goal is admirable, but the shine does not a shilling make, and all that glitters is not gold.

Both speakers pin their theory on the supposition that humans are influenced in their ethical behavior by subconscious or preconscious emotive impulses. I have my doubts (although they would find a friend in David Hume, I suppose). They imply again and again that they can explain how these impulses are created. Would the affirmative side be willing to provide that explanation now?

MODERATOR: Mr. Williams? Ms. Ibrahim?

MS. IBRAHIM: Passionate impulses connote a degree of not knowing. These stem from oppositions that enter our awareness when we recognize human differences—even shared ones. Mr. Frost used "passionate" here not in the conventional sense, to signal strong emotive force or ardency, although that may result, but as a counterpoint to compassionate impulses.

Unlike human samenesses (like the inevitability of aging, or the need for food, water, and sleep), human differences can be comprehended by the human mind only in relation to relevant opposites. Differences are not known—cannot be known, in fact—in and of themselves.

Let me illustrate this. Imagine you're an electrical engineer from Miami attending a conference on biospace technologies at Port Hikma University. Like most people attending the conference, you have come to hear a presentation by Dr. Marya Husain, a renowned Pakistani scientist and professor who is scheduled to present a groundbreaking paper on the first day of the conference. When you arrive at your hotel you are surprised to discover that the woman standing next to you at the reception counter—who is also in the process of checking in—is Dr. Husain herself. When she overhears that you have arrived for the conference, she turns to you with a broad smile and introduces herself. Over the next few minutes the two of you carry on a friendly conversation while you both fill out the hotel's paperwork. When Dr. Husain finishes, she stands, adjusts the shoulder strap of her bag, and graciously offers you her hand. You see that she is quite tall. She expresses the hope that you will enjoy Sanori and the conference and that the two of you will have a chance to talk again. With that she turns and walks away.

Let us further imagine that you learned the following during your brief encounter: that Dr. Husain is a beautiful woman, that she is kindhearted, is married, has dark olive skin, is Muslim, and is probably—judging by her clothes and jewelry—quite wealthy. You already know by reputation that she is one of the world's foremost scientists. Taken together, these characteristics compose the content of your awareness of Dr. Husain—of other.

At this juncture, is the content of your awareness of Dr. Husain a composite of human differences, human samenesses, or both? To answer the question, you simply apply the litmus test we've already mentioned. You ask yourself in regard to each of the things you've observed about Dr. Husain whether this is something shared by people everywhere, or not. If the answer is no, it is a human difference, which we place on Dr. Husain's silver sphere. If the answer is yes, it is a human sameness. It goes on Dr. Husain's golden sphere.

Is being Pakistani an experience shared by people everywhere? No. Therefore, that aspect of her life is visible on her silver sphere. Is being female an experience shared by people everywhere? No. That, too, is visible on her silver sphere. Is being a brilliant scientist and professor a universal human experience? No, clearly not. What about being married, being kindhearted, having dark olive skin, being wealthy, or being beautiful? Are these experiences shared by people the world over? No, none of them are. You have entered moral space at humanity's default position. Slide 16, please, Len. The content of your awareness of Dr. Husain is made up entirely of difference awareness. When you entered moral space, this is what you saw—slide 20, please.

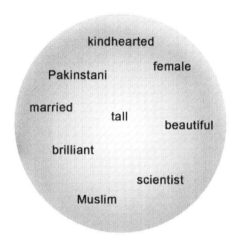

Slide 20
Dr. Marya Husain as seen from the default position in moral space

But we can improve on this illustration, for in truth it is incomplete and unsatisfactory. Human differences can be comprehended by the human mind only in relation to one or more relevant opposites. Defining oppositions, let's call them. When a moral actor enters moral space and sees other as attractive, he recognizes this quality because—and only because—he knows one or more defining oppositions, unattractiveness or plainness, applies to some other people. Both attractive and unattractive are projected upon his awareness, since neither can be comprehended in isolation. When he sees other as tall, he is able to identify tallness because—and only because—of his contemporaneous knowledge of the shortness of some people or perhaps people of average height. If all human beings were precisely the same height, there would be no idea or word for a tall person, and if everyone looked exactly the same, we would not have the idea of a physically attractive person. When I see dark skin, I recognize this as such because I am aware of lighter-toned people. If all humans had the same skin color, we would have no notion of dark-skinned people, light-skinned people, white people, or people of color.

In the same way, married inevitably enters human awareness with unmarried; wealthy with poor or middle class; Pakistani with non-Pakistani; Muslim with non-Muslim; female with male; kindhearted with mean-spirited or indifferent. You get the idea. Epistemically speaking, it is impossible to know, or to assign meaning to, any human difference—to anything visible on the silver sphere—without contemporaneous knowledge of its opposite.

In order to complete our illustration of your difference awareness of Dr. Husain, we must show the defining opposites as well as the perceived characteristics. Slide 21, please. The perceived characteristics, including Pakistani, woman, married, and so on, are shown here in bold, and below each, separated by a line, is a defining opposite for each.

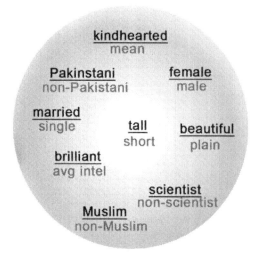

Slide 21
Difference awareness includes awareness of defining oppositions

Some combinations of opposed differences enter the moral actor's awareness without generating any morally significant impulses—that is, without producing impulses that will, or may, affect his or her moral treatment of other. Take, for example, "tall" and its defining opposite, "short." Although a morally significant reaction to another person's height is conceivable, let us assume for the sake of argument that Dr. Husain's height is a matter of no importance whatsoever to you, either consciously or subconsciously. To further simplify things, let's assume that the same holds for all of the differences (dyads) identified on Dr. Husain's silver sphere, save two: the fact that she is a woman, and the fact that she is Muslim.

If we imagine that you have been taught from an early age to believe that women are intellectually inferior to men, or that women who turn aside from more traditional roles to pursue a professional career in competition with men do so in derogation of God's plan for the world, then your awareness of Dr. Husain's gender will doubtless lead you to experience a kind of conscious or subconscious tension. An emotional response—a kind of cognitive dissonance—is inevitable when sensory input triggers strong evaluation in the moral actor. If we further imagine that you have a deep-seated prejudice against Muslims, your awareness that Dr. Husain is Muslim will likely produce a similar tension. These tensions, together with the negative passionate impulses they produce, are shown with dotted lines on slide 22 . . . 22, please.

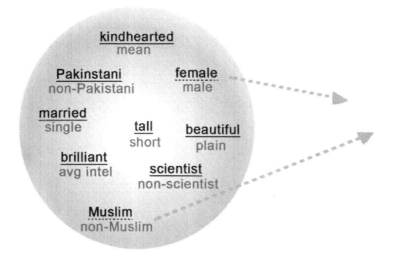

Slide 22
Passionate moral impulses are born of the tension between defining oppositions

Two points must be emphasized: first, that these psychological tensions would not be part of your awareness of Dr. Husain if she were male and non-Muslim; and secondly, that your awareness of Dr. Husain's gender, like your awareness of her status as a Muslim, is based entirely on—in fact, would be impossible without—your contemporaneous knowledge that some people are male and some are not Muslim. We are justified, therefore, in locating the tensions experienced by you in the cognitive space between female and male, on the one hand, and between Muslim and non-Muslim, on the other. The tension between these opposites is the spark that ignites our passionate impulses.

Passionate impulses need not be negative. They can be positive, as well, prompting the moral actor to endorse beneficent or positive moral conduct. As the Argentinean writer Jorge Luis Borges observed, "The reasons one can have for hating another man, or for loving him, are infinite."

Remove your imagined prejudices against women and Muslims in the case of Dr. Husain. If you are Muslim yourself, perhaps her faith is a source of pride for you, that you share your faith with one of the world's leading scientists. Or, let us suppose that when you meet her at the reception desk you are particularly in need of a smile and an encouraging word—the very things she supplies. Perhaps you have been stung recently by some rejection or maltreatment. Now the cognitive space between kindheartedness and its opposite, meanness, lights up in a positive way. Positive passionate impulses flow into your moral imagination where Dr. Husain is concerned.

I may see someone with great talent. My awareness of that person's talent may prompt me to feel awe or attraction, or I may feel jealousy and bitterness. But in every case, what I am feeling is rooted in an awareness that this talent is not universal—that some people do not possess it.

Passionate impulses are not bad. They're natural. Our lives would be dull and impoverished, indeed, if we could not discern human differences, or if we lost sight of each others' silver spheres and could not activate or experience our passionate moral impulses. In truth, however, there's no danger of that happening. Passionate moral impulses flow in an endless stream throughout our days. We humans never fail to see others' silver spheres. We are drawn to them—in fact, mesmerized by them—and, I believe, this force is such that we are bedeviled by the dumbbell effect: we see only the silver sphere when we encounter other. Other's golden sphere, his or her participation in the universe of shared human samenesses, is eclipsed, as shown in slide 16. Thus, compassionate moral impulses are not spawned, are not released to play what part they might in the moral imagination.

When the moral actor moves in moral space from the default position to a place where he or she can see not only other's differences but also part or all of other's golden sphere—when the more actor sees in other his or her participation in the universal human condition—compassionate moral impulses begin to flow into the moral imagination just as readily and naturally as do passionate ones. Slide 19, please. When I see in each of you, for example, the desire to be accepted for who you are, or your concern for the safety and happiness of loved ones—or when I acknowledge at the sight of you that there are people in the world whom you love unconditionally—I see these things not by virtue of a knowledge of opposites but by recognizing these experiences organically within myself. Looking within, I see that in this sense we are the same. I see myself in your eyes. This, I submit, is what it means to love another as oneself.

This is the fundamental difference between difference awareness and sameness awareness. Take the desire and the need for friendship and affiliation. We are social animals, and as with all morally responsible people, this characteristic informs our lives. I encounter you—or let's take someone else now, a stranger, someone I meet at a party. I encounter this person, and because of the draw of the silver sphere, the first thing I see is a composite of his human differences. I see his physical appearance, his manner of dress, his bearing; I see his ethnicity, his age; I may get clues to his intelligence, his approachability, his sense of humor, and the like.

Yet while I am struck at first by his differences, it is also possible to see in this person characteristics and experiences that are shared by people everywhere. By dint of an act of my own will, I can see in this man the desire for friendship and affiliation. I can also see other human samenesses.

All of the features visible on his silver sphere are, for me, dichotomized. But with human samenesses it is different. My knowledge of this man's desire for friendship and affiliation, my knowledge that he desires to be treated honestly and with respect, is not based on my knowing that some people do not possess these traits, do not want friendship and affiliation, or do not want to be treated with respect and honesty. It's not based on defining opposites at all. Instead, I know these things about him because I have looked within myself and found them there. I can say of other, "He is a person who wants to be accepted for who he is and treated fairly," not because I know of people who don't want this but because I experience this myself, internally, organically. It is there within me, just as it is there within you. And, significantly, this human sameness is an important part of me. I can look at him, in other words, and see important parts of myself. Do you see how adding sameness awareness at stage 1 of the moral continuum widens the human moral horizon?

Slide 23, please. Here's how we picture sameness awareness. This is the golden sphere of the dumbbell, and here are a few human samenesses I may see in other, if I apply myself.

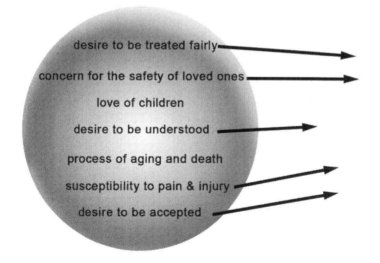

Slide 23
Sameness awareness spawns compassionate impulses that flow to the moral imagination

Again, notice that none of the features appearing to me on other's golden sphere are accompanied by a defining opposition. They stand alone. Not only do I, as a moral actor, not need an opposition to know or make sense of these qualities, but for the great mass of humanity no such oppositions exist. These are universal human experiences, characteristics, susceptibilities, and the like. I attest to them, and seeing them in you—seeing parts of myself in your eyes—involuntarily and automatically releases compassionate impulses into my moral imagination that may affect my moral choices.

You asked how the companion flag relates to these moral impulses. It is the world's first tangible symbol of all that human beings have in common, their differences notwithstanding. Therefore, it is a symbol of the golden sphere—a reminder that, in addition to the differences we see so prominently when we encounter each other (the default position), there exists *in fact* a separate but interconnected sphere of samenesses. Only when we see both spheres in our encounters with other have we seen other completely. The companion flag is a reminder of the need to see each other completely. Thus, we are creating a condition under which, owing to the release of natural compassionate impulses, more and more people will choose to do good.

(Applause.)

What Mr. Frost discovered, or I should say what he uncovered, is the need to identify *and label* for ourselves the content of our awareness of others prior to moral action. Only by assuring ourselves that we are seeing both differences and samenesses in others can we defeat the illusion called the dumbbell effect and access our natural capacity and propensity for compassion as a species. This is a first-level (or primary) bifurcation requiring us to distinguish two broad categories of awareness, whereas throughout history our forebears have focused exclusively on an unlimited palette of equally valid but secondary bifurcations—the oppositions visible to us all under the thrall of the dumbbell effect: tall/short, black/white, my tribe/your tribe, Muslim/Jew, friend/foe, neighbor/stranger, male/female. Our forebears have mistaken this for the last word on the content of their awareness of other. They have been seeing the part for the whole. *Pars pro toto.*

So, again, what does the companion flag do? It reminds us day in and day out that people are not just different. People embody two distinct spheres of experience, no matter who they are, where they live, or how pronounced their differences may seem to us.

Flying the companion flag below the national flag of Tashir does this in a way that is solemn, thought provoking, and perpetual. It captures our dual natures and makes this distinction-drawing—contrasting samenesses and differences—an important part of the backdrop of our children's lives. As I mentioned earlier, this will have a profound integrative influence on all children. It will increase their sense of inclusion, for one thing—of being at home in the world, and valued, regardless of their differences. It will increase their self-regard, their self-love, as well.

SEC.-GEN. ROMERO: Again, you've mentioned children. Do you not think, Ms. Ibrahim, that the companion flag would have an influence on adults, as well?

Ms. IBRAHIM: Yes, of course; but the greatest impact will be with children—future generations, especially the very young, ages three to eight, somewhere in there.

Very young children rely heavily on nonverbal communication from the trusted adults around them. They are particularly attuned to the significance of flying flags from the tops of buildings and other structures, at the entrances to parks and monuments, on bridges, at airports, museums, stadiums, libraries, and schools. Seeing both the Tashiri flag and the companion flag flying around them, our children will integrate both spheres of their own and of other people's experiences, understanding (or perhaps I should say "accepting at face value") the interplay and interpenetration of human differences and samenesses. Some would argue that the preverbal child does this naturally anyway; in that case, he or she will continue to do it, and in time will find the flags surrounding her harmonizing with—as opposed to counteracting—this natural inclination. Unlike previous generations, they will internalize rather than deconstruct this fundamental duality over time. Without abandoning received traditions and beliefs, they will embrace the paradox of humanity and this will translate into feelings of inclusion and self-worth and an unimpeachable belief in the connection of people everywhere. This will widen their moral horizon (or, if you prefer, keep it from shrinking). The effect will be permanent. Seeing the companion flag will add sameness awareness to "the space of reasons."

The child of the future will stop ahead of all moral choices and ask herself, "What have I just seen in other?" In the next instant she will look to the most telling features of other and ask, "Are these characteristics or features shared by people everywhere?" She will determine whether this or that feature is a difference or a sameness. If what she sees are differences only—a strong likelihood because of the draw of the silver sphere—she will know that she has not yet seen other completely. Acting without seeing other completely will be unacceptable to her, like dealing in half-truths and illusions. She will insist that she see both spheres of other's experience ahead of moral action, and so take a moment longer to identify one or more human samenesses in the example of other. Perhaps it will be the realization that this person is concerned for the safety and happiness of his loved ones, or is imperfect and aware of his imperfection. Maybe it will be, "this person desires to be accepted for who he is," or "this person, like people everywhere, wants to be treated fairly and with respect." The moral actor of the future will account for these to assure herself that she has seen other for who he is—completely— and that she is not succumbing to the irrational and irresponsible temptation to affect the well-being of another human being without seeing him completely, without—in a very real sense—knowing him as a human being.

The moral actor of the future will be highly skilled at labeling what she sees in other, not just according to the familiar oppositions tall/short, black/white, male/female, and the like but also labeling the content of her awareness of other as "a human difference" or "a human sameness."

Seeing that other is beautiful, she will say to herself, "human difference," and seeing that other is a Christian or a conservative, she will say to herself (if a moral act is being contemplated), "human difference." Brilliant—human difference. Doctor—human difference. Latino—human difference. Mexican—human difference. She has not seen this person yet. She knows it. She will not take a moral action of any kind until she has seen other completely. Oh look, he shares the trajectory of birth, aging, and death that we all share—a human sameness. He uses sounds and symbols to communicate—human sameness. He is susceptible to the same range of emotions that all people are—human sameness. Now he has been seen.

This is the key to the companion flag idea. Other is not just his differences. I am not just *my* differences. If I am a moral actor and all I see in other are his differences, I have not seen him completely. The differences I see are real, but to act in respect to another without seeing him completely is anathema to me. It is a kind of rational impossibility, and a source of intolerable cognitive dissonance.

We seek to leave the world a better, safer place for our children and grandchildren. With all the difficult choices mankind must make, and with the inevitability of conflict across human differences, the question we ask is this: What can we do to minimize the chances that our children and grandchildren will experience or perpetrate "man's inhumanity to man"?

The hope contained within this project is that a future may exist in which our children and grandchildren will eschew cruelty, violence, ridicule, and alienation in their dealings with each other; that instead, they will become guardians of one another's dignity and champions of compassion. This is not a utopian vision.

Recall Gandhi's admonition: we cannot make another man do good; we can only create the conditions under which he will choose to do good. Remember, too, that free will is not unhinged from reality. (I cannot will myself to fly unaided by machinery, or to be twenty-five again.) The free will of the moral actor entitles him to his own opinions, but not to his own facts. Because of the ineradicable draw of the silver sphere, generations of human beings have misunderstood the nature of other as he or she has appeared to them in moral space. They have contented themselves with the view that other's identity is a composite of human differences alone. They have formed opinions, codes of conduct, even moral philosophies, on the strength of difference awareness alone.

Once a moral actor has been made aware of the existence of a second sphere in moral space—one that he cannot see from the default position, but which he can see if he chooses to move in moral space—he is no longer free to view other's silver sphere as encompassing of his or her identity. He is not entitled to his own facts.

(Applause.)

SEC.-GEN. ROMERO: Aren't you indicting the current practice, common throughout the world, of flying flags that honor our national pride and distinctiveness?

MS. IBRAHIM: To a limited extent, yes. I'm indicting for its *incompleteness* the practice of identifying people on the basis of differences alone. People are not just different, yet that is the subtext of the world's flags. To proclaim—even to insinuate—with the world's most powerful symbols that we are different *tout court* is morally dangerous; history gives us more than enough proof of this. Once it is established that human beings are not just different, they are both different and the same, the question arises, "Why identify ourselves solely on the basis of differences?" That question turns urgent when we realize that, by limiting the content of our awareness of other to difference awareness, we block the flow of compassionate impulses into the moral imagination. We are blocking what would otherwise be the natural response of the heart to a recognition of one's essential connection to other, one's shared identity with other.

So, yes, now that the possibility of correcting this myopia is at hand, I am critical of the practice of flying flags representing groups of people tied together by shared differences without also flying the companion flag. Flags displayed without the companion flag represent an illusion—the illusion that our identity and value as people must be upheld solely by those who share our differences—our tribe, our nation, our religious community, our ethnic group.

It was Emerson, I think, who said, "The impoverishing philosophy of ages has laid stress on the distinctions of the individual, and not the universal attributes of man."

PROF. O'NEIL: So you are trying to correct this practice by offering the people of Tashir the companion flag. Why a flag, though? Why not just tell all Tashiri children that they must honor both human differences and human samenesses in themselves and others?

SEC.-GEN. ROMERO: Excuse me, but if you are against nationalism, you've picked an odd way of attacking it—and here again we have the problem of Occam's razor. In other words, if cleaving to our national differences is problematic, as you seem to imply, why not attack nationalism directly? Go for broke. Excise it outright. By adding the companion flag below our current national symbols, you seem to be trying to manage or counterbalance the purport of those symbols. Yet, won't the companion flag actually work to strengthen them, entrenching the problem further?

MS. IBRAHIM: Do you want to take this?

MR. WILLIAMS: Go ahead.

MS. IBRAHIM: Professor O'Neil asks, why a flag? Why not just insist that the children of Tashir remember and honor both human differences and human samenesses? The answer lies in the distinction between a *de*scriptive and *pre*scriptive act. *Is* versus *ought*.

The idea that someone ought to do this or that vis-à-vis another is philosophical, or at a minimum ideological. It promotes a metanarrative in which ideas of right and wrong conduct are identified (or implicated). Moral philosophies, ideologies, and codes of conduct are fine, of course—we rely on them—but like all prescriptions they impinge on the freedom of the person at the receiving end. When a parent or teacher tells a child that it is wrong to steal something from his neighbor, or to run out in the street without looking both ways, he or she is, strictly speaking, impinging on the child's freedom. A police officer impinges on the freedom of a driver when the officer pulls that driver over. When a prophet cautions that we should do unto others as we would want them to do unto us, that prophet is speaking prescriptively.

The companion flag does not speak prescriptively. It is not a philosophy, an ideology, or a code of conduct. It is descriptive. Joined below another flag representing our differences and separation from one another, the two flags together symbolize our true natures. Awareness of our true natures promotes the production of compassionate moral impulses across all differences and divisions. The key, as I said before, is to identify a new bifurcation or division in the content of our awareness of others. With sameness awareness naturally and involuntarily come compassionate impulses. No one is prescribing that we produce these impulses. We are not told by the flag or any outside authority that this is how we should react, psychologically or physiologically. It just happens.

To say that we are in some ways different and in some ways the same is not prescriptive. No one is saying this is how it *should be*. This is how it *is*. Because the healthy human mind is rational, it seeks reality over illusions and half-truths, and returns to those paradigms most conducive to truth. Once it was established that the earth circles the sun and not the other way around, people abandoned the old paradigm; they did not return to it and claim that the sun circles the earth.

Codes of conduct, ideologies, and moral prescriptions— which vary considerably across cultures and religions—are essential, but the companion flag is neither. We are not here to introduce a new philosophy or religion to the people of Tashir, but to free compassionate impulses that for centuries have been blocked by the dumbbell effect—by the illusion that difference awareness alone is the ground for moral contemplation. We seek to expose this illusion and the old paradigms that rely on a pinched and truncated view of humanity. I would like people to understand how maintaining this illusion harms people and keeps us all from the benefits that flow from the introduction of compassionate impulses at home and abroad. But that is different from telling people how to think or act.

The act of flying the companion flag is just that—an action. It is us doing something, rather than just speaking or instructing. Let us not forget that young people care much more about what we do than what we say.

Secretary-General Romero reads into the companion flag project an attack on nationalism or national pride. This is quite erroneous. The companion flag does not speak to our differences at all. It doesn't deny these differences, nor impinge on the right, habit, or preference of people to form evaluative judgments and strong, abiding opinions about the worth or import of their differences, some of which we see embodied in national flags. To argue this is to fall victim to the same either/or thinking that accounts for the dumbbell effect in the first place. The problem is not flying national flags, it's flying national flags without an accompanying symbol to represent the many ways we humans are the same. The problem with the half-concealed Mona Lisa is not the part we can see, it's the fact that we're not seeing the Mona Lisa in its entirety.

MR. WILLIAMS: In *The Power of Myth,* Joseph Campbell observed that we can tell what values inform a society by looking at the tallest structures within its cities and towns. In Medieval Europe, these were the Roman Catholic cathedrals. By the seventeenth century, political palaces had outgrown cathedrals. Today, in industrialized nations, commercial buildings tower over them both. I wonder if Campbell wouldn't agree that flags—so often placed *on top of* our tallest and most prominent structures and at the entrances to monuments, parks, universities, and public squares—carry a similar connotation, specifically in terms of the importance of identifying ourselves and orienting ourselves in a shrinking world?

RABBI LEVENSON: Okay, but surely you'll admit that telling people they should fly this flag is prescriptive?

MS. IBRAHIM: Yes, as far as it goes, that's true. I'm advocating that we adults adopt this symbol for the sake of our Tashiri children and grandchildren.

The companion flag is a descriptive tool that will usher onto the stage of their active minds an awareness of *the fact of* human samenesses and dispel over time the illusion that human differences exhaust the field where morally relevant facts are concerned.

PROF. O'NEIL: So in your ideal world, Ms. Ibrahim, you would have every person doing this inventorying you mentioned, before engaging in moral conduct?

MS. IBRAHIM: Yes. Every moral actor would inventory the content of his or her awareness of other ahead of moral conduct to make sure he or she was not acting on the basis of difference awareness alone. It takes only a split second to know if you are seeing only human differences. The mind is like a supercomputer; plus, ninety-nine times out of one hundred what we see ahead of our moral conduct is a composite of human differences. You are white, American, a college professor, a man of great intelligence . . . I will treat you this way. You are an Untouchable, a street beggar in torn clothes, with black dirt on your face and hands . . . I will treat you another way. It is at this point that the moral actor of the future will check herself and bring quickly to awareness one or two examples of human samenesses manifested by other *before* finalizing her intention to act. You are vulnerable to illness and injury; you desire to be safe and accepted for who you are; you are imperfect and aware of your imperfection. Now I see you completely.

SEC.-GEN. ROMERO: It's one thing to talk about compassionate impulses. It's another to prove their existence. What proof do you have of their existence?

MS. IBRAHIM: Do you doubt?

MR. WILLIAMS: A couple of years ago, an Uzbek woman employed at the United States embassy published a story about her brother, Ilhom. It proves, I think, the existence of compassionate impulses. I can read it into the record if you'd like.

SEC.-GEN. ROMERO: I have no objection.

RABBI LEVENSON: Yes, go ahead.

MR. WILLIAMS: It begins:

> Ilhom Rakhmatov had arrived at the train station early. He was glad to have his book as he sat on the hard bench, waiting for his friend, Rushtam, to arrive from Bukhara. The waiting room was alive with activity and incessant chattering, but in the last twenty minutes or so Ilhom had managed to relax, letting go of the tension that had built up over the long drive from the village. He was meeting the characters in his novel again,

recalling each with a fondness that approached gratitude.

Suddenly an abrupt noise lifted him out of the story. It was an eruption of high-pitched laughter, followed by a series of strange, rapid-fire utterances and more laughter. Ilhom looked to his left. Edging between the crowded benches were five African tourists—three adult women, a teenager, and a child of eight or ten. The tall, slender woman in front held four plastic bags bulging with souvenirs, fruits, and sundries; her sinewy biceps strained as she lifted the bags high in the air to avoid hitting the people she passed. All wore the brightly colored clothes and headdresses of their homeland. Their skin was as dark as any Ilhom had seen, and the whites of their eyes and smiling teeth shone in stunning contrast.

Ilhom saw that the woman in front was leading them toward the empty spaces on the bench beside him; in order to make room, he would have to move his backpack from the seat next to him. He decided against this. He looked down instead, pretending to read. *Don't sit here. That's the last thing I need.*

Ilhom hated Africans. His grandmother used to tell him a story from her childhood of six black men, all brothers, who had been hired by her father to work on a construction project near

Mashhad. She and her mother had traveled to Mashhad that spring to live with her father at a temporary camp built for the families of workers near the construction site.

When the black families arrived, they mostly kept to themselves at the edge of the camp. Their children did not attend the camp school and were considered off-limits by the other children. Things began to go missing from the camp a month or so after the black families arrived. Although none of the articles were ever found in their possession, rumors ran hard against them. Ilhom's grandmother recalled with bitterness the loss of her favorite doll, one her father had carved for her from a piece of hickory for her fifth birthday. "Ethiopians got it, sure as I'm sitting here," she would explain. When shortages caused by a labor strike in England brought construction to a crawl, her father fired the six brothers and evicted their families on ten hours' notice. That night, a foreman and twenty armed ironworkers ringed their shacks while the Africans gathered their things and decamped. "Father was right. It was the only way to make sure nothing else went missing."

The woman stopped next to Ilhom, the shimmering threads of her green, red, and black dress impossible to ignore despite his pretense of reading. "Excuse me, sir," she said in English. Frowning, Ilhom reached for his backpack and quickly placed it on the floor between his feet. He turned the page of his book, but his attention was now on the movements of the woman and her entourage. When she sat at last, he felt the sudden warmth of her leg pressing against his, and her perfume greeted his nostrils. This is too much! He sat for a minute or two (not quite sure why he waited), then abruptly grabbed his backpack and fled.

Two hours later Ilhom and Rushtam were driving north toward their village, enjoying shared memories and bringing each other current on all that had happened since Rushtam had left for the university. Ahead of them was a large, silver tour bus whose slowing and roaring to life again had punctuated the curves and switchbacks of the last twenty minutes.

They crested a pass and had started down the other side when suddenly the bus began to swerve drastically, first to the left, then to the right. The tall vehicle swayed precariously, its tires almost lifting off the pavement. Great clouds of dust and gravel flew up from both shoulders of the road.

All that they could see of the driver's efforts to control the bus were brake lights that seemed to oscillate at first, then grow brighter and more insistent with each passing second. Ilhom and Rushtam watched in disbelief as the bus swerved a last time to the right, broke through the barrier, and disappeared over the embankment as though it were a toy tossed by a child.

Ilhom screeched to a stop. He and Rushtam jumped out of the car and ran to the gaping hole in the barrier. They stared down in stunned horror past a rising column of thick, black smoke. The bus was resting upside down some thirty meters below the road. The roof had been crushed in several places, and bodies—four they could see plainly—were strewn about the wreckage. Ilhom stepped to his left and bent down, peering past bushes and rocks. Through the black, misshapen holes that had been the bus's windows human limbs (some seeming to move tentatively) were visible. Orange flames were jumping from the engine compartment and, below, a pool of black-ish fluid spread quickly over the earth like the arterial blood of a whale.

Ilhom grabbed Rushtam's shoulder. "Take the car, Rushtam! Go to the village and get help!" Rushtam nodded.

As the car's engine accelerated in the distance, Ilhom scrambled down the embankment, half-sliding, half-falling over the loose gravel. He arrived at the bus with both hands bleeding, covered in dust. He stopped to survey the sit-uation and heard the first awful moans from inside. Suddenly, the flames at the back of the bus exploded with a *whoof*!

The fire had spread into the passenger com-partment. Threads of black smoke began to rise from the rear windows like bubbles rising above a sinking hulk. The moans of the trapped passengers turned to weak cries.

Ilhom knelt by one crushed window frame after another, looking for a way in. He could see no more than a few inches into each blackened space before his view was blocked by crushed metal, twisted seats and seat backs, suitcases, and boxes—a tableau of incomprehensibility. The urgency of the spreading flames worked a strange but effective antidote to the horror that greeted him: protruding, lacerated arms and legs, the faces of the dead behind sliding veils of smoke. Only one window seemed to offer an ingress, but the passage was narrow and black smoke poured out of it in rolling billows. Where did it lead? There were more cries. The flames grew larger. Ilhom plunged inside . . .

. . . Forty minutes later, aid crews arrived from the city and the village. The bus was completely engulfed in flames now, and the heat of the fire was so intense that no approach was possible within ten meters. Seventeen meters to the east, on a ledge protected from the heat by a towering boulder, the rescuers found Ilhom, his hands and face severely blistered, tending (as best he could) to the seven people whose lives he had saved: two of them his countrymen, five of them African tourists—three adult women, a teenager, and a child of eight or ten.

You can see how the content of Ilhom's awareness of other changed in the midst of the emergency. He risked his life to save these people despite the fact that two hours earlier he could not stand to sit next to them. At the train station all Ilhom could think of was their differences. But of course their samenesses were there all the time.

SEC.-GEN. ROMERO: What samenesses are you referring to, Mr. Williams?

MR. WILLIAMS: Our shared susceptibilities to pain and injury. Our desire to be aided by others in an emergency, to be free from entrapment and danger.

SEC.-GEN. ROMERO: I see.

MR. WILLIAMS: Ilhom fashioned his initial response to the African tourists on the basis of difference awareness alone. He did this under the influence of the dumbbell effect. I'm afraid we all do this, or are prone to do it; but I'm equally certain that through an act of will this illusion can be overcome. In the story of Ilhom, it's a life-threatening emergency that jars him out of the illusion. We've all heard of similar stories where enemies are faced with a common threat and suspend their hostilities to meet the threat together. But I'm convinced—certainly Mr. Frost was convinced—that we don't need an emergency to arrive at this place. Why would we? The key event is not the emergency—those happen, they're part of life—it's the presence and persistence of the illusion and the resulting false belief that we are justified, as rational, caring people who are awake to the world, to fashion our moral commitments to others based on difference awareness alone. That's like saying we can describe the Mona Lisa without moving the butcher paper, without ever having seen the bottom half of the painting.

People can transcend this illusion and ultimately defeat it. But the first step is to understand that it's there, and to get our minds around how it arises and what sustains it in human communities around the world.

MSGR. DOYLE: Another supposition is that people, starting, as you say, with children, will be motivated by the companion flag to look within themselves and conduct an inventory of the content of their awareness of other. What proof is there that this will happen?

MS. IBRAHIM: The driving force will be truth, or a closer approach to truth than we have known before, combined with humankind's natural inclination to cleave to the truth as best we know it. It is the ingrained, illimitable practice of human beings everywhere to order their lives within a rational framework and to conform their aspirations to what rational and critical thought reveals to be sound, nonspeculative, and true. The companion flag reveals in symbolic space the true contents of moral space, and over time it will break the spell of the dumbbell effect. More and more people will experience compassionate impulses, feeling a profound new connection with strangers that stands apart unthreateningly from the hurried flow of passionate impulses, from the signposts of culture and custom, or from the waiting trains of our overlays and prescriptions. What will motivate us is the shared knowledge that we are not just different, we are both different and the same. I have not seen you if I have not seen that about you, if I have never seen parts of myself looking back at me through your eyes.

MSGR. DOYLE: So you're calling on people to stop and inventory the content of their awareness of other, not as to specific details, but simply to determine whether or not they are seeing only human differences. In most cases you believe that will be the case. You're saying that if people discover that the content of their awareness of other is limited to difference awareness, if they become aware that they are seeing only the silver sphere, they should pause long enough to find something about other that is a human sameness. They should refrain from acting until they've done so. So the steps are: inventory, then turn the dumbbell until you can see the golden spear. Have I got it?

MS. IBRAHIM: You've got the general idea, but you've phrased it prescriptively rather than descriptively. You're saying I'm calling on people to do this or that, or that they *should* do this or that. That's incorrect. What I'm saying is consistent with Gandhi's recognition of our moral autonomy, his recognition of free will. We can only create the conditions under which people will choose to do good. To see another person fully ahead of our moral actions is to do good. In other words, it's rational, and we are conforming our moral aspirations to what is demonstrably true: human beings *are* both different and the same. If you believe that we were all created by God, then God created us precisely as we are: in some ways different and in other ways the same. So, again, to see both spheres of other ahead of our moral actions must be good. We are honoring God's work. In contrast, if we treat others on the basis of an illusory, half-blind view of self and other, we dishonor God's work.

MR. WILLIAMS: Don't forget the two sides of the brain. We are specially equipped to see both differences and samenesses.

MS. IBRAHIM: Virtuous actions must come from within if they are truly virtuous, deserving of the name. So the idea is not to speak prescriptively, not to tell people that they must inventory the content of their awareness of other, or that they must turn the dumbbell. It's to create the conditions under which people will choose to do these things.

The companion flag project creates that condition by pointing out a mistaken impression. People avoid operating on the basis of erroneous impressions. They will change their behavior to conform to truth. They will choose to make correct use of the data on offer, and teach their children to do likewise.

RABBI LEVENSON: I think there's a bit of Orwellian doublespeak going on here. It sounds to me like the goal of the companion flag project is not simply to create an outcome where people *may* choose to do good, but, in fact, to create an outcome where they *will* choose to do good. (I'm reminded of Rousseau's comments that being forced to obey the General Will, people are forced to be free.) To say one *ought* to see both human differences and samenesses, and that one *ought* to inventory and consider both in interacting with others, is prescriptive. Let us not pretend otherwise.

PROF. O'NEIL: You alluded . . . Mr. Williams alluded to springs holding the dumbbell in place, which I took to mean holding the silver sphere in such a way that it's always pointed at the moral actor.

MS. IBRAHIM: Yes. Keeping us all at the default position initially.

PROF. O'NEIL: And I take it these springs—whatever they are—can be overcome. That's your theory. The moral actor can, with an act of will, turn the dumbbell despite these springs, or, as you've shown in your illustration, he can move around the silver sphere until he sees the gold sphere. Is that right?

Ms. Ibrahim and Mr. Williams: Yes.

Ms. Ibrahim: The dumbbell effect can be defeated.

Prof. O'Neil: Can you explain what these springs are?

Ms. Ibrahim: There are a number of sociopsychological forces holding the dumbbell in place, all of which account for the persistence of the dumbbell effect. One is the paradox of humanity, the fact that we are both different and the same.

A paradox, as we all know, is a seemingly contradictory statement that may nevertheless be true. "The only constant is change" is a paradox; so are "He who is everywhere is nowhere" and "This sentence is false." It's paradoxical to say that human beings are both different and the same. If they're different, how can they be the same? And if they're the same, how can they be different? How can we say this of any two objects: they are both the same and different?

The human mind doesn't deal well with paradox. We avoid thinking or speaking paradoxically. Abraham Heschel may have said it best when he wrote, "The human mind is one-sided. It can never grasp all of reality at once. When we look at things, we see either the features which they have in common, or the features which distinguish them."

It's preordained then. When we look at other people, when we encounter them, we are limited to seeing either their differences or their samenesses. We can't see both at the same time. We see either the silver sphere or the gold. That's how our brains work.

This doesn't mean we can't move in moral space, or reach out and turn the dumbbell. We can begin with difference awareness then add sameness awareness. That's what the companion flag project is about.

MR. WILLIAMS: A related spring is what neuroscience is finding out about the brain's limbic response to perceived differences, and our distinct ways of knowing depending on whether we are left- or right-brain dominant. The brain's left hemisphere tends to see things in parts. To deconstruct reality, largely for our own protection and safety—my tribe/other tribe, my ethnicity/other ethnicity, conservative/liberal, black/white. The left brain's approach is dualistic. The right brain, on the other hand, perceives things in unities, in wholes. It integrates the differences and oppositions seen by the left brain, and embeds them into a larger structure of understanding. Interestingly enough, the right brain has been associated with our ability to respond to symbols.

Studies show that males are more likely to be left-brain dominant than females, and females are far more likely to be right-brain dominant. But we all have been endowed with a two-sided brain, not a one-sided brain. Whichever hemisphere is dominant, it's possible to embrace that perspective then move gently but decisively to widen our moral horizons by utilizing the other side's viewpoint—our full moral potential. As James Olson writes in *The Whole-Brain Path to Peace*,

(Reading.)

> In the physical world, once we find a place where we would rather be or need to be, we move to that place. Movement is initiated by intent. Movement to or away from a mental position is initiated in a similar manner—by our intention to seek new perspectives and by the changing perceptions and judgments that we develop in the process of seeking new mental vistas. In effect, perception and judgment . . . guide our mental movement.

Olson describes what we have been calling the moral actor's choice to move in moral space ahead of moral action, to go beyond difference awareness alone to a state of difference awareness and sameness awareness. The companion flag and the host flag are reminders of this potential.

But the companion flag, let me say, goes a step farther. It's a reminder not just of the synthesis of perceived differences, but of all that human beings have in common regardless of their differences. It doesn't simply represent the integration and unity of those particular oppositions we have noticed on other's silver sphere; it represents all that human beings have in common, a separate cognitive sphere.

Imagine we are left-brain dominant. We come upon an Afghani woman who has been verbally abused by her husband in a public market. She is standing with her back turned to the crowd, bent over, sobbing uncontrollably. Reacting this way to a husband's abuse is a human difference. Not all women react the same way to abuse. We are able to perceive and recognize this difference because of our simultaneous awareness of a defining opposite (for example, our image of such a woman lashing out at her husband in self-defense). Our left brains have deconstructed the scene and supplied us with detailed information—including the bifurcation I've just mentioned—and this bifurcation appears on the woman's silver sphere (it is the content of *our* awareness of other).

Were we to move our perception to the right hemispheres of our brains, it's conceivable that we would discern as a "unity" the notion that all Afghani women are abused and will either cry or lash out in the circumstance. That is an integration of the information before us. However, neither is a universal truth. Neither experience is shared by people everywhere in spite of their differences. So, while the right brain seeks to integrate the information gleaned by the left, there is no guarantee that the result will be a human sameness.

I make this point because moving from left-brain analysis to right-brain synthesis is a step in the right direction but there is no guarantee that the moral actor will identify a human sameness without further reflection.

Using the litmus test implicit in the companion flag project (Can I identify one or more relevant experiences, characteristics, concerns, desires, or susceptibilities that are shared by people everywhere, in spite of their differences, that bears on the situation before me?) what results is quite plain. Visible to us on this woman's gold sphere are the desire to be free from abuse, the desire to be accepted for who we are, and the desire to be treated with respect.

PROF. O'NEIL: And what about neuroplasticity? Doesn't it render the right brain/left brain dominance argument moot?

MR. WILLIAMS: Neuroplasticity? You're talking about . . . ?

PROF. O'NEIL: The brain's ability to respond to stimuli, not always in a fixed, predetermined way, but, when circumstances require, by reorganizing its own structure, function, and connections. Hasn't science shown this in recent years, putting the lie to brain function lateralization—or at least casting it into doubt?

MR. WILLIAMS: I don't know, to be honest. I suspect plasticity has to do with the brain's ability to rewire itself after some assault like a stroke or traumatic brain injury, increasing the odds of recovery. Are you aware of research challenging the presence of left- or right-brain dominance in the *uninjured* brain?

PROF. O'NEIL: Not as such, no.

MR. WILLIAMS: Very well then.

Ms. Ibrahim: A third spring is nature, the instinct for survival. People's differences are part of what accounts for lethality and danger. We're constantly on the lookout for circumstances that might place us or our loved ones at risk, triggering the fight or flight response. We see other people's differences first. If we didn't, it's unlikely we would survive as a species.

So that's nature, and there's also nurture—what we've been taught to look for in other people, how to identify friend and foe, what to think of this person, that ethnic group, members of this profession or that. Ilhom's reaction to the African tourists was a learned prejudice. He had been programmed by his grandmother to fear and revile black people. The sight of the African tourists in the train station galvanized him. We're all subject to the influence of our parents and grandparents, our peers, our culture, the media. We're awash in messages about good and bad human differences, desirable and undesirable traits. Add to that the bonding effects of our particular national languages, our shared local customs, and our histories of victories and defeats. Flags as we currently use them mark our differences. They symbolize characteristics found on the silver sphere.

A fourth spring is the priority we humans give to the idea of justice, in whatever form, or by whatever standard that is measured. Justice—this thing that is valuable to us all—is measured on the silver sphere of human differences. As is success, by the way, the weft and warp of a meritocracy.

A related spring we might call the "now what?" spring. Does the person before me represent in some way a threat to the relative tranquility of life as I am currently experiencing it, or as I am seeking to come to terms with it? Here you are. I'm encountering you. I'm not a tree or a rock. I'm a person with a vested sense of living within the particular bounds not only of safety (which is the fight or flight trigger) but of rationality, freedom to move, the maintenance of my relationships, my habit of soldiering on, striving to actualize the life I've identified as mine or me.

But here you are. Now what? And of course I'll find the answer to that question, or clues to what might be the answer, by focusing my awareness on your silver sphere, not on what we have in common with people everywhere.

The number of springs holding the dumbbell in place is anyone's guess. I suspect there are dozens of reasons why we see each other's differences first. Much of this occurs at the subconscious level, as Mr. Williams has noted. The mind is constantly at work, comparing and contrasting. I'm aware of at least one physiological study where the subjects are shown a series of innocuous photographs, say, of different flowers. Suddenly, in the middle of the series, they are shown a photo of an entirely different but equally innocuous object, say, an automobile or a fish. Amazingly, researchers have found that the blood pressure of these subjects spikes at the change, or I should say at the moment their awareness shifts to the incompatible object. It's not inconceivable to think the same thing happens when we see other's human differences.

A sixth spring which may have ties to this I call "raw interest." This is the human preference for sensory and intellectual stimulation (new information). It follows that, given the choice between awareness of other's differences and of ways in which other is identical to all other people, including ourselves, we will choose the former. And we may persist in looking for differences for the same reason. We are interested in people's character traits, and in stories that almost always turn on the unique and interesting ways characters respond to conflicts and challenges. Silver sphere stuff.

Another spring that keeps us from seeing other's golden sphere is the illusion of completeness created by the oppositions we talked about before. When the moral actor sees other's human differences, we know that he or she attains awareness of those differences—that they have meaning for him or her—only because the moral actor is aware that some people don't have this or that trait, or haven't had this or that experience. In other words, the content of the moral actor's awareness goes beyond the relevant trait to encompass its opposite.

One of the effects of this "doubling" of the content of the moral actor's awareness of other is a sense that, by seeing the thing and its opposite for each visible difference on the silver sphere, the moral actor has seen it all. The moral actor feels justified—consciously or subconsciously—in believing that he or she has done enough—has taken in both sides, as it were, that his or her comprehension of other is complete. We've already talked about how the realm of opposites on the silver sphere represents—and *is,* for the time being—the operative bifurcation in the moral lives of most people today. And I've mentioned that the companion flag project introduces a new bifurcation, that of human samenesses and differences. In this new paradigm, the realm of opposites on the silver sphere of other becomes a subset of a more fundamental binary social world. Difference awareness is the source of passionate moral impulses, whereas sameness awareness in the moral actor produces compassionate impulses.

Prof. O'Neil: I understand your point. In Ilhom's case, he sees the ethnicity and skin color of the African tourists in the train station, but in fact the content of his awareness includes the oppositions of non-black and non-African.

Ms. Ibrahim: That's right, as well as the oppositions inherent in whatever other differences he sees in them. With acknowledgment of the adult travelers' gender as women, the content of his awareness necessarily admitted the idea of men. With their brightly colored clothes, his awareness took in the idea of plain or dull-colored clothing. When the woman sits next to him and he smells her particular perfume, his awareness extends to other perfumes or other odors, or to the lack of an odor. The defining opposites are there necessarily, and, again, because of this doubling, he feels that he has seen other against the background of all other reasoned possibilities.

PROF. O'NEIL: That is, until the bus accident, when he is forced by circumstances to recognize in them the universal desire to be helped in an emergency.

MS. IBRAHIM: Precisely.

MSGR. DOYLE: I find myself asking whether the act of inventorying the content of our awareness of other and turning the dumbbell is a hindrance to the prescriptions of religion, or a dilution of the faith-ordered life? Perhaps it is. How do you answer that?

MS. IBRAHIM: I'm not qualified to answer the way a theologian would. My off-the-cuff answer (although it's self-serving) is that every religion should be hospitable to the practice. In Islam we have the teachings of the Hadith, including "That which you want for yourself, seek for mankind." And this: "A Bedouin came to the Prophet, grabbed the stirrup of his camel and said: O the messenger of God! Teach me something to go to heaven with it. The Prophet said: 'As you would have people do to you, do to them; and what you dislike to be done to you, don't do to them. Now let the stirrup go!'" The Golden Rule requires us to look within ourselves for the essence of our shared humanity, not to fashion our moral conduct on the basis of human differences.

In the Bible there are several proofs, none more telling than the commandment to love your neighbor as yourself, found in both the Old and New Testaments. In the New Testament, this commandment is associated with the parable of the Good Samaritan. Another proof is the parable of the

Prodigal Son. I realize that these have attracted theological interpretations, but if we open our minds to other possibilities we find support for what I've been talking about. We can hypothesize, for example, that Jesus's intent in the parable of the Prodigal Son was more immediate and psychological than is often imagined, that he sought to introduce his hearers to the same hidden duality in moral space—that of human differences and human samenesses—for no greater reason than to unleash in the moral actor what I've been calling compassionate impulses.

MSGR. DOYLE: How do you mean?

MS. IBRAHIM: Here is the parable of the Prodigal Son. This is from the New International Version of the Bible:

> Jesus continued: "There was a man who had two sons. The younger one said to his father, 'Father, give me my share of the estate.' So he divided his property between them.
>
> Not long after that, the younger son got together all he had, set off for a distant country and there squandered his wealth in wild living. After he spent everything, there was a severe famine in that whole country, and he began to be in need. So he went and hired himself out to a citizen of that country, who sent him to his fields to feed pigs. He longed to fill his stomach with the pods that the pigs were eating, but no one gave him anything.

When he came to his senses, he said, 'how many of my father's hired servants have food to spare, and here I am starving to death! I will set out and go back to my father and say to him: Father, I have sinned against heaven and against you. I am no longer worthy to be called your son; make me like one of your hired servants.' So he got up and went to his father.

But while he was still a long way off, his father saw him and was filled with compassion for him; he ran to his son, threw his arms around him and kissed him.

The son said to him, 'Father, I have sinned against heaven and against you. I am no longer worthy to be called your son.'

But the father said to his servants, 'Quick! Bring the best robe and put it on him. Put a ring on his finger and sandals on his feet. Bring the fattened calf and kill it. Let's have a feast and celebrate. For this son of mine was dead and is alive again; he was lost and is found.' So they began to celebrate.

Meanwhile, the older son was in the field. When he came near the house, he heard music and dancing. So he called one of the servants and asked him what was going on. 'Your brother has come,' he replied, 'and your father has killed the fattened calf because he has him back safe and sound.'

The older brother became angry and refused to go in. So his father went out and pleaded with him. But he answered his father, 'Look! All these years I've been slaving for you and never disobeyed your orders. Yet you never gave me even a young goat so I could celebrate with my friends. But when this son of yours who has squandered your property with prostitutes comes home, you kill the fattened calf for him!'

'My son,' the father said, 'you are always with me, and everything I have is yours. But we had to celebrate and be glad, because this brother of yours was dead and is alive again; he was lost and is found.'"

A prominent theological interpretation would have us equate the father in the parable with God. We are told that the prodigal son stands for human beings who have sinned then repented and returned to God; his older brother represents humans who hold up their loyalty and accomplishments as a kind of entitlement to God's love, who deal in self-righteousness. The moral is that God waits with abundant patience for the return of his lost children, whom he will greet with great joy and celebration. But to the proud and self-righteous he is but an abiding father. In this interpretation Jesus is telling his listeners something about God.

But a different interpretation is possible. It's conceivable that what Jesus was describing in this parable was what we have been calling moral space; moreover, that he sought to prod his listener into understanding that something *in addition to* passionate impulses may hold sway in the moral imagination of men.

The story's protagonist is the father. Notice how the story begins: "There was a man who had two sons." We are enticed, just as Jesus's listeners must have been, to pass moral judgment on this man for the way he treated his two sons. No doubt intentionally, we are jarred to hear that the loyal son who has slaved in his father's fields for years has never received his father's celebratory bounty, yet the younger prodigal son returns and receives it unhesitatingly. When the older son confronts his father about the injustice of this, the father says, "Well of course I'm celebrating. This son was lost to me, and now he's found."

Monsignor, can you see how we might apply the dumbbell analogy to this?

MSGR. DOYLE: I —. No. Well, perhaps I do. But please proceed.

MS. IBRAHIM: First, take the story at face value. Rather than assume that the father is an allegory for God, let him be the earthly father of two sons, a man. And let the two sons be exactly as they are as well. It's clear from the story's structure that it is designed to invite the listener, you and I, to pass moral judgment on this man, the father, and yet we sense from its telling some hidden irony or meaning. (In fact, we more than sense it, for a great teacher, a rabbi, is telling this story, and because of this we know we are being challenged.) But then what is it? What are we to learn from this odd tale?

Let me suggest that Jesus sought to convey the fact that there are two distinct kinds of moral impulses available to us all in moral space. To highlight their separateness he conceived a story in which each type of moral impulse would be generated *in us*, the listeners, and yet they would work at cross-purposes, one kind endorsing a condemnatory attitude toward the father, and the other something else. You see, the story is not about God, it's about us. *We* are encountering the father in moral space, and what Jesus (silently) asks us is, "What do you see?"

Of course, he has set us up to be jarred by the backwards way this father has chosen to treat his two sons: to celebrate the return of the profligate son who has returned home out of necessity and self-interest, albeit with some contrition, while ignoring his older brother who has tirelessly worked his father's fields. How the father has chosen to treat these two is a human difference. To heap gifts upon a prodigal son who returns home in defeat while withholding gifts from a loyal son who has bent his back to his father's purposes is not an experience shared by people everywhere. Thus, when we encounter this man we observe this feature on his silver sphere. We are able to know it only through knowing its opposite. That is, we admit to awareness the fact that some fathers, some parents, would do just the opposite of this man: they would reward and celebrate the hard-working child, not the son who left in rebellion, squandered what he had been given, and returned with his tail between his legs to access more of his father's support. Most of us, I daresay, view this father's decision as unjust. Jesus understood this. The story is designed to excite negative passionate impulses, strong ones based on our view of other's silver sphere (difference awareness).

Jesus, a great teacher, sees something different. He tells the story matter-of-factly. He doesn't judge the father, and we sense that what the father has done is not blameworthy in Jesus's eyes. We don't hear Jesus praising the man, but in light of the father's uneven treatment of his sons, the absence of a critical word from Jesus is telling.

So what does Jesus see that we don't? The answer, I submit, is the father's golden sphere of human samenesses. He sees in the father the universal experience of all parents, of all human beings, really, when a beloved son or daughter or friend, someone they thought they would never see again, returns to them unexpectedly.

In other words, the content of Jesus's awareness of other extends beyond mere difference awareness to include sameness awareness as well. He may feel, or be subject to, the same negative passionate impulses we feel at the sight of this man's silver sphere, but in addition there are compassionate impulses released as he turns the dumbbell to see this man's golden sphere. These flow into Jesus's moral imagination and they counteract or neutralize in some fashion the negative passionate impulses such that the wick of condemnation or disapprobation is not lit for him. He stands in neutral regard of the man.

The story is meant to prod the listener into comparing his or her reaction in moral space to that of Jesus himself. Metaphorically, the listener is standing next to Jesus, and he is constrained by the obvious lack of judgment in Jesus to ask, "How is his experience in moral space different from mine?"

MSGR. DOYLE: Surely you're not suggesting that Jesus saw or thought in terms of a gold and silver dumbbell?

MS. IBRAHIM: No, of course not. That's just a construct or schema we're using to depict sameness awareness and difference awareness, and to illustrate the dumbbell effect. But no harm results from its use here, for my thesis is that Jesus was aware of, and sought to teach, the same fundamental bifurcation of the human experience. That he and other moral teachers throughout history have been alive to the distinction I'm describing, between difference awareness and sameness awareness, although as far as I know they didn't use these terms and they certainly didn't employ the image of a gold and silver dumbbell.

You know, Einstein, who was very interested in ethics, especially in the latter part of his life, described Jesus, the Buddha, Goethe, and other spiritual guides as "geniuses in the art of living." Whatever other claims one may make about Jesus, I think Einstein was right: he was, indeed, a genius in the art of living.

What the dumbbell analogy adds, if it adds anything, is a way to understand and even access the mechanism of Jesus's ingenious message of radical justice.

Msgr. Doyle: Radical justice?

Ms. Ibrahim: What do you see in moral space? If what you see is only a composite of other's human differences, you have not seen other completely. This is true whether what you seem to be feeling is negative or positive. Turn the dumbbell (as it were) before you arrive at a moral intention, before you act in such a way as to impact other's well-being. See in other some example or examples of all that human beings have in common. Now you have seen him completely. Now form your judgment or intention; now act.

There is justice and there is radical justice. The term "radical," as you know, has a double meaning. It means both fundamental—that is, going to the root of the matter—and favoring a revolutionary change, a departure from current practices, institutions, or understandings. We think of things like radical political thought or radical scientific theories. Jesus, I think we can agree, is regarded as a proponent of radical justice, and for me this is related to his recognition of the role of sameness awareness in the moral life of every moral actor. Justice, as we talked about before—the nonradical kind—is measured and accounted for on the silver sphere of other alone. It's one of the springs holding the dumbbell in place, for we are mesmerized by the presence and absence of justice, or by those clues visible on the silver sphere of other that speak of justice achieved or denied.

"What was the father thinking?" we ask. This son has taken more than his share. He has rebelled against his father and might never have seen his father again had he had better luck abroad. The other son resisted the temptation of a dissipated life; he stayed true to his father, and spent his days in his father's fields, asking little else than to be treated fairly, to have his measure in his father's time.

So the father acted unjustly and precipitously, yet Jesus does not judge him. Why? Because the father's failing (which we see on his silver sphere) does not end the inquiry of a moral actor who knows the true contents of moral space. Such a person eschews the temptation (although that is hardly the right word after a while) to determine his or her moral judgment or to fix a moral intention vis-à-vis any person until he or she has turned the dumbbell, until the content of his or her awareness of other includes sameness awareness.

MSGR. DOYLE: And once he or she has done that —?

MS IBRAHIM: Then they permit themselves to judge; to act. At that point their actions are informed by both passionate and compassionate impulses. This is radical justice.

MSGR. DOYLE: So justice is what we do on the basis of difference awareness alone, and radical justice is what we do when the content of our awareness of other includes both difference awareness and sameness awareness?

MS IBRAHIM: Yes, that's what I'm saying.

RABBI LEVENSON: Interesting. You started this by asking whether this religion or that, or this moral system or that, is hospitable to the dumbbell analogy. I guess you're telling us that for Christianity the answer is yes.

MS IBRAHIM: I believe it's yes; but bear in mind that I'm not a theologian or biblical scholar. People much smarter than I have interpreted Jesus's sayings and parables in other ways.

RABBI LEVENSON: I understand that. Your views are not universal. We can find them on your silver sphere.

MS IBRAHIM: Right. I'm interested in the ethical teachings of Jesus and every other spiritual guide. These men and women are, as Einstein said, geniuses at the art of living, and thank goodness for them. The question we're exploring now is whether there might be a correlation or resonance between the dumbbell analogy, this very simple idea, and their sometimes enigmatic bodies of work. If so, the dumbbell analogy could help us not only understand the thrust of what they were trying to tell us about the art of living, but something else: what I'm tempted to call their calmness or equanimity, the inner peace that comes over the soul when perspective is gained.

RABBI LEVENSON: And Judaism? Do you believe it is hospitable to the dumbbell analogy?

MS IBRAHIM: Based on what little I know of it, yes. We find in Leviticus: "You shall love your neighbor as yourself." And when asked to relate all that the Torah had to say while standing on one foot, Hillel famously replied, "Do not do unto your neighbor what you would not have him do unto you. This is the whole

Law; the rest is commentary." I maintain that these prescriptions are meaningless without sameness awareness.

MSGR. DOYLE: Can we stay with Jesus and Christianity for a minute? You said the parable of the Good Samaritan was another proof that the dumbbell analogy fits with the teachings of Jesus. Can you explain this?

MS IBRAHIM: Sure . . . okay, here it is.

> On one occasion an expert in the law stood up to test Jesus. "Teacher," he asked, "what must I do to inherit eternal life?"

> "What is written in the law?" He replied. "How do you read it?"

> He answered, "Love the Lord your God with all your heart and with all your soul and with all your strength and with all your mind; and, love your neighbor as yourself."

> "You have answered correctly," Jesus replied. "Do this and you will live."

> But he wanted to justify himself, so he asked Jesus, "And who is my neighbor?"

> In reply Jesus said: "A man was going down from Jerusalem to Jericho, when he was attacked by robbers. They stripped him of his clothes, beat him and went away, leaving him half dead.

A priest happened to be going down the same road, and when he saw the man, he passed by on the other side. So too, the Levite, when he came to the place and saw him, passed by on the other side. But a Samaritan, as he traveled, came where the man was; and when he saw him, he took pity on him. He went to him and bandaged his wounds, pouring on oil and wine. Then he put the man on his own donkey, brought him to an inn and took care of him. The next day he took out two denarii and gave them to the innkeeper. 'Look after him,' he said, 'and when I return, I will reimburse you for any extra expense you may have.'

"Which of these three do you think was a neighbor to the man who fell into the hands of robbers?"

The expert in the law replied, "The one who had mercy on him."

Jesus told him, "Go and do likewise."

Jesus is asked to explain the greatest of all the Judeo-Christian commandments: love your neighbor as yourself. Once again, he uses the parable form with an ironic and unexpected plot twist. In this case, the twist is that of the three men who had a chance to offer aid to the man lying in the road, only the Samaritan, a kind of outcast to the mainstream Jews of Judea at the time, stepped up. The priest and the Levite, men holding places of honor and respect in the community, crossed the road to avoid the man in need.

Only the Samaritan treated the victim as a neighbor in the sense endorsed by Jesus. In terms of our analysis, each passer-by encountered the victim and was, therefore, a moral actor in regard to him. The decisions of the priest and Levite to do nothing and the decision of the Samaritan to come to the victim's aid are all examples of moral conduct. As to each of the three moral actors, therefore, we may ask, "What was the content of his awareness of other? What did the priest and Levite see in moral space, and what did the Samaritan see?"

Staying within the facts given, we know little about the victim. He was a man traveling between Jericho and Jerusalem. He might have been Judean or Samaritan. History tells us that members of both communities used this road. He was beaten, stripped of his clothes, and left for dead. His wounds at a minimum required bandaging.

Are these traits human differences or human samenesses? Human differences, of course.

So this is what each moral actor saw on the victim's silver sphere upon entering moral space. The ability to know these differences was, of course, tied to (and dependent upon) the moral actor's simultaneous knowledge of the defining opposites. They recognized his gender as a male because they were simultaneously aware that some human beings are not male. They could comprehend that he was injured because some people are not injured, but go about in a state of relative health (and are at least free from the effects of violent attack). So these dualities composed the content of each man's awareness of other at the outset. That passionate impulses would arise at the sight of this man is hardly surprising, and we can understand, if we're honest with ourselves, the avoidance behavior of the priest and the Levite. There is nothing attractive about a stranger lying naked and bloody on the road ahead of us. Who is he? How did he get there? Is he inebriated? Is he truly incapacitated, or will he spring up and attack me if I approach? Here I am in the countryside, miles from anywhere. What could I do for him even if I did stop? What unwanted demands will be placed on me and my time if I get involved?

Not only must we recognize the negative passionate impulses that arise from this tableau, we must recognize, as the story implies, the role of free will in every moral choice, whether to act or forbear, in this case to give aid or pass by. We are reminded again that free will (freedom) is morally neutral, albeit a necessary element of the moral life. It is a sail that will fill to any purpose, fly to any port. On these facts we cannot blame the priest or the Levite for passing by and leaving this man to his fate, that is, unless they (and we) have missed something, unless we have failed, despite what we may think, to see all there is to see in moral space. What the Samaritan saw, I submit, was not some other human difference on the silver sphere; nor did he generate anything approaching a positive passionate impulse at the sight of this man lying helpless in the road. What the Samaritan saw in moral space was this man's desire to be aided by a fellow human being when in dire straits, when rendered helpless. It is Ilhom's story all over again. What he saw was part of this man's golden sphere. The Samaritan was motivated by awareness of the victim's participation in the shared aspects of life. It was not about his differences anymore.

We have every reason to believe that the Samaritan experienced the same, or very similar, negative passionate impulses as the priest and the Levite when he first entered moral space and beheld the differences visible on the victim's silver sphere. But he didn't stop there. He turned the dumbbell to see the gold sphere. He resolved not to form his moral intention until he had seen this man completely in moral space. That's what it means to love another as oneself.

The moral actor who wills herself to see other completely ahead of moral actions and decisions will always experience both difference awareness and sameness awareness. Turning the dumbbell so as to acquire sameness awareness is never a matter of turning it 180 degrees so that we lose sight of other's human differences and the dumbbell effect is merely repeated, with the gold sphere visible and the silver one hidden. It is a matter of turning it 90 degrees, or even less, just enough to generate sameness awareness and free the compassionate impulses that we all produce in that circumstance. Slide 13, please, Len. The Samaritan did not render aid in the absence of negative passionate impulses, but in spite of them.

Mr. Williams: If I may, that reminds me of Paul Tillich's definition of courage. Courage is the willingness to take life-affirming actions in spite of your anxieties. *In spite of.* It's not about waiting until our anxieties subside. It's about doing in spite of them.

Msgr. Doyle: Thank you. So your point is that the Good Samaritan saw this man's human differences, saw his silver sphere, but also turned the dumbbell and then was moved by compassion.

Ms. Ibrahim: Yes. I'm not suggesting that the Good Samaritan thought in terms of the spheres of a dumbbell, or that Jesus had this in mind. What I'm suggesting is that this parable, like the parable of the Prodigal Son, is consistent with the view that moral impulses flow from the content of our awareness of other and are of two varieties: what we are calling passionate and compassionate impulses. They flow from distinct albeit interconnected and interpenetrating categories of awareness, difference awareness and sameness awareness. The moral actor's cognizance of this singular bifurcation of the human life experience is determinative to the extent it allows him to see other completely and break the mesmerizing hold of difference awareness. Because of the draw of the silver sphere and the dumbbell effect, including, of course, the many springs holding the dumbbell in place, it is a challenge for most of us to achieve sameness awareness. I believe the Samaritan achieved it, and I think this was Jesus's point.

What did he so often say? Let he who has eyes see. Let he who has ears hear.

What I postulate is that justice, experienced as a force that can carry our moral intention and moral acts past lesser concerns, is not only measured by but rooted in difference awareness. We observe its precursors—the moral actor observes them—on the silver sphere of other, and from our observations flow passionate impulses. But radical justice differs: it is rooted in both difference awareness *and* sameness awareness, and both passionate impulses and compassionate impulses are implicated. The results can look different, even odd. It is a new world, but not an inscrutable one.

RABBI LEVENSON: Turn the dumbbell.

MS. IBRAHIM: Turn the dumbbell. Radical justice is what moral actors do—or are drawn to—when ahead of their moral conduct they will themselves to see both spheres of other's dumbbell. It's what they say, as well, having seen other completely—and what they think.

PROF. O'NEIL: But you're not a Christian or a Jew. You're Muslim.

MS. IBRAHIM: Yes. For me, Jesus is not a divinity but a great messenger from God, a prophet. Much of what is reported about him in the Bible leads me to think that he sought to bring people to this point. There is considerable evidence of his modeling behaviors that manifest a new way to see other in moral space: conduct that reflects the presence of compassionate impulses, conduct that is frankly meaningful to us (as readers or listeners) because we sense (and he tells us) that we are not far from realizing this ourselves. There is just something missing in the way we see those around us.

The Stoics, attempting to map the moral life, missed it by placing sameness awareness at the outer (virtually inaccessible) edge of our rational moral concerns. Slide 24, please, Len. They mistook the golden glow as the last of a series of steps traversed by difference awareness. But sameness awareness is not part of any series, not part of any hierarchy. It is separate, although it co-exists with difference awareness.

Slide 24
The Stoic model modified in recognition of a separate
but interconnected sphere of human samenesses

The result of mixing difference awareness with sameness awareness seems unpredictable and troubling to anyone who is focused solely on the silver sphere of other. Jesus ate and drank with tax collectors, prostitutes, and sinners. He befriended outcasts and lepers. He constantly reassured the meek, the poor, and the powerless. Many, including his disciples, complained bitterly about this apparent injustice, and I believe most of us would have experienced a similar discomfiture in the circumstances, had we lived at that time. Jesus, of course, was utterly unfazed.

There are numerous passages in the Bible that reflect Jesus's revolutionary understanding and orientation in moral space. It is self-serving to speculate that what he saw in moral space was the life experience of other bifurcated into two distinct categories, one encompassing human differences and the other human samenesses. That's our vision, not his. But, since we are testing the paradigm, it's at least interesting to note the seeming correlation between radical justice and compassion on the one hand and sameness awareness, or the moral actor's awareness of something, by whatever name, not tied to our differences, on the other.

PROF. O'NEIL: If Jesus were alive today what would he think about the 'Celebrate Diversity' bumper stickers I so often see around Cambridge? Do you suppose he'd have one on his car?

(Laughter.)

MS. IBRAHIM: I'm not familiar with that bumper sticker, I'm afraid. (Laughing.) However, I am aware of the movement. I think he'd reject the idea. The call to celebrate diversity, without more, perpetuates the old moral paradigm, that is, the view that once we see other's silver sphere—once we have taken note of other's differences—we have seen him or her completely. Diversity is a positive, postmodern term for human differences. The phrase "celebrate diversity" is a prescription telling people how they should think or feel about others' human differences and their own. Borrowing Gandhi's phrase, it is tantamount to "making another man do good" by telling him what to do: in this case, *celebrate* differences.

PROF. O'NEIL: But don't you think the idea is to get people to feel less threatened about other people in the world who are different from them, coming from a different culture, speaking a different language, that sort of thing?

MS. IBRAHIM: Sure. I'm not saying the motive is wrong. What I'm suggesting is that Jesus would find the whole program myopic; and I think he might object on another ground, that it doesn't acknowledge the role of freedom in our moral lives. The freedom (in this case) to celebrate or not celebrate diversity. The whole nature of freedom is that it's free. You said —

PROF. O'NEIL: Let me come back to that in a minute. I'm stuck on this idea that you don't think Jesus would be all over the 'Celebrate Diversity' bumper sticker.
(Laughter.)

MS. IBRAHIM: Like I say, I don't know. My thought is that he wouldn't be. I'm not an expert on Jesus. I cited these parables to suggest that Jesus had a different kind of understanding of moral space. He didn't ignore differences or diversity but he seemed to see them in a wider context. He talked about God causing the sun to rise on the evil and the good, and sending rain to fall on the just and unjust alike, and he suggested in the same passage that we should see each other this way, as well, which I take to mean we should see each other this way in moral space.

I'm tempted to say he saw others' differences in the context of their shared humanity, and he hoped that by telling the parables of the Prodigal Son and the Good Samaritan others would begin to do so, as well.

Besides, the prescription "celebrate diversity" cannot be taken literally. It must be rendered thus: celebrate all forms of human diversity except this one over here, or that one over there.

PROF. O'NEIL: How do you mean?

MS. IBRAHIM: I saw a television documentary a few years ago about the Kara tribe in a remote corner of Ethiopia. The members of this tribe believe in evil spirits, which, of course, is a not an uncommon belief in many parts of the world. However, they also believe that if the upper teeth of a baby born to the tribe begin to emerge before its lower ones, this is a sign that the baby is possessed by an evil spirit that will bring shame and misfortune to the tribe. Such babies are taken from their mothers and drowned in a river or left in the bush to be devoured by animals. As shocking as this sounds to us, it is an integral part of the religious tradition of this tribe. Obviously an extreme example, it nevertheless calls into question the open-ended prescription to celebrate diversity. The makers of the bumper sticker almost certainly didn't have this in mind as a cause for celebration.

What the bumper sticker maker probably had in mind was the much lighter fare typically offered up in present-day multicultural education classes in the West: an appreciation of the clothes, food, literature, music, customs, and holidays of a particular subpopulation. Take this class and learn about the Hmong in Vietnam;

take that one and learn about Mexican cuisine or the Japanese tea ceremony.

SEC.-GEN. ROMERO: There's nothing wrong with that, is there?

MS. IBRAHIM: No, absolutely not. But it's silver sphere stuff. It's important to learn about our world, including our differences. Mind you, I'm not against the silver sphere. I don't deny its existence, nor do I suggest that our differences are less important than our samenesses. I'm not a Rousseauian.

If I were back in high school I would sign up for multicultural education classes in an instant. I enjoy learning about other cultures and the way people live in other parts of the world. But you asked whether I thought Jesus would have a 'Celebrate Diversity' bumper sticker on his car, and I took that to mean, "Would the prescription to celebrate human differences be central to his ethical message?" I don't think it would be, or was.

To your larger question, I don't think the act of inventorying the content of one's awareness of other, and turning the dumbbell ahead of our moral decision making, is a hindrance to the prescriptions of religion, or a dilution of the faith-ordered life.

As Henri Nouwen wrote, "Compassion means full immersion in the condition of being human." You cannot know another person simply by knowing his or her differences.

RABBI LEVENSON: Tell me, are you familiar with the Charter for Compassion, spearheaded by Karen Armstrong?

MS. IBRAHIM: Yes, I know something about it.

RABBI LEVENSON: Why isn't this initiative preferable to flying a flag?

MS. IBRAHIM: Preferable? I don't know that one is better. Well, I do think the companion flag idea is better, but that's hardly relevant. Naturally, they coexist. (Len, can you find the Charter for Compassion and bring it up?)

MR. WILLIAMS: I'll try.

MS. IBRAHIM: While he's doing that . . . as I recall it, the charter calls on people around the globe to privilege compassionate actions over selfish ones; to celebrate diversity—there's our bumper sticker again; to work for justice . . .

MR. WILLIAMS: Here it is. (Shown on screen.)

MS. IBRAHIM: Yes. Now . . . if you'll look at this, you'll see the charter is prescriptive, not descriptive. It refers not just to compassion, but to "the principle of compassion," which impels us to work tirelessly to alleviate suffering, to honor the sanctity of other, to affect justice. We are called upon to refrain from inflicting pain, or from acting or speaking violently. As you read on, you'll see the operative words: "We call upon all men and women to restore compassion to the centre of morality and religion, to return to the ancient principle that any interpretation of scripture that breeds violence, hatred, or disdain is illegitimate," and so on.

There is nothing in this that I find disagreeable, but, you see, it *is prescriptive*. Just as the Golden Rule is prescriptive. Just as laws against murder, assault, and theft are prescriptive.

You asked earlier why offering instruction on compassion would not suffice in place of the companion flag. The answer I gave before applies here as well. You cannot make another man do good. You can only create the conditions under which he will choose to do good. Virtue cannot be taught. The individual, as Socrates discovered, must have—and *can* have, it must be stressed—direct insight into the knowledge of values.

You have not mentioned it, but let me bring up the naturalistic fallacy, the principle that you cannot derive an *ought* from an *is*. I want to argue on behalf of the companion flag that, while its underpinnings are decidedly naturalistic—citing the existence of human commonalities—it does not run afoul of the naturalistic fallacy, for no *ought*—no prescription—is claimed. This is an unusual but important feature of the companion flag. It does not tell people what to do, or how to think or feel, when human differences collide. It is simply an abiding symbol of our interconnectedness, of our human samenesses.

Again, the two questions posed by Mr. Frost: Are the things we have in common real? And, if so, are they worthy of a flag?

Prof. O'Neil: Defining once and for all what the "truth" is and trying to convince others of that is prescriptive. The affirmative side is declaring as an immutable truth that humans everywhere are both different and the same. Moreover, they are insisting that others ought to believe what they believe. They are telling us, "This is how you ought to see things." They deny the prescriptive dimension, insisting instead that the companion flag added below the flag of Tashir will result in a new descriptive, dual symbol, but this rings false. Dangerously false. They gesture at encouraging free will and offering people an open-ended choice, but in reality they are pushing people toward a predetermined and preferred use of that choice, and so it is an actual denial of free will.

Mr. Williams: Do you mean the freedom to have your own facts? The freedom to ignore gravity, or deny its existence, and step off a cliff? To label the sun a planet, or, as Ms. Ibrahim said, to ignore the charge of a li—?"

Prof. O'Neil: Excuse me, Mr. Williams. I wasn't done. A truly open-ended offer of free will and choice would have no regard for how people *use* the choice because *what* they choose is not the point, *that* they choose is.

Mr. Williams: And if you're saying that people are free to ignore facts, or choose their own . . . Perhaps that is true in academia, I don't know. What is not true on this planet is that some people die while others don't. What is not true is that some people require food, air, and water to survive while others don't. What is not true is that some human babies are born helpless and dependent while others are not.

This flag is concerned with how we see each other. Nothing else. It is a symbolic acknowledgement that despite our many differences, in some important ways we are the same.

You are mistaken if you think the companion flag prescribes that we treat one another with compassion. Ms. Ibrahim has explained at length that the most we seek is the opportunity for naturally occurring compassionate impulses to flow—which they do, when they do, involuntarily and spontaneously. They are not a choice, Professor, and no choice is being forced upon the people—particularly the children—of Tashir, *except this*: that we see each other entirely. They—like you and I—are both different and the same.

Msgr. Doyle: Let me interject something here. The affirmative side has made much of the Gandhi quote, "You cannot make another man do good, you can only create the conditions under which he will choose to do good." They posit that adding the companion flag here in Tashir is tantamount to creating such a condition. Won't they admit now that anything that will force people to do good, as they define it, is prescriptive *ipso facto*?

Ms. IBRAHIM AND MR. WILLIAMS: *Force* people to do good?

Ms. IBRAHIM: No, certainly not. You're ignoring the plain meaning of the sentence. He said ". . .will *choose* to do good."

MSGR. DOYLE: Yes, but if you are creating a condition that tells people they ought to act with compassion toward others, if their choice is for all practical purposes limited, or narrowed, to doing good (as you define that term), you are impinging on free will. I'm surprised you don't see this.

Ms. IBRAHIM: We see things differently which, of course, is not unexpected.

I see that we are running short on time. Allow me to speak to one last problem, or hurdle, that has not been raised. It is the problem of triviality—or I should say, perceived triviality. The view that a flag is a flag is a flag, and what does it mean to *me*? Speaking as a citizen of Tashir, I might say, "Why should I care about this idea? I have a family to feed. I am interested in fishing, or playing golf, or making my business more profitable. Don't you see? I have a life here. I am working, or spending time with my children, or meeting with friends. I have my health to worry about. I have my hobbies. Why would I be interested in a flag that will be flown off in the distance? The idea is irrelevant to me. At most, let it be someone else's concern."

I want to address this point of view. There is an old chestnut, a favorite in marketing and advertising classes: "Everyone listens to WIFM." W-I-F-M stands for "What's in it for me." The idea, which is not inconsistent with the Stoic and Confucian models of concentric circles of concern, or Maslow's hierarchy of needs, is that we humans will be galvanized to act on an idea only in proportion to its direct benefit to us. You want me to consider this thing called the companion flag? What's in it for me?

The negative side of this phenomenon might be called inertia or homeostasis, the strong tendency toward maintaining the status quo. Today, and for centuries now, we have used flags to celebrate and reify our differences from each other. Why would we want to add a companion flag now, forever changing this differences-only approach?

Of course, I have already answered this question in the main. But what I want to close with is a gentle challenge to those who would deny the inauguration of a new day in human perception and self-understanding on the false assessment that all of this, because it concerns a flag, is trivial.

No one who is alive today can, or I dare say would, argue that flags—the flag of Tashir, the flag of China, say, or the flag of the United States, are trivial symbols. They are far from it. And the companion flag, too, is far from it. It will have a direct bearing on the self-image of every child, and on his or her ability and willingness to see him- or herself in the eyes of others. The day the companion flag is adopted will be a bad day for bullies, a bad day for those who would scapegoat others, or trample them underfoot on the basis of their differences alone. The world's cruelties are differences-based. We have all heard, have we not, the following:

> When the Nazis came for the communists,
> I remained silent;
> I was not a communist.

> When they locked up the social democrats,
> I remained silent;
> I was not a social democrat.

When they came for the trade unionists,
I did not speak out;
I was not a trade unionist.

When they came for the Jews,
I remained silent;
I wasn't a Jew.

When they came for me,
there was no one left to speak out.

The companion flag is the farthest thing from trivial, and there is much in it for all of us. It is, above all else, a gift—our gift—to future generations.

MODERATOR: Thank you; and thank you all for this interesting debate. The agreed upon time has expired. (In fact, we are a few minutes over.) I would ask each side to sum up. Ms. Ibrahim or Mr. Williams? Please limit yourself to one minute.

MS. IBRAHIM: For all the reasons mentioned, we urge adoption of the companion flag for the people of Tashir. This is a historic opportunity, a moment of profound self-awareness, of species-wide integration never before seen, of uniting. Here is a chance to bring into the physical world—the world of time and space—a constant recognition of the source of compassionate impulses in people everywhere. Let us begin this process here in this wonderful country, my home, Tashir.

Will the impact be felt immediately? Probably not. But over time an awareness of our interconnection will play a larger and larger role in the moral lives of the people. Imagine, in conclusion, how different the world would have been had the companion flag been adopted three hundred years ago. Can you see how populations in the industrialized West would have turned their backs on the evils of slavery and exploitative colonization, how mass exterminations such as the world witnessed in the nineteenth and twentieth centuries would have been unthinkable?

Is it in the best interest of the people of Tashir to adopt the companion flag? It is.

Thank you.

PROF. O'NEIL: No one doubts the sincerity of this effort. And no, it is not trivial. It is a grand design, but it is also a misguided idea. Truly these liberal nostrums "litter history like tanks abandoned in the desert." This one, too, will be abandoned—*should* be abandoned, and hopefully this debate will speed that result.

One supposes that it can be said that people are both different and the same. Certainly, we agree that the elimination or reduction of "man's inhumanity to man" is a worthwhile goal. But to urge, as the other side does, that people in pursuit of their legitimate ends will impose a check upon themselves at the sight of this flag is incredible.

We know we are all people. We know we share common traits. But it is our differences that propel us, that give us our true identities, our sense of place, purpose, and belonging. Our moral choices will always conform to the nearer, thicker, warmer affiliations: family, tribe, profession, culture, nationality. Accordingly, we urge the Tashiri parliament to reject the resolution.

Thank you.

ABOUT THE AUTHOR

Scott Wyatt was born in Portland, Oregon in 1951 and grew up in Sandpoint, Idaho. He has earned degrees from Stanford University and the University of Washington, and has worked as a lawyer in the Seattle area since 1976.

His first novel, *Beyond the Sand Creek Bridge*, was released in 2012. Like *Dimension M*, it explores and ultimately challenges humankind's primary moral paradigm—the "habit" of formulating our moral commitments to others on the basis of difference awareness alone. As he explains in his online profile:

"As passionate as I am about writing, I am even more passionate about an idea that came to me out of the blue in 1985, following a trip to the former Soviet Union. This is the notion that the moral dimension in human interactions and behaviors—how we treat one another—is shaped as much by 'the content of our awareness of other' as by those rules, mores, symbolical thoughts, religious tenets, prescriptions, and what not, that we call our own, or that we embrace throughout our lives. Yes, I know that's a mouthful!

"At its core, though, is this idea: that human beings—all of us—are both different and the same (we are made up of both human differences and human 'samenesses'); that, when we encounter one another, we are naturally drawn to, and mesmerized by, the human differences we see in *other*—including some that we share; and that, for a variety of reasons, we formulate our moral commitments to other based exclusively on 'difference awareness:' my family/your family, my tribe/your tribe, my ethnic group/your ethnic group, my nation/your nation. The content of our awareness of other, in other words, which gives rise to the moral impulse, is difference awareness alone, not a combination of difference awareness and 'sameness awareness.' The compassionate impulse, which is the fruit of sameness awareness, is lost.

"This is more than can be conveyed adequately in a paragraph or two. You'll find this theme developed in attorney Jason McQuade's closing argument in *Beyond the Sand Creek Bridge*, and again in "The Sanori Flag Debate," the appendix to my second novel, *Dimension M* (2013). It is a dominant theme in my own life, as well. In 1999, I founded the Companion Flag Project to elevate and sustain public awareness of all that human beings have in common, their differences notwithstanding. I have traveled throughout the world introducing the companion flag idea (as well as the companion flag, a symbol of all that human beings have in common). At this writing, the companion flag has been adopted at schools and universities in over fifteen countries."

Mr. Wyatt has four children and five grandchildren. His wife, Rochelle Wyatt, is a talented Seattle area actress. Since 2009, they have lived in a home overlooking Lake Sammamish, fifteen miles east of Seattle in the foothills of the Cascade Mountains.

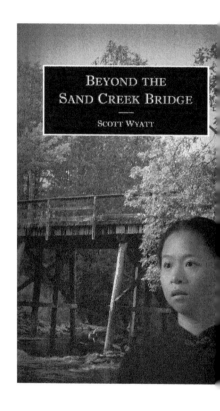

DISCUSSION GROUP QUESTIONS*

1. How did you experience *Dimension M*? Were you engaged immediately, or did it take you a while to "get into it"? How did you feel reading it—amused, sad, disturbed, confused, bored . . . ?

2. Describe the main characters—personality traits, motivations, inner qualities. For example:
   - Why do characters do what they do?
   - Are their actions justified?
   - Describe the dynamics between characters
   - How has the past shaped their lives?
   - Do you admire or disapprove of them?
   - Do they remind you of people you know?

3. Do the main characters change by the end of the book? Do they grow or mature? Do they learn something about themselves and how the world works?

4. Is the plot of *Dimension M* engaging—does the story interest you? Is this a plot-driven book: a fast-paced page-turner? Or does the story unfold slowly with a focus on character development? Were you surprised by the plot's complications? Or did you find it predictable, even formulaic?

* Questions 1-10 used by permission. *LitLovers.com*

5. Talk about the book's structure. Is it a continuous story . . . or interlocking short stories? Does the time-line more forward chronologically . . . or back and forth between past and present? Does the author use a single viewpoint or shifting viewpoints? Why might the author have chosen to tell the story the way he did—and what difference does it make in the way you read or understood it?

6. What main ideas—themes—does the author explore? (Is the title a clue to a theme?) Does the author use symbols to reinforce the main ideas?

7. What passages strike you as insightful, even profound? Perhaps a bit of dialog that's funny or poignant or that encapsulates a character? Maybe there's a particular comment that states the book's thematic concerns?

8. Is the ending satisfying? If so, why? If not, why not . . . and how would you change it?

9. If you could ask the author a question, what would you ask? Have you read other books by the same author? If so how does this book compare. If not, does this book inspire you to read others?**

10. Has this novel changed you—broadened your perspective? Have you learned something new or been exposed to different ideas about people or a certain part of the world?

11. Did you read "The Sanori Flag Debate?" If so, what did you think? Did you conclude that one side or the other "won" the debate? Which side . . . and why? Having read *Dimension M*, how do you think the Tashiri Parliament would have voted? Would they have adopted the companion flag, or rejected the resolution?

** Feel free to contact the author through his website (http://www.scottwyattauthor.com) or on Facebook. Mr. Wyatt endeavors to respond to all reader messages.

12. What were the strongest reasons for and against adoption of the companion flag? Did you think of other arguments for or against adoption of the companion flag? What were they?
13. Can you think of reasons why the author chose to set the debate in a fictional country?

Made in the USA
Charleston, SC
21 November 2013